Lieutenant Jacob Starke and Calypso
Michael T. Ribble

Apalachicola Publishing—Dumfries, VA
ISBN: 978-1-7330842-0-8
LIEUTENANT JACOB STARKE AND CALYPSO
Michael T. Ribble
Available Formats: eBook | Paperback distribution

Dedication

To:
Commander John Guy Strohaker,
Dr. James Stanford Bradshaw,
and most especially, Baerbel, my love and muse.

Disclaimer

This is the first book in a series following a fictional navy officer through the months leading to the Spanish-American and Philippine Wars. Trying to avoid conflict, the United States Navy and Revenue Cutter Service carried out tactical operations to prevent illegal military supplies and fighters from entering Cuba, but these have been largely forgotten. While no coordinated effort such as this novel describes appears to have taken place, it would have been possible. Actual people with political, military, and public roles, alive during this period, were included, however, all fictional characters are wholly imaginary and any likeness to actual persons, living or deceased, is coincidental. The actual and fictional events timeline is constructed to achieve as much accuracy as possible. This is equally true for ancillary events included to approximate the period's environment. Certain long-standing institutions, firms, agencies, and public offices included in this novel are mentioned and their activities taken from historical sources, or assigned tasks that could have occurred within normal operations.

Table of Contents

CHAPTER ONE
THE PROPOSAL

Department of the Navy occupied the State, War and Navy Building's east wing, overlooking the Executive Mansion, Presidential Grounds, and Treasury Building. The 1884 French Second Empire edifice, or the Building to Navy officers, contained three departments, was the nation's largest office building, and tourist attraction. At an east wing window, newly promoted Captain Sidney Albert considered his future, the Cuban Junta, and avoiding war; while slowly swirling a second coffee around the worn, white china cup. Monday was unusually cold and gray outside, but the cup warm and aroma comforting. Unlike some others, his office lacked a fireplace, which meant chilly winter mornings, but those were less trying than a Washington summer afternoon's heat and humidity, with the only protection a striped-cloth awning extended out and over the window casement.

Of fifty active duty captains, he became most junior, after decades of hard work, risks, and fighting. There was scant opportunity to rise further, except in seniority. A handful of commodores existed mostly as courtesy titles for specific positions; the 1873 Congress abolished admiral and vice admiral ranks, and the six rear admirals were always nearing mandatory retirement. Captains mostly controlled the Department, but authority came from competing and shifting blends of seniority, assignment, and personality. For Albert, this meant working for the Assistant Secretary of the Navy would soon end.

Admiral Porter reestablished line officer supremacy over steam engineering within the Department, and they still held the greatest influence, but there were staff officers, enlisted men, civilian clerks, typists, craftsmen, and others. Many civilians were still hired and fired under the spoils system, sometimes requiring them to balance navy and party demands. Line and staff officers disputed many things, but the prize was status, and through that, power. Line's competitors were naval constructors, paymasters, medical officers, and chaplains, but the most serious contenders were the steam engineers and Marine Corps. Marines were never popular with line officers on ships, and thought better employed guarding naval stations, while steam engineering, buoyed by the rapidly expanding technology, believed their power and status should do the same. Leaching away, but still smoldering after thirty years, was a war between the states, mostly referred to as the war, and forbidden wardroom topic.

This was familiar territory to Captain Albert, who felt opposing attractions of obtaining a final ship and Building politics. With this promotion, he entered the small cadre controlling five squadrons and eight independent bureaus; confirmed by the number of personal congratulations. Although future assignments would be even more sensitive to power, influence, and association, he was positioned well with his present assignment under the Bureau of Navigation; arguably the most powerful because it controlled personnel.

Captain Albert's record, listed in the *Register of Navy Officers*, was an additional asset. In the Home Squadron before the war, he was on *Saratoga* when she pursued and boarded the *General Miramon*, a renegade Mexican warship, off Anton Lizardo, and when she took the Cuba-bound slaver *Nightingale* off Africa. When *Saratoga* returned to Philadelphia, the ship was decommissioned and her officers forced to take sides, but, as a New Yorker, he did not "go South" or have his loyalty questioned like many comrades. He first went to a gunboat flotilla, saw hard fighting, then to a Gulf of Mexico blockading squadron. After the war, he rose slowly in an atrophying navy until 1880, when he commanded *Appalachicola*, a steam screw sloop in the European Squadron. For the next fifteen years as a commander he carefully orchestrated staff billets leading to his current position. Since 1895, he initiated, then nurtured, liaisons with the Naval War College, Office of Naval Intelligence, Marshals Service, State Department, and War Department; for Assistant Secretary William McAdoo.

Most recently, he worked the Cuban morass, coordinated Department actions to prevent or delay war, and projected European reactions. The Assistant Secretary was satisfied with the last six months' progress, although hampered by Spanish diplomats, adversarial jingoes, and passionate Cubans. The unstable island erupted soon after United States Marshals seized *Lagonda*, *Amadis*, and *Baracoa* at Fernandina, Florida, in January 1895. The Cuban Revolutionary Committee, usually called the Junta, chartered these ships to carry José Julián Martí Pérez, or Martí, with weapons and insurrectos to Cuba. Their libeling forestalled the revolution until April when arrangements were complete for a British schooner to break her passage along Cuba and cast off a small boat with Martí and others. Once ashore, he began the promised short revolt, fell in combat, and bequeathed stalemated guerrilla war. After a year, the United States was increasingly effected since the Junta, headquartered in New York City, sent filibuster expeditions south, and slowly gained popular support.

Despite their efforts to sway the public, Americans were more concerned with surviving and recovering from a recession lingering since the 1893 financial panic; and public rancor overseas focused on Britain. Not only did their America's Cup contender fail in a maelstrom of incidents, conflicts, and accusations, but both nations threatened war over the Venezuela border dispute. Like a previous incident with Chile, conflict was narrowly avoided, in this instance because African Boers defeated Jameson's Transvaal raid and Britain needed an ally to offset Continental censure, particularly from Germany. Besides this, Italy's Abyssinia invasion, France taking Madagascar, Armenians in the Ottoman Empire, and more, competed with Cuba for newspaper space; and the coming national election would mean even less coverage.

Cleveland's two terms, split by a Republican interlude, were ending. While President, he avoided war, damped expansionists, jousted a recalcitrant spoils system, and supported Secretary of the Navy Hilary Herbert's efforts to reconstitute the fleet, an effort begun in the 1880s. Three steel battleships were in commission, with more building, planned, or authorized. Lesser ship numbers were increasing as well, and the quality recently demonstrated by *Columbia* handily beating a crack liner, *Augusta-Victoria*, on their return from the Kaiser-Wilhelm Canal opening ceremony. New technologies appearing at home and overseas were also included or incorporated, such as a ram, dynamite cruiser, and submersible torpedo boat; which was why the Department closely watched the war in Korea where modern Chinese and Japanese ships engaged.

The day's first visitor, Lieutenant Jacob Starke, recently returned from the Far East and was temporarily assigned to the Office of Naval Intelligence, but Albert's subject was a plan to dissuade filibusters. While waiting, he slowly sipped the last coffee as his eyes wandered from the Treasury Building, past the Executive Mansion grounds, walkways, trees, and statuary, then continued northeast past its greenhouses to Executive Avenue and Lafayette Square. The panorama of buildings, moving people, and horse-drawn vehicles was mostly unobstructed since winter denuded intervening trees, and the city prohibited streetcars from using overhead wires or horses. Instead, the cars' steel shoes traveled through a slot in the roadway between rails, drawing electricity from an underground cable. While he watched, a yellow, white, and mahogany Capital Traction Company streetcar paused near the park to transfer gray canvas mail bags from its trailer to a waiting horse-drawn cart. Although a majority of passengers leaving were men, the number of women increased during his tenure, even as government clerks; most were young and would stop working beyond the home when married. It was on his mind because Abigail, his thin, redhead wife, and two daughters discussed high school for girls and college for women all evening. Suspecting something, he deployed light gray pipe smoke as a screen, then assumed an attentive, thoughtful, and uncommitted posture, thinking all would soon be revealed, but neither wife or unmarried daughters, Olivia and Isabella, enlightened him before retiring.

Morning ritual complete, Albert crossed to a carved oak desk, set the worn, white china cup with embossed gilt eagle down, pulled back the rolling chair, sat, then scooted forward over a Persian rug. Several sharp knee pains resulted, which he attributed to shore girth and sea arthritis. A wooden correspondence box filled the desk's right corner, beside a mahogany pipe stand next to a small wooden device with four rollers displaying weekday, month, day and year; which he set earlier to "MON MAR 2 96". Morning sun passing through the window lit the desk, but should it fade, waiting above was a white glass and brass gas lamp suspended from an ornate ceiling medallion.

The Evening Times from Friday was on the writing pad where he left it because Cuba seemed that day's theme. A line drawing of the Junta flag was dead center, just below the banner and dateline. Besides calling for Cuba Libre, the caption proclaimed it would fly alongside American flag over their offices. An earlier story about the Cuban general Antonio Maceo's demise was retracted; which was not surprising since the press regularly reported the Bronze Titan's death. The Senate Foreign Relations Committee hearing on Cuban belligerency was covered, albeit leaving out legal issues and costs; along with the administration's refusal to support House or Senate resolutions being conveniently buried in the back pages. With equal objectivity, it applauded insertion into committee records, General Máximo Gómez y Báez's pamphlet boasting of the humane treatment Spanish prisoners received, affirmed its accuracy, then contrasted it with Spanish barbarism. The paper was not unique, similar coverage was eroding an already deteriorating relationship with Madrid. Most stories were rumor, fabrication, and sometimes fact, usually coming from New York, Tampa, or Key West, and often straight from the Junta. This edition included an article describing Tampa's civic leaders hosting a Junta reception, with luminaries showing personal commitment by wearing American military uniforms. Albert's pipe released a small, blue-gray cloud; State would soon hear of it, followed by the formal complaint. He also suspected the affair would be equally unappreciated in the Executive Mansion across the way. It was worse in Madrid, with Cuba's Governor-general, Don Valeriano Weyler y Nicolau, cautioning a call for elections would harm island campaigning due to war fatigue at home. Each day, Albert read several papers to stay informed on filibuster facts and rumors. What delayed this edition's plunge into the reed wastebasket was mention of the *Horsa* case. Since mid-January the steamer's first and second mates were in court, but now an appeal was filed, new trial requested, sentence suspended, and defendants returned to custody. Despite Albert's frustration, he knew the Justice Department considered just getting them to trial a success.

After making notes, the paper finally entered the wastebasket as clerks, stenographers, and staff passed down the corridor outside his door. He looked up at a clucking wall clock, then, preparing for his nine o'clock appointment, began a final review of Starke's service jacket, left by a clerk from the Navigation Bureau's Division of Officers and Fleet. Lieutenant Jacob Jefferson Starke was born a Virginian less than two years before the war, entered the Naval Academy in 1876, graduated in 1880 as a naval cadet, went to sea for two years, then returned for examination. Commissioned as midshipman, or junior ensign, in 1882, he reached full ensign the next year, lieutenant (junior grade) in 1891, then lieutenant this year. Several documents spoke to his actions during the Alexandria bombardment, Brazil's naval mutiny, and Sino-Japanese War. Albert was also aware just before receiving his appointment to the Naval Academy, he accompanied the Montana expedition to force Sioux onto reservations, as a civilian mule packer.

Starke was stashed with the Chief Intelligence Officer, Lieutenant Frederic Singer, after returning from *Detroit* and the Far East, so he was available; but Albert was also convinced Starke was perfect for his filibuster project. The recently promoted lieutenant had more fighting experience than most postwar Academy graduates and a reputation for seamanship that included merchant ship cruises during leaves of absence. Midshipman Starke also served under Albert on *Appalachicola* when the British bombarded the Egyptian city of Alexandria and American ships sent a landing party ashore to protect the embassy. He also wrote the odd essay on various topics, some outside the profession and others contentious. One included in the folder, echoed the French response to Mahan's sea power theory by arguing for a broad mix of coast defense, torpedo boats, submarines, and commerce raiders; despite the Department's recent conversion to Mahan. Another promoted more sail-capable ships to reduce cost and oversea coaling dependencies. Starke was never foolish in manner, act, or position, and Albert was about to offer him a command with high personal risk and little reward, so his acceptance was not certain, especially if Singer countered with an Office of Naval Intelligence position.

The intelligence office moved from the Bureau of Navigation to Secretary's office in 1890 and now had twelve officers and clerks gathering information from squadron commanders, and officers overseas in any capacity. Most possessed strong language, drawing, or writing skills; with a private income desirable for attaché assignments, since London, Paris, and Rome societies outstripped the Navy salary and expense account. Albert knew Starke would fit perfectly there as well, since he came from a prosperous family, was fluent in Spanish, passable in German, and possessed Academy French.

Albert was also competing with an uncle, who controlled the Starke family's shipping, railroad, and other interests; and wanted his nephew to join him. Albert always thought it strange Starke remained with such opportunities available, since the American navy offered a moribund promotion process with front-line ships considered relics until recently.

Besides these impediments, the father, Jefferson Augustus Starke, provided another. He was one of *Saratoga*'s wardroom forced from the Navy when they returned from Africa. Although strongly believing military officers should avoid politics, he refused to fight seceding states when the constitution did not prevent them; and particularly Virginia where his wife's family owned a plantation. He reluctantly submitted his resignation, but instead of the customary acceptance, was dishonorably dismissed by Secretary Welles just as Radical

Republicans began secret arrests of Southern officers and those thought sympathizers. Albert helped him slip away South, where, like many, his services were offered to the emerging nation. Innovative and aggressive, he began as a shore battery commander on the Potomac River, then blockade runner, and, finally, commerce raider. Although his wife and child were sent to live with the brother in Washington for their safety, she died there of typhoid fever. Grieving from her death, and facing arrest if he returned from Havana, he asked his brother to raise the child. Albert heard he was in Egypt for a time before settling in Rio de Janeiro where he started the Southern Caribbean and Atlantic Shipping Company. The firm currently operated a route along South America's east coast, with charter and tramp shipping as far north as its Havana office. Now crewed by the usual nationality mix, after the war many were Confederates desiring to avoid the States, ex-officers forbidden to sail under the American flag, or both. While startup funds were thought to have come from his family, the two firms had no business relationship beyond agents in Havana. Several older politicians and Navy officers claimed the money was from a captured Federal ship's gold shipment, and denounced Starke as traitor and pirate. Most Confederate naval commanders were accused of piracy, especially after commerce raiders devastated Northern merchant shipping and whaling, but missing gold and Starke's refusal to submit meant the old Republican enmity passed to his son.

Checking the clock, Albert thought it was partly the uncle's influence Jacob Starke was allowed in the Academy; then Congress limited commissions after 1882 to open vacancies. The result was, following six years of study and serving at sea, any graduate in excess, despite the degree, was given a year's severance pay and no commission. Albert thought Starke would have been among those leaving for business, medicine, law, diplomacy, the Revenue Cutter Service, or some unique endeavor. One such cadet, Philo McGiffin, offered his education and training to China, taught at their naval school, then fought Japan.

As Albert resumed work, a Capital Traction Company streetcar jerked and squealed down shiny tracks between Pennsylvania and Executive Avenues. Inside, Jacob Starke grabbed a seat back to pull himself up. Lean, but muscular, he was average height, fashionably dressed, with dark hair, bowler hat, and sparse, neatly trimmed beard. Visible under his black wool frock-coat, unbuttoned for sitting, was a white wing-collar, gray silk cravat, and pale red-silk waistcoat transversed by two gold chain loops. His trousers were single-creased, and left hand grasped gray leather gloves wrapped midway around an ebony walking cane with silver mushroom head and worn tip. Lifting it above other riders, he carefully shuffled down the car's short aisle to a rear platform.

As the streetcar braked south of Lafayette Square, Starke stepped down on Executive Avenue then, once clear, turned to wave thanks. Skirting scattered globules of frosted or steaming manure, he stepped over rails and slots in the asphalt, then continued over bare ground on the Executive Mansion's west side to the Building. Merging with a small party, he walked through the nearest decorative gate in a black, wrought iron fence surrounding the grounds. It was a striking structure compared to the usual Federal and Grecian style government buildings, with three departments sharing five floors and basement with nearly fifteen acres of offices; a mile and a half of black and white checkered corridors; 550 rooms; and 150 fireplaces. The Navy Department was mainly in the east wing, but began absorbing State's spaces before construction completed in 1888. There were four main entrances with the one closest to Captain Albert's east wing office also nearest. Ascending two flights of marble steps below four stories of porticos separating layers of double fluted columns and windows, he entered the Building through massive doors.

Albert's office was a short climb and walk from there. Crossing a corridor, he ascended to the fourth floor on fitted granite stairs, turning left twice after each flight, to enter the next staircase. As he climbed, with one hand tracing the brass baluster, Starke occasionally glanced up to the fifth floor rotunda's colored glass skylight. He also paused briefly to look down through stairs and floors shaped like pie slices to the basement, and exchanged greetings with other arrivals. Turning left on the fourth floor, he walked noisily north down a white-walled corridor with checkerboard marble floors bounded by black borders. Passing recessed pine and mahogany doors with overhead transom windows and heavy framing, he reached Albert's office near the hallway's turn west, knocked, grasped its brass door knob with embossed anchor, then twisted. As it opened, Captain Albert pushed back from his desk, offered a quick handshake and greeting, then motioned him to a compact settee. After congratulating the captain on his recent promotion, Starke settled into its worn leather upholstery.

Albert returned to his desk, sitting slowly, then began sorting items scattered over its cluttered surface while Starke considered the captain's short, stocky frame. It always moved with a rolling gait, and included thick, powerful arms and legs suggesting he could easily climb ratlines, cast a lead, or row a pinnace. Melded to the thickish torso by a short neck was a round head of close cropped, receding gray-white hair. Unlike most, he was clean-shaven and intentionally wore an immaculate service dress blue uniform, even with civilian attire allowed for officers assigned to the Building. The blouse was trimmed with braided black mohair as were four stripes on each sleeve. Peeking from the high blue collar with anchor and eagle devices was the upper perimeter of a white standing collar clamping his neck and wrinkling slightly reddened skin above. Service coats were required to end just below the hips and conform to the figure, which accentuated his rounded paunch. Smartly creased blue trousers, stressed at waist and thighs, rose over and partly covered polished, black calfskin, not patent leather, shoes.

From serving under him and aware of his reputation, Stark knew Albert was as much Building creature as seaman, and seldom acted spuriously. The uniform cultivated a specific impression, particularly with civilians. Even social events were planned and selected to achieve results; and he exploited every opportunity offered, even if it occasioned minor disruption or irritation. Despite this, Albert could be equally decisive, clear, and precise. In the fleet, Starke recalled him as humorous, professional, and competent; with few passions beyond Navy and family. Wherever Albert was, he was successful because he built, nurtured, and relied on a reputation for honestly, consistency, and follow-through. He was equally enthusiastic about sail and steam, an uncommon trait in senior line officers, so steam engineers and naval constructors trusted him, despite their predisposition to view older line officers as myopic when dealing with steam engineering or shipbuilding.

This musing ended abruptly when Albert leaned forward, then selected a meerschaum from the pipe stand, after hesitating near a briar one. Sitting back, he dredged it through a supple leather tobacco pouch, gingerly packed the bowl, then lit up by passing a match over its center while creating a draught. As a match carcass arced into an ashtray, Albert's forehead wrinkled, then piercing near-black eyes lined up on Starke, as he began, "Will you remain in the Navy, Jacob?"

Starke tightened his grip on the walking stick and sat upright, as Albert went on, "If so, what's your next assignment?"

Ignorant of interview's purpose, Starke felt both rounds strike home. He was leaning towards resigning, or applying for another leave of absence, but not before completing the Office of Naval Intelligence assignment. Even so, he made inquiries about a new torpedo boat, from the class named for Rear Admiral Foote, but his chances were poor. Singer sounded him out about staying where he was, but office tasks were too academic and attaché positions of interest already filled. That left a gun division on a large ship, where he would be one of many, or, if fortune favored, navigator; but some pedestrian assignment ashore was more likely, which was why Captain Albert's summons peaked his curiosity.

Watching Starke struggle, Albert recalled the *Appalachicola* officer who seemed in the Navy, not of it. That subtle detachment deepened over years and it was doubtful Starke would advance far beyond his current grade, despite excellent capabilities and qualities. He was one of the men large organizations sought to prop up those favored, who fell short on capability or were shy of risk. Starke was resourceful, reliable, consistent, and possessed a fine sense of situation. Exceptionally self-disciplined and introspective, he often came across as pleasantly unsociable, which, for a reason Albert never understood, seemed to attract women. Some traits were clearly from the mother, since Albert recalled the father as companionable, often impulsive, and addicted to action. However, father and son definitely shared one attribute; both were exceptionally cold-blooded in a fight, or similar circumstances. These qualities, including Starke's career ambivalence, meant he was the officer most likely to achieve success with Albert's scheme, yet the least hurt should it fail since Albert believed Starke's interests were best served outside the Navy anyway.

Albert made these points to Rear Admiral Ramsey, Chief of the Bureau of Navigation, when submitting his name, since Ramsey saw all line officers as interchangeable, and thought the candidate should be senior on the list. Unbending and honest, the admiral was unforgiving about chain of command, discipline, and those maneuvering for convenient or comfortable billets, as the much celebrated Captain Mahan discovered when he enlisted others to suggest the Navy was better served leaving him at the Naval War College. The reluctant mariner received a choice sea command, the cruiser *Chicago*, bound for Europe; which displayed Ramsey's unique mix of iron and fairness.

The bureau chief was approached months earlier about Albert's plan to disrupt Junta filibusters, since nothing would happen without agreement or acquiescence from the thin, white-haired rear admiral with walrus mustache and dark eyebrows, who, unlike Albert, wore dark civilian clothes of conservative cut. He was also on the river campaigns, before returning east to serve with the Army, then commanded nine ships and two shipyards, was a London naval attaché, and served as Naval Academy Superintendent. Although they had *Saratoga* and the river war in common, this would not sway Ramsey, and, like many senior officers, he would abruptly end discussion when he felt there was enough to decide or the message became unclear. If that point came too soon, the original proposal might be discarded, or extemporaneous decisions made. To avoid this, Albert considered all possible questions and ensured everyone positioned to halt, delay, or promote the project was brought in. He finally made his case while leaning forward from the wooden-framed, pleated-leather chair between a tall bookcase and the admiral's desk; covered with papers, books, reports, and other material. His delivery speed increased while adjusting the pitch mid-flight to fit unspoken reactions, then, when this soliloquy ceased, relaxed back into the chair, expecting questions, but was only asked if Secretary Herbert and Speaker Reed were on board before receiving the blessing.

Albert successfully repeated this on Friday, this time for permission to offer Starke command of the critical unit. Ramsey asked more questions, then reluctantly approved; and today would determine if that lieutenant would accept. Pausing to relight his pipe and take a long draw, he held it to one side, then took the plunge, "I've a proposal, but it's no torpedo boat. They're a senior lieutenant command and there's less than a handful. I may locate something on one of the three *Indiana* class ships, or *Iowa* since she commissions next year. If you're willing to wait, and I relieve Captain Crowninshield next year on *Maine*, there may be an opening. She was too long in the builders, more slow armored cruiser than battleship, and an experiment that seems to attract misfortune, but has her uses and some qualities I appreciate."

Taking another draw, Albert chuckled, "*Texas* being worse, for one. Anyway, I might be in position to offer you a department or possibly navigator."

Starke liked Albert, but had no interest in *Maine* and hesitated, allowing the captain to ask, "You've sailed as mate and master on family ships?"

"Yes, sir. Passed a deck officer examination and shipped on a brigantine, schooner, and ocean tug. All small, but I've supercargoed larger ships. The family also keeps a yacht I race when in Newport."

"I remember you took no offense being called a soldier, have a relative in the Tenth Cavalry, and once had similar inclinations."

"Yes, sir, but I seldom advertise it."

"What happened?"

"Long time ago, captain. I was sixteen, out of Jefferson Classical & Military Academy, and enamored with cavalry. My uncle warned it sounded good in books, but was considered the worst duty for a reason. Even so, he once met the Seventh's lieutenant colonel and was acquainted with a navy family whose son, William Reily, was just assigned. Jefferson Academy taught riding, shooting, and how to pack wagons or mules, so it was arranged for me to go as a civilian packer on a summer expedition to push hostiles onto the reservations."

Starke ran fingers through his hair, looked at Albert who was sitting back, leisurely drawing on a pipe. It seemed he wanted more, so Starke added, "I didn't keep a journal so my recollection's images and events that come in bits and pieces. Companies from the South and local posts were pulled in to Fort Abraham Lincoln, then we left, and it was miserable. I sometimes rode a mule, but more often walked. When fighting started, the pack train and company with it joined others in a depression on a bluff above a river. It was filled with horses, mules, and wounded men; with the thirst intolerable, firing constant, and shrieking animals terrifying. I was too scared to panic, then accepted I would die, crawled to the perimeter, and begin shooting. My Springfield jammed with the Army cartridges, but a soldier showed me how to clear them with a knife. After the hostiles left, we moved upwind of the dead. A single bottle-green fly still reminds me of them swarming on food, carcasses, corpses, and us. From there to Washington's a blur, but I was cured of cavalry and it probably helped with the Academy appointment. Afterwards, the experience made Academy incidents seem petty and left me a better understanding of my uncle's view war is mass insanity, and the alternative must be worse to contemplate it."

"You still volunteered to go ashore with Goodrich at Alexandria. By the way, he and Chaillé-Long spoke well of you.

Chaillé-Long returned to Egypt a few years back as a lawyer to settle claims. Also writes and lectures. A remarkable dandy. Goodrich is with the Asiatic Squadron, but returning to the Naval War College."

Albert then quickly changed course, "You're recently back from China?"

"Yes, sir. After *Detroit,* I was supercargo on a company ship. Saw Philo McGiffin. He was badly wounded off Yalu River and may not recover fully."

"I believe you worked with Lieutenant Simms, so there's likely more to it, but your Cuban connections are my interest."

"My uncle's firm keeps a Havana agent and my father a small office, so I've used the port, and several others on the island. There's also a Pinar del Río sugar plantation and mill, but insurgents have shut them down, like most other American investments."

Albert pulled the pipe stem from his mouth's corner, briefly leaving a thin thread of spittle, instantly removed, then, through the smoke, asked, "Are you working Cuba for Singer, and what do you know of it?"

Starke took time to respond, then began, "No, I'm researching torpedo boats. What I know is mostly from newspapers, reading, and a friend at *The Sun*. It seems Spain can neither stay or leave, and the fight's bleeding out them and Cuba. Even if the Spanish support their army long enough to crush the insurrectos, I doubt peace would last ten years, so continuing's probably honor, investments, and not knowing what else to do. Besides, to declare Cuba independent and leave means they desert their loyalists, and there's fear it could become another Haiti. I believe there's talk of us buying Cuba, or assisting the Junta, but we're better off staying clear."

"And, filibustering?"

"Ignoring it strengthens the Junta and risks repeating Britain's missteps that led to the *Alabama* claims, but actively supporting Spain's equally short-sighted, since they must fail at some point. Which reminds, didn't the *Horsa* trial end last week?"

Starke saw this touched a sore spot as Albert scrapped his pipe over an ashtray saying, "Yes, her officers were found guilty and are appealing the verdict. So how do we deal with Cuba?"

"Stay away. Investors knew the risk, and, while Europe's hard to predict, monarchies are sympathetic by nature. An army sent to the island, even if it didn't fight, would falter from disease until the rainy season, then disintegrate. Besides, I doubt the Junta wants us replacing Spain."

"Specifics?"

"For the time being, halt Junta filibusters using our ports."

"And, should war come with Spain?"

"Blockade Cuba and Puerto Rico. Choke off what's needed to fight the insurrectos. Spain would have to break through, or lose their army in Cuba through attrition. I doubt they could raise a blockade, so any war would be decided at sea. We can't invade Spain, landing troops on either island risks disaster from disease alone, and there's no reason insurrectos already fighting would welcome us."

"And, Spain?"

"Spain loses Cuba in any war, but might get better terms and keep Puerto Rico if fighting could be prolonged; which means abandoning their army in Cuba. If they preserve their fleet to attack our coasts and shipping, like *Shenandoah*, our blockade would be weakened from ships pulled to placate the public. However, Spain's treasury wouldn't support it, they could lose a large part of their army, and the Philippines remain unpredictable."

Captain Albert weighed the response while pausing to reload the cinnamon-brown pipe, "The Naval War College's developed a Spanish war plan along those lines, but Admiral Ramsey's not fond of Newport, so he'll have Kimball develop another this summer, and there's talk of blockading Cuba with small ships."

Starke grinned, "Kimball favors gunboats and torpedo boats."

Albert leaned back, "In part."

Sensing he wandered off topic, Albert pointed his pipestem towards the hotel used for Washington's Junta office saying, "Then you believe filibustering must be stopped."

"Yes, sir, but any liaison with Spanish authorities would be unwise and unpopular."

"Exactly. By the way, Singer's due for relief, a Lieutenant Commander Wainwright; but I can offer you command."

Starke was stunned. Senior lieutenants, like Singer, Wainwright, Simms, or Kimball would jump at this, and, despite Albert's political acumen, how could he offer? Always a skeptic when unanticipated fruit landed in his path, Starke responded, "I appreciate the opportunity, captain, but there's more?"

"It's a small command, Jacob."

Declining might dry up future opportunity, but he knew Albert well enough, "It's the mission then?"

"I'll explain, but it must remain close-held, even in the Building. Junta ears are just beyond the door."

"You've a feel for the Cuban situation, especially our investments," Albert continued, "but most have no idea of Cuba or its politics; fewer have been there. The Junta feeds newspapers, holds rallies, and lobbies for the public support providing them money, men, and acceptance of illegal filibustering.

Thanks to the *Horsa* affair, I can almost recite *United States Revised Statutes 5286* verbatim."

With this, Albert paused to relight, then went on. "The President wants to keep us out. Despite temporarily stopping the filibustering during their last revolution, we were nearly at war with Spain. After *Virginus* was taken, I was with Cushing on *Wyoming* when it looked like our relics would fight Spain's modern fleet. Supposedly, Cushing, or HMS *Niobe*'s commander, informed the Spanish another execution and their nearest warship, or Santiago, would be fired on. Spain proved unwilling to fight both countries."

After a quick shake, the extinguished match's smoldering carcass joined a growing pile in the ashtray as Albert recalled his old commander. Cushing's health collapsed on that cruise, but Albert remembered his taste for action, total calm during it, and knew Starke had these traits. He pressed on, "We must avoid repetition. A Spanish gunboat fired on the mail steamer *Alliance* and a second sank the British schooner *Honor*. President Cleveland's proclamation last June is being ignored, and Charleston authorities stopped *Laurada*, the largest filibuster yet."

Briefly distracted by corridor noise, Albert explained, "After *Laurada*, I was assigned to work filibuster coordination. Mostly with our North Atlantic Squadron, since it has the ships; and Rear Admiral Meade's sudden retirement made that easier. When he commanded Washington's navy shipyard, his temper was legend, and it didn't improve."

Seeing Starke's expression, Albert grinned, "He's retired, so I can be candid. Bunce is easier to work with, but still needs ships in exercises, not on filibuster patrol. When the squadron was in Newport last August, Secretary Herbert met him on *Dolphin* and they agreed to move annual Caribbean maneuvers to Norfolk's drill grounds; because of Venezuela and Cuba. However, Bunce did agree to free up more ships for patrols."

Albert, set his pipe on the ashtray, freeing both hands, "Jacob, I coordinate with Bunce's staff, Revenue Cutter Service, and Justice against filibusters. Since there's not enough navy ships, and revenue cutters are tied to districts, a rat terrier, ferret if you prefer, is needed to flush filibusters and disrupt the Junta's expeditions. The ship will be under the Special Service Squadron, with a roving commission to go after them from Port Royal to Key West; or entire Caribbean, if necessary. Bahama Islands, Straits of Florida, Gulf of Mexico; specifics can be worked later, but Junta expeditions would be engaged to the legal limits, or near enough to be arguable. Taking individual ships wouldn't be necessary to disrupt operations. If Junta expeditions constantly worry over the next ship to appear, they'll make more mistakes, costs will rise, and planning disrupted. Treasury might contribute a cutter, but I'll believe that when it happens."

While Starke considered this, Albert's fist landed firmly on the desk, for him an unusual gesture, "We must gain the initiative." Then, he grinned, "That's the mission, now the ship; an 1880s composite hull bark with lines lifted from blockade runners and foreign gunboats; built for merchant service but easily converted to a cruiser. She's under conversion now and will have water tube boilers, a triple-expansion engine, and two 4-inch rifles."

Disbelieving, Starke looked at Albert, "You can't mean *Illusive*?"

"*Calypso*, lieutenant, *Calypso*. Neither previous name fit. Your uncle was approached last summer regarding a lease with option to buy, but offered outright sale."

Albert paused, emptied and scraped the Meerschaum's bowl, recharged it, passed a match over the center, then waited. Like a raider or privateer, *Calypso* would have a roving commission, freedom of action, and no local control. Independent command, familiar ship, potential for action; Starke's father would have snapped it up and Albert surmised this apple had not rolled far from the family tree. Albert was no angler, complete or otherwise, but quite confident his bait taken and the hook well and truly set.

CHAPTER TWO
Decision Made

Albert gave Starke overnight to consider the offer, believing he would be unable to resist *Calypso*, and no other viable candidate was immediately available. Starke knew vacillation about joining his uncle's firm, Starke Shipping and Shipbuilding, must end by morning. However, accepting *Calypso* committed him for two more years, and a mission with few attractions except command. Albert seemed to sense he was inclined to resign, so why him? If the offer were made by anyone else, he would have declined, but *Appalachicola* created a trust Starke hoped was shared. Still, he never underestimated Albert's infectious enthusiasm and persuasive abilities.

This did not free him of the day's obligations, so he was soon working in the Navy Library's two-story reading room. Sitting at the massive mahogany table dominating it, he began reviewing a submersible torpedo boat analysis, and, once started, worked hard and well inserting notes and proposing edits regarding size, engineering, seakeeping, and torpedoes. However, he periodically laced fingers behind his head, leaned back, and looked up to study the suspended electrolier, stained glass dome, and intricate dark ceiling above ornate off-white statuary. *Calypso* promised return to sea in a unique ship, and few lieutenants were offered commands. The price was a vague undertaking Albert warned might be professionally detrimental if successful, and end his career if it failed. There was also Albert's recent promotion. He could move to a new assignment, like *Maine*, and the project lose its champion. Finally, Starke realized he was drawn to the unknown, and, like any addict, cycled through lust, exultation, satiation, then revulsion.

Still undecided at day's end, Starke filed the torpedo boat analysis then left for his family's mansion north of Dupont Circle. The late afternoon was cold and damp, skies overcast, and little change anticipated beyond rain and slight late-week warming. Along his path through a soft, gray winter stillness, he passed mottled white, gray, and black snow mounds receding from midday sun but reluctant to decay, while traces of burning coal supplanted summer fragrances. Head down, hat sloped forward, and cane tapping asphalt, he pushed easily through a light breeze.

Retracing the morning route past the Executive Mansion greenhouses, he saw a Capitol Traction Company streetcar board passengers then squeal east to Pennsylvania Avenue. He could have taken it home, but Metropolitan Company tracks were just north of Lafayette Square, so he waited for their next car under leafless trees near a hotel and duplex mansion. The competing lines paralleled the park, one north, one south, but both had stops a short walk from Starke mansion. He soon boarded one, greeted the conductor, surrendered his fare, then claimed a vacant spot on the aisle side of a mid-car bench seat. As they accelerated, he would intermittently brush his neighbor, a rotund man with beard and bowler who slouched comfortably against the window. When Starke sat down, the gentleman nodded, then shifted attention to passing homes and businesses. Neither spoke, only tourists did that. Starke enjoyed streetcars in pleasant weather, but not to the extremes of House Speaker Thomas Reed, who also rode for pleasure and to observe the lines' eclectic passengers. Besides servants, clerks, merchants, attorneys, lobbyists, and the like, embassies and other international establishments added foreign ambiance. There were also a number of middle class Colored and Negro riders, especially on routes passing near the Strivers Section or government buildings. Men returning from work dominated evening runs, and women those running around midday. Flocks of tourists during the season meant declining civility, with their chatter spiking during conventions.

Starke was about to drift off when they halted at the Grafton Hotel and he saw a woman's hat push through dark coats, bowlers, and homburgs to secure first place in line. Its owner dressed well, but not extravagantly, suggesting a clerk, copyist, or similar. As she boarded, he saw her hat floated on rolling auburn hair, pinned to a pompadour framing a classic face. As she edged down the aisle, Starke saw innocently suggestive brown eyes move under flawless eyebrows, which his aunt said was achieved through meticulous eye make-up use respectable women denied; and even suggesting it was tantamount to insult. Similarly, the face might have received lemon or vinegar juice, nothing more, and both cheeks blushed light red from the sidewalk wait. Shielded by a Brussels carpet bag guided by tightly gloved hands, she stifled several sniffles while scouting a roost. The double row of buttons for closing the dark over-frock coat, reaching from knee to collar, was partly undone, and fell open as she walked, exposing a traveling suit. This suggested she was inclined to strain conventions in favor of practicality, since ladies seldom unbuttoned in public.

The coat spread further as she scrutinized passengers, revealing a fine, blue-black wool jacket and matching full-length, flared skirt. As she walked, its hem swayed slowly just over the floor to reveal black leather shoes with light stains at the soles. A wide, black-cotton belt covered the junction where her skirt waist passed over a lace-decorated white blouse with leg-of-mutton sleeves, if coat bulges were any indication. A long, black necktie suspended from her throat barely covered the blouse's constraining bone buttons, and the fashionable S-figure meant a stylish, less restrictive corset with modest bustle.

While trying to curb his curiosity, her eyes paused on him, then moved on, so he rose, touched his hat and offered the seat. She accepted with indifference, although they briefly faced each other before he backed away and she took the proffered seat. Twisting down into it, the woman adjusted her coat then placed the bag on her lap, base forward like a shield. As she settled, the other occupant acknowledged their exchange with a quick touch of his bowler's brim, before returning to the window. The remaining new arrivals behind her joined Starke and others standing on the northbound car.

As she sat upright, looking forward with accomplished poise, Starke worked his legs while grasping an overhead brass rail with one gloved hand, freeing the second to control his cane. Like going aloft, streetcars demanded one hand for them and the other for yourself, or, in this case, a heavy cane; although the drop was considerably less than a yardarm's. Moving northwest up Connecticut Avenue, they squealed past embassies and churches amongst homes, businesses and open areas. Several short stops brought no boarders, but riders thinned and few were left standing. Those near the windows were dozing or watching for twilight when, around seven, gas, naphtha, and electric streetlights were lit. They soon entered Dupont Circle with the bronze admiral standing above dormant flower beds and surrounded by leafless trees, just as tracks took the streetcar left to Denmark's embassy and the Georgetown transfer point. While Starke would continue up Connecticut Avenue beyond the Spanish Embassy to line's end near St. Margaret's Episcopal Church, the woman glanced at Starke, then began gathering belongings and adjusting clothes. Just before the car halted, she rose in a single smooth motion then passed unimpeded to the front platform. As she left, her recent companion winched himself upright with low grunts and groans, then trailed in a crabbing motion to clear benches; since his unconfined bulk consumed greater space working its way down the short aisle than inertly spread over a seat. Starke shifted in the aisle as several behind exited by the rear platform, then, through a window, saw her stand away from the rails, waiting for the Georgetown connection.

Fully awake from standing, Starke regained the vacated seat, and watched what passed near the car's window and whatever interested him up the side streets. Through open areas and cross streets, he saw the Cairo Hotel, a new twelve-story building, the city's tallest, whose Romanesque architecture defied the lingering recession and offered its residents refuge, including a manicured rooftop garden, where he spent several evenings with a Havana cigar and thick-bottomed glasses of amber whiskey. Near the modest Spanish Legation, he went forward, waited until the car stopped and its safety gates opened, then stepped down through them to the street. After glancing at St. Margaret's red-brick Episcopal church, he started up Florida Avenue into a light breeze.

Dusk was near and lights flickered in a row house cluster on his right and larger homes to the left. He soon saw the mansion several blocks away and turned west towards it. Like their Newport, Rhode Island summer cottage, it was not used year around, but only during appropriate seasons, and never the Washington summer. For those months, his aunt, and uncle when business permitted, escaped north to avoid the heat, humidity, and disease. The mansion held no special attraction for Starke, being only a few years old in a growing neighborhood. That association went to Oxen Grove, a Virginia plantation on the York River, left to him by his mother's family, but almost lost because of Radical Republicans' Confiscation Acts. His father's family saved it by assuming quasi-legal owner-ship, paying taxes, then financing a postwar recovery. If pressed, it was his home, despite seldom visiting and run by a local manager.

He was familiar with the mansion's Romanesque design. A red stone exterior reached four stories, if ground floor and heavily gabled attic rooms counted. Three corners were rounded and the fourth superseded by a tall turret with cone-shaped top and massive lightning rod resembling a flagstaff. The centered main entrance opened to a massive whitish-gray stone porch flanked by marble steps sweeping up and around a utilitarian concrete stairway leading down between stone arches to a ground floor front door. Between this porch and corner, a smaller half-turret was grafted to the front. The same stone used for the ground floor wall and porch reappeared as a single course separating upper stories. Spread amongst its peaked roofs dressed by small glass-globed lightning rods, were chimneys of different heights with gray concrete caps.

A grass median separated house from sidewalk, and broad side lawns set it apart from neighbors. An expansive rear yard extended out from a conservatory and carriage house attached to the mansion's rear wall, but separated by a concrete apron and rear entrance. Set further away was a large red-brick sta-ble capable of housing a half dozen horses, but containing two.

Behind the ground floor's rear door was a kitchen, pantry, scullery, bathrooms, laundry room, central heating complex, china closet, storage rooms, small office, and servant's hall converted from a smoking room. Stairs and dumbwaiters rose to the upper floors. Above, on the main floor, two heavy oak doors opened from the front entrance into a short passage be-tween a small butler's office and cloak room. Beyond was the paneled, two-story center hall, splitting the house, and ending with curved staircases below Tiffany stained-glass windows that led to the second floor.

To the hall's immediate right was a large Louis XVII off-white ballroom with parquet floor and small rear portion raised to form a band dais. On the street-end was a half round alcove formed by the partial turret. Suspended along the ceiling's centerline were three intricate cut-crystal gasoliers falling just below the tops of windows lining one side, and large wall mirrors on the other. From this arrangement, a grand ballroom illusion was created from the large space. Directly above, on the second floor, was the formal dining room, along with a smaller salon and, more often used, breakfast space.

Left of the central hall was a large reception room or parlor with its front corner formed by the larger turret. Two folding doors extended from hollow pillars on either wall to create a pair of smaller rooms, when required. The library, to the parlor's rear, included built-in shelves, oriental rugs, floor globe, leather chairs, and large wooden desk with brass lamp and high backed chair. Above parlor and library were four bedrooms with attached dressing rooms.

Near the second floor's rear wall was an enclosed staircase to attic guest rooms on the servants' quarters level. Shaped to fit gables and turrets, the small guest rooms were to the left, opposite servants' quarters that also conformed to the roof, but split into male and female areas. This side was also accessed by a smaller staircase twisting up from the ground floor.

The mansion included a great number of features. One was extensive indoor plumbing, with second floor en suite bathrooms having tubs and showers; and a washroom next to the breakfast room. Third floor guests shared two bathrooms, one for males and the other females, duplicating the servants arrangement. The first floor powder room was next to the cloakroom with an equivalent gentlemen's facility beside the butler's office. Two more bathrooms with cage showers were on the ground floor just off the mud room. For heat, a coal-fired boiler supplied hot water to cast iron radiators crowned by wood and velvet covers. This was supplemented by several fireplaces, with some using the same gas that powered lights and fired a large kitchen range.

As Starke climbed to the main entrance through the winter air then pulled a mechanical brass doorbell, he noticed flickering, translucent fumes, rising from chimneys to disperse in the colder air and gentle breeze. The ringing summoned Joshua Altman, former purser with the Starke firm, now butler. After the door closed, Starke surrendered hat gloves, coat and cane, then thanked him as the voices of his aunt and an older man escaped the parlor. Moving through double doors into the matriarch's realm, he saw Aunt Constance seated in the alcove beside an end table with a light pink, globed lamp. Sitting across from her, bulking over a second table, with coffee and cake remnants, was a heavyset man in suit and vest.

As Starke entered, they stopped talking and his aunt smiled. Afternoon visiting was a common and well-defined custom. House calls were made and cards left from two to five or eight to eleven. Visitors to the city made initial calls. Cards not left by strangers required a return call within three days. For this reason, all cards received at the Starke mansion remained in a silver salver by the cloak room for Aunt Constance's daily review and attention. Most were engraved or handwritten, since printed cards received less consideration. Any with right-hand corners turned down meant the call was made in person, while "p.p.c." in the bottom corner meant the person left town.

His aunt controlled mansion operation and the Starke social calendar, although daily domestic activities and tasks, excluding work done by the cook and her two assistants, went through the butler. This currently included a senior maid and three more assisting her, two footmen, a groom, and two laborers. All were steady, experienced, and loyal since most had some family or business association before arriving. She was also expert using social custom to best advantage. While the Starke family traced back to a small, south German state, hers came from Dorset just after New Amsterdam fell to the British, and remained in New York society. However her marriage to Immanuel Starke was encouraged by both families, since it fused Thomas railroad interests with Starke shipping.

Formidable, well-read, and grounded in consistent, unshakable beliefs, buttressed with absolute Episcopalian faith, she mostly tolerated Christian competitors, was suspicious of Rome, and firmly applied her shoulder whenever needed for church business. Local ministers often took advantage, with nearby St. Margaret's being the latest. She partitioned the world between believers and nonbelievers, then ranked each halves' constituents by their actions. Convinced all possessed souls, she was attracted to the abolitionist cause as a young woman, but not radical abolitionists' acts and rhetoric, which she believed treasonous, along with their secessionist contemporaries and fellow travelers, which included her nephew's father. As a result, she refused further familiar association, so Starke was astonished when he recognized the guest. His aunt smiled, then directed him to a nearby settee with, "Welcome home Jacob. May I present Governor Fitzhugh Lee."

A broad range of political, business or artistic classes were welcomed to his aunt's domain. Some, like those from Mrs. Lodge and Mrs. Cameron's circle, were younger, but most persuasions were tolerated, if civil, since the mansion was to facilitate social liaisons as much as it was a home. Even so, they were usually women, mostly Republican, and never, in Starke's experience, ex-Confederate generals. The guest, obviously enjoying her company, led Confederate cavalry, farmed in Virginia, and was a solid Democrat who championed reconciliation, maintained the war decided all issues causing it, and became Virginia's governor. His diplomatic skills obviously extended beyond politics, since the parlor's congenial atmosphere suggested extraordinary progress towards reconciliation had been achieved with his aunt.

Starke turned to him, "I'm honored, sir."

With that, his aunt interjected, "Perhaps you gentlemen prefer the library? Jacob, could you show Governor Lee the way?"

Lee and Starke rose together, passed back through double doors, then walked to the library. Once inside, Lee occupied a chair near the fireplace as Starke took its adjacent twin, "Brandy or whiskey, governor?"

Through thick white mustache and goatee, Lee responded, "Thank you, sir, but no. Your Aunt already plied me with coffee and cakes. My intent was to leave a card, but accepted her generous offer of refreshments since you were expected and your uncle away."

"In New York."

"No matter, I want to discuss your father."

Starke was again caught off guard, "Sir?"

Lee repositioned his bulk, "This must be close-held."

"Of course"

"Cuba."

Starke sensed Albert's hand, "Cuba, sir?"

"I may be going to Havana as consul general. Ramon Williams lived there and was our representative for years, but forwarded his resignation. Worn thin promoting our interests in the face of economic threats, filibustering, press antics, and years, I suppose. Since February he's also been contending with General Weyler, whose selection as Governor-general means Madrid has no intention of yielding to the Junta. He fought there during the last war and has dealt with similar situations. During our war he was in Washington and has the reputation of a professional soldier who takes the field with his troops. He'll move to end the stalemate but, while Cuba should have independence, we must look to our interests."

"Williams departure will be a loss. He's been fair."

"Perhaps too much so, but I was interested in an appraisal of your father's willingness to assist with his Havana office and contacts. Nothing specific yet, but what might be possible or could prove useful. I believe he had some previous business with Williams."

When Starke delayed, Lee added, "My father was also dishonored by the Lincoln administration, but we're one nation again."

Starke was certain his father did not share Lee's forgiving views, so he chose his words carefully, "Governor, I'll approach my uncle, but it may take time. My father seldom speaks with the family and refuses to deal with our government. I visited with him while in Rio de Janeiro and his allegiance is to Brazil. To his mind, any claims this nation had on him ended with Secretary Stanton's letter."

The governor rose slowly, "It's no surprise, but gives me an idea how to approach him, if necessary. Captain Albert said you'd be candid. Should you receive a response, or need additional information, feel free to visit in Virginia, and I will endeavor to repay your aunt's kindness."

Walking together towards the cloak room, Starke saw their butler emerge from his small office, "Mr. Altman, could you get Governor Lee's things and alert his driver?"

After Lee dressed, the pair went outside as a black Studebaker sedan brougham clattered to a halt. With brake set and carriage door opened by the driver, Starke walked Lee to it as a muscular black-maned Cleveland bay, marked by one white and three black socks, pawed the roadway with shod hooves. Impatient shakes of the gelding's head rattled his harness against the shafts while condensation rose from large, wet nostrils, and two pointed ears shifted back and forth. The governor planted his foot on the single steel step, then swung through the door, sagging its rear springs. As they rebounded, the door shut, its driver returned to his perch, and Lee's head appeared in the window, "Good evening, lieutenant. We may meet again shortly. Give Captain Albert my regards."

After the brougham was safely off, Starke changed for supper. Monday's meal was chicken, with in-season vegetables or what was stored, and the cook's choice of pastries. His aunt's menus held to a specific main dish type each day in a weekly repeating cycle to increase efficiency, and accommodate customs such as Friday fish. Supper began precisely at seven-thirty with twelve hours between it and breakfast. Morning meals were invariably ham, bacon, eggs, toast, and coffee, with afternoon coffee and cake. Starke often took a light mid-day meal near the Building, but had not eaten since breakfast.

While waiting, he returned to the parlor where Cynthia, their senior maid, was clearing plates, cups and other debris. Starke looked to his aunt, who was obviously waiting for them to be alone again. She was closing sixty with long, black hair turning gray, tightly piled and secured with invisible fastenings. Neither heavy or thin, Starke's father and uncle claimed she was a beauty at her New York coming out; which matured to elegance over time as poise, security, and confidence accumulated. After their marriage, she became the loving, childless wife who raised Starke, governed her realm benevolently, and complemented his uncle, whom she loved deeply.

Before Lee arrived she already dressed for supper in a gray day dress that rose from the floor to end in an upright collar and oval broach at the neck. Lace pads like epaulettes broadened each shoulder while the simulated waist coat closed snugly over her ribs to mold the figure. Lace overlaid sheer sleeves ending just below each elbow with a slight flare, and vertical facings of the same material ran from hem to collar. Her only jewelry was a gold wedding ring and small bracelet.

Once Cynthia left, closing the door, Constance smiled, "I received a telegram. A cousin's children, Edward and Katherine, are over here on business and will be down from New York on the thirteenth."

She was pleased and eager, Starke not so much. While house and staff could easily accommodate them, his aunt's look when she mentioned the sister, brought foreboding. Unless this Katherine had taken Holy Orders, an unmarried female would descend and remain until he left for *Calypso*. If his aunt deemed her eligible, there would be more than the intermittent evening of subtle encouragement to consider a union and children, since his aunt wished her ersatz son to marry well and continue the line.

Starke endured these social skirmishes with consideration, tact, and strict adherence to protocol after his aunt explained young women near twenty-six saw prospects decline as they became spinsters. While most middle and upper class women feared this, some did not. Those with financial security saw less expectations and restrictions, especially Americans, who could then share apartments, retain jobs, and travel unescorted. His aunt's female relation, however, was upper class English, a species he thought more mercenary than romantic after coming out. Each knew the window to secure a comfortable future was brief and competitive, so they spent their youth in preparation. As young women, they were schooled in languages, running large homes, etiquette, then, from sixteen to twenty-five, every activity became dictated and driven by social expectations, under strict protection.

While understanding and unwilling to take advantage, Starke acknowledged social and family obligations, then avoided matrimony. However, now in his mid-thirties, justifications were falling away and pressure increasing. Wherever he was, invitations with potential matches lurking or shunted in his path blossomed. Even the Navy's unmarried officer preference reversed as his seniority increased to the point he was grateful Albert had not yet put forward his unmarried daughters. This matrimonial reluctance partly grew from observing his aunt and uncle. Except for lacking children, which they seemed to have overcome, it was an ideal union. His father also married an exceptional woman, though of uncertain lineage. Forty years later Jefferson Starke never remarried, still carried a lock of her hair, and visibly grieved when Florence Starke was mentioned. Jacob Starke saw little chance to obtain anything like this, but inherited their romantic proclivities and knew, should it be less, he would be miserable. He also inherited a sense of loyalty, which excluded liaisons, mistresses, or divorce in obtaining relief. Considering this, he cultivated a polite detachment that perversely stimulated an opposite state in unmarried women and their mothers.

"Jacob?"

The voice wrenched Starke back from impending matrimony to the parlor, realized he was staring through Aunt Constance, then recovered with, "I don't remember you mentioning them."

"Their father's a baronet with a Dorset manor called Brydian Grange, near Bridport, but they've also a London house."

"When do they arrive?"

"The telegram said Baltimore & Ohio's Royal Blue Line at eight next Friday evening."

Starke was considering how to get them from station to mansion when his aunt loosed a ranging round, "Katherine's nearly twenty-six."

The expected salvos followed and he failed to shift topics, so a gentle duel continued until supper was announced. In the breakfast room, where informal meals were taken, he was allowed a respite, but discussion over evening coffee consisted of fond family remembrances salted with subtle advice and hints regarding the refined, moral, religious, and apparently available Katherine.

When his aunt retired, Starke took the same library chair occupied for the governor's visit, to peruse the *Evening Star*. While the Cuban belligerency resolution received greater coverage, a mob attack on Barcelona's American consulate was reported as an affront organized by city merchants to protect Cuban trade and instigated by a bullfight's blood lust. State dismissed it as ruffians, along with Spain's minister in Washington, who pointed out similar incidents with more dire results than broken windows were visited on Spain's consulates. A Baltimore & Ohio Railroad article reminded readers the panic's effects continued. Another reported several Colored men and boys received a year's sentence for assault, while a similar story on a different page claimed three Georgia and Louisiana lynchings occurred for similar transgressions. Navy items were scattered throughout, including a relatively accurate comparison with Spain's armada, and a less welcome one about the Brooklyn navy yard dropping *Katahdin*'s conning tower lid in the river. All warship movements were covered and there were reports the Senate authorized a thousand more sailors. After this morning, one item caught his attention more than it might have in the past, Albert's *Horsa* was sold, renamed, and returning to sea.

Starke finally retired and drifted off, still uncertain of *Calypso*. He slept fitfully at first, was awakened by clambering through Egyptian rubble, returned to sleep, then woke in a Montana depression filled with wounded men and braying pack mules. Finally, after a desperate swim through flotsam and drowning sailors to clear a dying ship, he fought back to consciousness, abandoned all attempts to sleep, moved to a chair, then poured two-fingers of sipping whiskey into a water glass. While waiting for the house to wake, he reasoned *Calypso* might be his only chance to command a Navy ship; but he could always resign. He was also lured by the prospect of returning to sea, where each voyage brought purpose and destination. It was good there. He always slept well, with few dreams, and was comfortably severed from matrimonial pressure. In the morning, his aunt would caution him about the family predilection for action, and attraction to the unknown, which Starke could not deny, but he already decided to accept *Calypso*.

CHAPTER THREE
A Die is Cast

Confident of landing his catch, Albert scheduled two morning discussions in a room between his office and Navy Library. State promised a clerk to give status and views. A second session would brief the U.S. Marshal Service and Revenue Cutter Service on the status of Albert's efforts, then his afternoon was clear to spend with Starke on *Calypso* and mission details. As anticipated, Starke came directly to his office and accepted the command, then left with him for the nine o'clock meeting; Albert in his undress blue uniform and Starke wearing civilian attire. As it was Albert's meeting, he came early. If a flag officer, he would have taken equal care to arrive on time or within fifteen minutes to avoid embarrassing a host; who should come early to deal with conflicts or oversights. Albert reserved the small room weeks before and checked the previous day, but always arrived early since his first days in the Building when he watched a humiliated officer try to breach a locked door while participants jested or stood mute in frustration.

The small conference room entrance resembled his own and others along the corridor but differed inside. The single door, with framing and transom window, took most of the inner wall, and a single large four-pane window filled the other. The entrance, ceiling, walls, and trim, were buried under chipped and dented layers of off-white paint, encircling the dark pine floor. A single row of small brown-framed ship photographs hung equally spaced above an inconspicuous chair rail.

Albert requested water and glasses, then sat below the window with Starke taking the chair to his right. Placing note paper and Eagle pencils on the table, Albert noticed a broken lead, retrieved his penknife, then began trimming over the single black ashtray. Starke shifted his chair to gaze out the window overlooking an interior courtyard below translucent cirrostratus clouds promising warming weather and rain. The water pitcher and glasses came at nine, followed by a knock and turning doorknob.

Albert and Starke rose, using calves to push back chairs, as a State Department clerk entered. Their guest's age was indeterminate but attire impeccable. A gray three-piece, striped suit constrained a billowing white cotton shirt with starched wing collar, not the more comfortable banker's variety. His thick reddish neck was further constricted by an encircling black bow tie, and high quality vest, traversed by a heavy gold watch chain, that partly concealed matching trousers and suspenders. Of average height, but thick build, his soft fingers displayed several large gold rings. Meticulously center-parted, brown-blonde hair glistened with a light sheen of Macassar oil, matching a mustache and goatee displaying equal care and attention. Starke also thought he noticed an effort to avoid appearing apprehensive; suggesting the arrival's position, ambition, and energy might exceed experience, knowledge, and insight.

Clarence Newcomb shut the door, appraised his hosts, then selected studied deference as the optimum approach. The uniformed one appeared in charge, but the second's manner was suspicious. While probably an officer or senior clerk, the well-dressed man's poise, detachment, and expensive apparel alerted him to wealth, influence, or high position. Newcomb moved quickly for the advantage by half-sliding notes to the table's end, then extending his right hand to the captain and gambled, "Captain Albert and *Calypso*'s future master? Clarence Newcomb, Diplomatic Bureau senior clerk working the

Cuba desk, and reporting through the Third Assistant Secretary to our Second Assistant Secretary."

Albert's Building tenure provided passing familiarity with State's structure. Richard Olney, Secretary of State, was Attorney General until last year. His Assistant Secretary, William Rockhill, just moved up from Third Assistant Secretary. However, the key player was Second Assistant Secretary, Alvey Adee, who was Olney's principle policy advisor and Albert's contact. An avid bicyclist, or wheelman, he was unique among political appointees in having a full State Department career, augmented by an exceptional memory tapping years of experience. Although he once served as Third Assistant Secretary, Albert was more appreciative of Adee's tenure as Chief of the Diplomatic Bureau, since it was State's most influential office and included a stable of expert clerks assigned by country to draft reports and diplomatic responses. This meant Albert must carefully manage the discussion since Newcomb was likely a senior clerk instructed to obtain rather than provide information. He hoped Starke divined this as well, but Albert had yet to observe his protégé's political adroitness. His hand quickly reached out for Newcomb's, "Captain Albert. I work for Assistant Secretary McAdoo."

Once free of Albert's hand, Newcomb reached for Starke's, "Congratulations on *Calypso*."

Newcomb made a poor first impression on Starke, who remained cautious but followed his habit of never acting on it; believing he could alienate someone who might prove valuable, or the reverse. However, unblinking eyes bored directly into the clerk's, "Thank you, sir; Lieutenant Jacob Starke."

After sitting, Albert offered Newcomb water, who thanked him then went to the table's far end, near the door. Once settled, with the freshly poured glass in easy reach but safe from overturning, the clerk scanned his documents, shuffled them, extracted a handful, then began, "You requested a summary of State's views on Cuba. Let's begin with the Civil War's close."

Albert and Starke flinched. North and South named the conflict differently and Newcomb's term offended Southerners who called it The War for Separation. Albert just referred to the war, since its national trauma left no doubt what he meant and most had no objection. Oblivious, the clerk continued, "Spain's control has deteriorated, causing several insurrections. Their Ten Years War continued to '78. In '73, a war between our country and Spain over *Virginus* was narrowly avoided. Another revolt in '79 and smaller ones since, including the '93 uprising, have occurred. We attempt to curtail filibustering, but arms, funds, and men, including Americans, still reach Cuba. Even between outbreaks ships, like *Galena* in Key West during '85, were assigned to prevent filibustering. Last year's three-ship expedition was intercepted in Florida, but Martí still landed in Cuba. Now, it appears our merchant ship *Alliance* was recently fired on by a Spanish gunboat, and when the British schooner *Honor* ran aground after an alleged filibuster run, Spaniards supposedly killed the crew. Not only have filibusters reached Cuba between May and June, after the President's proclamation, more attempts were made in October, with *Horsa* taken, a filibuster sinking off Long Island, and the Marshals Service stopping *Bermuda*."

Albert and Starke remained silent. Newcomb, paused, then reshuffled papers before continuing, "Cuba's trade with us was about 96 million dollars in '94; down from the previous year due to the '93 panic and Wilson-Gorman Tariff. Spain's restriction of our imports to Cuba aggravates this. Besides trade, our investments, estimated at thirty to fifty millions of dollars, are at now risk, although some sugar mills, plantations, mining, railroads, and so forth, were obtained for little or nothing after the last revolution."

Starke looked up. His uncle's sugar mill and small plantation were acquired for a fraction of their value, but both were now closed, burned, and unoccupied. Sensing a question, Newcomb raised his head. When neither man spoke, he sipped some water then pressed on, "These are threatened because Gómez, the top insurrectionist general intends to force Spain's departure through destroying the island economy and value, while increasing Spain's costs. They've responded by reducing small towns and plantations' protection to reinforce ports and cities. The Governor-general's re-concentration policy was announced on 16 February, trochas are being constructed or repaired to prevent rebel movement, and Madrid is sending additional troops. We estimate greater than a 100,000 more will come to support the campaign, despite Spain's financial state. It's difficult to predict who will prevail, but either way, American interests, citizens, and investments are threatened."

Newcomb looked for reactions. Albert was leaning back with elbows on the table edge, while Starke's head was down, finishing a note. After a sip of lukewarm water, he went on, "Cuba's increasingly less governable and our Cuban communities swelling with refugees, which means fertile ground for the Junta to gather support. This revolution's better organized than the last, and to end its filibustering means patrolling more coastline than was blockaded during the Civil War; with less resources and little public support. Madrid's been unsuccessfully approached about selling, but should they be forced out, the island risks occupation by a foreign government or following Haiti's example. Autonomy is the most palatable option, and Secretary Olney will meet Spain's minister to push for it and other reforms. Should they agree, we will announce they're moving towards resolution, which may erode Junta support. However, Spain's unpredictable, due to recent conflicts, the regency, a weak government, and almost bankrupt treasury. Even if they agree, autonomy may prove impossible because island loyalists and insurrectionists violently disagree with each other, and internally, regarding this. It also requires Junta support, and they don't trust Spain, are fragmented, and oppose all opposition to independence. They even approached Secretary Olney for support, or acquiescence, regarding burning sugar cane crops. He informed them it was called arson, then ended the meeting. In summation, our interests are at risk and State does not support the Junta, but meeting Spain's demands to end filibuster expeditions entails suspending the Constitution and declaring martial law."

Laying the papers down, Newcomb interlocked his fingers, and with elbows laid over the disordered pile, finished by asking, "Questions?"

Albert considered, then inquired, "The belligerency resolutions in Congress?"

"The President won't sign, so they're off the table until fall."

"What's the European position?"

"Spain made discreet overtures to several nations. Many are sympathetic but none willing to act without others. Our sources claim the British were approached to lead a coalition, and Queen Victoria is concerned Spain's monarchy could fall, but their prime minister's case against involvement carried."

When Albert posed no more questions, Newcomb turned to Starke, "Sir."

"What occurs if the Junta's granted belligerency status?"

"Spain and the Junta receive equal treatment. However, both must be a coherent entity, such as the late Confederacy claimed to be, which the Junta isn't. Spain would no longer be responsible for American investments in Cuba, either side may freely acquire arms, and both could inspect our ships for contraband, although only Spain is capable."

"Thank you."

"Captain Albert. A question. For what purpose did you request this briefing?"

Albert anticipated this. The Diplomatic Bureau wanted specifics from his discussion with Olney, which he would not provide if their Assistant Secretary saw no reason to divulge them. Besides, it was better if fewer people knew project details, since the Junta had many friends in the Building. However, fair questions required honest answers, so he responded, "We're exploring actions to discourage filibusters."

"And, *Calypso*?"

"Lieutenant Starke will assist existing Navy and Revenue Cutter Service ships in the Caribbean."

Satisfied, or concluding the well dry, Newcomb checked his watch, then offered an off-the-shelf smile, "Thank you, captain. I must be elsewhere in ten minutes, but should State be required, I'll make myself available."

Newcomb departed after ritual handshaking. As his footsteps faded, Albert turned to Starke, "Thoughts?"

"Hearing the Diplomatic Bureau position is useful. Sounds as though they're straddling business interests and public opinion. They don't favor Spain, won't support the Junta, and find their situation uncomfortable."

Albert tapped a pencil several times before responding, "They live on the fence, Jacob. Great Britain caved on Venezuela after Jameson's raid raised French and German hackles; and chose not to add us to the offended. State claims victory, but their smart money realizes no stars will align so conveniently a second time. Let's break. We'll return at ten-thirty."

While Starke called on Singer, the pitcher was refilled and glasses replaced just before two Revenue Cutter Service officers arrived slightly early; wearing their new uniform style, similar to the Navy's, but differing in cut, rank insignia, and other features. The service was established to control smuggling, since most government revenue came from tariffs, then tasks were added: assisting mariners, slave trade suppression, ending north Caribbean piracy, seal protection, and, now, Junta filibuster expeditions. Originally under the Treasury Department as its Revenue-Marine Division, two years before it was reorganized as the Revenue Cutter Service, but without full bureau status. During this, its previous rank structure, established as a master and mates on each cutter, became four tiers, with captains at the top followed by first, second, and third lieutenants. The service head was a senior captain, there was no flag officer, and a cutter's commander could be any of the four ranks. Because this became confusing when working with the Navy, Revenue Cutter Service captains were given lieutenant commander equivalency.

Today, Captain Gibson Fischer and First Lieutenant Boyd Hunter were depositing hats and coats on a chair near the door, then edging along the wall. Following introductions, they sat next to Albert. Fischer was almost jovial, but it did not detract from the perfect master mariner stereotype, complete with full, graying beard and weather-damaged nose. He looked around, then announced, "Since we're waiting, there's time for a pipe."

With that, a battered instrument swiftly appeared, preparations undertaken, and a yellow flame passed slowly over center bowl, which glowed with each puff. The spent match arced into the ashtray trailing thin gray smoke. Starke saw Albert regretted leaving his pipe behind. The mustached first lieutenant also settled in, deferred to his senior, arranged notes, then glanced occasionally through the window behind Albert.

Ten minutes later the Justice contingent arrived. Neither Arliss Spencer or Brian Fields were the marshals of dime novels. On the street, Starke would have thought the almost rotund figures with short hair, large mustaches, three-piece brown suits, banker collars, and bowlers, were businessmen, clerks, or politicians. Their hats and coats went in the chair opposite the Revenue Cutter Service pile as they slid along the wall on Starke's side. Before they sat down, everyone was on their feet exchanging names and handshakes over the ashtray, which just received a second match.

As Albert invited everyone to sit, the last arrivals dropped to their chairs, causing cane backs to creak and legs scrape. The older one, Spencer, with nearly joined eyebrows over deep-set eyes and prominent jowls, explained, "Sorry about showing up late, came from another meeting across town, we've too many small offices in the city."

Because it was the common Justice complaint, Albert commiserated appropriately, as Spencer grinned and winked at Starke, "So Sidney gaffed you, too."

It seemed the remark pricked Albert, but Starke decided the two were familiar since he ignored it and began, "*Calypso* will commission at Norfolk, complete workups off that port, then enter the Caribbean by late summer to harass and disrupt filibusters."

Fischer asked, "Fernandina, Nassau, Jacksonville, and Key West?"

"Yes and no. She'll have a roving commission in the northern Caribbean and Gulf of Mexico."

"Excellent. With *Calypso* confirmed, Treasury will contribute the new cutter *Vanguard* fitting out in Baltimore. First Lieutenant Hunter has taken command and she was specifically requested to complement *Calypso*. *Vanguard*'s the second *Windom* class cutter, around 170 feet, and capable of fifteen knots or a bit better, more than enough to outpace filibusters. She also has twin shafts, less draft to get in close, especially along the Keys, and carries a three-inch mount. The Secretary's agreed *Vanguard* reports to headquarters, not a district, although Hunter's familiar with the Key West area and has local contacts."

Spencer interjected, "As discussed with Sidney, the Marshals Service is tied to judicial districts so no comparable arrangement is possible. However, Fields works Florida's Southern District and will liaison for the Caribbean. I'll do the same north of Fernandina."

After pausing, he continued, "I assume *Calypso* won't be using any Pinkerton detectives engaged by the Spanish minister?"

"We welcome any information, but cannot be seen as coordinating with Spain."

"Agree, we've contacts with them and might obtain something, but formal liaison must go through State to the Spanish minister."

"Absolutely, and direct contact with the Junta also requires State's involvement."

After each detail was reexamined several times, talk slowed then faded, with Albert achieving what he intended; although concerned this might only be the harmonious lull before a raft of misunderstandings and misconceptions. Consequently, he closed the meeting with, "Well, gentlemen?"

That brought another round of handshakes and card exchanges, then Albert's guests walked down the corridor, discussing lunch and leaving the two officers alone in the room; where they agreed to meet in Albert's office at one.

CHAPTER FOUR
Steam Bark *Calypso*

While waiting for the afternoon meeting, Albert lingered at his office window watching an Executive Avenue streetcar, distinct against greenhouses, grounds, people, and carriages. He gave up the meeting room and brought what he needed to the office, so a Caribbean chart and other material blanketed his desk. The vacated room went to a relieved clerk from the basement's Hydrographic Office. Albert smiled, a novice waited too long to reserve a room, learned of their scarcity, and now owed a favor.

Starke would lunch until one o'clock, and it was just shy of noon, so Albert filled his cup with warm coffee. Turning, he saw three gingerbread cookies covering an off-white porcelain saucer perched on the desk's right corner. Abigail slid them into his worn leather satchel that morning. While Albert preferred standing at the window to think, taking cookies with coffee proved irresistible, so he returned to the desk. He alternated between sips and bites, reevaluating tasks delayed or needing attention until cup and saucer emptied, then retrieved a briar pipe, carefully packed the bowl, passed a match over its center, and began drawing. Once Singer released Starke, the plan's operations would largely shift to *Calypso*'s future commander, freeing him to work other aspects.

This was his latest task for the Assistant Secretary. Commander Albert reported to the Building in 1893 for a Bureau of Yards and Docks' assignment, but Admiral Ramsey made him special assistant to William McAdoo, the Assistant Secretary, who knew his work promoting Port Royal's naval station. Located on the South Carolina coast, it was occupied for Federal blockaders, then remained a coaling station until Albert's suasion and staffing skills, assisted by Republican animosity towards Charleston, created Port Royal's navy shipyard; with improved coaling pier and largest dry-dock south of Norfolk.

The Assistant Secretary came from Ireland as a boy, worked as a reporter, practiced law, represented New Jersey in Congress, and, while there, chaired the House Naval Affairs Committee, and Committee on the Militia. When his party failed to nominate him for reelection, he joined a New York City law practice, then returned as Assistant Secretary in 1893, under Hilary Herbert. McAdoo was delegated oversight of navy yard repair and construction; the survey and investigation boards; and Naval War College. Albert soon earned his confidence and, during a meeting with the Secretary and his assistant about the Fernandina affair, McAdoo turned to Commander Albert, seated directly behind, whispering, "Put a plan together, Sidney."

Working late, he established requirements, identified alternatives, then culled the list. Within a week, a mission was defined, then McAdoo and Herbert were briefed. Since Navy did not have the lead in dissuading filibuster expeditions, he developed relationships with departments and agencies having authority, responsibility, and resources; then offered contributions. Although stopping arms smugglers appeared straightforward, it was far from it. Only ships leaving from or registered in the United States could be stopped, so the rest fell to Spain and other nations. It was an ancillary Navy mission, so commitments and expenditures must be minimal. The Justice and Treasury Departments bore primary responsibility, but had competing internal priorities and political stress that limited what could be accomplished. There was also no intelligence organization to work the Junta, because it would be illegal or the capability did not exist; leaving the Pinkerton National Detective Agency, hired by Spain, the only entity organized and capable. Finally, the administration wanted to avoid anything resembling the 1891 *Itata* fiasco, that possibly cost Republicans the last election.

The North Atlantic Squadron was Albert's primary Departmental resource since it controlled ships. However, squadron commanders always wanted to retain them, and the Secretary wished to improve its ability to operate as a whole. This made negotiation difficult with any flag officer, but Albert initially dealt with Rear Admiral Richard Worsam Meade III. His reputation as an advocate for reform and technology existed alongside a demeanor shared with his late uncle, a general who acquired as many Northern as Southern adversaries during the war; and earned several snapping turtle sobriquets.

Consequently, Albert built and strengthened liaisons with other departments, while obtaining what he could from Meade, before concluding a more active element was needed. This was a dedicated ship that did not target individual filibuster expeditions, but created the same dynamics as a commerce raider; drive up risk and cost. Assigned to the Special Service Squadron, it would operate with loose direction from the Building, haunt favored routes, and threaten every expedition setting out by obscuring what the Junta knew of its movement and intent.

Success required the right ship and commander, but he tackled the ship first. Some torpedo boats were in the water, but only *Cushing* was operating. She was eight years old, made twenty-four knots, had a small crew, needed constant coaling, and was known for poor seakeeping. Her high speed was also unnecessary since filibusters used schooners, small freighters, or seagoing tugs seldom exceeding ten knots, and almost never fifteen. Another source was wooden relics like

Yantic or *Appalachicola*, but whether in use or ordinary, they required large crews, were slow, and most worn out. While a small cruiser or gunboat might suffice, those were unavailable for any length of time. Since battleships, armored cruisers, and monitors were excluded, Albert choose a merchant ship conversion.

He never balked at getting counsel and honed an ability to seek expert advice, then listen, evaluate, and exploit it. This began during his first cruise when a frustrated lieutenant loudly berated Albert when he attempted to bluff his way through a rigging question. He was told, with obvious frustration, "You're here to learn, so get with the bosun, understand the answer, then try again; but don't waste my time with farce. Ignorance is not stupidity, you can recover." Albert took the reproach to heart and learned from it.

Consequently, he read James Bulloch's books, then asked Lieutenant Colwell, the London attaché, to press him for additional information on commerce raider design, blockade running, and whether any blockade runners were available. Meanwhile, Albert donned civilian attire to tour Jacksonville, Key West, and Fernandina. Returning through Georgia and Virginia, he attempted to speak with ex-Confederates such as John Kell, Conway Whittle, and Joseph Barney. A number were reticent or suspicious, but some proved helpful, and knowing Jefferson Starke opened more than one door. He even considered going to Rio de Janeiro to approach his old shipmate, but decided time was short and the elder Starke probably sympathized with the Cubans.

Instead, he approached the brother's Starke Shipping & Shipbuilding firm, since some of those visited mentioned it once planned four commercial ships designed for conversion to small gunboats or privateers. The Baltimore firm was familiar in most East Coast ports, where its blood-red swallowtail house flag of three interlocked black S's in a yellow circle flew from the mainmasts of thirteen freighters and two small liners. The firm moved cargo throughout the Caribbean and along the East Coast in smaller ships; hardworking sail and steam freighters that entered and departed with little comment. For larger ships or long voyages, the firm chartered, while its small West Point, Virginia shipyard served company ships and local customers.

His first meeting with Immanuel Starke proved the rumors partly true, and the working names were *Cutlass*, *Claymore*, *Rapier*, and *Broadsword*. It seemed the firm wanted to mitigate high risk and insurance rates should the nation go to war with the Navy weaker than most in Europe, and some in South America. Immanuel Starke saw an opportunity to offset losses by selling these ships to the Navy at a war profit, or send them privateering, since the United States declined joining the 1856 *Declaration of Paris* that ended the practice.

British architects were contracted and studies made using lines and information from the Confederate *Alabama*; German aviso *Zieten*; Royal Navy's *Doterel* class; and Russian cruiser *Asia*, then tradeoffs made and a final design approved. The result was a yacht-like hull that optimized steaming and sailing capabilities with a clipper bow to slip through the sea, and aesthetic, but outmoded, fantail stern. Her single large stack rose from a deckhouse beginning just aft of the main mast and continued forward to lift slightly at the pilothouse foundation; above it was a flying bridge surrounded by lifelines and canvas windscreens. Aft were two round bar, or rotary, boat davits either side of a cargo hatch. The bark rig was chosen to provide high performance with minimal crew, so under sail she had almost unlimited range for long passages. There was also a double-expansion 850 horsepower engine that easily handled steam transits. A single screw arrangement was selected over twin for better performance under canvas and more hull volume, although it gave up some maneuverability and drove a fourteen-foot draft. Wrought-iron keel, framing, and bulkheads provided strength and greater interior space, while the wood hull allowed coppering below the waterline to reduce fouling. It also meant less dry-docking and opened more ports for maintenance or repair. Deck space topside, aft of the mizzen and ahead of the foremast, included foundations for heavy muzzle-loading pivot guns. Besides this significant battery, if converted, her cargo holds became berthing, magazines, storerooms, and additional coal bunkers to increase range without losing sail lockers. The result was a 1,150 ton ship of 220 feet with a thirty-one foot beam, capable of steaming nearly 2,300 miles at ten knots. Two were laid down, but growing costs and Navy expansion made railroad investment more appealing. One ship was broken up on the ways, but *Cutlass* was too far along. Since completion would cost less than stopping work, she was launched, named *Illusive*, given a light schooner rig to steady her, and the long, elegant bowsprit bobbed. While in service, she was occasionally chartered for special cruises, but mostly shuttled small cargoes and passengers between Philadelphia, Havana, Caracas, and other ports; returning adequate, not exceptional, profits.

Albert returned to the company offices with a Board of Inspection and Survey member when the firm offered to sell, since the design was seventeen years old, her steam plant required updating, and a full overhaul due. The Navy was equally receptive since it lacked small gunboats after Congress halted their construction six years earlier. With events in Mediterranean, seal protection, and filibuster patrols, pressure was building to fill temporary gaps, which, in the case of filibusters, found battleships' steam launches on patrol, warships being diverted, and, recently, calls to award prize money, or issue letters of marque. To strengthen his position, Albert courted offices positioned to assist, delay or halt any sale and conversion. The Bureau of Construction and Repair was assured design work and Norfolk's navy shipyard given some tasks. The Bureau of Steam Engineering was offered an immediate opportunity to install Normand fire-tube boilers and a triple-expansion engine, then test them at sea. The Bureau of Ordnance was lured with installation and field testing of the latest 4-inch, 40-caliber quick-firing rifles, and Bureau of Equipment and Recruiting enticed with two suits of sails and other items. However, acquisition became possible when the Secretary and Assistant Secretary, having chaired the Naval Appropriation Committee, obtained unexpended funds, so no party could object because they lost funding. With that, survey and transfer negotiations began, his rat terrier idea moved to conception, and, since Starke accepted, he had a commander with the potential to succeed in the unique assignment.

Albert was enjoying a spurt of self-congratulation, briar pipe jutting from a corner of his mouth and supported by his right hand, when Starke returned with an empty folder, "Afternoon, captain."

"Afternoon, Jacob. Ready?"

Starke scanned the desktop, obscured by a chart, notes, and the odd book. Hanging his coat on a rack, he walked to the desk, "Yes, sir."

Albert lowered the pipe, stood, and lifted a handful of papers, "*Illusive* was renamed *Calypso*, as a sale condition, to sever her from the Starke firm. The name's from a small gunboat with no real history."

Jefferson Classical & Military Academy naturally exposed Starke to the classics, so he recalled Calypso was the beautiful nymph who delayed a mariner's return home. Albert sensed hesitation, laid a sheaf of notes over the chart, grinning, "You won't recognize her. New masts have been stepped and a bowsprit with jibboom added."

"I wasn't aware her bark rig existed."

"Didn't. Our navy constructor substituted masts and spars left off another ship. Lower masts are steel, uppers pine. Drawings called for wood, so this should be stronger and reduce top weight. Spars required shaping, but they're finished."

"Where's she berthed?"

"In dry-dock for hull sheathing, boiler replacement and engine change-out. Towed from your uncle's shipyard at West Point to Newport News four months ago. Removals, tow preparations, and some conversion work occurred there; mainly storerooms, staterooms, and crew quarters. Your uncle insisted that be in the contract since West Point would have overhauled her."

"Who's in charge?"

"Lieutenant (junior grade) William O'Leary, a steam engineer assigned naval constructor duties. Unusual, but Newport News Shipyard's government department is just forming, so people are used where needed. Seems professional, enthusiastic, and has water-tube boiler experience. Perhaps he wants a billet."

"We need to talk crewing."

Albert retrieved his pipe, passed a match over the bowl then, with it in hand, remarked, "Last subject, back to *Calypso*."

Setting the pipe aside, Albert pulled several sheets from a stack and passed them to Starke, "This covers sails. About 19,000 square feet. Main and fore mast spread topgallants, topsails and courses; mizzen carries a gaff topsail and driver; plus jibs and staysails. Both light and heavy weather canvas sets are being made up; sail flax canvas, numbers 1 through 5.

A storm-sail set's sewn from number 1 canvas and load-out of eighty-yard canvas rolls requisitioned for repairs."

With pipe aroma from a fading gray wisp of smoke permeating the office, Albert handed the papers to Starke then moved on, "Plant's a triple-expansion reciprocating steam engine with two Normand water-tube boilers good for 180-pound steam; same as some new gunboats, so you're operationally testing the combination. It's similar to *Detroit*, so it won't be entirely new, but high steam pressures require experienced steam engineers. A full speed run's needed to learn her top speed over distance, but our calculations suggest 1,227 horsepower may drive this hull to fifteen knots. There's also two donkey boilers included in the plant."

After passing more paper to Starke, Albert hefted the next pile, "I've started talks with Bureau of Ordnance. Main battery is two 4-inch 40-caliber breech-loading rifles; same that *Iowa* gets for secondary batteries. They were designed in '92 and weigh about two tons. The first version uses bag ammunition, so confirm the Washington Navy Yard's gun factory ships you fixed ammunition variants. Probably more useful for our purposes, a Driggs-Schroeder 3-pounder quick-fire mount goes on either side just behind the main deck bulwark near the pilothouse. Gatling guns will mount on deck, or for the landing force, carriages. *Calypso*'s unique, so there's latitude, except in main armament, so you may consider exchanging the 3-pounders for 1-inch Nordenfelt machine guns. I telephoned Lieutenant Commander Leutze, in the yard's ordnance office, to arrange a ten o'clock Friday sit-down. Once you agree on those guns and the small arms load out, we can tell the shipyard how to arrange magazines."

The Bureau of Ordnance letter detailing the proposal, and more notes followed the first papers into Starke's folder. Looking up at Albert, he inquired, "Boats and searchlights?"

"Next subject. She had davits for two pairs of whaleboats on either side, which didn't suit her new role. I wanted steam launches, but their size and weight numbers were so bad stability calculations were abandoned; although handling problems would have done for them anyway. In the end, existing davits were replaced with round bar davits and she'll receive a pair of whaleboats and two steam pinnaces."

Starke again watched Albert paw through papers until a small folded sheet emerged, "There's also two electric generators with enough power for searchlights. You get two lights aft of the flying bridge, and the Ardois system for night communication."

Searchlights and the Ardois signaling system were new, so Starke decided to study how they were best used. While considering this, an idea emerged, "Hull color?"

"Gray, but you could have white or torpedo boat green." Albert chuckled.

"I suggest black, gold, and straw-yellow. White's too showy and a Spaniard seeing gray may think we're at war. Our old ships and Spain's cruisers have black hulls, so the color scheme could contribute to filibusters' discomfort and be useful at night."

Noise intruded from the hall as people passed and Albert concentrated on writing in a notebook, before responding, "Excellent. I'll get those instructions to Newport News. They were planning gray, but paint's not bought."

Albert briefly raised, looked at the electrolier, then appeared to calculate, "Boilers, condensers and hull should last eighteen to twenty-four months before major overhaul, so *Calypso*'s good until June of '98."

Starke's forehead formed successive ripples, Albert noticed and intruded, "Different thoughts?"

"Fire-tube boilers are new, so's a triple-expansion engine. There's canvas replacement, bottom fouling, crew changes, and so forth. I'd suggest an interim dry-docking."

Albert added it to his list, responding, "Good point. Port Royal shipyard has docking and repair facilities, besides it's near your patrol area."

After finishing, Albert set his notebook aside, smoothed the chart, then began, "It's March and the conversion must complete by June, so you'll need to get down there. Remember, ships are a yard's meal ticket. Unless another project's pushing, they'll do anything to stay at the trough. However, Newport News is building two gunboats, so your problem may be gaining attention. Now the mission. You'll need to flesh out what I've drafted, then provide recommendations. We'll write the orders after sea trials."

"Yes, sir."

"Assuming you leave Norfolk in June, *Calypso* enters the Caribbean during hurricane and yellow fever seasons. Yellow fever ends in late August, hurricanes in November. Let's plan a return to Port Royal around June next year, two weeks in dock, then upkeep through July; might help avoid that year's worst seasons. Coaling there may also throw off the Junta, and you won't have to pry it from commercial venders."

Then, grinning, he added, "… and less chance for a coal torpedo," before finishing his notes. Setting them aside, he looked to the chart where, using his pencil to circle then successively point to different locations, said, "Your patrol area. Concentrate on Straits of Florida, Nicolas Channel, and Old Bahama Channel. If you're not long away, some cruising northeast of Dry Tortugas, through the Windward Passage, or Yucatan Channel might prove useful. Use the personal cipher provided for messages to me, but continue normal reporting, including Navy regulations' arrival and departure reports. I'll be your operational contact, and Special Service Squadron the administrative one."

Another paper emerged from Albert's stack, "This lists ports with undersea cables. Cap Haitian, with the United States & Hayti firm, suites our purpose, but local conditions may close it. Western Union Telegraph Company's in Key West, Tampa, Nassau, and Jupiter Inlet, but the Junta will hear immediately. Kingston and Cockburn Harbor have cable access, but it's under British control with messages going to Nova Scotia before coming to Washington over landlines. Spain controls and monitors Havana, Cienfuegos, Santiago, Caimanera, San Juan, and Ponce. Enough said there, and here's the latest information on others, but you'll want to update it before entering the Caribbean."

With cable information fattening the folder, Starke realized Albert was delegating tactical planning and he must double down to stay free of Building direction. Shifting topics, Albert said, "I've included the latest navigation notes. Usual points, winds generally veer from northeast to southeast, the Straits of Florida current can reach three knots, but most currents circle Cuba clockwise at one. Since Caribbean charts are inaccurate, several additional ones have been added to the Hydrographic Office's chart allowance. If you need anything else, get in touch with the fellow using our conference room."

Starke considered this, "That's appreciated. Perhaps we can suggest the mission is partly chart survey?"

Albert considered this, reopened his notebook, then responded, "Agreed, I'll get with Lieutenant Commander Moser at Coast Survey," then, while fondling his pipe and glancing anxiously at the slightly ajar transom window above the door, continued in a lower voice, "Commodore Bunce relieved Rear Admiral Meade last year and, despite Spain, wants the squadron in the Caribbean as a single group. He's also established seven-week rotations in Key West to slow local filibustering. *Montgomery* and *Newark* completed stints and three more ships are being considered, but that would probably over-stretch the squadron. Although not involved, the Seventh Lighthouse District operates the lighthouse tender *Mangrove* out of Key West, so we might look into her for assistance."

Eyeing the transom window again, as he dredged through his papers, Albert continued, "While visiting Cuba must be coordinated with State, there's a contact working the Plant Steamship Line if you need to get something to the consul-general. By the way, do you have any business there regarding the mill or plantation?"

Starke's thoughts immediately returned to Fitzhugh Lee, "I don't believe so."

"Shame. Might have been useful. Anyway, if you do, we'll arrange leave. Now to the crew, *Calypso*'s proposed comple-ment's eleven officers and 124 enlisted, but see if it fits what you think is needed since we've latitude there, so long as the total doesn't change and people are available. I've arranged with east coast receiving ships to send *Calypso* their best, not those they want to offload. Your wardroom will be provided two officers for watchstanding, deck, and gunnery. I've asked for three, but if that doesn't happen, we'll get naval cadets. There'll be a navigator and executive officer, of course, and the Steam Engineering Bureau's committed to a very junior chief engineer, an assistant, and possibly three watchstanders; most likely engineer cadets. There'll be a paymaster and sur-geon, but you'll not be blessed with a chaplain."

"Marines."

"Not resolved. Your thoughts?"

"The crew's small, sir. Marines don't stand useful under-way watches, and petty officers resent them. We'll have a scratch naval landing party at best, and not enough marines to change that, so engineers and sailors would be more useful."

"I'd have thought Alexandria might make you more an advocate."

"For *Calypso*, I see no role, and if there was, the number assigned would either be too few or turn her into a troop transport. Anyway, they concentrate on marching and drills, not marksmanship; and I've seen those results too clearly."

"Montana, I suppose. Well, a squad's proposed, and Colonel Commandant Heywood's staff claim they've emphasized shooting. It seems he plans to argue for their manning large ships' secondary guns, like the British, and may push to operate your 4-inch mounts. Rifles are problem since he's refused to issue new Lee rifles until everyone's outfitted, so they still use black powder Springfield Model 1884s; while sailors have three or four types, including magazine rifles."

Starke, almost grinned, "If the Marine Corps is refusing Lee rifles, there may be enough for *Calypso*, I'll bring it up with Leutze this Friday and perhaps visit the firing range."

"Meanwhile, I'll start your orders to *Calypso* and work today's changes. You'll need time to turn over with Lieutenant Singer, so we'll speak next week."

After they shook hands, Starke shut the folder, retrieved his coat then walked down the black and white checked corridor. Albert restored his desk while Starke left the Building for Lafayette Square. Unlike Monday, he took the Metropolitan Company line, with different scenery and no mystery woman.

CHAPTER FIVE
Navy Gun Factory

During the two days following Starke's afternoon conference, midweek rain cleared away remnants of the scattered, gray-black snow redoubts with off-white cores. He completed his intelligence work or shifted it to Singer's officers and clerks. Albert was also visited several times, and they spoke in the corridors. Both evenings he left late and once ate at a nearby hotel. Altman met him at the mansion door both nights, with his aunt asking what kept him on the second.

When the next day's navy yard meeting with Leutze was mentioned, he discovered she met his father as a young woman. The Württemberg painter from Stuttgart was well-known beyond the art community, where he organized Dusseldorf writers and artists. When Prussian authorities dispersed or jailed them, he returned to Washington, and now, like Starke's father, professed allegiance only to his adopted country. She recalled the son was born in Prussia and appointed to the Naval Academy by President Lincoln.

To meet Leutze, who worked for the ordnance officer, Commander Jewell, Starke wore his seldom-used undress blue lieutenant's uniform. Besides going beyond the Building, Washington Navy Yard marines and watchmen knew their regulars, but an unfamiliar civilian would be stopped, so the uniform prevented delay. After buttoning the blouse, he added overcoat and cap, then left the mansion. Earlier than normal, he walked under clear skies to the streetcar stop, took one to Lafayette Square, then continued on foot to the Building.

After brief visits with Singer and Albert, he left through the 17th Street entrance to hail a yellow Herdic cab from the sidewalk. It was the single horse version. Larger ones were pulled by a team and carried eight passengers. As it approached, he remembered transportation was still needed for next week's excursion to meet the English visitors, but, with rates set by distance, a cab would be readily arranged, like today's driver, who was especially satisfied since there was the potential for a return passenger following a good fare. The uniformed driver, perched on his open seat over small front wheels, smiled as Starke entered between the cab's large rear ones. After settling on one of the seats lining either side, he lay the satchel beside him, then heard a sharp whistle as the cab pulled from the curb into the morning bustle.

Between the Building and navy yard, he studied Washington. Southbound, they turned left on B Street, paralleling the mall until Center Market, then south on 7th Street past the Baltimore & Potomac station. Constructed of red-brick with black mortar and trimmed with stone bands, its clock tower rose above lesser spires, gables, and long train shed extending south. Then came the Capitol, dominating everything from its rise, as they moved southeast on Virginia Avenue's combined street and railbed. Passing Garfield Park and the large switchyard, they reached 8th Street, where the navy yard main gate could be seen two-blocks south. This last leg passed down an asphalt boulevard under streetlights hung from poles with wide sidewalks lined by nude saplings, their cast iron surrounds, and an occasional bicycle. The main gate was the central archway of a four-story, white-brick building bulging the shipyard's brick wall. Centered at street level, it was flanked by internal Greek columns and included wrought iron gates. On the entrance's right was office and guard house, and left, the Marine officer's quarters, with the entire upper level dedicated to their barracks.

The air was cool and sun making headway when Stark left the cab, paid its driver, then entered. Passing through, he returned the Marine sentry's salute, nodded to a civilian watchman, then entered a broad park enclosed by red-brick industrial buildings and whitewashed quarters. It was familiar because his uncle's firm once did business there, as did William Reily, now almost twenty years in nearby Mount Olivet Cemetery. Reily was ship-breaking obsolete monitors when Starke met the handsome man with a thirst for adventure that already landed him on a survey expedition to Nicaragua. He befriended Jacob, then played host at Fort Abraham Lincoln. Starke last saw him ride off with Captain Yates' troop on a large bay, but he intermittently returned in dreams or flashbacks.

The shipyard formed a right trapezoid, with 5th and 9th Streets making up its top and base, M Street the right-angled side, and the Anacostia River waterfront its angled face. Three sides of the compound were brick walls, buildings, or fencing; with the commander's quarters east of the gate, and other houses backing to 9th Street. More officers' quarters were just to the west, with red-brick industrial buildings filling areas south and west of a central park leading to the river. Several large buildings enclosing a courtyard gave the impression of a single, immense building that dominated the view. Beyond, two huge, faded-white, ship houses sat on the waterfront. The largest, a four or five story barn-like structure, was near the southwest corner, while its smaller sibling was southeast near the waterfront's opposite end, with a dry-dock and marine railway. Since most of the shipyard became the Navy Gun Factory, both stood deserted except for unpopular offices at their shore ends.

However, his destination was a small brick building with wooden veranda and widow's walk, just visible between two large brick buildings beyond the park. He walked briskly to the commandant's office and shipyard administration building where Leutze worked. The morning was clear and atmosphere laced with smells of burning coal, mixed industrial odors, then the river's. He located Leutze's office just inside the front door, hung overcoat and hat on a cast iron wall hook, then introduced himself. Since the Academy, Leutze acquired a graying mustache, goatee, and girth. He greeted Starke with a firm handshake, motioned him to a table overlooking the veranda and across the yard to the smaller ship shed, then began, "I received Captain Albert's phone call. Congratulations on *Calypso*. I've another year or so here, but hope for the same."

"Yes, sir."

Leutze then extracted notes from previously ordered piles on the table, "I've reviewed the *Calypso* arming proposal. Two 4-inch 40-caliber guns is a useful main battery, although new gunboats like *Wilmington* mount eight. The guns should be in Norfolk next week, but I'll track the shipment."

Starke saw his opportunity, "I understand they're not Mark 1 Mod 0 guns. *Calypso*'s a small crew, there's no hoists, and the magazines are converted so I anticipate cooling problems. Fixed ammunition would allow faster firing and safer storage than bagged."

"Albert's agreement specified the latest version. If not, I'll see it corrected, but that could delay delivery if they're not available."

Starke needed his support, but risked a nudge, "The magazines must be configured soon."

"*Calypso* will receive a fixed ammunition version, Jacob. If it's an inventory issue, I'll get them from *Iowa* or a new gunboat, since *Calypso* commissions first."

Leutze then pulled a different sheet from the pile, "This requisition's for two Driggs-Schroeder 3-pounder quick-fire mounts. I believe one will be located on either side behind the bulwark near her pilothouse. *Calypso*'s also slated for two Gatling guns. She'll not be over-armed, but well enough for any filibuster; and most Spanish gunboats in the Caribbean are slower or mount large muzzleloaders."

Starke ignored the filibuster reference, but noted rumors of *Calypso*'s mission reaching the yard, then passed his own sheet with figures and sketches across the table, "I believe there's some discretion. Four-inch guns reach 12,000 yards and fire around eight rounds per minute with a good crew, but their field of fire is obstructed by bowsprit, deckhouse, and masts. Captain Albert suggested 1-inch Nordenfelt machine guns instead of Driggs-Schroeder."

Leutze considered the calculations, then looked at Starke, "Your notes advocate a rapid-fire 3-pounder gun. That Nordenfelt fires bursts, and is most effective under 2,000 yards. That leaves the 4-inch guns covering a 10,000 yard gap with a slower rate of fire, and best accuracy below 2,000 yards. Your calculations correctly show 3-pounders reach nearly 7,000 yards, which gives better coverage, and a Hotchkiss five-barrel gun is good for thirty rounds a minute, although they claim sixty. A six-pounder would improve range, but reduce firing rate. I agree the Driggs-Schroeder 3-pounder's not the best choice, and suggest a Hotchkiss of the same size. It's more reliable and includes a gun carriage for landing parties."

Starke agreed, then moved on, "*Calypso*'s to receive .45-70 Gatling guns, which use black powder. If possible, I'd like to outfit the ship with 1895 Colt–Browning machine guns and Winchester-Lee rifles since they both use the 6mm smokeless cartridge and a single ammunition type would be useful. With

Gatlings, that means .45-70 trapdoor Springfields, which I would like to avoid."

After extracting and studying another form, Leutze saw the ship was to receive single shot Springfields. Making a note in pencil, he replied, "That makes sense, but Colt-Browning's an air-cooled automatic gun firing something over 4,000 rounds a minute. While it passed Newport Torpedo Station tests, the single barrel cooks-off after long bursts. Some may be available, but the Winchester-Lee rifle contract was only awarded in January, and 6mm cartridges are scarce."

Starke was resigning himself, when Leutze looked up, "I suggest we consider what's in storage. Perhaps we could pry out some 6mm machine guns, rifles, and ammunition as an operational test, but it's unlikely. There's another approach. The Navy bought small quantities of .45-70 magazine rifles, the Remington-Keene, Winchester-Hotchkiss, and Remington-Lee. There may be enough Remington-Lee's."

"The 1885 model?"

"Yes, the five-round, bolt action magazine rifle. Good for 2,000 yards, not that anyone's that accurate. If not in the armory, they could be pulled from a Naval Militia unit."

Admitting, this was better than expected, Starke confirmed, "Four Gatlings, with them?"

Leutze returned Starke's notes, "Yes, and you'll receive .38 caliber double-action revolvers. As to quantity, I agree with your calculations. For a crew of approximately 135, the proposal of 75 rifles and 25 pistols fits."

With negotiations at an end, they spoke generally on Cuba and filibustering, shook hands, then Starke lifted his overcoat and hat from the hook and left. The midday sun outside was welcome, but clouds were gathering; as Thursday's paper predicted. Even so, it was an enjoyable walk across the park to the main gate, which he passed through, then, since he was not committed elsewhere, waited for the next yellow, white, and mahogany Capital Traction Company streetcar.

CHAPTER SIX
A Horse and Three Women

Starke slept strong, hard and dreamless after committing to *Calypso*, and Albert's mission, but also because he would ride that morning. Somehow, a familiar mount's companionship relaxed him, while allowing time to think, so Washington weekends often included an early ride using a Starke carriage horse.

Gemini was his favorite, although both neck-reined and exercised with saddles. Like all Starke horses, they were geldings. Mares grew unpredictable with age, while stallions served best as studs or statues. Society scorned mules, despite their qualities; and often being favored by generals on campaigns. Assigning him a tall, gray mule years before, an old packer quipped, "Mules is smart, horses cunning." He found it a true observation over the years. Starke often considered buying a horse, but riders developed an attachment to favored mounts, so he would feel disloyal selling each time he left. Hiring a Washington Riding Academy horse was unpalatable because multiple riders turned stable animals into barnstormers, hammerheads, or passively defiant mounts inured to beating, coaxing, and reason.

He woke slowly in a burled walnut high-back bed under a green, goose-down comforter to a soft sun filtering through overcast skies and draped window. *The Evening Times'* warming and rain prediction stood, which meant less riders and bicycles, so he folded sheet and comforter back on themselves, then abandoned their warmth for the dressing room's morning chill. As every morning, he trimmed his beard, lathered, stropped the straight razor, and shaved. While doing so, he was reminded to lay in a safety razor and blade supply before returning to sea. A breakfast buffet was set out in the morning room at seven-thirty, where he joined his aunt for eggs, ham, toast, and coffee, then returned to powder a carved boar's hair toothbrush and clean his teeth.

Starke owned proper riding attire, but preferred a more utilitarian outfitting, so he stripped, retrieved a folded union suit from the bureau, slid into its gray flannel, then closed the buttons. Light-blue wool cavalry trousers followed, with sewn-on side and watch pockets. Then came a long-sleeve pullover shirt, light-gray wool with five bone buttons closing it to the collar. He buttoned three, then pulled wide canvas braces over each shoulder. His jacket stayed in the armoire, since the heavy duster was adequate for the day's weather. Gray woolen socks followed, then supple, brown leather cavalry boots, almost to the knee, completed the assemble. Leaving for the stable, he draped the butternut gray duster over his arm and picked up the center-creased cavalry hat.

Set back from the carriage house attached to the mansion, the cinder-brick building's second floor hayloft spanned a four-horse stable and second small carriage house. On its stable side were two stalls with wooden partitions curving down from the rear wall to a square newell post. Between the stalls and sliding door to an exercise yard was a large room for horses to shelter. Although stable and carriage sections began with the same stone floor, shod hooves had worn the stable side smooth. Halters, bridles, leads, and feedbags hung from the wall near a tall cabinet filled with ointments and grooming tools. Two bins containing corn and grain were locked to prevent foundering, and dry, green hay forked down through a ceiling trapdoor.

Their groom, Darius Sutton, enjoyed a local equine reputation and meticulously cared for his stable and horses. Before coming to the family sixteen years earlier, he was a Tenth Cavalry trooper until hit by a nearly spent .44 Henry round. While hard living showed on the small, sinewy man, he was active and keen. Dressed for stable work, his battered wide-brim hat fit tightly on short, graying black hair. A voracious reader, he consumed books, old newspapers, and shared *The Colored American* subscription costs with several friends. He just finished checking grain bin locks and was reaching for a five-tine pitchfork hanging on the wall when Starke entered.

Sutton greeted him with, "Dreary morning Mister Jacob. Gemini's in the first stall."

Seeing the groom favoring his right leg, Starke replied, "Much appreciated, Darius. How's the leg?"

"Weather's discomforting, but our Lord's looking after me."

From the large room just off the stalls came sounds of frantic neighing and shod hooves striking stone, provoking Starke's gelding to lift his head in reply. Darius chuckled, "Castores don't like being left. Saddle's on the tree."

Gemini and Castores were matched bays of seven years with black tails, manes, and socks. Although Castores had the paler belly and lighter forelock, it showed less until long winter coats gave way to summer ones. Gemini swung his head rearward until restrained by the halter lead, observed Starke, then pawed stone and straw with a single front hoof. As the horse stood with a rear leg cocked, Stark approached from the side, lightly dragging his hand across the rump and continuing forward until he slipped a rope over the gelding's neck, removed his halter, then attempted to slide a curb bit in the mouth. Gemini resisted the cool steel, but Starke used the horse's overbite to leverage it through clenched teeth, then slid it behind the last molars as Gemini began positioning, and warming the bit. Starke held it place and pulled the bridle over the bay's head, adjusted ears and forelock, then buckled the throat latch.

Castores whinnied and Gemini responded by shaking his head. Led to an outside ringbolt, the tethered Gemini remained motionless until Starke returned with the Nolan saddle, consisting of a wooden tree overlaid by layered leathers to form a deep seat, elevated pommel, higher cantle, and no horn. With steel stirrups swung from leather straps passing over large skirts directly under the rider, it sat like a stock or McClellan saddle but adjusted to the horse. Using slightly yellowed teeth, the gelding lunged for the black saddle blanket, but Starke was faster; quickly landing the Nolan with one stirrup flipped back over the seat. Although Gemini inflated while it was cinched, Starke tightened the belly band, waited for him to breath, placed a knee in the horse's flank, then pulled to secure it.

After donning the duster, Starke unhitched the bay, sandwiched the reins between his left hand's fingers, edged his boot toe into the stirrup, then swung into the saddle, just as the gelding twisted left to unbalance him. Once mounted, he adjusted the reins then guided Gemini from the stable. Seeing this, Castores entered the exercise yard where he paced back and forth along its board fence's well-chewed top rail, whinnying.

Starke preferred neck-reining. With the horse guided by neck pressure, the rider's left hand controlled the horse and right remained free. He rode bareback before saddles, so synchronizing knee pressure and shifting weight while reining came without thought. After years of riding, he disliked direct reining and preferred the basic walk, trot, or gallop.

Starke pointed the horse to a dirt road leading northwest as Gemini's attempt to reach the paddock behind the exercise yard ended with an obligatory half-buck and sideway shuffle.

At the walk, Starke adjusted duster and hat brim while using leg muscles to match the horse's rhythm. Walking or trotting, they moved generally northwest along the road, north of Washington Heights but south of Mount Zion cemetery and national zoological park. Without Castores' distractions, the large bay settled into long, smooth strides as Starke became absorbed in thought.

Yesterday, the newspapers reported Spain fitting-out eight commerce raiders capable of twenty knots, with nine or ten-inch guns. Princeton students burned the Spanish king in effigy, unaware he was ten years old and the country run by a regent, Maria Christina. As they dragged Spain's flag through the streets, their Spanish counterparts, with equal enthusiasm, forced campuses to close from rioting. In Cuba, Havana's Chamber of Commerce debated Cienfuegos' trade boycott of the States while Governor-general Weyler forbid anti-American protests and warned order would prevail. The *Evening Star* reported the cutter *Morrill* intercepted a filibuster schooner, just as Tampa's district attorney directed the Collector of Customs to release *Mallory*, another ship loaded with weapons. Unfortunately, her cargo was legal unless destined for Cuba, it was difficult to disprove a manifest beforehand, and she carried no insurrectos. Meanwhile, Spain's minister, believing all delays useful, had detectives charter the yacht *Roi*, to search for *Ardell*, another filibuster schooner reported out.

Rock Creek bridge interrupted these thoughts, since he always stopped, dismounted, and tightened the cinch. After crossing, he passed over the Chevy Chase streetcar tracks then worked north along Carlisle Avenue, with Mount Zion Cemetery and national zoological park visible through a light mist drifting down from low clouds.

Starke met with few riders and no carriages, although a fashionable equestrian with English saddle, cord pantaloons, jack boots, and oilskin dipped his brown felt hat in greeting, then waved a leather quirk. Starke nodded and observed the mare's tail was bobbed, leaving no horsefly defense. He and Darius disliked bobbing tails or cropping manes, and saw little purpose in quirks or spurs. However, weather and rhythm soon took him back twenty years to cavalry, infantry, wagons, and mules pushing through spring rain, sleet, and snow. On that trip, work went to midnight, with reveille at three or four o'clock to load mules and repack wagons. He shivered, recalling the chilled weakness and gnawing hunger. Shifting in the saddle, he thought of pleasure riders moaning about saddle-sores after a short outing, while troopers endured weeks with chafed crotches burning as battered flesh ground between leather and bone.

Starke's thoughts then shifted south as Gemini shook his head without breaking stride. In winter, Florida's coast was livable, but its interior was mostly swamp, heat, mosquitoes, and snakes. In summer, the entire southern coast saw heat rise, humidity soar, and yellow fever arrive. Further south, the Caribbean's islands had changed little during the century. Communications were improved, piracy eradicated, and the slave trade ended, but hurricanes, disease, and malaise flourished amidst seas that rocked gently over deadly reefs, dropping to immense depths, or turned violent by sudden storms.

The Caribbean crown jewel was Havana, a fortified city with parks, hotels, shops, restaurants, and yacht club; hosting cosmopolitan residents from the United States, Europe, China, Africa, Philippines, and other regions. Since the sixteenth century, it was the social and trade center anchoring Spain's western empire and building immense wooden ships for the Armada Española. Starke visited as a child, then returned on company ships and business, including visits to the Pinar del Río sugar mill and plantation. His favorite haunt was Hotel Inglaterra with its balconied rooms overlooking the Paseo del Prado and central park. Recalling mornings of coffee and pastries at street-side tables watching the city wake, Starke wished *Calypso* would enter the narrow channel separating it from Morro Castle.

Gemini whinnied at a green milk-wagon with yellow trim, tall rectangular doors, and company name in white letters. Its gray-white horse snorted a halfhearted reply and the uniformed driver half-waved. Riding on, Starke sorted through what must be accomplished in the two weeks before leaving for Newport News. By then, the British guests would arrive, Newport summer preparations would be complete, and Washington's December-to-Easter Sunday social season petered out. After that, heat, humidity, and disease would close many city businesses and suspend receptions, dances, and socials. By late spring, the wealthy's annual migration to northern states, or high ground near the city, would be well underway.

As the road lifted, he spotted a handful of Mount Zion tombstones reflecting what rays of sun pierced the overcast; and indistinct animals in zoological park pastures. After recrossing streetcar tracks, the road ended and he turned towards President Cleveland's summer home, then, rejecting the first two southbound routes to the mansion, wheeled southeast on the third, paralleling a brook. As they walked, water flowing over and around rocks melded with shod hooves striking dirt and gravel; then Gemini hesitated, lifted his tail and jettisoned steaming, greenish-brown balls to form a twenty-foot column strung out over dirt and gravel.

Starke let the easy walk increase to a jolting trot then the gallop's smooth undulations as the warmed and enthusiastic gelding ran full out a quarter mile. With nostrils flaring, breathing labored, sweat darkening Gemini's coat, and white spittle foaming around bit and chest, Starke brought him back to the walk before dismounting a short distance from the stable. While the excited horse paced about, Starke loosened his cinch, signaling ride's end, then walked Gemini the remaining distance. Besides discouraging barnstorming, he never returned a heated horse and would have done more, but Darius always currycombed, to examine his charge's condition.

Ignoring occasional nudges from Gemini's nose, Starke reflected on the rapid change in sports over five years. Sailing was now fashionable, baseball gaining popularity, and bicycling, or wheeling, a national passion. Advertisements and wheeling news filled Washington papers. It was also viewed as a new woman sport, so females were guided by a plethora of dress, fashion, and protocol information. European bicycle tours were also popular, like those the State Department's Addee favored. Even the North Atlantic Squadron had a bicycling club, so he bought a Stearns Yellow Fellow for Rock Creek Park and other wheeler locations, but his interests tended to riding, fly fishing, an occasional hunt, and fencing. The last had also gained adherents as exercise. Since it was taught at Jefferson Classical & Military Academy, and in the Naval Academy curriculum, Starke was proficient with several blades, singlestick, and canes.

The stable-yard was empty until Gemini's neigh brought Castores outside to race back and forth along the fence, kicking up his heels. Gemini tried to pick up the pace, but a firm yank on the reins checked him. At the stable door, Sutton took them, observing, "You sit like a trooper, Mister Jacob."

"Not bad for a sailor, but thanks, Darius."

"Tell me when you next want to ride, helps exercise 'em."

Starke left Sutton unsaddling Gemini at the ringbolt while Castores neighed loudly and frantically shifted between stable and exercise yard. Smelling of horse sweat, Starke headed for his dressing room shower. Entering the house, he removed his hat and felt cool air pass over wet, matted hair where the brim rested. Later, exiting the cylindrical curtain draped from a steel ring centered over the white-enameled tub, he toweled, then dressed for a quiet afternoon in the library.

Although Stephan Crane's novel was popular, Starke extracted an orange-brown book with a sphinx sitting sedately between title and author on its cover. H.G. Wells' time machine was more contrived than the translation of Jules Verne's underwater ship tale Starke just finished, but the reader was moving rapidly between epochs when the wall clock returned him to the present, and Saturday afternoon tea with his aunt.

He heard feminine voices while approaching the parlor, then realized a "Woman's Times" reporter was interviewing her. The woman in Lee's old chair appeared familiar, but they were never introduced so recalling her name was unnecessary. The woman added more unintelligible shorthand to a notebook while his aunt excused herself to greet him with, "A good ride, Jacob?"

"Yes, Gemini's excellent for a carriage horse."

She then turned to the visitor, who paused working her pencil and pad, then lowered it to the lap of a floor-length, light blue skirt trimmed with gilded beading at its hem. He was certain she was from Monday's streetcar; brown eyes, perfectly formed eyebrows, a classic countenance beneath an auburn pompadour, and the Brussels carpet bag alongside her chair. The woman's pale neck rose from a high white collar with a silver and blue ribbon girding its base. Below, the open bolero jacket with braided cuffs clung to her shape, then parted for a billowing white blouse with black onyx buttons and loose folds gathered at the waist before passing under an embroidered v-shaped black clincher belt, to create the fashionable, low, full bosom look.

Accompanied by requisite hand gestures, his aunt began, "Miss Cassandra Evans, Lieutenant Jacob Starke, my nephew. Miss Evans is from *The Evening Times*. We've finished speaking of St. Margaret's, so please join us."

The woman spoke in a pleasant, but inquisitive, almost challenging, manner, "Mrs. Starke said you were riding. Rock Creek park?"

"No, southwest of there."

"I prefer wheeling. She said you'll soon leave for a ship in Norfolk?"

"Newport News Shipyard."

"She thinks you'll be in the Caribbean?"

"Possibly."

Obviously his aunt and Miss Evans discussed more than church funding; and this reporter not only sensed more than a routine cruise but saw through his effort to avoid a direct answer. She cast bait a second time, "With Cuba in revolt, I'm trying to persuade my editor to finance a Havana trip, but would settle for Jacksonville or Tampa."

Starke was contemplating risks reporters ran in Cuba, when Aunt Constance added, "Cassandra's father owns a newspaper and she graduated from Wells College, same as the First Lady."

Evans quickly added, "I worked with my father after leaving university, before he helped arrange the Times position, and I've stayed with Georgetown relations four years. It's a pleasant change from home, where every conversation was newspapers, grammar, or politics."

Starke was thinking Miss Evans was attractive, articulate, and must enjoy a young spinster's freedom, when Cynthia entered to serve coffee and gingerbread cookies. As she lowered the tray, Starke remembered her arriving from Oxen Grove after her parents passed, and thought she must also be in her mid-twenties. Although lacking Miss Evans' formal schooling, he did not doubt her intelligence. Like Darius, she constantly read the library's books when not working and effortlessly mastered domestic skills. While attending to Aunt Constance, Cynthia had grown, blossomed, then matured between his intermittent visits, and was now de facto housekeeper.

Neither short or tall, her oval face included nearly black eyes, dark eyebrows, and well-shaped, translucent cinnamon brown lips. Long, rich black hair worn up, framed the face but left earlobes visible. The attractive nose separated two slightly hooded almond eyes, giving her an exotic, but enigmatic aura. Habitually solemn, Starke occasionally witnessed an unguarded smile which began demurely then climaxed with a crescendo of flashing white teeth. She always dressed to conceal a figure Starke thought attractive, and perhaps some internal passion. That she stayed single was also unusual since the local Colored community seldom viewed marriage as ending work outside the home. As always, she gracefully completed the task, exchanged a few quiet words with his aunt, then slipped away.

Cassandra Evans was equally guarded, polite, and intelligent, but relentless in learning what Starke knew of Havana and the insurrection. This grew more uncomfortable as it continued, because women usually avoided discussing such things with men, and the reverse. An hour later, with coffee gone and only cookie crumbs left, she explained it was time to leave for the St. Margaret's streetcar stop, then thanked his aunt for the interview. After wedging notebook and pencil in the carpet bag, Starke went with her to the front door, where Altman retrieved a plain, well-crafted coat from the cloakroom. Starke helped her slip it on, which she seemed uneasy about, then Altman passed her hat. After declining an escort to the streetcar stop, Starke watched hat and coat advance purposefully towards St. Margaret's alongside a bobbing carpet bag, until she passed safely from view.

With the obligation complete, Starke returned to find Aunt Constance and Cynthia restoring the parlor, and resumed his seat. When Cynthia left, his aunt renewed her campaign, "Miss Evans seems attractive and intelligent."

"A new woman, it seemed."

"Perhaps. I suspect she's different when at ease. Women blessed to be pleasant, attractive, and intelligent find they're excluded as a threat. Until age or situation makes it irrelevant, women tolerate intelligence, looks, or an agreeable nature, but no more than two. Three's intimidating, so they respond. She's intelligent, and peaked your fancy, but changed when you entered. I suspect she finds men troubled by her intellect, and women hostile, so she's defensive. That's what you saw."

When Starke realized his aunt also described herself, he set cup and saucer down, said nothing, then looked at the woman who raised him. She noticed and smiled, "We're a mercenary sex; territorial and unyielding when home or society is disturbed because everything's always at risk. Disease or childbirth took most of my childhood friends. Others were trapped or impoverished by circumstance. That's why I support Louise House. Except for God's grace, family, and chance, your mother or I might have sought refuge there, or with relations."

Before Starke replied, she straightened her dress then continued, "I wanted to provide your uncle a son, although terrified of giving birth. It's no longer possible, but I've no complaint. I've kept my figure, suffered few aliments, and Immanuel's faithful and loving."

Uncomfortable with his aunt's frankness, he began, "Aunt Constance..."

"Consider Cassandra Evans or someone like her. She appears reticent, but will soon desire a husband and children. Perhaps another strikes your fancy, someone associated with the Navy. After all, Commander Davis' daughter married Senator Lodge. The right woman will bring more than you imagine, and you'll do the same for her."

His aunt ended as unexpectedly as she began, by adjusting her loose tea dress, announcing, "I must away. We'll use the dining room tonight, since your uncle arrives Tuesday." He stood, watching her cross the entrance hall to the stairs, then returned to the library, poured two fingers of amber whiskey, retrieved H.G. Wells's book, and sipped through time.

Monday morning, Starke took the Building's stairs, not its hydraulic elevators. Unlike many, he did not fear the new contraptions, but preferred the exercise and meeting people on the stairs. Today, they were considering *Calypso*'s executive officer and chief engineer, with Starke's rank and seniority limiting candidates. His second in command must be junior but able to manage daily ship routine and assume command if necessary. The chief engineer was equally critical, but that selection depended on the idiosyncratic Steam Engineering Bureau chief, Commodore George Melville. A swift resolution was needed since Starke would depart on the twenty-sixth for Newport News, aboard the Norfolk & Western Steamboat Company's overnight liner, *Newport News*. This allowed Starke a week with his aunt's guests and time to resolve armament and personnel items.

Early the next evening, Starke left to meet his uncle at the Baltimore & Potomac train station, between the Building and Capitol. The city's two stations were within blocks of each other, but set apart by a no-man's land in the Pennsylvania

Railroad and Baltimore & Ohio lines' struggle for control. The Baltimore & Potomac station was operated by the Pennsylvania Railroad because it owned the smaller line, but served all roads, except Baltimore & Ohio. Trains using this station entered and left the city from the southwest, after crossing the Potomac River over Long Bridge. Baltimore & Ohio trains came from the northeast, then used that line's older and smaller New Jersey Avenue station.

Allowing ample time for an eight o'clock arrival, Darius harnessed Gemini and Castores to the large carriage, then brought it to the street where Starke waited. The unmarked black landau was their most fashionable vehicle. The lower body was glossy wood trimmed in silver and ebony, with center half-doors and lowering glass windows, while the upper's oiled leather clam sections kept it relatively light. A matched team was handled from an open bench seat over the front wheels, with rectangular coach lights attached to its railings. The body was comfortably sprung, using elliptical springs on spoked wheels with rubber tiring. Each wheel had thin mudguards and between the larger rear wheels was a folding luggage rack. Inside, two red-leather bench seats with coil spring cushions faced each other.

Baltimore & Potomac station parking was tight when trains were in, and the trip took longer than anticipated, so an engine and tender protruded from the long train shed when they arrived. Seeing this, Sutton dropped Starke at the B Street entrance then looked for a nearby parking spot. Entering, Starke went though the ladies waiting room to the central hall, where his uncle waited near the baggage room, across a large chamber filled with rows of benches. Beside him was an older Colored porter expertly balancing a baggage dolly burdened with a substantial trunk. Seeing Starke, his uncle tugged a heavy gold chain and extracted a fat Waltham hunters pocket watch from his vest.

Nearing sixty, he still dominated any space. The full beard and muted dress only accentuated this, as did a tendency to move in rapid thrusts. His hair was short and thinning, but that and hoods developing over the eyes buttressed a natural authority and disciplined inclination for action. Seldom jovial or trivial, he possessed a rough kindness and loved his nephew, but business and Constance were his passions. As that nephew neared, the thick beard almost hid a slight smile, "You finally made it, Jacob, and I trust the landau's out front?"

Starke responded to the familiar routine, "Yes, sir. Darius is waiting outside."

They retraced Jacob's path across the ladies waiting room, where his uncle habitually paused to look over rows of arm chairs at ochre wallpaper separated from a paneled lower wall by a thick chair rail. Protruding from it was an ornate plaque and star. Restarting for the entrance, he reflected, "Garfield's murder was a national disgrace that shouldn't be commemorated."

Outside, Darius Sutton positioned himself to move quickly alongside the curb at the entrance, which he did when the trio came through the door. Setting the brake, he climbed down and approached Immanuel Starke, who extended his right hand, "Good evening, Darius. Should have let someone else drive tonight. How's the leg?"

"Get'n better with warming weather, Mister Starke."

"It's all we can expect at our age."

While they spoke, the porter positioned the trunk on their rear carriage rack then secured it with buckled leather straps. As Sutton checked the load, Immanuel tipped twice the going rate while thanking the baggage man. Starke's uncle venerated honest labor as much as he loathed those avoiding it. He also ensured those deserving were rewarded when possible, in contrast to most of his class, who seldom parted with more than necessary, or let all know an extra penny was freed from captivity when they did.

After his uncle was seated, Starke placed a foot in the stepping bar, swung aboard, then shut the door. Sutton climbed to the driver's position, arranged himself, gathered the reins, then released the brake. Although muted by the oiled leather top, shod hooves striking pavement were audible as the carriage eased from the curb into late evening traffic that thinned beyond the Executive Mansion. As darkness drew closer, the landau continued rolling north with carriage lights flickering.

Starke waited for his uncle to begin, which he did with, "I understand you accepted *Calypso*?"

"I couldn't refuse, but have concerns."

"Decision's made, Jacob. Deal with it and move forward."

With that, his uncle pulled a large cigar from its leather case then clipped one end with a silver cutter. Returning the instrument to a pocket, he stripped the band, moistened the tobacco leaf, then passed it through his beard. A match flared, followed by two quick draws, before he cracked the window and turned to Starke, "Sugar and tobacco interests got what they wanted with the Wilson-Gorman Tariff, but it's played hell with Cuba. As always, corrupt politicians and their backers never pass an opportunity to expand the public trough, and won't be satisfied, even if they get an income tax, which the Supreme Court thankfully spiked."

Starke suspected this was the dying quiver of a lively debate with other businessmen or a politician during the journey. After another draw, bringing the cigar tip to a glow, its moist, darkened end emerged from his uncle's beard. As the city passed by, he held the cigar midway with thumb and forefinger as if balancing it, then said, "Nothing surpasses a good Havana. I'll keep my Cubans and pay willingly."

Their conversation paused as the carriage passed Dupont Circle, the Spanish Embassy, and St. Margaret's church, then turned on Florida Avenue. Sutton finally deposited his passengers at the mansion's front door, and received a Cuban before taking the landau to the rear. Inside, Altman greeted Starke's uncle as he took the heavy coat, hat, and cane, then Aunt Constance added her formal welcome. Stark excused himself then left for the library and Wells' time machine, but looked back to see them enter the parlor, with his uncle's right arm encircling her waist.

Following the next evening's supper, Starke was in the library for evening whiskey with his uncle. Sitting before the fireplace, Immanuel considered his Cuban, then turned to Starke, "Never believed sons must follow fathers, or uncles, so I've not pushed you to join the firm."

They often had this discussion when traveling together, but his tenor this evening was different. Immanuel was the elder brother who presided over an extended family, and supported Jacob. Starke often considered what his uncle would do, before taking any action. However, he knew little of his past because the man never rambled or bragged, even with provocation. He obtained respect rather than deference from associates and maintained a reputation for fair dealing, honesty, and reliability. Plying those near him for true thoughts, he was known as a tough negotiator, who seldom made decisions before considering every aspect, evaluating risk, and probing for opportunities. Once decided, the problem, situation, or adversary's weakest point was engaged without emotion. He also possessed the enduring fatalism often experienced with long-serving soldiers. As Starke's aunt remarked, when their love produced no child, unlike many, he did not blame her or become unfaithful. He accepted it as their joint fate, but with less attribution to divine intent than his wife.

Starke thought him a gifted strategist, who favored small armies and just enough navy for trade protection. Besides cost and mischief potential, he felt anything larger invited overseas adventures. Despite this, he supported his nephew's studies at Jefferson Classical & Military Academy on the James River, arranged for a place on the Montana expedition using his contacts, then contrived a Presidential appointment to the Naval Academy. With greater enthusiasm, he placed his nephew on company ships Starke found harsh, demanding, and unforgiving. However, that experience matured his composure and gave him confidence when facing challenges or distasteful tasks; and he later discovered his uncle explicitly warned masters about favoritism. Now, sitting beside him, that uncle swallowed a sip of whiskey before invading his thoughts with, "I sold *Illusive* because she'd become a liability, but nearly walked away when Captain Albert hinted you might command."

"Why, uncle?"

"I suspected you were considering the company and welcomed it. However, selling her still made the best business sense."

Setting down the glass, he took a long, pull from the cigar, then went on, "I've a fair guess what Albert's up to, so you should know your father and I remain in contact and Lee's inquiry was passed on, but he shouldn't expect anything. Your father and I saw our nation ripped apart by northern abolitionists and southern radicals. Your grandfather and I believed it good business to avoid politics, as did your father, but while he was at sea we watched insanity prevail. When *Saratoga* returned from Africa, he found Lincoln's crowd preparing to invade the South, felt he must resign, was dishonorably treated, then accused, and now completely disowns the States, as you learned in Rio de Janeiro."

After another draw, he rested his forearm on the chair as thin smoke tendrils floated up, "Unlike others, your grandfather and I assumed a long, disastrous war, so our ships were immediately registered in other countries and no contraband shipped. The entire operation went overseas and operated from Havana. We were not popular, but did well while competitors were bankrupted by high insurance rates and had ships captured, sunk, or taken by the government. As you know, I paid Lincoln $300 to avoid fighting for his radicals, and don't regret it. Others couldn't buy their way out or were forced to enlist for the bounty. I've no quarrel with any who did or didn't fight, but those who agitated for war then avoided it, live without honor. I've never spoken with several since, and now their ilk are back, so I support the President and Albert, which is also why I sold *Illusive* for conversion."

Pausing for a sip, he mused, "Warmongers seldom pay full freight. The country your father and I knew is dead and won't return. Your father's a hero in Virginia, while your aunt and I are tolerated; only because I avoided politics and kept the West Point yard running. If not for that, we'd be thought scalawags or carpetbaggers."

The unguarded mood enticed Starke to probe deeper, "What about *Woods Rogers*?"

Increased cigar gnawing and wrinkling forehead revealed his uncle's discomfort, but the half-smoked cigar entered the ashtray as he began, "You've a right, but it goes no further."

"I understand, uncle."

The remaining whiskey disappeared and another finger slid into his uncle's glass from a matching decanter, "As the war ended, he was number two of a thrown-together raider sent after Federal transports bound for New Orleans. The captain died of fever after running the blockade and Jefferson was unaware the Confederate government fled Richmond, so continued the cruise. He speaks little of it, so I've no idea how a large paddlewheel steamer like *Woods Rogers* was taken. However, as the prize was more valuable and seaworthy, he transferred to her, along with his crew and those willing to join. His old ship, under the steamer's master with *Woods Rogers* crew and passengers, was sent to Havana as a cartel. Your father failed to run the blockade and was low on coal when one of those who joined revealed she carried hidden gold for New Orleans banks. Since gold was needed in Europe to buy weapons, your father made for Havana. The cartel ship never arrived, so he assumed the master broke parole, but learned after the war she vanished at sea."

Finishing the whiskey then relighting the cigar, his uncle went on, "The Confederacy was collapsing, but not yet extinguished, so ship and gold were prizes with no one to accept them; and your father would not surrender either to the Federals. Like the *Stonewall* ram, *Woods Rogers* and cargo were sold to pay the crew, but the gold was not listed on her manifest, so it vanished and I believe went to Confederate refugees in Canada, Europe, Mexico, and South America. Your father kept nothing. His Southern Caribbean and Atlantic Shipping Company began with a family loan and was repaid from profits. Since your mother had passed, he wanted you raised with us, but refused to return and couldn't visit after the gold and cartel ship's disappearances. Even now, he might be prosecuted, with or without grounds, and assets seized as compensation for *Woods Rogers*, or through the Confiscation Acts."

His uncle then changed tack, "Albert thinks well of you, but sees your future spent supporting more favored and less deserving officers, and I agree. Constance and I've no children, and your father's unable to inherit, so all Starke holdings will pass to you. Should I go first, she and others will rely on you, as will the servants, which must be treated as family, especially Cynthia."

Starke already owned Oxen Grove, and anticipated some inheritance, but was shocked to hear he would receive the entire legacy and head the family. Reacting more than responding, he observed, "You're in good health, uncle?"

"Yes, but of an age. While I don't share Constance's faith in any hereafter, I want our people looked out for," which Starke knew was genuine.

"Knowing this, what are your thoughts on marriage?"

The inheritance was a shock, but Starke was prepared for this, "It must be more than convenience. The desire was there when younger, but damped by voyages or curbed by service custom. I admit to some anxiety, but also less desire to compete for women or seek romance as years pass."

"You're considering it anyway. Perhaps the British cousin deserves a look; and I believe Constance planned something while they're here."

"She'd prefer a ball, but they're less fashionable, so a dinner party's in the works."

"You're probably right, and balls require longer notice. Which reminds me, when do you leave for Newport News?"

"On the twenty-sixth, Norfolk & Western's overnight steamer."

"Chesapeake & Ohio goes to Richmond, with connections to Newport News, and dining car if memory serves, why not the train?"

"I can carry more on the steamer, and it's comfortable."

His uncle relieved the ashtray of the cigar stump, studied it, then continued, "Makes sense, besides it allows time to adjust. You've sailed our ships and the Navy's, but never commanded. That reality won't take hold until they're all looking to you for a decision. Until then, choose the best people, build a solid crew, and prepare."

"Captain Albert said much the same."

The unlit cigar was again in motion, "I also telegraphed Aron Sharett, a discrete ship chandler may prove useful."

"I do have one concern. Are any of our ships filibustering?"

"No. War must be prevented because its aftermath could be anything. We ship cement, wood, and the like, even if used for trochas, but not military goods for Spain or the Junta; and your father's doing the same."

Starke thanked his uncle, who relit the neglected cigar then settled back in the chair. They sat quietly together for a few more minutes, before Starke retired. The older man lifted one hand up, palm forward in a tranquil wave before taking another draw.

CHAPTER SEVEN
Second Chances

Starke and his aunt concentrated on their own projects over the next few days, although his efforts were less obvious than those at the mansion. Preparing for foreign guests and subsequent dinner party disrupted routine far more than working late at the Building. While some staff cleaned and polished, others made trips to Washington's stores and markets with the landau or stanhope.

He spoke with Leutze several times, including an awkward conversation using a telephone connecting the Building to Washington's navy yard. The week ended with confirmation *Calypso*'s 4-inch breech-loading rifles used case ammunition, not bag; and no 6mm Lee-Navy rifles or machine guns were available; although, Leutze did obtain 1885 bolt action Remington-Lee rifles with box magazines. An excellent weapon, except for a black powder cartridge which created clouds of smoke and limited rounds sailors carried. Its effective range was near 1,000 yards, despite claims of nearly 3,500, and was accurate to 300 yards, although few sailors would consistently hit targets much beyond a hundred, despite Leutze obtaining the 500 grain rounds with better ballistics. While there was no way around the rifles' socket bayonets, Starke doubted his sailors would be proficient using them in any case. As promised, *Calypso* would receive four Gatling guns, and latest Model 1895 double-action revolvers.

While Starke worked *Calypso*'s weapons, Albert focused on her wardroom. The Bureau of Navigation controlled line officer distribution, but other assignments meant talks with the steam engineering, paymaster, and medical organizations. The first resolved was the executive officer, and *Calypso* needed the best. If the man chosen proved weak or curried favor, discipline fell to the commander, but a tyrant sapped initiative and cowed crews. Since *Calypso* was Starke's first command, Albert wanted a consistent, fair, and experienced officer who only required monitoring. A Division of Officers and Fleet clerk put forward Lieutenant (junior grade) Benjamin Watson, then pressed Albert to consider his service record. The unassigned officer was being forced to transfer from an older Coast and Geodetic Survey ship by a commander threatening charges. Although the clerk did not know the man, he saw injustice, Albert's requirements, and put the lieutenant's hat in the ring. Watson's qualifications and experience were excellent, his ability under sail reportedly superior, he possessed exceptional navigational skills, and was Starke's junior.

Starke wore his undress blue uniform with high collar, black braiding and insignia to the initial interview, held in a large office Albert borrowed. When he entered its anteroom, Watson was seated in a wooden chair against the wall. Although thin and drawn, his eyes constantly scanned and evaluated everything within range, like the hunter who stays motionless until prey approaches, then moves decisively. Seeing Starke, the officer lifted seamlessly from the chair with, "Lieutenant (j.g.) Watson, sir."

No doubt, a crisp salute, would have accompanied the greeting outside, but Starke disliked meeting the candidate before the interview. He politely acknowledged him, then went through to the office, where Albert waited. The officer was available, qualified, and fit perfectly, with gunnery and executive officer experience; but Starke's reservations rested on the last commander's letter, tucked in the service record, with its "prejudicial to good order and discipline" phrasing. Albert would only advise, "Ask him yourself, Jacob."

Watson was summoned, preliminaries completed, and the interview began. Although uneasy at first, he recovered, then crisply answered questions, impressing Albert and Starke with his operations, administration, and discipline knowledge. Finally, Starke asked, "Can you explain your commanding officer's comments?"

Shifting uneasily, but speaking precisely, Watson responded, "There's nothing specific to refute or explain in the letter, so I'm left claiming them unwarranted with nothing to address."

Little more came from attempts to probe one or two of the letter's passages until Albert looked squarely at Watson, "*Winston A. Capps* has an excellent reputation, correct?"

"Yes, sir. We took soundings, corrected charts, and plotted navigation hazards across the southern Caribbean, and off Nicaragua for the proposed canal."

"My experience suggests she must then be led well, or driven hard with no concern for crew. Which is it?"

The lieutenant paused, weighing his response, then said, "I'm forced to leave that evaluation to others, captain."

"I understand. Lieutenant Starke, a final question?"

Starke turned to Watson. "What rumors have you heard regarding me?"

Albert started to preempt him, then stopped. Watson's knowledge or reservations should be heard. It also went to honesty, since, believing his career over, would he be candid and risk an opportunity, say what he thought they wanted, or dodge the question? Albert rethought his evaluation of Starke's diplomatic capabilities as Watson looked uncomfortably at him, then, finding no reprieve, began, "This interview was unexpected, so I made inquiries and learned it was for your command. There was more about your father, but most said, you've sailed merchant and navy. A few warned you've a propensity for grim situations. Alexandria's bombardment, the recent Asian war, and Brazil's naval mutiny came up. Others said you were a soldier, but did not offer it as an insult, and a number claimed you're well-off. Several said to wait for any other ship."

"…and?"

"My family ranches near Gunnison in Colorado, but I chose the sea over haying, cattle, and freezing winters. Given the opportunity, I prefer not waiting in the Building with make-work until this is resolved, so I'll accept, whatever you offer, if it's at sea."

Starke looked through the window at a seagull flying some distance off, until it saw a promising item then dove from view. Returning to Watson, he responded, "I can't go deeper, but this is no ordinary cruise. There's little reward if success-ful and real risk of failure. Waiting was sound advice. Do you want to think it over?"

"No sir, I decided to take what you offered before coming."

Albert interjected, "Has the billet been explained to you?"

"I hoped navigator."

Starke looked at Albert, who gave a nearly imperceptible nod then turned to Watson, "I need an executive officer for a merchant ship under conversion to gunboat."

Before the surprised Watson answered, Albert raised his hand, "Admiral Ramsey knows Commander Gagnon's posi-tion, but believes an opportunity is deserved. *Maine*'s in Hampton Roads, and Newport News has two gunboats build-ing. Starke will soon take *Calypso*. You may go with him or be assigned one of the others."

"I'd prefer *Calypso*, captain."

"Very well. You'll have an answer today."

With that Albert rose and the others followed. Watson passed through the anteroom to the black and white tiled corridor and could be heard walking away. Albert retrieved his notes, then turned to Starke, "We'll talk in my office."

Captain Albert felt more relaxed at his own desk with Starke on the settee. After selecting a pipe then charging it, he began, "Commander Gagnon's a martinet lacking confidence, a sundowner, and my inquiries suggest his complaints aren't valid. Ramsey unquestionably supports the chain of command and his commanders, but shares my opinion. However, there is maneuvering room here since Navy officers and crews are technically assigned to the Coast and Geodetic Survey only if available. Should Watson be required for *Calypso*, and transferred as Gagnon demands, all things get temporarily resolved. Watson appears to fit the bill and is familiar with the Caribbean, but it's your call Jacob. Don't feel pressured, Admiral Ramsey will assign him to another ship, and I'll ensure a rebuttal is drafted, either way."

"As you say, except for Commander Gagnon's letter, he's best qualified."

"Excellent. I'll have orders written, but the mission and *Calypso* come first. Any problem, contact me and he'll be replaced."

"Yes, sir"

While Albert and Starke decided, Watson was settling into a borrowed desk feeling better than he had since reporting to *Winston A. Capps*. At the time, he thought the Treasury Department's Coast and Geodetic Survey Service suited his ocean and mathematics affinities. Numbers spoke to him and calculations were comforting since procedure and accuracy produced correct answers. When not, errors could be revealed with time and effort. His other passion was gunnery and he often engaged in debates about reliance on gun captains, new armor, long-range guns, torpedoes, and ramming. While siding with the higher rates of fire camp, he was intrigued with larger calibers' possibilities if aiming could be resolved. While at the Academy, he meticulously followed rules and escaped with few demerits. Watson never considered cadets who lacked his talents inferior, and often tutored them, so he was well-liked. Although solemn and strict, he was considered professional, consistent, fair, eschewed favorites, and not subject to outbursts. Everything changed after reporting to the obsolete brigantine *Winston A. Capps.*

Her few officers and crew were anxious, apprehensive and guarded. Nothing was too small to escape notice and reprisal. No one was taught, only tested, with the smallest negative action or event determining the individual's personal worth. Wardroom and petty officers completed tasks expecting blows, avoiding public berating, and quietly rejoicing when someone else fell victim, since innocent speech brought unacceptable risk. Gagnon's application of regulations, not improper action, darkened the ship's mood then encouraged crew hard-cases to set up those above for gain or whim. Watson spent nearly eighteen months, steeling himself each day, until, off St. Lucia, a sudden squall bore down on the ship. He sent for Gagnon, let sheets fly, and began taking in sails. Wind and water struck, just as the commander arrived on deck, rolling the old ship nearly on her beam ends before she paused, shuddered, then slowly righted. Although they would have capsized if Watson delayed, he was dressed down before officers and crew, called a human failure, and his only salvation, Gagnon. When he stood mute, the commander became apoplectic, then put him ashore at the next port with a letter for Ramsey.

The day after his interview, Watson was preparing his resignation letter when a short memorandum arrived assigning him to Norfolk's receiving ship, then to *Calypso* as executive officer when she commissioned. Albert's *Maine* or gunboat offer was unexpected, but nothing compared to this. Although his new commander seemed an enigma and likely difficult to serve, he had taken a chance on him, and resurrected Watson's long-dormant loyalty. Later, in Albert's office, he received official orders, the forcefully advised to respond to the Gagnon letter and schooled in avoiding an accusatory response while thoroughly discrediting vague accusations. In three days, he completed the minor task he was working, went to the station, and boarded Chesapeake & Ohio's Richmond train.

For *Calypso*'s chief engineer, Albert and Melville agreed on Passed Assistant Engineer Adrian Osbourne, although too junior for formal designation. Stationed at California's Mare Island Navy Shipyard, he commissioned in 1884 as a steam engineering officer, so, until just recently, held a relative rank of lieutenant (junior grade), then attended the Academy's advanced course in marine engineering.

Summoned to the Mare Island administration building, Osbourne was surprised by unanticipated telegraph orders to report to the Newport News shipyard's senior naval constructor for further assignment as chief engineer on a gunboat conversion. He disliked leaving the Pacific, but had anticipated several years before this opportunity, so, within a week, he boarded the new steam tug *Unadilla* for San Francisco. Surrounded by shipyard wives, under clear and nearly cloudless skies, he watched the yard's single, cut-stone dry-dock pass, then the roofed-over receiving ship *Independence* at the end of a long finger pier. Built as a ship-of-the-line to fight Britain, she instead sailed against Barbary Pirates and Mexico. When the tug passed two four-masted barks at the coal piers, he saw its wake move slowly across the still channel to ripple against their flat iron sides, smelled the coal dust, then took a last look astern. After leaving the channel separating Mare Island and

Vallejo, he watched the four-story, red-brick naval hospital shrink until both towers disappeared. Then, balancing against a slight chop, he entered the deckhouse to contemplate the next week's journey, beginning with a Central Pacific ferry to Oakland, train to Omaha, several more to Richmond, then on to Newport News.

CHAPTER EIGHT
The British Widow and *Calypso*

While Lieutenant Adrian Osbourne journeyed east by rail, Edward Curtis and sister, Katherine Ledford, traveled from New York City to Washington on a Baltimore & Ohio Royal Blue Line train. At Baltimore, a slab-sided electric engine towed their blue and gold steam locomotive, tender, and five cars through Howard Street Tunnel, uncoupled then motored to a siding. Once clear, the steam engine reawakened with a piercing whistle, clanging bell, then successive thuds and shudders as the train jerked forward, gained momentum, then accelerated until it raced over oil-stained ties and ballast. Soon, only clicking rail joints, a rasping engine, and steel wheels' irregular squeals reached passengers. Outside, a smoke plume rose in dark bursts, drifted away, dissipated against overcast skies, then settled off the right-of-way.

Katherine Ledford watched passing Maryland cities, towns and farms through leaded glass windows with etched and frosted trim. Seated in a comfortable blue chair with gold trim, she occasionally looked inside the parlor car to its royal blue ceiling and varnished mahogany walls. Beyond convenience, safety, and comfort, she had little interest in railroads, but painstakingly choose the best train to Washington; then reserved parlor car seats believing coach travel meant second or third class despite assurance Royal Blue Line passengers received identical treatment on the five-hour runs departing Washington and New York simultaneously at three o'clock.

Her brother stood with several men at the car's far end exchanging details on train and line. Custom Royal Blue Line 4-6-0 steam engines capable of devouring ninety miles every hour pulled cars selected from a stable of baggage, coach, diner, and parlor cars; with sleeper or combination cars available, but seldom used. Each run included a dining car staffed by French chefs preparing turtle, duck, and other entrées. These were served by white-uniformed waiters to passengers seated in booths outfitted with folded white linen napkins, matching tablecloths, and fresh flowers. The steam-heated cars' saxony blue exteriors with gold leaf trim and ornate ironwork were connected by vestibules; with pintsch gas overhead lighting, fed by undercarriage tanks that exhausted through ceiling vents.

Katherine's first travel beyond Britain began on a rainy Liverpool morning by boarding Cunard's RMS *Lucania*. Arriving six days later at New York City's Pier 40, she kept to her relatives' mansion and was apprehensive of this Washington excursion, since she viewed the city as no less onerous than New York; but more provincial and plagued by disease and hot, humid summers. While her brother came to explore business opportunities for a London syndicate, she was attempting to escape pressures and vexations visited on young widows with income. It was her first significant journey, so Paris or Vienna would have been preferable, but male escort was obligatory for women travelers, and her brother offered. She disliked the few American women she met at home, mostly young, rich, and intent on marrying poorer aristocracy. Having met no American men socially, Katherine did not dispute her father's disdain for the former colonies' social crudeness and awkward interference which recently caused the formation of a flying squadron to defend Britain's western Atlantic interests.

She was an exuberant and fearless young girl, but adolescence brought disconsolate inclinations that grew to stretches of despondency commingled with short flashes of her earlier nature. Perhaps the worst came during her presentation at court while coming out. Sitting in a long column of open carriages carrying young women, she slowly rolled through a writhing gauntlet of obscene invitations and insults hurled in earnest or sport. She stared ahead, persevered, saw discipline brought salvation, then embraced the attribute to conceal and bridge her dark spells. Inquisitive and intelligent, she concealed her ease mastering the requisite accomplishments, to avoid any suggestion of being a bluestocking. Expected to marry soon and well, she often relied on her self-control to squelch romantic notions and complete the task with assessment and acquiescence, not passion. Because her large dowry ended all claims on her family's wealth, and be managed by her husband, she accepted a distant cousin's proposal. Philip Albert Ledford was a titled family's second son whose own wealth and disposition meant her dowry was neither an interest or enticement; so marriage negotiations gave her broad discretion, with control passing to her brother should it end.

Philip proved an ideal match in temperament and proximity. After boarding school and short visit home, he went to HMS *Britannia*, then left the training establishment with a Royal Navy commission. Once the province of Britain's middle class, by mid-century the navy became fashionable for aristocrats' second sons, excluding its engineering branch which was viewed artisans at best. Neither romantic or passionate, Philip loved her deeply and proved considerate, caring, and, unique among his peers, faithful. This shielded her from disease and brought domestic calm. In response, she honed her social acumen to become a popular hostess and valuable consort, since her French, polite conversation, social etiquette, and literature interests were seen as impressive enough for guests to feel entertained and comfortable, but not threatened.

Alone with Philip, she discovered he was an enthusiastic conversationalist who eagerly exchanged ideas on all topics; and when he was away, Katherine not only had the house, social obligations, a large library, and riding to occupy her, but the pair wrote so profusely fellow officers ribbed him about having a passionate wife who absorbed every desire for other women.

Their letters seldom touched more earthier topics, and each reunion collapsed Katherine's comfortable equilibrium while she adjusted to his physical presence and her duty to provide potential heirs. They both desired children, but bearing one so unnerved her, their first awkward attempt proved painful, and subsequent exercises truncated, distasteful, and unrewarding. Sensing this, Philip would lessen his demands and, despite the absurdity, Katherine's thoughts shifted from frustration with his appetite to her failure to whet it. She would then set out to revive those urges, until reaching an equilibrium that held until he left; when correspondence resumed, as did the cycle. While she considered this, Edward claimed an adjacent chair then, chin on chest, dozed to the train's soft rhythm of sound and motion. She looked at him, then outside, as a long smoke plume drifted up and away, gained breadth, grew nearly transparent, then settled like gray ground fog.

Several miles on, head pillowed against a gloved palm, Katherine caught herself nearly following her brother, then resumed musing. Three years after they wed HMS *Victoria* was rammed; then sank eighty fathoms to the Mediterranean floor off Tripoli, taking nearly 300 of her crew, including Philip. Ever since, he lived in her mind, an elegant hand on preserved letters, and, somewhat less so, in brief inscriptions on Portsmouth's memorial obelisk and Ledford family crypt. While the nuptial arrangements left her well off and not reliant on his family, she was his childless widow who gradually realized how much she loved him, then sought solace in discipline and protocol to become an exemplary mourner, wearing black two full years before adopting partial mourning's gray and muted colors. Despite the Ledfords' kindness, she realized it was impossible to remain without a function and surrounded by reminders. This melancholy grew until she returned home, where, expecting sanctuary, widow Ledford found married friends aloof, husbands overly attentive, and no explanation for either. Preparing for her coming out, she critically surveyed her physical attributes; concluding they were less appealing than many but not unattractive, then retained the image. Unaware a natural molding continued, with marriage and maturity adding an indefinable sensuality men found enticing, she felt preyed upon and sought camouflage in her wardrobe, deportment, movement, and discourse by muting all things demonstrative or suggestive, excluding bicycling and riding sidesaddle.

While considering her situation, she was seduced by the car's motion and woke with a start when several short whistle blasts signaled they crossed a switch diverting the fast blue train, trailing black smoke and white steam, down the Washington branch line. Later, with evening approaching, the conductor announced their arrival and passengers began gathering and repacking items. Katherine held everything close, had little to attend to, and quickly returned to observing countryside. Entering Washington from high ground to its northeast, she watched farm and forest yield to homes, businesses, then a racetrack, cemetery, and structures she overheard was a deaf and blind institute. The Capitol's dome rose above nearby buildings, as the blue train slowed, testing air brakes, and the raised roadbed gave way to city streets. Cutting across several blocks to I Street, then west for a wye junction, the train reversed direction to back down Delaware Avenue through sidings and rail yards, before curving southwest to the Baltimore & Ohio's New Jersey Avenue Station train shed. This station was less grand than its competitor, with a tall, square clock tower rising from the northwest side and train shed extending out to the northeast. The single story depot had a cross-gable main roof, with smaller gables, and a main entrance opening on New Jersey Avenue; under the large canopy separating arched windows.

Waiting on the platform, Starke watched the distinctive train pass empty boxcars and a yard engine coupled to wooden gondolas. Since the British pair were new to the city and unknown to him, Starke and Sutton left early with the black landau, planning to hire a cab for the two large steamer trunks and smaller bags expected. They took Massachusetts Avenue to New Jersey Avenue, then turned south to the station, located between C and D Streets. Since Starke wished to meet their guests at the train, Sutton was left outside to negotiate a single-horse, yellow Herdic cab.

Against the engine's smoke column, white steam flashed from a long whistle blast as the rear car approached. Its vestibule door became distinct, then the brakeman, a coupling knuckle, and, just before the blue train slowed to a walk, two dangling air brake hoses. After filling the left archway's vista, the arriving train emitted a succession of crashes, brakes, and squeals before halting close to a buffer stop. The accompanying rush of air carried hot engine smells that dominated coal, steam, grease, and oil odors lingering from previous arrivals and departures.

Once stopped, a uniformed conductor and assistants, carrying metal foot stools, dropped from car stairs to the station platform. Placing their stools to address gaps between the lowest steps and platform's concrete, passengers were assisted down. Starke observed some went to those awaiting their arrival, while others headed for the station. Finally, a disoriented couple fitting his aunt's description exited the parlor car, with the woman guided to the platform by a serious Colored man wearing the gray railroad uniform.

Approaching her male companion, wearing an Ulster coat and bowler, Starke inquired, "Mr. Edward Curtis?"

"You must be Mr. Jacob Starke, sir."

"Welcome. Our carriage's outside; once the luggage's unloaded."

The young man bowed slightly, then turned, "My sister, Mrs. Katherine Louisa Ledford."

The woman was short to average, and wore a caped overcoat securely buttoned up through its high collar, making her appear taller. A flat boater with ribbon was anchored above long, light-brown or perhaps dirty-blond hair, center-parted then coiled to a bun behind her head. Starke bowed slightly, received a slight nod, and felt relief. A safely married sister, blunted, diverted, or ended matrimonial machinations, which was always welcome, but especially now he was committed to *Calypso*.

Two porters emerged from the baggage room with carts containing a pair of Louis Vuitton steamer trunks, smaller cabin trunks and several bags; then the procession went to the carriages. Within minutes, the Herdic cab was filled, an extra cabin trunk lashed to the Landau's rear rack, and porters tipped. With passengers settled in red leather seats, Sutton headed up New Jersey Avenue to Massachusetts Avenue, then home at a fast walk. An overtaking streetcar worried Gemini and Castores, but, coaxed by Sutton, continued without interruption past Mount Vernon Square to Dupont Circle, where familiar streets reassured the bays. Keeping station behind, the cab's single gray mare remained disinterested in anything beyond her worn leather blinders.

Inside, Starke sat across from his charges, answering Edward's questions, and thinking him a young English version of Captain Albert, albeit without a uniform and sporting a neatly trimmed mustache. At his side, the gloomy sister feigned looking forward, but was unobtrusively snatching glimpses of red-brick and marble buildings turning gray at dusk. While her coat concealed what lay beneath, Starke surreptitiously examined the face, while responding to the brother. Her long, thick hair was rolled and fastened in a large bun. The wide, oval head was halved by a longish nose between large faded-blue eyes just under curving eyebrows. The forehead gained slight horizontal furrows when she concentrated and, just below her nose, a slight channel lead to the thin upper lip compressed against its much fuller companion. Taut facial muscles accentuated her cheekbones and a distinct jawline curved up from the slight chin dimple. Her mouth seldom opened, and never more than necessary to speak or yield the occasional stillborn smile. Although married and unresponsive, Starke felt an undefinable attraction in her firm, sophisticated countenance that overcame the conservative dress and aloof demeanor. She obviously excited something in his being, but he thought it transitory and concentrated on the brother's questions.

After explaining the District of Columbia was neither city or state, but ten square miles carved from Maryland and Virginia, until the latter reabsorbed its contribution due to slavery and neglect of the residents. He then characterized the capital as a Southern city, run by appointed commissioners after nearly bankrupting itself on municipal projects to block the government from moving west. Starke also explained the intermingling of mansions, businesses, houses, and shacks; then its racial integration, Colored sections, streetcars, and local establishments. Responding to Curtis, he ran through notable hotels and restaurants such as the Ebbitt House, Willard, Raleigh and Wormley hotels. Starke noticed great relief when Edward learned alcohol was not yet prohibited, despite a plethora of local religious congregations. When asked about the war, Reconstruction, and Cuba, Starke subtly shifted topics.

During the ensuing days, Curtis' interest exceeded his sister's and proved far from superficial. He explored the city by foot and streetcar, especially public buildings, which included the Capitol, National Museum, Botanical Gardens, and State, War and Navy Building. Katherine seldom accompanied him, except for an evening at Albaugh's Opera House. Her primary interest was the Washington Riding Academy, where horses could be obtained to explore Rock Creek Park. Although inundated with work, Starke exchanged riding Gemini for a Saturday outing on sedate, or stubborn, stable horses; since riders outnumbered mounts, and the Starke horses were required elsewhere.

Formal riding attire proved equally annoying. Starke owned a set, and came up with a second for Curtis, but Katherine declined Aunt Constance's offer, and instead the two women visited a tailor. This produced a blue-black riding habit consisting of a straight-legged, trouser-concealing skirt accompanied by a mandarin-collared tunic with buttons laid diagonally from right shoulder to left waist. Its lightly veiled helmet fit her center-parted hair and bun; with leather riding boots and gloves completing the ensemble. The conspicuous style, a departure from her normal dress, set the widow apart from other riders, as did the smooth, effortless way she rode sidesaddle on stable horses.

Katherine grew more at ease as days passed, unlike Starke, who learned she was widowed. While their acquaintance consisted of meals and awkward meetings, the bond between her and his aunt strengthened. Several times Constance let slip the widow's mourning would soon end, especially as dinner party preparations matured. These meticulously planned affairs were replete with social conventions and rules, reflected status or advanced business, political or social goals. Starke's aunt was a veteran of such events, but also part of several social circles having members whose disruptive proclivities when invited were equaled by their offense if not. To skirt this, she let it be known Edward, and Katherine, were guests of honor at a dinner party tied to the ship's sale. While those not invited were unlikely to suspect Curtis had no involvement, most were aware Constance supported the business with such parties, so few would be offended; and it easily addressed class, status, and dress implications.

While Jacob Starke was annoyed with inserting *Calypso*, he quietly acquiesced after learning his uncle and Albert were tasked with the guest list; and the captain's daughters employed to balance *Calypso*'s prospective executive officer and chief engineer, since the sexes' parity was essential. Starke suspected the officers' acceptances were less voluntary than his aunt anticipated, since both were in the city on business when Albert personally delivered their invitations. Constance's artistic bent insured Lieutenant Commander Leutze and his wife, Julia, were included. Less welcome to Starke, *The Evening Times* reporter Cassandra Evans was as well. She would not only view the affair as social column fodder, but an opportunity to collect other items of interest; and his aunt asked Starke to escort her. The Revenue Cutter Service's Captain Fischer, and departing, Lieutenant Singer, with wives, completed the list. Wednesday, March 25, at eight o'clock was agreed and handwritten invitations delivered by messenger if possible, otherwise the person was informed and a formal invitation promised.

As cards arrived and calls made, to accept or decline, there were two regrets, which was what his aunt expected. Fischer and Singer pled prior commitments. Starke suspected Fischer attended no more of these than necessary, and Singer was turning over the intelligence office to Lieutenant Commander Wainwright. Starke would see Fischer again, but regretted losing the opportunity of sharing an evening with the stout lieutenant, whose bear-like countenance and full bushy beard were headed for a cruiser as its executive officer.

When Starke brought up dress for *Calypso*'s two prospective officers, Captain Albert observed they, "...damn well better have every uniform, including dinner dress," paused, as though trying to recall something, then added, "Besides a commissioning ship's commanding officer must report officers' uniform status to the Department." The remark also neatly committed Starke to Navy dinner dress. However, the captain was correct, and the service formal wear was nearly the same as, and no more or less agreeable than, civilian black pants, jacket, white waistcoat, shirt, and gloves. He also guessed Albert's intransigence might reflect domestic chaos arising from Abigail and her daughters' purchase, maintenance, or repair of three low-necked, short-sleeved gowns with gloves; obligatory for these functions.

While dinner party preparations moved forward, Starke spent evenings reviewing the *1893 Regulations for Government of the Navy of the United States*, which laid out watch-standing, management, correspondence, legal requirements, medical administration, recruitment, finance, contracting, honors and other ship, shore, and shipyard activities. Starke scanned its nearly 600 pages, but studied and made notes mostly about duty descriptions, ships in shipyards, and commissionings. Between reading, writing, and slow sips of rye whisky, he sensed an approaching juggernaut's breath and book's transformation from reference to *Calypso*'s command backbone. While doing this, he saw Albert's adroit machinations, especially in the article defining a lieutenant's command as, "...a tug, tender or any ship not rated ...," which explained why *Calypso* was classified less than a fourth-rate, as did an 1869 general order specifying marines required by class, which also ended with fourth rates.

One article could not be sidestepped. Navy ships in a yard for major repair or conversion were taken out of commission and placed under the local commandant until the work finished and commanding officer accepted. This limited Starke to observing and offering advice until commissioning, when he must accept full responsibility for what the yard provided or decline the ship.

A surprising number were not accepted, which was why he and Albert worked the Building's bureaus that independently controlled shipyard tasks through district commandants. He could confront their officers and clerks while in Washington, but once in Newport News, any bureau inclination to shift priorities, evade contact, proliferate correspondence, or force his return to coax critical tasks through was less restrained. Since everything could not be complete before he left Washington, Starke concentrated on arming *Calypso* and shaping a crew. Enlisted personnel were placed under the Navigation Bureau several years earlier, so Albert sent official requests to Navy receiving ships. *Franklin*, in Norfolk, was building *Calypso*'s crew, but most on the East Coast were approached. Included were *Wabash, Vermont,* and *Richmond,* in Boston, New York, and Philadelphia; but not the Newport station and training ship for boy apprentices, *Constellation,* because taking boys would require *Calypso*'s crew provide training, care, and religious instruction.

These receiving ships were permanently moored, roofed-over wooden frigates and ships-of-the-line located in key ports or shipyards to collect recruits, berth sailors between ships, and assemble crews. They supplied the fleet with men from across the globe, since the service still relied heavily on merchant seamen, sought and enticed with better pay and conditions. Within this broad palette of colors, nationalities, and religions, any draft might contain past adversaries, American citizens and Indians, Irish, German, Colored, Negroes, Spaniards, Europeans, and a few from more exotic locales, such as the Sandwich Islands; although the Chinese Exclusion Act limited most Asians. These sailors' hard-earned seamanship skills were in such demand officers were detailed to teach English on some ships; but change was coming. New weapons technology, more electrical equipment, high pressure boilers, mechanical systems, and less reliance on sail was shunting this eclectic mix aside in favor of native-born from the Midwest. *Calypso* straddled this fissure since both were needed to operate an advanced steam plant, maintain modern guns, and handle her under canvas.

Calypso's small wardroom required officers who could work well in these circumstances, so Starke and Albert moved quickly, using Bureau of Navigation contacts, to acquire line officers, then other bureaus to fill staff billets. After finding two promising ensigns to head departments and stand watch, a more experienced third one, stepped forward for the navigator billet. The lanky, sandy-haired Ensign Walter Dunbar just returned from the Far East, and viewed the unanticipated billet far more promising and preferable than Pensacola's comatose shipyard. For engineers, Captain Albert met with Commodore Melville, the Engineer-in-Chief who controlled plant design, maintenance, operation, and steam engineering billets. Another staff billet worked was paymaster. For that, Albert called in Bureau of Supplies and Accounts favors to get the best; working through the assistant bureau chief, Paymaster Michler, a wealthy and popular Building veteran Albert met regularly since that bureau occupied first floor offices below his own.

Returning from a meeting with Michler, Albert had leaned back in his chair, selected a pipe, gently pressed moist tobacco into a fresh-scraped bowl, then ruminated, "Paymasters have a legitimate gripe, Jacob. There's no formal training and little guidance, only an initial certification board to evaluate education and experience, then promotion boards to consider what they accomplished. Consequently, the breed's best make things happen, while steering you clear of pitfalls, but many cling to regulations, and the worst are addicted to cabin and wardroom. We need someone with initiative, who sees opportunities but knows the limits; and Michler has a fellow in mind."

After shifting the smoldering pipe to his left hand, Albert added notes to his journal, paused, wrinkled his brow, then looked up, "We're not where we should be with Bureau of Medicine and Surgery, but their assistant, Surgeon Boyd, has three candidates, so concentrate on getting *Calypso* ready. I'll work the surgeon, apothecary, and baymen."

The remaining morning was spent on other critical staff and specialty billets. Obtaining a gunner, boatswain, sailmaker, and carpenter all demanded suasion to land the best, but marines proved most onerous. Albert was aware of the general order Starke found that assigned them only to fourth rate ships and above, but believed invoking it would do more harm than good. He explained it might insert *Calypso* into the acrimony existing between Navy line officers and the Marine Corps, which could result in interminable delay or even re-rating the ship. Many officers were advocating removal of all marines from Navy ships, then assign them to guard shipyards and naval facilities. Marine headquarters was resisting and arguing for a greater gunnery role. Consequently, Albert felt pushing the colonel commandant might entangle *Calypso* and, he explained, their headquarters seldom retreated once a position was taken.

Calypso's conversion continued at the Newport News shipyard, a new business venture constructed in what had been a farming community until 1881, when the Chesapeake & Ohio built a rail line down the peninsula to haul West Virginia coal to Hampton Roads. The yard opened ten years later, and concentrated on commercial work until awarded the *Nashville* and *Wilmington* contracts; initiating a government department. That fledgling organization, employing only two constructors, two engineers, a carpenter, and clerks, temporarily relied on Norfolk's navy shipyard and frequent workarounds; but was likely to balloon in the future since the shipyard was after more government business. This also meant the *Calypso* conversion enjoyed greater accommodation and urgency than anticipated in most government or private yards. Starke was made aware of this through the government department status reports he began receiving after accepting *Calypso*, due to Albert's connections.

During his last days, Starke moved from the intelligence office to a small table in Albert's. While there, he took up pipe smoking and grew familiar with the captain's daily routine. Each morning began with coffee near the tall window, then one administrative task after another, punctuated with brief excursions to the Assistant Secretary, bureaus, or other offices. There were also scheduled or gratuitous meetings and visits, with pauses for a quick lunch or occasional pipe. Albert once took Starke to brief the Judge Advocate on his filibuster project, before seeing the Secretary. They returned with a sheaf of questions and Albert grimaced, "Lawyers won't say how to do anything, but usually explain why you can't pursue an attractive approach. They're natural impediments, but don't ignore them."

Starke also visited the navy yard and gunnery school looking for good seaman gunner graduates, and to subtly progress Leutze, who tolerated it. One afternoon, for no reason, he walked to a 300 foot, seven-story ship house. The seventy-year-old building's dirty windows across its roof and sides partly lit a shadowy interior pierced with dust drifting down through sunbeams. Other than several offices at one end, the interior's stagnant atmosphere was impregnated with disuse, dried grease, and river mud. Along the roof's peak were track and lifting tackle remnants, while under its thick wood framing and rusted fastenings, neglected shipway rails emerged from stagnant river water to run beneath an unused ship cradle littered with hull blocks. At the forward end, a large chain coated with rust scale, lay limp at the cradle then rose into a large winch crammed with gears, levers, sprockets, and two partially filled wire rope drums. It left Starke in a pensive mood, more impatient than ever to commission *Calypso*.

Lieutenant Watson was the first officer returning from Norfolk. Albert arranged the trip to complete the *Winston A. Capps* transfer, discuss a draft response to her commander, and get firsthand status. It also occurred during the dinner party window, which served to eliminate any attempt to avoid attending. Starke found Watson slightly heavier and less overwound, but still slender with an ability to transition seamlessly from rest to action. During the interview, Starke sat at his small wooden table covered with notes and the open Navy regulations book. Albert remained behind his desk, where he questioned, listened, and frequently plowed the worn leather tobacco pouch with a well-used briar pipe, tamped the bowl with a thumb, then tended to its fire.

Albert had opened with, "Sit down Ben, it's good to see you."

Like many senior officers, he referred to those of less or equal rank by first name in private or more casual situations, unless frustrated or upset, then they were formally addressed. Subordinates knew better than to take similar liberties, so Watson responded, "Didn't think I'd return so soon, sir. Hated to leave when I was getting familiar."

"That's partly why you're here. Lieutenant Starke will be down there soon and should know what to expect, so I'd like your thoughts. Where are you staying?"

"New Atlantic Hotel near the Portsmouth and Berkley ferry. The accommodations are good, it has a restaurant, and the ferry runs hourly to Old Point Comfort."

Watson looked at Starke, then went on, "When reporting, I spoke briefly with Captain Terry then several times with *Franklin*'s XO, Lieutenant Commander Jasper. They've the Secretary's correspondence regarding our crew and briefed their commandant, Rear Admiral Brown. He's offered to do whatever's needed to commission *Calypso*."

Albert took a long draw on his pipe, "If you see Admiral Brown, convey my appreciation and ask if there's anything he requires."

Watson paused, assessed the two officers, then continued, "*Franklin*'s still moored in Portsmouth near the shipyard and handles Norfolk sailors since there's no naval station ashore. The ordnance officer said *Calypso*'s 4-inch guns arrived, with our small arms. No sign of the Gatlings, but they're expected in the next shipment. Captain Terry's begun a crew draft and training. Until *Calypso* commissions, I report to Commander Jasper, who's helped move things along."

"You've been to Newport News?"

"Twice, captain. Once after Lieutenant Osbourne arrived from Mare Island. He's staying at the Warwick Hotel, near the coaling piers, ferry, and train station. It's convenient and the city's best."

Watson stopped to observe Albert through a pleasantly pungent gray haze floating over his desk and Starke finishing some note, then continued, "I met Lieutenant Osbourne at his hotel's restaurant just before taking the train north. Naval Constructor Woodward at Newport News passed him to the navy shipyard's senior engineer, who put him on their books, then reassigned him to Newport News. He's examined the entire ship, not just the steam plant, and said her major installations and modifications are complete, the hull's being recaulked, masts are stepped, bowsprit's in place, and stern tube's overhauled."

While they considered this, he pressed on, "Is the ship's complement set? If so, I could tailor the watch, quarter and station bill."

Starke replied, "It's still early. Wardroom's not settled, two seaman gunners are allowed but not selected, and we're hoping to get a few sailors who've completed the Newport torpedo school's electrical course."

Albert questioned Watson further on navigating Hampton Roads, then subtly confirmed he was prepared for the approaching dinner party. Finally, Starke excused himself for lunch so the other two could work the Gagnon response. Walking the corridor's black and white tiles, he thought Watson fortunate to gain Albert's expertise refuting Gagnon without directly accusing him.

After Starke returned, Albert added, "When you speak with Admiral Brown, get his insight on working with State. Five years ago, they put him in extremis. I suggest you don't mention your father since Brown's ship was taken during the war and he was a guest in Libby Prison."

Albert worked a letter and Starke reviewed active circulars and general orders modifying Navy regulations until Passed Assistant Engineer Adrian Osbourne knocked twice on the white pine door, then entered as they rose to greet him. The young engineer, having just received the relative rank of lieutenant, already reported his arrival to the Bureau, even before checking in at the Army-Navy Club. The ship's future chief engineer was from Mobile, Alabama, and spoke slowly with a deep southern accent. Equipped with a laconic veneer, he often emphasized major points or significant facts with a nod or grin. While his features were unremarkable overall and height average, a stout build stressed uniforms and chairs; and the stubby fingers slid forward in greeting were cut and cracked from probing pumps, valves, or other machinery. An unrepentant Melville loyalist, he considered the bureau chief, and Benjamin Isherwood, role models. When not working ship machinery, he devoured technical journals and, unique within his community, was fascinated with gunnery and possessed a talent for handling ships under sail or steam; which attracted him to *Calypso*, and Starke to him.

Osbourne had come from the Steam Engineering Bureau's third floor offices where he reported to their chief engineer, Lieutenant Commander Harrie Webster, before navigating a half-hour interrogation by Melville. The bald captain with flowing white beard dominated steam engineering and won a Congressional Gold Medal for saving *Jeannette*'s men in the Arctic. Osbourne found him committed, mentally agile, forceful, and endowed with an astounding store of knowledge. He also avoided Melville's inclination and capacity to shred fools and fakers. While discussing *Calypso*'s triple-expansion engine, also selected for new gunboats, and water-tube boilers,

Melville and Webster stressed their need for operating information, then allowed him to contact Webster directly should anything go awry during the conversion or future operations.

In Albert's office, Osbourne settled on the same settee Starke used before his present small table and chair arrived. At his desk, Albert selected a meerschaum pipe from the rack and, while charging it, began, "You've reported to your bureau?"

The settee creaked as Osbourne repositioned, "Yes sir. Spoke with Commodore Melville and the chief engineer this morning. I understand *Calypso*'s testing the new triple-expansion engine and Normand water-tube boilers."

"Testing's secondary."

"I understood she was commissioned for it."

Pointing his pipe stem at Starke, Albert responded, "*Calypso*'s after filibusters, but will test to the extent feasible. She's been given a sail rig, so you may spend a great deal of time under canvas."

With a slight grin, Osbourne's bulk shifted, "Captain, I never expected a chief engineer designation this soon, so I'm grateful, but a fender between two bureaus?"

Albert, released a puff of smoke, then continued, "Decline if you've strong feelings, but work with Starke and there shouldn't be a problem. Your bureau maintains a tight rein with little interest outside the steam plant, so you must please them, but stay loyal inside the lifelines. Now, your impression of *Calypso*?"

Osbourne aligned his thoughts, then began, "I examined engine and boilers during my two days there, but need to go through them again, then condensers, piping, and particularly the coal bunkers that were added. I want to be confident in their design, construction, ventilation, and alarms, especially if she'll often be under sail. While not my area, I'd also like to inspect stuffing tube, dynamos, winches, and other items before undocking. From shipyard talk, if there's any delay, or a re-docking, work could be deferred months; probably because *Wilmington* and *Nashville* launched last October and sit pierside. They won't commission before next year so *Calypso* can still get a few months attention, but that dries up as their dates approach. The Norfolk engineer's assigned me to the Newport News government department, which gives us a foot in the door, and they've a steam engineer as lead inspector for the conversion since they're short naval constructors."

Captain Albert listened, relit, then drew from the light cinnamon pipe, "Lieutenant O'Leary. I assume you've met?"

"Yes, sir. Took me through *Calypso* and answered questions."

"What do think of him as assistant engineer?"

Osbourne had never before been asked to influence a fellow officer's career, but quickly responded, "Seems excellent, and no one knows the ship better."

"Good, speak to Commander Webster and I'll support you. Get with Lieutenant Starke on the black gang. If there's anyone you want, we'll help get them assigned."

"Yes, sir."

Starke looked at Albert then Osbourne, "We'll inspect the entire ship together before she undocks. I understand you're in the Building for several days reviewing steam plant conversion drawings?"

"Yes, sir."

Albert also probed Osbourne with subtle questions about the dinner party before he left; then returned to his tasks, wreathed by faint, pungent, pipe smoke. Unlike Europe, most Americans preferred loose-leaf or twist tobacco chews. Starke tried both but stayed with cigars, until his confinement with Albert. He also thought pipes more convenient at sea, where tobacco tins would store better than cigar boxes. Old sailors claimed they could be packed to stay lit upside down in wind and rain, but Starke never saw it done. Cigarettes were out of the question, partly because of storage, but more because they were predominately a woman's choice; although favored by his best friend at *The Sun*, a New York paper.

When not in the Building, Starke's free time was mostly spent as host to their British visitors. Besides riding, he invited Curtis to the Cairo Hotel's rooftop gardens, and regularly joined him and Uncle Immanuel for evening cigars and drinks in the library. During these sessions, it was clear Curtis' interests were broad and questions incisive. Besides asking Starke to compare the American navy with Britain's, he wanted to understand how Utah became the latest state with a Latter Day Saints government and polygamy. The approaching election, predicted to pivot on the gold standard and 1893 panic recovery, were of particular interest. When asked about Cuba, Starke deferred to his uncle, whose information came from the press, contacts, and the firm's masters. Since Washington papers carried international news, the three also discussed Italy's Ethiopian defeat, Jameson's disastrous raid, and Britain's invasion of Sudan to end Mahdist rule, which Curtis argued was less about avenging General Gordon than helping Italy and blocking France's African aspirations. Overall, Starke found Curtis agreeable, except for viewing these events as a great game, like American jingoes.

After learning Starke watched Alexandria's 1882 bombardment, a Sudan precursor, then went ashore with American marines and sailors to restore order, Curtis pressed for a description. Starke was not inclined, since he, and a father who once served Egypt, saw more duplicity than necessity on Britain's part; but provided a few snippets to avoid offense. He paid for it that night revisiting the panic, rubble, and butchery, as he fought to escort refugees to four American ships anchored just beyond floating debris and corpses. The images, sounds, heat, insects, and stomach-turning stench kept waking him in a sweat, so he obtained little more than an hour's deep sleep.

Starke was seldom with the sister, except when riding or during evening meals. Otherwise, it was a glimpse of her with Aunt Constance in the parlor, or boarding a carriage on warm days. He thought little of her since *Calypso* demanded full attention, but noticed she was unguarded with Sutton, who seemed equally at ease, unlike Cynthia. Between the two women, a stiff, proper guest-servant facade laced with tension existed that both seemed comfortable maintaining.

Religion occasioned one of his rare exchanges with widow Ledford. Most people in his aunt's social strata were Episcopal or, for the more liberal, Unitarian. Consequently, she was pleased to learn Katherine was Anglican, not Catholic, then invited her quests to St. Margaret's. Starke limited his church attendance to special days, and when unable to avoid it. One Sunday morning, on his way to the library, where *Calypso* documents and work blanketed the large desk, Katherine asked why he did not attend service. His rote answer response was well-polished to avoid conversion attempts or give offense, but she was taken aback, crevassed her brow, then replied, "A freethinker," before making for the door. Her disapproval upset him, although he saw no reason it should.

CHAPTER NINE
Dinner Party

Rain was coming, but fair weather forecast for the evening's dinner party. Starke retrieved his Newport News steamer ticket and had luggage arranged by noon since it was his final day in the Building. What could be accomplished had, so his attention already shifted south, except for that last social obligation and its distractions. Cassandra Evans was definitely one of those since his aunt's motivation for inviting her might be clear, but not the acceptance. Unescorted ladies did not attend, and their introduction barely adequate, yet his aunt deftly maneuvered him into an evening with Evans, including the trip to and from her Georgetown relatives. Starke did not dislike women, but learned escorting marriageable ones meant navigating a complex minefield of implications, expectations, and conventions.

This apprehension was relieved in Georgetown. Arriving in uniform at the relatives, it was clear they, and she, viewed her attendance as a professional event with few obligations on his part. During the ride, she discussed unique buildings and prominent families while Starke listened and sometimes replied; being preoccupied with *Calypso*. He was less than forthcoming on some subjects because her many skills included an ability to accumulate every bit of information, with or without carpet bag and notebook.

The landau returned to the mansion slightly before eight o'clock, just as Constance Starke prepared to receive guests during the customary fifteen minutes before; and insure all ladies were paired with their evening escorts. As each guest entered, Altman assisted with coats, shawls, and hats at the entranceway, announced their arrival, then guided them to Constance and Immanuel standing at the parlor's double doors. Both Starkes wore gloves to permit female guests to retain theirs, although a few society arbiters might wince. Constance, stepped out a pace to greet each arrival and, since she was receiving, wore a tea gown, customary for the hostess. Starke's aunt carried off the light-blue and white satin gown with elegance and poise. Although worn sans corset, hers included a small bustle and train; with shoulders, cuffs, and high collar of pale-blue lace. From collar to hem, the single front and back panels in white were unobstructed, except for three dark-blue lace soutaches bridging the front at bust, waist, and thighs. Sleeves came to the elbow, with long lace cuffs falling down and away, just above matching silk gloves. Her jewelry was drop earrings, two plain silver bracelets, and wedding band. The gown and jewelry accentuated a fine countenance, etched with delicate facial lines that moved when she smiled, complementing thin lips and penetrating eyes that often twinkled like a young girl's.

Beside her, Immanuel's black wool tailcoat struggled to contain a muscular frame becoming less angular and more corpulent, but retaining formidability. A white shirt under a shade darker waist coat displayed its single line of Mexican silver studs leading to a white-silk bow-tie, adding to the already constricting standup collar. The ensemble also included straight-legged trousers, sans side stripe, black patent leather shoes with pointed toes, and white kid gloves. His newly trimmed beard rose to merge with short hair, thinnest near the crown.

Attended by Starke, Cassandra Evans removed her shawl to reveal an attractive, but appropriate dress for women near or at spinsterhood. The green velvet gown began with a cone-shaped skirt and minimal bustle, rising to a jacket-shaped corsage with mutton sleeves. The low-cut rectangular front displayed unblemished breast tops with breadth added from the corset's upward thrust. Corsage and skirt were trimmed with black lace, and her smooth auburn hair anchored by a discrete tiara. The ensemble finished with pearl earrings, a matching choker necklace, and light gray gloves to her elbows.

After Evans greeted his aunt, who introduced Starke's uncle, she entered their parlor with Starke in tow, for light conversation without refreshments. Although politics were customarily avoided, Evans' instinct and interest soon took them to Cuba, a Raleigh Hotel interview with Gonzalo de Quesada, then Dynamite Johnny O'Brien. Starke was unconcerned about the Quesada interview, although he was the Junta's Washington man, but O'Brien was more than an adversary. He was an incorrigible filibuster, who, with his wife's help, constantly outwitted police and Pinkerton operatives trying to build a case or block expeditions. A perennial player in the Caribbean's near constant revolts and revolutions, his sobriquet allegedly came from running explosives, or employing them to discourage pursuit, so Starke grew even more circumspect.

Lieutenant Commander Leutze and wife, Julia, were announced then greeted by Starke's aunt and uncle. While speaking with Evans, Starke saw Leutze calmly endure his uncle's thrusting handshake as they exchanged greetings. Although it was their first meeting, Starke provided what details he knew about each Navy guest to prime conversation and avoid embarrassment. Leutze's success arming *Calypso* confirmed rumors he was an artist achieving results, although Aunt Constance was more familiar with his father's painting. Captain Albert mentioned Leutze taught languages at the Naval Academy and believed him fluent in a number, including German and Russian, and read several more. He also mentioned Leutze just received orders to the West Coast, steel-hulled gunboat *Alert*. Born in Dusseldorf, Prussia, a dozen years before Starke, He was tall with large nose, and deep-set light blue eyes. Dark eyebrows contrasted with a graying mustache and his goatee concealed a small chin and thin, angular countenance with prominent cheekbones. Like the other officers, he wore a uniform of black patent leather shoes, blue trousers without striping, and white shirt with bow-tie, under a waistcoat and tailcoat. Two decorative gold buttons were on either side of the open tailcoat, while four smaller ones in a square pattern closed the low-cut waistcoat. Below a line officer's star, three rows of gold braid encircled each sleeve near the cuff. Julia was well-dressed, with an easy poise acquired from similar events, and passed a quick exchange with Constance while lightly holding hands. Her long, gray gloves added to the paneled sleeveless gray gown cut fashionably low, front and back. A lace triangle inserted at the base expanded the hem and accentuated the corset's effect.

Captain Albert and Abigail arrived next, trailed by two daughters, with the youngest last. Other than four gold stripes and leather shoes, his dinner dress uniform matched the others, but the family caught Starke's attention. Abigail, was not the large, unpretentious, and good-natured woman he envisioned. Instead, she was thin with red-hair showing the first gray wisps; and nearly as dynamic as the barely constrained daughters in tow. As the family's exuberance pervaded the parlor, Starke's future executive officer and chief engineer crossed the main threshold seconds before the fifteen-minute deadline, attracting the captain's notice.

Starke suspected they lingered outside until Albert arrived, then followed him in; which said much for one or both's social acumen. Watson's uniform matched the others, apart from quality and fewer gold stripes, while Osbourne's was that of the steam engineering corps, with red cloth sewn between gold stripes, no star above, and different hat device. The marked difference was in physique and demeanor. Starke thought it fortunate tail jackets were worn open, as Osbourne's already strained waistcoat stretched threateningly when his uncle's thrusting handshake was returned with equal vigor. Watson's uniform, however, seemed slightly large, and he shook hands in a firm, slow, and respectful manner that was submerged in the uncle's pumping.

Starke was introducing Cassandra Evans to Leutze and his wife as the Albert formation tacked in their direction. Slowing towards the end of their approach, Albert fell in beside Julia Leutze, with the family taking station on their patriarch. Starke introduced Evans, but the others were already acquainted through work or the navy yard dances Starke seldom attended. He enjoyed dancing and was accomplished, but invariably weighed this against the sticky web of social obligations lurking in the tight community.

Abigail lacked physical features that might be thought beautiful, beginning with her fine red hair that resisted the pompadour and was so dark it appeared brown at a distance. Around the ears, and where it stretched over bone, her skin was nearly translucent and heavily dusted with faded freckles. Overlarge, green eyes moved constantly and pressured dark eyebrows further up a taut, red-tinged forehead. Nearly bisecting her thin face was a large nose balanced above a vibrant smile and noticeable overbite that displayed a single row of teeth, accentuating the small chin. Eschewing subdued colors, her shimmering, reddish-orange gown, with bustle, rose from the floor to a Swiss waist concealing a corset that failed to push a nonexistent bust upward. The material above her waist crossed to form two broad shoulder straps and 'V' front. She also wore a modest gold necklace, matching earrings, and long black-silk gloves. The disparate combination proved strangely fetching, and was accentuated by her being the most naturally vivacious woman Starke ever met; one who glowed in Albert's shadow with exuberance that was neither forced or deceitful.

The daughters unequally inherited her features and personality, although both were slightly broader and bustier, probably Albert's contribution. Olivia, the elder, had muted dark brown hair, lacked freckles or translucent skin, and wore a red satin dress with scalloped black lace trim, hemmed to ride just over the floor. Rising from the garment's trim, pleated red material converged at the Swiss waist that broadened to contain a modest neckline dip and puff sleeves. The waist's lower edge was trimmed in black lace imitating a V-shaped belt. She also wore a two-strand pearl necklace, drop earrings and long kid gloves. The hair was pulled back and rolled to a bun with a tuft left free to hang down over brown eyes. Her younger sister, Isabella, was their mother's untamed version, with impatient eyes, rebelliously springy red hair, and vivid features. The green dress she wore was similar, but less bold, to fit her more distinct features and younger age. It was trimmed in white with clean lines rising from hem to shoulder without distraction. The neckline was cut modestly open, though more shallow than her sister's, with vestigial puff sleeves. The hair was wrestled into the same style as her sister, and she wore single-strand pearls, drop earrings, and long cotton gloves. Although deferential, the sisters' contagious effervescent lit the room like flares, even breaching Evans' professional demeanor while speaking with them.

Edward Curtis and Katherine Ledford finally entered through the double parlor doors with the brother leading slightly, although not enough to suggest intent. His hair was trimmed and mustache waxed before donning Savile Row apparel consisting of a black dress coat of fine wool with step collar, worn over a low-cut double-breasted white waistcoat, evening shirt, and bow tie. The close-fitting trouser's seams were concealed under black side braid. He wore no jewelry beyond studs and cufflinks, but finished the ensemble with pearl kid gloves and fashionably pointed, black patent leather shoes. The interval between the two widened as Curtis walked to the room's center, unaware Katherine hesitated, appeared to reconnoiter, then warily advanced.

Curtis dressed well, but Katherine was breathtaking. Confident, poised, and graceful, the widow transfigured an all-concealing black silk mourning dress into a sensual garment ripe with eroticism. The gown rose from the floor to a high standing collar clasped tight to her neck. Black half-sleeves over full ones fell nearly to short, black gloves rising slightly above her wrists. A laced, black silk corselet confined her natural shape from waist to ribcage and accentuated what lay above and below. The lower section leading to her waist consisted of several ruffled layers with more starting at each hip, then converging in the rear to eliminate the bustle. Just below her waist, the ruffles passed under two panels resembling a protective armor belt, while nearly sheer material above her bust strained noticeably as she moved. The effect was further enhanced by the absence of a train or distracting jewelry. She wore only a gold-rimmed shell cameo from Naples, fastened to a black silk band around her neck. Starke later learned the piece arrived from Malta on the same day HMS *Victoria* sank, and its hand-carved face was taken from a picture of her Philip always carried. Invisible, except for a small bulge in one sheer black silk glove, was the mourning ring she was never without. A black garnet and wire diadem was pinned to the hair, which was up in her preferred style.

Starke's aunt and uncle smoothly escorted them through the guests because no one was sitting; women with bustles seldom sat for short periods, and gentlemen never did while a lady stood. At every pause, the cousins were introduced, then light chatter resumed as guests observed and surveyed their supper companions, especially Albert's daughters and Stark's future officers.

Cassandra remained near Starke, quietly asking questions until, reconnaissance complete, she sortied. Uncle Immanuel was an early objective, but abandoned when, with Nicaraguan canal press interest rising, she learned Leutze participated in the survey twenty years earlier. Starke offhandedly mentioned it when asked about a friend, on the same survey, who later obtained an army commission and died in Montana. Briefly free of escort duties, Starke joined Curtis and Albert. Meanwhile, his aunt circulated through the guests, ensuring formal introductions were made, and each pairing ready. Throughout, she constantly monitored the parlor's Waterbury banjo clock ticking down a schedule developed several days earlier, then reviewed just before starting fruits and jellies that morning.

Two unseen dumbwaiters were lifting food and drink from the ground floor where the cook, Martella Young, reigned. She was formidable, stout, dark, and possessed a natural ability to prepare food that was a passion aided by near photographic memory. Starke did not recall how long she had been with his aunt, whom Martella still referred to as Miss Constance. His uncle was invariably Mister Starke, and he remained Honey, or Mr. Jacob if more formality or chastisement was appropriate. An inveterate hugger, Starke expected a soft crushing between powerful arms when he came home after any extended absence. Work, age, and kitchen attractions smoothed her classic West African features, but the nearly circular face contained a pleasant mix of high arcing eyebrows, deep brown eyes, broad nose, and pronounced cheeks. Full lips revealed large white teeth when she laughed, but an iron-straight line when upset or taking an unassailable position. Like the others, she often borrowed from the library to read in the servant's hall during afternoons, when all cooks were idle. Martella Young spoke little about life beyond the family, but Starke's uncle mentioned she learned the profession in her parents' small restaurant; lost when family savings vanished in the Freedman's Bank collapse.

At nine o'clock, without confirming preparations were complete, Constance Starke invited guests to the upstairs dinning room. As hostess, she and Edward, a guest of honor, led, trailed by her husband and Katherine, then Captain Albert and Abigail. The remainder fell in by rank, beginning with Lieutenant Commander Leutze and Julia, Starke and Cassandra, Lieutenant Watson and Olivia, then Lieutenant Osbourne and the barely controlled Isabella. The column moved across the main hall, then upstairs at precise intervals with each woman's right arm lightly grasping their escort's crooked left.

Edward and Aunt Constance stood aside as the column reached the dining room to let Uncle Immanuel and Katherine pass. Everyone entered from the side of a long rectangular room with windowed alcove at the street end; matching the ballroom below. For formal dinners, the morning room at the far end separated guests from staging operations. An oval mahogany table with oak leaves set for additional guests was centered on a light oak parquet floor under a high ceiling framed with heavy square beams and dark-crystal gasoliers. Each oak door frame was varnished then polished until its wood seemed embedded in glass and, except for a black marble fireplace, paneled walls that matched the door frames rose halfway before turning into intricately patterned gold and rust wallpaper. A large buffet set against the wall opposite its fireplace and chairs encircled the table. Other than a half-dozen oil paintings, there was little decoration, despite the popularity of filling rooms with small items. The room was the decoration, fit the house architecture, and might be from a Renaissance castle, except side windows and broad alcove at the end flooded the space with daylight, then exposed it to the night. A floral arrangement centerpiece on white linen tablecloth was flanked by two dishes of cakes and surrounded by off-white bone china, crystal stemware, glasses, silverware, handwritten placards, precisely folded napkins, and menus.

Constance Starke never committed the social lapse of communicating with staff during dinner, yet logistics remained firmly under control. Altman would insure every move was correct in the dining room, while, in the adjacent morning room, Cynthia was in charge of dumbwaiter lifts and ensuring all debris and used items were loaded for return to the ground floor. Martella ruled there, and stood ready to prepare and send every course up on schedule. Since she refused strangers in her kitchen, the only additional help was two footmen Altman hired from a large hotel.

Immanuel Starke went to table's head and stood facing the alcove with Katherine on his right, until Constance and Curtis, entering last, went to the far end where Curtis faced Starke's uncle with Constance on his right. After sitting, the meal began when the seated guests, alternated by gender, removed gloves. There was no prayer and throughout, Starke's aunt orchestrated table conversation with practiced ease by setting topics, ensuring no one was left out or dominated; and preventing food, politics, or other unacceptable topics' intrusion. Leutze described Germany and Nicaragua, Cassandra her New York school, and Curtis the Atlantic crossing. Starke and Katherine mostly responded to questions, while Albert spoke to Port Royal. Everything interested Abigail, and the two daughters made headway with their escorts, or the reverse.

Observing his future officers, Starke noticed they followed his lead and found the evening less tedious than anticipated. He was pleased with them and impressed by Olivia and Isabella. The four understood and followed proper etiquette. Gloves came off, hand gestures were avoided, servers were not addressed, and, most challenging, an appropriate familiarity between escorting and escorted observed; well barely. None overate or drank excessively, and unwanted dishes were not refused but returned with empty plates and bowls.

Footmen rotated serving direction to give all equal time and ensure everything was appropriately, hot, warm, cool, or cold. A tureen of consommé was followed by oysters on the half shell with chicken and rabbit side dishes. After a sorbet came the main course of roast sirloin, with vegetables, salad, and fried potatoes. White or red wines and spring water separated courses, with desert consisting of chocolate, nuts, jellies and candied fruit in cut-glass bowls. Lemon-water filled finger bowls arrived at nine o'clock, and soon after Aunt Constance looked to Katherine and the ladies; signaling them to rise and end dinner. Her husband followed suite, the column reformed, and everyone left for tea and coffee in the parlor, since Constance preferred men and women not be separated following dinner.

Starke noticed Evans heartily approved of his aunt's choice, and for the next hour guests conversed while sipping tea and coffee, with escorts supplying charges with all they required. Uncle Immanuel, Albert, and Leutze stood near the double doors, while Abigail and Julia found common interest at the alcove. Near the casement door concealment, Starke's future officers seemed unable or unwilling to escape Olivia and Isabella, while Cassandra herded Starke between clusters. Katherine remained near his aunt until ten o'clock, when the hostess began her final pass though the parlor then stood near the door as guests took their leave. Within a week most would make a return call to thank her; a point Captain Albert already made with the two lieutenants. Cassandra Evans would certainly return, not only out of courtesy, but for details needed to finish her article. Each guest spoke briefly, then crossed to the entrance where they used the facilities and dressed for departure. Since Starke would leave for Newport News in the morning, he bid farewell to Captain Albert, Lieutenant Commander Leutze and their wives.

When Evans indicated her readiness to depart, word went to Sutton, who quickly brought the landau around. She and Starke were soon rolling through dark streets permeated with the smell of approaching rain. Her Georgetown relatives were up, so, after wishing all a good evening, Starke returned to the landau and its impatient horses. Unwilling to tolerate another stint in the closed carriage, or lower its leather top with rain near, he dismissed Sutton's halfhearted protest and joined him on the broad driver's seat; pointing out they would be seen as an empty carriage with driver and footman. Habitually, Starke did, or attempted, what he asked of others, but expected they know their trade better. He wanted to drive, but, accepting the achievable, sat quietly beside Sutton as the carriage rolled through a still, spring night, ripe with rain's promise.

Altman came to the entrance when they returned, but the others could be heard cleaning above and below. This would continue for more than an hour, with each knowing their mistress would offer some reward. In that, Constance resembled his uncle; each event's success was entwined with personal gain for those carrying it off. After speaking briefly with Altman, he left his outer garments, then went to the library since, except for the dinner dress uniform and other necessities, he was packed for the Newport News trip and awake from the open air ride. In the library, he poured a brandy, settled in a leather chair facing the fireplace, then opened *The Evening Times*.

It reported the steamer *Bermuda* completed another filibuster expedition after being released by New York authorities although her intent was obvious. It appeared the officers were freed while authorities confirmed documents consigning the cargo to Kingston, Jamaica, were forged; once General Garcia arrived, the ship left and he jumped bail. The newspaper claimed her cargo included rifles, revolvers, machine-guns, machetes, and ammunition. Starke thought machine guns unlikely, but the remainder was what might be expected from a small filibuster schooner. Steamers would also carry clothing, medicine, and explosives. The paper's tone left little doubt it supported the Junta, not current law, and made Starke feel greater urgency for *Calypso* to reach the Caribbean. He considered this while sipping the biting amber liquid; until surprised by Katherine. As she glided into the library, he folded the paper then set it aside on a small table. Standing, he turned to welcome her, "Good evening, Mrs. Ledford."

She eyed the chair beside him, saying, "May I join you?"

"Certainly, Mrs. Ledford."

"Katherine, please."

Starke was surprised she was up and wearing the black dress. He offered a brandy, which was declined, then she sat without speaking. After glancing at *The Evening Times*, Katherine broke the silence, "I was unable to sleep or sit alone in my room. I read that newspaper while you took Miss Evans home. Did you see women served on a South Dakota jury, and one at Cornell University earned a doctorate? Such things are almost unheard of in Britain."

"No, something different."

"What?"

"A filibuster reaching Cuba."

"I see that often. Are they important?"

"The Junta in New York smuggles weapons to Cuba. They take our sanctuary, then break the law and risk war with Spain."

"Shouldn't Cuba be independent?"

Her lips snapped to a hard straight line when he responded, "The same could be said about Ireland and British colonies in the Caribbean."

Until now they spoke only in passing, and she thought Jacob polite, but hard; a man whose presence unsettled her, which is why she could not understand waiting up for him. The flat tone of his response left her confused, but was not patronizing, which was much like Philip. Without allowing time for a riposte, he added, "But, it's not that clear. Cuba is almost a Spanish province with people from Spain, Spaniards born there, those from other colonies, and many freed slaves, or their descendants. Some favor an autonomous region and a few, annexation by the States. Even those supporting independence split on politics, wealth, and race. Most Cubans just want to survive, and not be shot, starved, or macheted. Business interests prefer stability. For instance, our firm has a plantation and small mill near Artemisa that's closed."

"Then you accept Spain's position?"

"No. My uncle and I avoid politics, although he'll sell the Cuban holdings because of the insurrection. The island's poorly governed and Spain cannot stay or leave without disaster. If they remain, people and resources will continue to pour into a war that's likely to resume in a few years, even if they prevail this time. On the other hand, the Junta lacks broad support, so their strategy is to increase Spain's distress while destroying the island's value. In addition, many, even in the Junta, fear Cuba could follow Haiti, which means worse fighting just off our coast. The compromise position is autonomy, but that's not likely to succeed."

"I see you're no jingo, but politics is inescapable. Serving British officers are often in parliament."

"My father might agree now. He tried to avoid taking part when radicals took the States to war against each other. Thirty years later, nation and navy are recovering, but there's still resentment. Our wardrooms forbid discussing it, and, like many others, my father's in Rio de Janeiro, with no allegiance to his birth country."

"I wonder what Philip thinks?" she replied aloud without thinking. Katherine sometimes felt he still somehow spoke to her.

Confused, Starke asked, "Your husband?"

"Yes."

"You miss him?"

"Very much. We wrote often, and I keep his letters."

"My aunt receives the odd letter from me, and those to my uncle are usually business. On rare occasions, I post one to my father. Anyway, my apologies for going on."

Starke wanted to explore her thoughts but lapsed into silence, perhaps because less admirable signs of attraction arose. He concluded the cause was *Calypso* temporarily absent from his thoughts, they were alone, excellent brandy was having an effect, and her dress seemed an enticing barrier; or perhaps because she came to him alone at night, even if in the library. The result was a struggle to subdue more powerful urges than previously experienced with attractive women, especially those who showed no inclination of seeking more than company. However, knowing it would soon pass and *Calypso* was waiting, supplanted those primal urges and brought salvation.

Katherine appraised the man across the small table. Tonight, in uniform, he resembled Philip, although the two were utterly different in looks and manner. She never thought her husband aggressive, and expected he would some day enter the Foreign Office, since his wide interests and liberal outlook were unusual in the Royal Navy; except for young officers coalescing around Jackie Fisher and Percy Scott. Always proper, even when frustrated what was right did not take place, he inevitably acted with unquestioned honor and courage. Captain Bourke, an earl's son, family friend, and HMS *Victoria's* commanding officer, told her Philip was last seen going below to order the engine room watch to leave; but instead died with them as the ship capsized with still-turning screws driving her to the bottom.

Philip was a professional, who prepared for war, but Jacob seemed a warrior by nature, albeit one who failed to realize the personal toll exacted. She recalled one gathering when Philip's guests debated foreign navies over cigars and brandy. The others dismissed America's as a quaint mix of monitors and wood relics with scratch crews unable to face a proper European squadron, or even some from South America. Philip swirled the liquid around a crystal glass, looked at it, then interjected, "Germany and the United States are our greatest threats; with growing industries to provide them powerful ships. However, Americans are more dangerous because they've bested us ship-to-ship and their junior officers approach war with the same innovation and energy yankee merchants show in business. Many of their senior officers have fought capable adversaries during their civil war, while ours, other than Fisher, Tyron, and Percy, are grandmasters of protocol, painting, polished deck fittings, and opera wakes. In war, I doubt Americans will show equal concern for such niceties."

Katherine was uncomfortable. She refused temporary liaisons, or anything else, since being widowed and saw no reason to change. Besides, a proper relationship was impossible. He would not fit her world, she could not survive his, and her father loathed colonists. She already ventured too far by visiting him alone at night. At home, most would see this as an invitation for a nocturnal visit, so continuing was absurd and risked her honor. While there was no indication he would take advantage, she suspected Starke did not possess Philip's softness and restraint. While not handsome like Philip, his leanly athletic appearance must hold some attraction for her since she felt heated and discomfited. While vacillating between attraction and aversion, Katherine was shocked to hear herself quietly ask, "Will you write?"

Starke was caught off-guard. Katherine displayed little interest before this evening, and was now more forward than he thought capable. He impulsively replied, "Certainly, Katherine, my aunt always has an address."

Retreating to silence, she watched him quietly sip the last brandy, then grew ashamed of not only staying up to accost him alone at night, but suggesting they correspond, which implied she sought a commitment or understanding after less than two weeks acquaintance. Growing more distraught, then uncertain, embarrassed, and uncomfortable, she rose, saying, "Good evening, Jacob. I'll see you at breakfast."

Jacob responded, "Yes, Katherine, I'll look forward to it. Sleep well."

With that she passed through the door, walked across the hall, then began climbing the stairs, unaware Starke could not ignore the black dress moving with and against her body. When she reached the landing, he replaced the crystal decanter top, then passed though her faint scent as he went to his bedroom.

CHAPTER TEN
Potomac Steamer

Alongside a wooden finger pier jutting from the Washington Channel's east bank, *Newport News* readied for overnight passage down the Potomac River, then south through Chesapeake Bay to Norfolk. With stern facing the waterfront and bow pointing to the channel's west bank spill area and Potomac River beyond, the steamer's bulk eclipsed river freighters, schooners, and workboats; whether underway or alongside adjacent piers and wharfs. Grayish-white gulls glided above in loose spirals over water, wharfs, and piers; searching for a late meal, then diving. Since mid-afternoon, the nondescript gray sky accentuated stagnant harbor air that smelled of coal smoke, steam, mud, sewage, decaying garbage, and approaching rain.

Traveling to Newport News in civilian clothes, Starke waited in a loose crowd on Norfolk & Washington's 7th Street wharf. His black derby and single-breasted Chesterfield overcoat with velvet collar, covered a light wool sack coat, vest, and loose trousers. The ensemble also included gray leather gloves and a solid cane for fashion and protection. Starke's aunt favored less proletarian dress, but he wanted utility and convenience. At his feet was an off-white canvas socking containing scabbard and sword, bound loosely to a well-used leather Gladstone bag. Darius Sutton brought him to the wharf early, and, after checking Starke's abused steamer trunk and smaller cabin version, they shook hands, paused briefly with them clasped, then the veteran trooper began an uphill return that should have him home before night overtook dusk.

Less than a year in service, *Newport News* was one of three Norfolk & Washington ships running daily between the capital and Norfolk, with stops at Old Point Comfort and Newport News. Restrained by doubled spring and breast lines, some ninety feet of her three-decked white hull extended beyond the pier into the narrow channel. A shimmering gray-black haze lifted from smoke pipes rising up through the steamer's decks and thin stack. Starboard side amidship, a wide gangway inclined gently from the pier to a main deck entry port. Projecting slightly from the black steel hull, her white superstructure, trimmed in black, included two decks lined with large rectangular windows. The saloon and gallery decks began about a third of the length from her bow and ended with a gallery deck open area under a white canvas awning stretched taut over wire rope strung between stanchions. Above the gallery deck, her pilothouse, crowned with a huge gilded eagle, was followed by a long deckhouse, black stack, and three boat davit pairs. Starke's stateroom was comfortably distant from stack and pilothouse on the gallery deck's starboard side.

He surmised the ship handled well, or would not remain on the river. The pilothouse was on or near her pivot point, keeping the conning position over ship's course when bow and stern swung in opposing directions during turns. A jackstaff towering over the straight stem could also assist steering her, if not too near the pilothouse. Her precursor's side wheels had apparently been replaced by a single screw, although twin screws would serve better on the river. A single-screw arrangement was less maneuverable, but could be partly addressed through confident ship-handling and the stockless anchors housed in the bow; more useful for shiphandling than stocked anchors on billboards.

With her starboard side to the pier, a slight channel current would set the ship away when freed of mooring lines. However, tugs were needed to hold her starboard quarter off during the tight port turn down channel. Starke was thinking through getting her underway when the steam whistle's long screeching blast summoned passengers. Although many lingered to finish farewells, Starke worked through those standing and milling to the large boarding port, entered, was greeted by her purser; then immediately engulfed by a ship's familiar smells, droning ventilation fans, steam line vibrations, and more. Following directions, he climbed two wooden staircases to the upper deck and located his room on the balcony surrounding her grand saloon. Using the small brass key, he entered a single-bed stateroom; having decided against sharing a berth room. On the outboard wall was a tall double-paned window overlooking waterfront, city, and surrounding countryside. Although he caught glimpses of the Building, Washington Monument, Arlington House, and Long Bridge from the pier, the vista improved markedly three levels higher. The Capitol loomed over a mostly red-brick city from its mound, as did the Arlington plantation house on National Cemetery high ground across the river. While contrasting it with Oxen Grove plantation, an inbound freight train crossing Long Bridge distracted him.

Starke laid cane and luggage on the brass bed secured to the inner wall, then hung hat and overcoat on peg hook. Looking around, he saw the walls and square overhead beams were painted white and dark pine floor thickly varnished. There was electric lighting, and a small steam radiator beneath the window. Walking to a wicker chair in an outboard corner, he saw its counterpart contained a triangular porcelain sink, varnished wood shelf, and towel rack.

While waiting, he retrieved the briar pipe Albert gave him the last day in the Building, then filled its bowl from a new leather pouch. As a novice pipe smoker, he struggled with compacting the soft brown fibers just enough to stay lit but not so loose they would instantly incinerate. Between relights of the pipe, he revisited the decision to remain in the navy, despite his uncle's advice to concentrate on what had been decided, until the sword and scabbard on the bed caught his attention. His uncle gave it to him at commissioning and the blade traveled with him on all Navy duty because it was his father's, one was required, and it fell within the loose specifications. Unlike dress swords, it was a weapon, not a light accoutrement. The 1860 model's cut and thrust blade was sharpened enough to cut but not weaken or ruin its edge, and the heft and balance fit perfectly. He disliked dress swords' pretense, thinking they were better discarded, or an honest blade specified, but also believed it folly to carry a weapon one could not employ; so he learned to handle it, along with canes, singlesticks, foils, and sabres.

Starke planned to eat just after *Newport News* was underway, since most passengers stayed on deck watching the shoreline, then locate his old friend, Darwin Tyson. When their paths crossed, usually in Washington, they spent time together over dinner and drinks, although there was little difference in Tyson's case. They met in the Bond Building lobby and discovered both were there for *Newport News* tickets. Tyson, on assignment for *The Sun*, would disembark at Old Point Comfort, finish a story on Hotel Chamberlain's opening, then board the Chesapeake & Ohio train to Richmond, where he would transfer to a Southern Railway Company express for Florida.

It was difficult to recall Tyson in the Jefferson Classical and Military Academy's gray cadet uniform, although he wore it well and truly. Even then, his friend was a volatile concoction of eccentricity, intelligence, and perception; tinted with reliably dismal views. Arcane poetry, history, mathematics, or military tactics, he went after everything with skill and enthusiasm. Unfortunately, his sense of discipline and honor reliably conflicted with the school's, so he left for University of Michigan's College of Literature, Science, and the Arts; where a degree came in less time than most, with little apparent effort. His father owned a small watch factory that prospered from the war, and anticipated Tyson taking over, but the heir was drawn to reporting politics, crime, war, debates, scandals, and the like. After working on several newspapers for varying tenures, Tyson earned a reputation for rooting out leads, meticulous research, and compelling stories. This culminated in his current position at *The Sun*; where his persistence, passion, and honesty pricked interests, constabularies, and governments.

At the ship's second whistle, his pipe was abandoned to the ashtray as he left the cabin for the starboard side. Placing gloved hands on a stanchion and woven wire railing, he looked over at men pulling the brow onto the pier while others singled-up mooring lines. The pilothouse was sectioned off because *Newport News* lacked separate bridge wings, but he found a spot to observe the first mate direct line-handlers as the master watched for channel traffic or port side problems. A small tug from upstream crossed the bow, pivoted, then tossed a heaving line to the forecastle crew, who pulled it through the bow chock, followed by a small hawser for the headline.

The purser once worked for his uncle's firm, so he stopped to talk. From him, Starke learned *Newport News* was 274 feet long with a thirty-seven foot beam, and carried up to 300 passengers. Using two boilers, her triple-expansion engine drove the 1,320 ton ship to twenty-two knots. He also confirmed a single screw, which meant, with a high hull and tall superstructure catching wind, she was awkward in restricted water. Today, however, the large steamer was moored on the pier's downstream side, the predicted light breeze was holding, and what current existed flowed almost imperceptibly south from the channels' tidal reservoir.

Starke watched the small tug's stack belch black smoke and headline's belly flatten, but saw no strain taken. When the mate ordered, "Take in all lines," using a brass speaking trumpet, line-handlers lifted mooring line eyes off cleats, walked them to the pier edge, then released them to the deck crew, that pulled rapidly to avoid a wetting. Her deck vibrated slightly as the screw began turning, adding thrust to wind and current, now that mooring line resistance ceased. As turns increased, forces against the hull changed with some results felt immediately and others anticipated. Although the ship inched forward, her rudder could not immediately influence the equation, a major handicap alongside piers. Consequently, Starke waited to see how the conning officer would clear, then turn south into the channel; without swinging her starboard quarter against the pier or being set down on two small schooners.

As the current slowly breasted ship from pier, engine and rudder orders were given and repeated between master and pilothouse. When the gap opened, power was increased several seconds then eased. After a slight delay between engine orders and effect, the hull began moving down the pier, disturbing refuse floating in the black water alongside and giving her rudder increasing bite. When the stern cleared, a full starboard helm began the port turn, to run south down channel. As the pier head cleared, the small tugboat, again belching smoke, took a strain on the headline, increasing the turn, then steadying the larger ship. When the steamer was aligned mid-channel the headline was cast off; freeing the tug to clear the large ship's course, slow, then retrieve its hawser. As the eye flopped onto its fantail, it tooted, then returned to the piers under light smoke, leaving a dirty, gray-white wake.

Starke went to the port railing as shaft turns increased and *Newport News* surged forward. He watched the long peninsula with Washington Barracks and arsenal pass, then looked up Anacostia River to the navy yard and ship house visited a few days before. At Fort Washington the steamship would turn, then again at Mount Vernon, Quantico, and Acquia Creek, before reaching Maryland and Mathias points. Afterwards, the course to Point Lookout and the Chesapeake was relatively straight, but the deceptively broad river with large shallows lining the channel also concealed snags, with weather, traffic, and floating debris adding more hazards. However, it was not Starke's responsibility and the Norfolk & Washington steamers were known for à la carte seafood dinners, so he left for the dining room.

Starke descended a broad staircase from the main deck to a dining room that consumed the ship's width; and accommodated four rows of tables split by a wide central aisle. Supported by stanchions, the two overhead I-beams on either side of its main aisle ran lengthwise with smaller beams crossing athwartship. The entire room was painted dull white, contrasting with a dark diamond-pattern carpet. There were portholes along each side, but electric overhead lights in globe fixtures furnished illumination. White linen cloth was draped over square tables surrounded by four bentwood chairs and preset with silverware. Large, white linen napkins protruded from water-glasses at each setting and surrounded a centerpiece outfitted with menus and condiments.

As Starke entered, a waiter in black jacket and white shirt offered a port side table with clear view of the stairwell. Once seated, he examined a menu, considered roast duck or stuffed shad, then selected rockfish, fried oysters, and corn bread. After he ordered and requested tea, the harried waiter bowed slightly, then moved quickly away. While fingering his unlit pipe and thinking of *Calypso*, Starke spied a boney, balding, and clean-shaven figure at the staircase foot. Darwin Tyson, paused, scanned the space, saw Starke, then advanced. A floor manager's attempted interception barely slowed him as he crossed to the table where Starke had risen. Pulling back a chair, he sat with a perfunctory, "May I join you?"

"My pleasure, Darwin."

"Have you ordered?"

Starke replied as Tyson flashed through the menu. When the waiter returned with tea, he selected canvasback duck and Beaufont Lithia Water. Replacing the menu, his familiar sardonic grin appeared, "Raw oysters, fried oysters, and oyster stew; all sorts of oysters. Covered Virginia and Maryland's oyster wars ten years ago. Now, there's less oysters, fighting, watermen, and shuckers. Still plenty of oysters here though."

Before Stark responded, Tyson drank from the just delivered water, pulled a large silver flask from his inside jacket pocket, then added enough alcohol to restore the original volume. The newly fortified water looked benign, but gained significant potency. Tyson looked across at Starke, raised the glass, swirled it slightly, then stated, "Nothing like clear spring water with lithium salts. Great for health and attitude. Now, about this ship the Navy's giving you?"

"*Calypso*?"

"Yes, late of your uncle's firm. If memory serves, *Cutlass* and *Illusive* before *Calypso*; and has a privateer pedigree?"

"You're well-informed."

Tyson, sipped the muscular spring water, set it down, then continued, "You're obviously not superstitious about renamed ships and I smell story, Jacob."

"*Calypso*'s old and would have been overhauled or sold off, but the Navy needs small ships, so everyone came out ahead. She's a lieutenant's command, same as a large tug or lighthouse tender, and will be sent to the Caribbean to test a propulsion system, possibly do some surveying, and carry out patrols."

Tyson knew his friend would not lie to him, but could be less than candid, if necessary. With the Caribbean mentioned, he was convinced there was more, but Starke moved first, "What's your assignment?"

"Hotel Chamberlain. Opens in April after six years building. I'm next door at the Hygeia getting background; then it's Tampa, Key West, and Havana's Hotel Inglaterra. My editor wants more than peanut club rumors or Key West fiction on the reconcentrado. Then it's back to New York for the Cuban-American Fair in May."

"I'll still be in the yards."

Tyson, took a belt of spring water, "No sale on your Caribbean ruse, Jacob. You attract stories and can't help yourself: Montana expedition, the Alexandria bombardment, Brazilian naval mutiny, and China's war with Japan. If I'd been with you from the beginning, the first story I filed would have been front page news."

"I doubt you'd have filed. That reporter's buried there. I was young and ignorant then, like you, and no one expected what happened."

"Perhaps, but I can't accept this ship was selected, rebuilt, re-rigged, then armed with the latest 4-inch gun mounts, of which there's a shortage, for what you claim."

Starke welcomed the waiter and server arriving with their food since Tyson obviously nosed about after leaving the Bond Building. While enjoying fresh-grilled fish and fried oysters, the waiter attempted to refill water glasses, but Tyson intercepted him, declined a refill, then thanked the man; but later asked for water instead of any dessert. The puzzled waiter brought it with Starke's cake. Once he left, Tyson added his personal elixir and began sipping the clear liquid. When the dining room began overflowing, Starke proposed they shift to the smoking room or grand saloon. After leaving something for the waiter, Starke looked back from the stairs to see their table being reset for a waiting family.

The smaller, spartan, and less crowded smoking room included a line of rectangular windows along one side, matching those in the staterooms, and was furnished with the same chairs and tables, without tablecloths, used in the dining room. Wood benches were also placed against its walls and one corner had a brochure rack. The overhead lighting matched the dining room, but brass sconces with electric bulbs and flower-shaped globes were fixed at precise intervals along the interior walls. Choosing a window table away from other patrons, they sat on either side, looking out at the passing shoreline of trees and fields interspersed with clusters of houses, some near the river, but more on higher ground beyond.

Tyson observed, "Plantation houses, built back from the river against pirate raids."

Without responding, Starke pulled out a pipe, then filled and tamped its bowl with his thumb. Although cigarettes were thought feminine, Tyson retrieved a gold-trimmed jade case partly filled with a Turkish variety, tapped one against the edge, then lit up. Afterwards, the match was tossed to the ashtray, as he continued, "What do you know of Weyler's strategy?"

Employing Captain Albert's ruse, Starke lit his pipe, took a draw, then lifted it, considered the smoke, and constructed a response, "What good choice does Spain have? Beyond fortified areas, people are supporting, supplying, or terrorized by insurrectos. The Spanish can't afford to remain and don't feel they can leave. Perhaps Madrid's gambling the reconcentrado and troop surge will end it. The general they sent will certainly try; and take the field against insurrectos. He fought in Cuba before, has been successful elsewhere, and was an attaché during our war; which supposedly convinced him less intense, prolonged conflicts are more costly than short violent ones. It's also Spain's last roll of the dice since they cannot absorb much more."

"What would our old history lecturer say? The one who left a leg at Fort Fisher."

Starke recalled Jefferson Academy's large brick building, with classrooms occupying one wing and living quarters the other. The lecturer was a paunchy man with a bushy, gray beard who hobbled to the blackboard armed with chalk. Savagely assaulting the slate, he would suddenly pivot towards the class, continuing the lecture adorned with blotches and streaks of chalk dust. Starke coaxed the pipe into drawing well after sacrificing two matches, then responded, "The one who echoed my uncle's belief war's mass insanity?"

"Yes. Remember his six sequences: naivety, fear, resignation, barbarity, remorse, then denial."

"Whatever happened to him?"

"His wound finally killed him, or consumption. Tried to sell an obituary, but New York papers have no interest in dead Confederate captains."

Starke's pipe was unexpectedly staying lit, "I didn't believe him then."

They smoked silently for a time, then Starke spoke, "Did you ever meet a Miss Cassandra Evans in Washington?"

"Attractive woman with auburn hair. Met her briefly in the Times office. Writes for their women's section, but wants more hard news. Women use pseudonyms for bylines, when they get one. She's Boudica Brown. Nellie Bly was Elizabeth Cochran's until last year when she married an old fellow with money and stopped reporting. Cochran worked for the *World* and we met several times. Someone mentioned it to Evans, and she buttonholed me."

Tyson crushed a cigarette carcass in a brass ashtray, took a quick nip from the silver flask, then continued, "Anyway, she wants to move on from covering theater, women's topics, and social news. A lot in her situation do, but men are better suited for hard news. Their nature is to understand or control what surrounds them; women create. Good reporting's unvarnished, so their nature and predisposition interfere."

As Tyson sipped, Starke added, "Said she hopes to get to Havana."

Brushing his lips, Tyson replied, "It's where correspondents make reputations, so a gaggle's there and in Key West. Hope you're not interested. She'd do almost anything for a story, although rumor has it her virtue is more disinclination than restraint; like Chinese eunuchs sacrificing part of themselves to advance. Anyway, about *Calypso*?"

"As I've said, there's nothing."

"So you say, but I suspect we'll meet in Florida or Havana. How does our fleet compare with Spain's?"

"We've four battleships to their one. Advantage in armored cruisers and torpedo boats goes to them. For speed and range, only *New York* or *Brooklyn* match their *Infanta Maria Teresa* class, or new *Carlos V*. They're also ahead on small gunboats. Overall, it would depend on whether Spain had an ally and how their ships are used."

Starke's pipe died often as time passed and empathy grew for Albert's constant search for matches. Foregoing a return to the dining room, he finally announced, "I think I'll get some sleep; and you?"

Tyson rose smiling, "I'll go as far as the grand saloon, but for me and Napoleon, it's three hours a night. I'm condemned to prowl while the world sleeps. Probably read or take some air in a deck chair."

Starke forgot Tyson's sleeping habits. Even Jefferson Academy instructors conceded their mandatory six hours sleep amounted to confinement and torture for their charge. He was eventually allowed unfettered access to the library; and later said there was nothing to do with those extra hours but learn or go insane.

Passing through two wood doors with framed glass upper panels, they climbed the dark-pine Grand Staircase to the saloon deck, entering just forward of its large, square stack enclosure with mirrored side panels. The saloon rose through the gallery deck to curved beams supporting a ceiling with ornate electroliers. State and berthing room doors ringed both decks, opening directly to the saloon or, on the gallery deck, a balcony with varnished wood railings. The large space was furnished with a mix of bentwood chairs, leather arm chairs along both sides, and large, round leather divan near the Grand Staircase railing. Pausing, Starke confirmed their breakfast arrangements, then left for his stateroom. Looking down from the balcony, Starke saw Tyson approach a small gathering passengers, then introduce himself. He obviously intended to pass time or troll for information, since Washington's wealthy and influential favored these ships over trains.

In his stateroom, Starke checked for bedbugs, opened a window, undressed, and was soon sliding between clean sheets in a buttoned night robe. He slept lightly, but well, soothed by the steamer's slight rocking, three pistons' rhythm, and the faint sound of water passing along the hull. He was occasionally semiconscious from slight course changes or a whistle blast, then returned to sleep as familiar at-sea habits took hold. He woke fully at Point Lookout, when the ship made a major course change south, but returned to sleep after checking his father's plain gold Patek Philippe & Cie hunter pocket watch. Starke rose early next morning, then moved quickly to the corner commode to wipe arms, chest, and head with a washcloth. The water poured into the porcelain basin from its matched pitcher was bracing. His aunt called these a whore's bath, which shocked him the first time she said it. Once dressed, he met Tyson for a breakfast of fried eggs, ham, toast, and coffee. Starke took sugar in his coffee; Tyson a quick injection from his flask.

After finishing, the friends went topside. *Newport News* was making good time, running nearly due south, through a crisp morning under cloudless skies, so her seven o'clock Old Point Comfort arrival looked good. The shoreline off their starboard bow was growing more distinct, with the Atlantic just visible beyond the bay's mouth over the Middle Ground to the southeast; and a large island could be seen some distance off the port bow. The steamer held her course past Horse Shoe Flats, then, in sight of Old Point Comfort, heeled slightly to port as she came west, cutting a long, curved wake through the gray, glasslike Chesapeake. Starke reveled in this Friday morning underway on the bay, with the tang of steam and coal smoke; even as a passenger.

Tyson lit a cigarette, finished, then flipped the butt overboard, "Forgot to ask. Heard anything about your family's Cuban investments?"

"They're mostly shut down after fighting around Artemisa. My uncle won't ask workers to defend them, pay protection to insurrectionists, or, until peace returns, rebuild. He's sent money to help and retain key people needed to restart operations , but that can't continue, and there's rumors they're being threatened for receiving it."

With Fort Monroe off the starboard bow and Fort Wool to port, Tyson touched Starke's sleeve, "Enjoyed the trip, Jacob. Met some useful folks last night. Best of luck."

"Be careful in Havana."

Tyson retorted with a grin, "See you at the Inglaterra," then went below before Starke could respond.

The shoreline, Old Point Comfort, and Fort Monroe closed rapidly, disentangling the elongated Hygeia Hotel from fort, trees, and other buildings inhabiting the point. The popular vacation destination catered to visitors with wealth, connections or prominence. Starke expected Tyson would penetrate that society like a barracuda striking a school of fish, seeking more stories than the Chamberlain Hotel, now rising above the Hygeia.

Bay and shoreline scents grew stronger after passing between Fort Monroe on the point and Fort Wool on its man-made island. Just south of Newport News lay Hampton Roads, then the Elizabeth River, which separated Norfolk and Portsmouth. *Newport New*'s steam whistle loosed several blasts as she approached Baltimore Wharf, causing figures on it to grow more animated. Starke felt the ship bleed way as Engineers Pier and Old Comfort Point lighthouse passed serenely down the starboard side; then, by sighting along the railing, gauged the shallow angle used by the master for his approach.

Baltimore Wharf was a large octagonal platform on heavy pilings at the end of a broad pier extending out from the street starting at Fort Monroe then passing between the Chamberlain and Hygeia hotels. Small finger piers sprouting from it were filled with small, steam-powered tourist launches, while wharf center hosted a large, single-story, gabled building serving as ticket office and waiting area. Immediately to the west, straddling beach and bay, just past the peninsula's southern point, was Pavilion Pier, a small circular structure for entertainment.

The landing spot was a shade longer than *Newport News*, so the master approached at bare steerageway, angled slightly towards the wharf, then, when the deck crew was confident, heaving lines arced out. All but one bounced across thick planks, where they were taken up by deck hands and used them to pass mooring lines over. One failed because the monkey fist struck a tall piling, but the backup went over as it sank. When the bow spring line's eye slid down over a piling, the master ordered it held, put his helm over, then walked the hull in. Judging momentum, he backed a touch, then ordered all stop. As the ship settled against the pier, slack was taken from mooring lines, but they were left singled since *Newport News* would quickly discharge passengers and luggage then leave for Newport News and Norfolk. Once secure, a short brow came over from the pier and passengers emerged though the amidship entry port, followed by their luggage, which was collected by hotel carts.

Starke saw a streetcar waiting beyond the pier and guessed it connected with a new line to Newport News that allowed shipyard workers to live well beyond the city limits. Nearby were vendors and carriages waiting for passengers coming off arriving ships. The new fortress-like Chamberlain Hotel, with six stories, massive gabled towers on each corner, and balconies, was less familiar to Starke than the elongated Hygeia across the street. An extremely long building of four floors running along the beach, it had mansard towers and beach-front pavilions covered by red and white striped canvas.

Newport News' whistle soon signaled her departure, the gangway rolled back on the wharf, and line-handlers made ready to cast off. When mooring lines were retrieved, the ship backed from the wharf, stopped, then surged forward, setting course for Newport News, a short distance west. Starke looked astern at a thin man waving his fedora before entering the wharf's central structure.

Standing on the starboard side, Starke could make out the Chesapeake & Ohio roadbed and nearby light rail line. Both followed the peninsula then crossed Mill Creek to Hampton as more development appeared along the coast. In the distance to port was Hampton Roads, then Elizabeth River with Nor-folk on one side and navy yard the other. A ferry was leaving the channel under a dark cloud, and smaller smoke plumes were visible across the horizon and up the James. Besides sev-eral steam ships, small schooners were underway, and a large, ship-rigged collier under tow passed Fort Wool with courses draped limply from yards; except when small gusts caused barely discernible shivers. Once past the fort, she would be released, her canvas sheeted home, and, with a favorable wind, sail past the Middle Ground into the Atlantic.

Approaching Newport News from the east, the first visible structures were an eleven-story grain elevator and tall coal piers; used by ships entering Hampton Roads as landmarks. Next came the railroad station's tall clock tower, then its com-bination train shed and pier; with the Warwick Hotel on high ground beyond. Starke remained topside partway, then re-turned to the stateroom for his belongings before going to the entry port.

Sixteen years earlier, Newport News was a farming and fishing village with so few White residents, only Colored children had a school, and that an impromptu affair in a house. Now there was a rail terminus, coal piers, grain elevator, growing shipyard, burgeoning businesses, and thriving market for local farmers and fishermen. Two school buildings, White and Colored, were constructed, along with Newport News Academy, the substantial First National Bank Building, a trolley system to Old Point Comfort, and the Italianate red-brick county courthouse with tower. Not surprisingly, the county clerk's office and jail beside next door, were not only kept busy with routine administration, but miscreants from the brisk saloon and bordello trade in a dock area that served sailors, laborers, and others.

Starke waited at the closed entrance port with others disembarking at Newport News. Unable to see outside, he felt the ship heel slightly starboard as she rounded Newport News Point and began her approach on the rail station pier. Other slight course changes came as *Newport News* threaded through ships anchored or loitering off the coal and grain piers. Finally, a slight nudge announced they were alongside the 600 foot combination pier and train shed. Once mooring lines were singled, the entry port doors slid open, a brow positioned, and passengers flowed into the red train shed with open sides and gable roof capped by a ventilation structure running its ridge. Carrying his off-white canvas sword sheath, leather Gladstone bag, and cane, Starke walked across double railroad tracks in pleasantly brisk weather, amid mixed smells of coal dust, river shore, grain, and fish; then entered the light yellow station. While still inside, he heard *Newport News'* steam whistle sound as she backed from the pier, pivoted, then went south, past the Middle Ground to Norfolk.

Assured his luggage be at the Warwick Hotel before noon, Starke went outside, then paused under the station clock tower to study the multistory, black coal pier constructed four years earlier. Its massive unloading arrangement allowed railroad cars to dump dusty black loads into hoppers, then used chutes to fill colliers brought alongside. Beyond was the even larger, eleven-story grain elevator with its own pier. The Warwick Hotel was the largest inland structure, two blocks west and long block north; occupying higher ground inland. Between station and hotel, the vacant land was laid out in blocks with tall saplings lining streets girded by single-rail, waist-high fencing. An impromptu footpath cut diagonally over one block, adding to the scene's fading pastoral flavor.

Starke saw the streetcar line served the hotel, so he boarded when a car arrived. Its fully enclosed passenger compartment provided shelter, the conductor managed entry through the front vestibule, and riders disembarked from the rear. Electric power came from a trolley pole centered on its roof, while the short wheelbase and four wheels gave agility. Within minutes, it squealed to a halt in front of Warwick Hotel, a four-story red-brick structure shaped like a reversed L, with the base paralleling the shore and open side facing west. Chimneys were scattered across its roof, and where the legs converged was a small cottage-like roof structure. Its ground floor, under a line of white porches, contained shops and offices opening directly to the street and shaded by individual awnings. Nearby was the customs house and post office building, with a large white flagpole midway between them and the hotel.

Starke entered the lobby where the clerk stood behind a broad counter in front of the manager's office. Moving forward, he passed a substantial table surrounded by chairs of dark wood and leather, lined with brass tacks. To his left was a large fireplace facing an additional half-circle of them. The walls were paneled and painted white for the lower third, with the remainder wallpapered. Overhead, a beam framework partitioned the ceiling, with electroliers hanging from several of the larger squares' centers. As Starke approached, the clerk in black suit and bow-tie continued entering notes in a large green book until he stood directly in front of the counter, then the head rose with a, "May I assist, sir?"

"Please. Lieutenant Starke, I've reserved a room."

"Yes, sir. Top floor facing the river. Room 407. A Lieutenant Osbourne is on the second floor. Perhaps you prefer to shift?"

"Would you want your boss next door?"

"If you'd sign the register, sir."

Starke took the black dip pen, wet its nib in the inkwell, signed, replaced it, then rotated the large book towards the clerk. After confirming his luggage was expected by noon, he began reaching for his bag when a bell clanged, and a young Negro in gray uniform stepped forward to show him upstairs. The room was square, utilitarian, and clean, with the entrance in one corner. Two single brass beds with prominent head and footboards half-filled it. A small leather settee occupied the second corner, a commode with electric fan the third, and a walnut armoire hid the fourth. The faux-French carpet pattern was set off by a high ceiling white, smooth, and unencumbered, except for a three-globe electric light fixture at the end of a long brass tube. A small writing table and chair were at one bed's foot.

When alone, Stark crossed to his window, overlooking the James River. Little shoreline was visible beyond the coal piers and grain elevator to the east, but it offered an excellent view of Hampton Roads. Moving west, was the railway station with tower, train shed, and pier. Beyond, ships were leaving the James and moving through Hampton Roads. A road ran the riverbank west; passing two small piers before turning north at a large bluff. At the turn was a short ferry pier with a shelter structure. On the bluff was the large casino with its own pier. Just west was Newport News Academy. Between hotel and river, the low fence girded empty blocks with the worn footpath clearly visible across the eastern one. Another was landscaped as a park with broad paths to a circular center etched in the grass; and three large trees remained from a previous life as pasture or forest, before the streets were lined with electrical poles and telephone lines.

Besides a streetcar making its way from the station, and carriages, Starke watched a tug back from train station pier. Nearby, rectangular barges shared smaller piers with rowboats, scows, and other craft. Repacking his pipe, he observed a small steamer leave the ferry pier, while its sister remained moored on the upstream side. Four three-masted schooners were anchored in the stream, waiting to load coal or grain, while a dark-green bark was shifted to the coal piers by two tugs shrouding its deck with their black smoke. He sympathized with masters carrying coal or grain since they were dirty, difficult, and dangerous cargoes. Grain was always ready to shift, swell, or explode, while coal, especially when poor quality or damp, could smolder deep in a hold. If discovered, burning lumps might be dug out, holds sealed while the ship raced for the nearest port, or cargo and ship abandoned.

Starke's luggage showed up well before noon. He transferred items from steamer trunk to armoire before changing to an undress blue uniform for visiting the shipyard; since Monday would be dedicated to making his official call on Rear Admiral Brown in Norfolk. Returning to the street, he hailed a cab for the shipyard's main administration building, ten blocks away. The carriage rolled smoothly towards the river through a clear day and warming sun, then turned right on West Avenue near the casino and Newport News Academy. Most structures, mainly row houses mixed with other buildings, lay north of the avenue, but even they thinned as Starke continued west. The cab finally turned north at the shipyard boundary for a block, then left on a street paralleling its north side. They immediately passed the main entrance, a tall, white-framed gate and gatehouse, then continued along a brick wall, only slightly higher than pedestrians walking beside it. Inside the compound, he could see large red-brick industrial buildings with gable roofs and an abundance of windows. Here and there, gray smoke exhausted from a tall, cylindrical chimney built into some buildings; although most had ventilation structures along their roof ridges with open and closed windows.

The wall gave way to a white picket fence just before the main administration building; a two-story, red-brick structure with white cement trim and large chimneys on either end. At the center was a square tower over the main entrance, which was a glass-filled arch over double doors. On the second floor, he found the government department's offices and entered through a plain wooden door with frosted glass window. Inside were rows of desks occupied by a military and civilian mix. One officer stood, came around his desk, extended his hand, and grinned, "Lieutenant William O'Leary. Welcome to Newport News, sir."

CHAPTER ELEVEN
Ship Conversion

Newport News Shipbuilding and Dry Dock Company's ways and piers were crowded with three steel gunboats, several commercial ships, and two tugs building; plus their constant repair work. In the center of this construction, overhaul, voyage repairs, inspections, and hull cleaning, *Calypso* shared the Simpson's Basin Dry Dock with a large, bark-rigged collier.

The yard's James River waterfront bristled with piers, quay walls, and building ways. Inland and south of the dry-dock lay an outfitting machine shop, paint shop, and large kiln. To its north were tall cranes, a ship shed, carpenter shop, store room, and the lofts for riggers and sailmakers. Further inland came a row of large, red-brick buildings housing the lumber department, joiner and woodworking shop, machine shop, boiler department, and smithy. A fitting-out shed included a heating and bending shop just below the second story molding loft. Tall brick chimneys with cement caps rose from the power house and buildings having a furnace or boiler.

Farthest inland, the main gate opened on Washington Avenue, as did the administration building, some distance east. The second floor government department was directly across from the yard's clerical and accounting offices, next to the drawing and design division. Two weeks after welcoming Starke, Passed Assistant Engineer O'Leary sat behind a battered desk in his comfortably-worn wood swivel-chair, with both hands interlocked behind his head, watching shadows transit a nondescript entrance door's frosted glass window; with thoughts shifting between *Calypso*'s docking plan and his future.

The ship increasingly captivated him after having had her at the Starke firm's West Point shipyard, then through the Newport News conversion. *Calypso*'s unanticipated contract stressed an infant department with meager staff already making do and forced it to stretch traditional bureau boundaries. His own Bureau of Steam Engineering possessed total control of Navy steam plants, while Bureau of Construction and Repair's naval constructors controlled ship design and yards. They clashed so often on technical authority it seemed a continuous feud. Despite this, the senior Newport News naval constructor, Lieutenant Joseph Woodward, having few options, approved O'Leary's request to manage the ship's West Point work.

This included tow preparations, removing ballast, offloading coal, and draining fresh water tanks. In addition, some deck gear, supplies, and equipment were recovered by the firm; with the remainder inventoried and stowed. Coal bunker cleaning, and modifications such as roughing in magazines, were also contracted. Except for tow preparations, all work complied with original *Cutlass* drawings for conversion to a commerce cruiser.

He also managed to meet schedule, despite a Bureau of Construction and Repair distraction. The culprit, an unidentified clerk, constructor, or combination, directed coal bunkers be relocated to shield magazines. While a coal bunker fire's potential threat to munitions was debated on new designs, *Calypso* would not be fighting warships or land batteries; and the directed changes would delay the project. O'Leary recognized this, obtained Captain Albert's support, then worked different bureaus until advocates were neutered by demonstrating cost and schedule risk, then requiring full technical justification and accountability. O'Leary resented the wasted time, but gained reputation in three bureaus. This, and the ship entering

Newport News on time, encouraged Woodward to retain him as lead inspector for the conversion.

Woodward was uneasy assigning a steam engineer to work outside that bureau's boundaries, but O'Leary welcomed it. He believed *Calypso* offered more opportunity than ships under construction and still owned by the yard. That proved true, but now commissioning was near and a disturbing harbinger peeked from under the docking plan. It was Starke's note asking future *Calypso* officers to meet Wednesday afternoons; although none reported directly to him before commissioning. While meaning little to Osbourne and Watson, since they possessed orders, O'Leary wanted to confirm his inclusion resulted from approaching them about an assistant engineer billet, not just courtesy. Woodward already agreed to support the transfer, but advocated a different command. He stressed modern gunboats were building in the yard, while *Calypso* was on the navy list as a sailing ship, or eighth rate. O'Leary knew her type was passing, but the steam bark was well-found with a modern propulsion system. Other aspects, however, weighed for and against pursuing her. O'Leary not only enjoyed shipyard sights, smells, sounds, and work, but his recently earned reputation required nourishment. While an early return to sea risked this, especially on the wrong ship; his expanding department's formality was increasing. Captain Peter Rearick would relieve as chief engineer and engineering division head in May, then three independent divisions controlled by their Washington bureaus would congeal. Woodward would become hull division chief inspector; with the office transformation continuing throughout the year, especially when Ordnance and Equipment inspectors arrived.

In April's third week, he requested *Calypso* after constant deliberation, observing those he would serve, and taking heed of a chief engineer who advised him to go where loved.

Osbourne, the prospective chief engineer, initially seemed excessively casual, but proved a superb administrator and technician who immersed himself in yard and ship, seemed an expert shiphandler, and was an exceedingly junior chief engineer. O'Leary was not as familiar with Watson, who stayed in Norfolk to build the crew and ship administration. Although equaling Osbourne's professional manner, and similar in age, he seemed less genial, more driven, and sometimes mercurial; perhaps because he remained languid until flaring to action. However, he never admonished publicly and proved fairminded. Overall, O'Leary concluded he was probably wellsuited for an executive officer. Even more important, Osbourne and Watson enjoyed a close personal and professional relationship, unlike some engineering and line officers.

Starke remained stubbornly undecipherable. O'Leary retained little Irish accent, but inherited a broad face, black curly hair, chalk-white skin, green eyes, a Catholic family, and younger sisters who offered running commentaries on men. He concluded the prospective captain's physical attributes probably appealed to their sex; and rumors alone would quench any romantic cravings acquired through dime novels. Rocking back in the chair, legs crossed at the ankles, he closed his eyes, and pictured their future commander. Starke's slightly receding dark hair was never oiled but well-tended, except several rebelling locks over an athlete's angular, taut countenance. Distinct eyebrows crowned faded blue eyes sited in bone casements below a solid forehead and between high cheekbones. From either side of a generous and round nose, they easily trained and pointed with precision above small, well-formed lips, pressed to a nearly straight line above the narrow chin. A well-trimmed beard partly obscured much of the face, perhaps to cover small pockmarks, while unremarkable ears lay inconspicuously alongside a head pivoting securely on the solid, but not overlarge, neck. Lean and muscular, his gait and carriage suggested authority, knowledge, and propensity to act. Never overtly friendly or aloof, he listened with equal intensity whether the speaker was yard rigger, official, or senior officer. Polite, proper, lacking swagger, and enigmatic, O'Leary suspected he possessed a readily tapped, dark underpinning; which left him uneasy, since ship captains set the tone. However, he also visualized Starke in full control during any emergency, especially storms at sea; although he admitted this perception might be influenced by learning Starke was a respected mate on merchant ships, whose crews were often far less deferential and more judgmental.

During his West Point stay, he heard the Starke family came from a small south German state, then assimilated with other immigrant streams to become uniquely American. They operated several businesses and amassed considerable wealth, though not at the Vanderbilt or Carnegie level; and Starke inherited a plantation downriver from West Point that *Calypso* passed under tow. His father, a hero to some, traitor or pirate to others, abandoned family and country for Brazil, where he operated a small shipping company. It seemed the son learned from his uncle and inherited from his father, since rumors had him with cavalry in Montana, fighting Alexandria's looters, involvement with Brazil's naval mutiny, and the fleet action off Korea. O'Leary suspected some of these rumors were heavily embroidered, but none seemed overtly false, except the far-fetched Montana story; and there was a murky Office of Naval Intelligence connection. Finally, while Starke's antecedents, looks, and manner might excite his sisters' interest, he had no idea how his prospective commander viewed him.

O'Leary soon dropped this midday conjecture to review the docking plan. Written with the dockmaster, using updated *Cutlass* drawings, it included schedule, mechanics, planned work, weak hull areas, projections, keel and bilge block locations, and whale shore positions needed to prevent rolling. A weight baseline was also established before engine, boilers, stack, and some deckhouse sections were removed pier-side. While in dock, every addition or removal's weight and location was recorded to calculate stability, determine ballasting, and prevent listing or capsizing when re-floated. Thirty days were planned for *Calypso*'s hull work, boiler installation, engine replacement, and smaller jobs before the 650 foot dry-dock shared with the collier astern must be flooded. Should *Calypso* be unready, the Navy could face lay day penalties, but the yard was also eager to free their only dry-dock.

While out of water, wood sheathing was removed, her hull cleaned and inspected, then stern tube and stuffing box overhauled and repacked. Zinc plates were also renewed, valves replaced, an upgraded propeller fitted, and hull penetrations made for the new boilers and engine. Where iron framing was weak, doubler plates and stiffeners had been fitted then fastened by three-man ironworker teams with one person holding the red-hot iron mushroom with tongs while right and left-handed men hammered away until it fused with the plate. Hydraulic water riveters were not used on *Calypso* because her tasks were scattered and small; but whether by hand or machine, O'Leary observed boilermakers, ironworkers, and riveters grew hard of hearing, and some became odd, if too long at the trade. Wood planking was also replaced where there was damage or rot. Each board was measured, cut, fitted with grain matching location, then secured with galvanized iron bolt fasteners. All hull caulking was pried out with raking irons, then oakum and marline worked into the seams, just ahead of men pounding it tight with caulking hammers; then another team sealed it with hot pitch. When her hull sheathing work completed, *Calypso* looked less a hulk; and especially so when the yard began applying black hull paint over primer.

Her wood hull, unlike steel, supported copper sheathing below the waterline to slow tropical marine growth. Albert advocated this, but its cost was high and arguments existed for and against. Coppering prevented her from ever mooring alongside unsheathed metal hulls, and corrosion was a problem, but it would also help maintain her speed for two years. The larger debate grew so acute the Office of Naval Intelligence was asked to examine foreign navies' experience; and returned enough promising information to justify experimenting with gunboats. Albert immediately offered up *Calypso*, secured additional funding, and exchanged upgrading her anchors for the remainder.

One morning, four weeks after spring officially arrived, Starke enjoyed ham, eggs, and coffee at the Warwick before boarding a trolley to the administration building. Once there, he reviewed the work schedule with Osbourne and O'Leary, then left with them for the waterfront through a rear door. As the day warmed, they walked between red-brick buildings, immersed in competing riparian, industrial, and burning coal smells. The trio soon reached the dry-dock where two long brows spanned a twenty-five feet deep chasm between *Calypso* and its wall. Both portals were guarded by veteran laborers with pencil and green notebook to track description, weight, and destination of the material and equipment crossing. At the forward brow, Starke approached a thin, older man with deep creases tracing a browned face and sparse white hair escaping from under a work cap, "Morning Ned, how's the day look?"

Sliding the pencil into the notebook's spine, he replied, "Pleasant, Cap'n, pleasant. Work's started aboard and on the floor."

"Excellent. Hope the rheumatism holds off and you get more sun. Always feel better knowing you're on the weights."

The man responded "Yes sir, Cap'n." Starke nodded, grabbed a handrail, then began crossing. Midway, he paused for a ritual ship inspection while O'Leary, several steps behind, wondered how many passed Ned without acknowledging his contribution.

Calypso's three lower masts were stepped and new bowsprit pushed out over her stem like a tusk, but the deckhouse remained incomplete aft, and her single large stack was absent. Above an intact pilothouse, the flying bridge was draped with protective tarps. Aft, two unrigged round bar boat davits were secured to deck-edge cleats. Looking through whale shores, hoses, and lines between dry-dock and ship, *Calypso*'s exposed hull, from clipper bow to fantail stern, revealed her fine lines. Also visible, small paint teams worked the sides on planks swung from lines to the main deck then, absent hogging-in padeyes, were pulled close by a single manila line encircling the hull. On each suspended plank, two men sat, dipped brushes in pails lifted from the floor, then worked this glutinous mix deep in the wood grain. While he watched, a light wind gust washing over the dry-dock sucked out paint vapors and carried them past the brow, briefly vanquishing all other odors. Below and further aft, scaffolding rose from the floor for trades fixing copper sheathing to the skeg.

The three officers' undress blue uniforms, stood apart from yard workers who, except for a supervisor or two, dressed for their trade in what was useful and available. Denim overalls, hats, and vests predominated, but there were some boiler suits and leather aprons. Once across, Starke's party headed for the pilothouse where they could confer without interfering or being interrupted. The mahogany structure included tall, single-pane windows in its forward wall, sides, and doors. At the rear, two smaller windows flanked a combination cabinet and chart table. The space above was filled by shelves and pegs for navigation instruments and material. Centered forward, even with the side doors, a magnetic compass topped a tubular brass pedestal supporting the thin-spoked ship's wheel, also brass. The brass voice tube overhead to the flying bridge was similar to those clustered near the pedestal base. Each ended with heavy cap, hinged to allow insertion of a speaking funnel. The engine order telegraph, or EOT, for communicating with engineering, topped a second brass pedestal, and the conning pelorus was mounted under the forward wall's center window.

O'Leary opened a small notebook to began his morning status, "We should undock on schedule, but late boiler delivery ate any slack. We're beyond halfway, so regaining schedule's impossible. Some deck leaks were uncovered, wood rotting against metal, but were repaired during the delay. Hull penetrations are complete, and the replacement propeller to match the new engine's power and shaft rotation fitted."

Starke nodded, "So undocking's just achievable?"

"Yes, sir."

The walkthrough started aft, with rudder stock and steering. *Calypso*'s design allowed more cargo, centralized ship machinery, accommodated limited space over the rudder, and supported an aft gun mount. Consequently, a steam-operated steering engine was placed in the auxiliary machinery room below her pilothouse, unlike newer ships; and connected to a shaft, cable, and clutch arrangement linking three helm stations to a balanced rudder. While only the pilothouse was assisted by this steering engine, her balanced rudder helped all three; especially the aft helm, used for sailing, that required two helmsmen, and emergency steering, which employed a block and tackle.

Moving forward below deck, they examined storage lockers and berthing, then entered the three large midship compartments where firemen, machinists, electricians, and oilers labored. The engine room surrounded a Navy-designed vertical, triple-expansion engine. From its base, anchored to the ship's bottom, three massive cylinders rose nearly to the main deck. Capable of 1,227 horsepower, it produced nearly 400 more than the double-expansion engine replaced. Designed for warships, the engine demanded rigorous maintenance and could not run continuously at top speed. Because its three pistons reused steam at successively lower pressures to increase range and power, boilers producing higher steam pressure were needed. While *Calypso*'s officers were eager to learn how the ship, already thought fast, would perform with the additional power, a Steam Engineering Bureau office wanted shaft horsepower measurement added to the work list for similar reasons. Since this was unplanned and require the ship to steam in dry-dock, it would destroy schedule. O'Leary struggled to convince them to see reason, but without success until Albert and Osbourne asked the Bureau's chief engineer to intervene.

Since several trades were working, they moved on to the cavernous boiler room where two Normand water-tube boilers dominated. By passing water through small tubes in the firebox they generated steam more rapidly and efficiently than fire-tube boilers that passed flames through tubes surrounded with water. However, producing high pressure steam required skilled operators, painstaking maintenance, and quality feedwater. Two small, fire-tube auxiliary boilers offered a second steam source for winches, dynamos, distillers, and more. Also sharing the compartment were the main and auxiliary steam systems' condensers, pumps, piping, valves, and miscellaneous equipment. When operating, the space's trimmers, passers, stokers, and water tenders worked in temperatures over a hundred degrees while plagued by coal dust working into clothing, hair, and skin. On the steel grating platforms above the deckplates, no one lasted beyond a few minutes.

Since the trades were also working the boiler room, Starke's trio quickly passed through to the smaller machinery room, under the wardroom, that contained the steering engine, pumps, and auxiliary equipment. At sea, it was noisy, hot, and humid from steam piping, valves, and, like the engine room, permeated by lubricating oil vapor. The adjacent dynamo room held three steam-driven units, two large and one small. Navy ships began rapidly adding new electrical equipment after the first lighting installation thirteen years before, but *Calypso* came with a rudimentary system. During conversion, the ship's dynamo room was expanded and new switchboard installed for distributing electricity to internal lights, an Ardois system, searchlights, and other appliances. Osbourne believed steam engineering should control this space and equipment, but Navy regulations assigned it to the navigator.

While locating engineering compartments roughly midship increased cargo space, after conversion it vastly improved crew comfort. Unlike the latest warships, scattering machinery throughout, then wedging crews in leftover space, *Calypso* offered roomier accommodations. That, and the wood hull lined with port holes, or more accurately air ports, just below the main deck, achieved better insulation and ventilation than her steel counterparts, especially with wind sails rigged. After passing through the dispensary, galley, windlass room, and magazines, the officers left the ship then walked to the main administration building where Osbourne and O'Leary returned to undocking preparations.

Meanwhile, Starke took his temporary desk in the open bay office to complete a status report for the next day's interview with Rear Admiral Brown and Captain McCormick, aboard Norfolk's receiving ship *Franklin*. After that, he would cross the Elizabeth River to meet with Commander Todd, head of the navy yard's Ordnance Inspection Division, and Green, its Equipment Division, since they would fit out *Calypso* and install ordnance after Newport News. He looked forward to the excursion, since these ferry trips offered a break from Newport News and its increasingly tedious routine.

At each workday's close he invariably left for his Warwick Hotel room in early evening, then kept mostly to himself. Consequently, his never enviable social life withered further from *Calypso*'s demands and approaching departure. Even so, he admitted it was largely his own doing. While industry and agriculture dominated Newport News, the prosperous and wealthy vacationed at Old Point Comfort, Virginia Beach, and nearby areas, so there was society, hunting, fishing, a nearby casino, and nightly hotel bridge games. There was also the local Navy community, although it was not convenient and he was a transient, which relegated him to the periphery. Still, he made the requisite calls, left cards, and received some invitations. This would change if *Calypso* operated out of Norfolk after commissioning, but Albert's ferret would be a gypsy, so he saw little need to become deeply enmeshed. He also remained distant from prospective *Calypso* officers, which snuffed the last flicker of significant companionship.

On one or two occasions, he considered temporarily acquiring faith and join some congregation, but an agnostic persuasion and desire to avoid feminine entanglement kept that at bay. Shifting to a boarding house was another option, except the Warwick Hotel was not only a local social center, but offered weekly rates, a restaurant, laundry service, stream of people, and nearby small gym where he fenced. In addition, the Richmond paper was always in the lobby, along with Norfolk's five, and *The Daily Press*, a new, local four-page newspaper published from the post office. Although he used the time to perfect pipe-smoking, and developed a partiality for specific tobaccos, his salvation came from a routine that included an evening walk past the desk and lobby bridge game, then across the park to the ferry dock, with neighboring pleasure pier and casino, to watch ship traffic on the James. However, by mid-April the small hotel room felt more a secular monk's cell; and during more discouraging moments he reflected on his uncle's offer, riding Gemini, brief exchanges with Sutton, and, more than anticipated, Katherine.

During one low period, Katherine's promised letter appeared at the front desk and, while reading the beautiful, feminine hand, Starke visualized her in the erotic black gown. After his aunt's dinner party, he thought it boorish to refuse a proposal that was forward, uncharacteristic, and risked her reputation; but now the letter's subtle, hesitant verbiage gently probed for a response. She revealed brother and sister were remaining longer in Washington while Curtis built political and business contacts; and his uncle was often at the Baltimore office. Consequently, Katherine and his aunt spent a great deal of time together and planned a Hygeia Hotel stay before traveling to Newport for the summer season. It seemed she also discussed saddles with Sutton, but would not try the Nolan, believing it scandalous to sit astride in society. She was now riding Gemini, with her brother on Castores, instead of stable horses. Several exchanges with Martella on English, French, and more extravagant Southern cooking were mentioned, but nothing about Cynthia.

The letter lurked on the table, wanting reply, when Tyson reappeared and, except for light sunburn, was little changed since leaving *Newport News*. He was returning to New York, but diverted to Old Point Comfort for additional information on Hotel Chamberlain's medicinal attractions. From there, he booked an Old Dominion liner to New York City, but finagled a Warwick room for the night to visit Starke. They ate well in the restaurant, with Tyson fortifying his spring water, although Starke found him unusually restrained and, strangely, asking after Cassandra Evans.

Deferring to Starke's routine, they left the hotel then walked into the future park through a clear spring evening. At its center, Tyson paused, extracted his gold-trimmed jade case from a coat pocket, tapped a Turkish cigarette on the hinge, lit it, then tossed the match away with a flourish. Starke dragged his pipe through a plain leather tobacco pouch, packed the bowl, then passed a flame over its center while slowly sucking fire through moist tobacco. Tyson watched, looked furtively around, then began, "Stayed briefly in Tampa, then took *Olivette* through Key West to Havana. Weyler's moving fast. Trochas are being strengthened or built. At least one has electric lights and land torpedos. Inept or corrupt officers are going home, including a half-dozen generals. Additional troops are arriving, mostly unpaid conscripts, and rumors have it they'll reach 200,000; but disease is already thinning them, and the rainy season's not yet here. Pacificos that fled farms to safe areas before the reconcentrado can't return and the army's unable to feed them. They're arrested by troops if not carrying a pass, which means the wall or prison, but insurrectos will shoot, hang, or machete them if they do. General Gómez ordered plantations, outbuildings, and railroads destroyed; anyone working sugar factories is to be shot, but more often it's a rope or machete. Entire families've been killed. Weyler's curbing protests against Americans in Cuba, but those not taken for the army in Spain are rioting against us for supporting rebels and allowing filibusters. Many, especially anarchists, believe Spain's in Cuba for the aristocracy and Barcelona's big business. Weyler keeps tightening the noose, but can't maneuver Maceo into a decisive battle. My sources weren't consistent, but several towns have been attacked after *Bermuda* landed General Garcia. Consolacion del Sur, Jaruco, and Batabano definitely were, and government soldiers apparently fired on each other near Cano. Both sides also claimed victory in some fight or skirmish near Cienfuegos."

Tyson retrieved another cigarette, lit it, then sent a second expended match arcing into the dusk, "Our newspapers attack Weyler, who doesn't distinguish them from individual correspondents, so there's always new restrictions. Although there was only enough time to gather low-hanging fruit, I left Inglaterra often enough to get a flavor. There are good correspondents in Havana, but most lounge about the hotels and report rumor. Even so, the Tampa and Key West maggots are worse. Most won't look beyond cigar factory gossip. Sorry about rambling, it's just something I can't stomach. By the way, Fitzhugh Lee replaces Williams as consul-general in May or June."

After Tyson finished, Starke exhaled before responding, "You've a more interesting time than myself, but *Calypso*'s on track for a June commissioning."

"Perhaps we'll meet in Constantinople."

Starke quickly lowered his pipe, "What?"

"Paper's considering sending a correspondent, and the missionary lobby wants ships. *Calypso*'s well-suited and this is exactly the thing you always walk into."

"Still don't follow?"

"Since the Armenian uprising two years back, missionaries keep demanding Navy protection for them and the Armenian Christians. It's now a campaign issue, along with economic recovery and free silver. Even Cuba runs fourth. No one's certain if the Ottoman army's protecting Armenians or supporting attacks, but the Kurds are involved, and it appears Assyrians are also being killed."

Tyson took a long drag, releasing it through both nostrils, "Our influential God-fearing gentlemen want the Navy, and my paper, a correspondent. Frank Lenz, the bicycling journalist, was killed doing it, so my editor was clearly told I will not replace the wheeling reporter; besides the country's dry."

His friend's information was usually accurate, so Starke lowered his pipe, "I doubt our navy would get involved. A fleet wouldn't be enough, and sending most of what we have past Spain into the Mediterranean's unthinkable."

Another cigarette was burned by *The Sun* correspondent, "True, but missionaries are powerful, it's an election year, and sending an inexpensive, expendable gunboat before the vote may become irresistible. If *Calypso* completes in June, she's available and perfect."

Starke could not respond without revealing *Calypso*'s true status, and Tyson's mental agility was legend, so he retreated behind the cliché, "*Calypso*'s testing new boilers and engines, then patrol or survey."

Both looked at each other as Tyson grinned, "Everything at face value, my friend."

As they resumed walking, Tyson changed subjects, "I'm only gone from the city a few weeks and Raines passed an ordinance to keep New York's unwashed from drink. Won't succeed, but should do for a few lively stories."

With that, he flicked a cigarette carcass into the night, grinned at Starke, then pulled the concave silver flask from his coat. At the pier, they walked past the ferry's night watch to its head, then stood, looking out over the river. The vast sky had scattered light gray clouds that let endless stars illuminate a still, cool night. The James River was wide, flowing, and black, with its main current far enough out only the slowest water slid under the pier, eddied lightly against pilings, ghosted around splintered wood, then slipped downstream to the bay. Lights flickered on the river, then in bands beyond its far shore. The furthest were homes and businesses, the nearest ships, with downstream traffic sprinting through Hampton Roads, and those close aboard offering fleeting silhouettes.

Tyson lit another cigarette, then flicked his match into the water where a disappointed fish struck; leaving behind a gulping sound and pock mark on the ink-smooth surface, before asking, "You fish?"

"Fly fish when I can."

"Lately?"

"No."

"Still have the plantation?"

"Yes, it's my mother's family home, but Oxen Grove's no longer a working plantation. Sharecropping maintains it and provides income. I don't often go there because it's forty miles by train from Richmond to West Point, then downriver by boat since the poor roads make for a miserable trip, even in good weather. You feel marooned, if not prepared."

The two paused, watching a dark, silent shape slide quickly past, before Starke mused, "Schooner," then took another draw. He looked down at his pipe, rotating it slightly. The thin figure beside him, with uncanny perceptive abilities that always sharpened after a night's sipping, entered his thoughts with, "Cherchez la femme?"

Starke saw no reason to deny it, "Yes, There's a woman. A British widow visiting my aunt with her brother."

"Aunt Constance's next candidate to fill your marital void?"

"I suppose."

Tyson grinned, "Well my friend, if your aunt is orchestrating matches, the sea's your salvation, and there's safety in distance, so the Levant's better than Cuba. She's a formidable woman, and I've greater respect for her than she for me. What about your not-yet-intended?"

"Nothing beyond casual conversation until the evening before I left. She suggested writing, I agreed, so now her letter requires a response."

"Odd she was that forward. A proper lady?"

"Very."

"Find her attractive?"

"That last night, yes. Until then, an inconvenient guest who rode well, was never easy to speak with, and just about tolerated me."

"What happened to her husband?"

"Lost with HMS *Victoria* off Tripoli."

"You say she approached you?"

"Apparently waited up for me after a dinner party, since she hadn't changed from evening dress when I returned from taking Miss Evans home."

"Cassandra Evans is attractive. Perhaps she saw her as the competition and decided to act."

"I doubt it; she showed no interest for a week."

"Did you, my friend?"

"Not really, and I have *Calypso*. Besides she called me a freethinker before leaving for church, so I never thought her inclinations went beyond courtesy."

"She's English, religious, and scents forbidden fruit. No, she saw competition and took action. After the family jewels?"

"No. She possesses a fortune, and I've only the plantation and navy incomes."

"You'll have more."

"Yes, but she dislikes the States."

"Where is she now?"

"In Washington with her brother, but she'll accompany Aunt Constance to Newport this summer."

Tyson worried a rapidly disappearing cigarette between stained thumb and finger, "Dislikes it here but stays, Aunt Constance likes her, and she asked to correspond?"

"Yes."

"You're standing into danger, my friend. Convicted on your own words. It seems you're attraction enough to approach alone at night, and she wants to continue even though she won't live outside England. She's got your scent. May not know it herself. Perhaps you both need your ashes hauled."

"Somewhat indelicate, Darwin?"

"Men need the occasional liaison, why not women? I don't subscribe to female hysteria, but she's beyond my advice. For you, however, I can recommend several top drawer New York establishments, and another in Havana."

"Not sure that's helpful."

"You asked. Otherwise, lay low until this mutual interest fades. If you must reply, remember anything beyond bare acknowledgment will be taken as commitment."

Starke thought Tyson was baiting him, which he occasionally did, and often found his friend's allegedly dry sense of humor pushed a murky line. Changing subjects, he asked if Tyson would be in New York through the Cuban Fair. Learning he would, Starke considered a bordello quip, then recalled skilled debaters quickly vanquished in repartees with Tyson. Instead, they returned to the hotel and finished off discussing the Chamberlain hydrotherapeutic department's salt water pool. The next morning, Starke boarded the first Norfolk ferry while Tyson breakfasted before taking a streetcar to Old Point Comfort.

CHAPTER TWELVE
Undocking *Calypso*

Nearly two months after interviewing with Captain Albert, and a week since his friend left, Starke completed a letter summarizing Tyson's Cuban observations for the Office of Naval Intelligence, without identifying him. Katherine remained a conundrum, but he still posted a cautious response. While more than Tyson suggested, the risk appeared small since she must return to England, and *Calypso* would demand attention. Albert was asked to bring up O'Leary's transfer with the engineering bureau since he sought the billet and was capable, although Starke felt Woodward's advice to the young engineer sound.

Watson visited several times each week, but remained mostly on *Franklin*. Starke disliked receiving ships despite arguments of convenience, economy, and instilling shipboard habits. *Franklin* was arguably one of the best, constructed forty years before at the navy yard in Portsmouth, Maine; with enough of a predecessor's components to convince Congress the new screw frigate was a repair. Placed in and out of commission, and twice a flagship, she served in the Mediterranean and North Atlantic. Finally, the large frigate was decommissioned, modified, then recommissioned as Norfolk's receiving ship. Her masts and most guns were removed, then a barn-like structure constructed over the main deck for instruction, drilling, and muster. Other changes included electric lighting, a large galley, administrative offices, and new living quarters. She accommodated near 300 sailors in her new role, although thousands passed through each year, entering the navy, between duty stations, or awaiting discharge. Their sewage slid from scuppers into the river, where it was mostly carried downstream, and her propulsion boilers, abandoned twenty years before, generated nothing more than clouds of summer mosquitos. A maze of small piers lined with davits and small craft married her to a riverbank across from the navy yard.

After Starke met Admiral Brown on the ship, his respect grew for the Navy's senior admiral. He was stocky, with large drooping mustache and short neck that rolled over a confining standup collar, eyes peering over noticeable bags, and forehead advancing well up his scalp. The almost benign appearance was at odds with a fighting reputation, ashore and afloat.

Besides *Calypso*, they regularly touched unrelated topics. Since Brown read Starke's report on *Blanco Encalada*'s torpedoing in Chile, one visit's topic was the inexpensive torpedo boat's threat to capital ships. Since they were discussing Chile, Starke asked about the Department of State; as Albert suggested. Brown emphatically responded, "I spoke with Albert regarding *Calypso*. Suggested you may find yourselves in extremis if Republicans win this fall. You've heard about *Itata*; tried running guns to Chile five years ago. State couldn't decide to support their president, congress, or stay neutral. Their Third Secretary resigned over it. Anyway, a schooner was waiting for offshore to load rifles for the Congressional side, so she was detained in San Diego and a marshal put on board."

The admiral leaned slightly forward, then settled back, "Her crew put him ashore, met the schooner, then ran for Iquique; where British and German ships were waiting. Admiral McCann and I were sent with *Charleston*, caught her off Iquique, and persuaded the crew to return with cargo. The federal prosecutor declined to prosecute, but the administration pressed on, and lost, as did the faction State backed."

Leaning forward and looking Starke in the eye, he took a conspiratorial tone, "When that happened, State went to ground and left us hanging. I retire in a year, so let me point out they've not changed and you've a father some may wish to pillory, but would settle for a son. If you continue with Albert's scheme, never forget that. Flag officers travel in political orbits, so as long as Captain Albert's scheme remains within law and policy, you've my support; for the next year anyway."

Soon after that interview, the scheme's prospective ferret took a major step forward when *Calypso* floated from the dry-dock during slack water at high tide. Beginning at seven-thirty that day, yard workers checked both ships in the dock, cleared its floor, inspected the caisson gate, tested pumps, then rigged backing gear to a pair of diminutive steam locomotives called mules. The day before, O'Leary and their dockmaster examined preparations. Even Watson crossed from Norfolk to join him and Osbourne scouring every compartment, tank, and void for problems, then walked the dock floor. An hour before the event, two tugboats passed lines to the entrance basin's wall and received the dockmaster's instructions while line-handlers gathered in groups near their stations. Once every station reported ready, Starke and his officers located a suitable spot to observe, but, to avoid interfering and legal issues, well back from the dry-dock area; except O'Leary, who was still lead inspector.

Once the dockmaster, O'leary, and commercial bark's representative completed final checks and ensured men stationed below deck were alert for leaks, the brows and whale shores were removed, then flooding began. Although pumping dry took an hour and a half, filling from the river took less. The floor soon disappeared as water climbed dock walls until the bark's bow slowly lifted, followed by *Calypso*'s. Flooding paused periodically for the dockmaster to confirm there was no leaks, then resumed. The hulls rose easily off keel blocks without incident, then several large wood blocks surfaced alongside the bark and *Calypso* listed slightly starboard. Flooding was halted until *Calypso*'s list was determined to be a minor ballasting problem, then resumed. When the dry-dock filled to river level, the caisson gate floated and tugs towed it clear while the bark's backing gear took a strain, coaxing her across the dry-dock's concrete sill to the entrance basin where returning tugs shifted her to an upstream pier. While they were away, backing gear was attached to *Calypso*, so mules were soon inching her back under black clouds of smoke and straining cables. At first *Calypso* moved imperceptibly, then faster as her bulk gained momentum. After clearing the sill, both tugs made up to port, eased her through the entrance basin into the James River, then positioned her bow out and starboard-side-to at the shipyard's southern pier.

Once alongside, *Calypso* was allowed to settle while brows were placed and mooring lines adjusted. From her new berth, those on the main deck had an unobstructed view downriver, past the pleasure and ferry piers to the Chesapeake & Ohio coal docks and grain elevator. The casino and Warwick Hotel were also visible, slightly higher and set back from the river. Looking upriver over the pier was the yard's waterfront, with *Nashville*, *Wilmington*, and *Helena* in different construction phases, and commercial ships building or under repair. With undocking complete, Starke returned to the office, placed his cap on a clothes tree, then went to a small table where Watson, already seated, was opening a folder and arranging contents.

Starke began, "So where are we?"

Watson replied, "Well, sir. The crew may have to remain on *Franklin* until fitting out, since there's no berthing here. I received the Bureau of Equipment watch, quarter, and station bill, but it needs tailoring. The navy yard equipment office continues to order and store Bureau of Allowances items for an eighth rate, which means we get the same as *Alert*, *Ranger*, and *Yantic*."

Stark nodded, "Let's move on board soonest to take ownership and keep the crew healthy."

"Yes, sir, and Captain Albert's still looking out for us. Crews usually come as a draft before commissioning, forcing the ship to examine and justify any found unfit, but we're allowed to pick ours beforehand."

"Let's not advertise that."

"Yes, sir. We're mustering as a crew on *Franklin*. Most chiefs have been selected and a proposed petty officer list's almost complete, but master-at-arms is open. Assigning billets and messes should finish before the crew moves on board, so they'll arrive with stations assigned and most cooks elected."

"Fine, remember crews crawl before walking. For the first day, just get them on board, settled, and fed. Beyond that, insure the fire bill and flooding stations are covered."

"One more item. A Chief Boatswain Mate Weaver requested *Calypso*. He's on *Franklin* but assigned to *Maine* and waiting for her return."

"Weaver? First name Braddock?"

"Yes, sir."

Braddock Weaver was on *Detroit*. Roughhewn and ungainly with a demeanor implying a slow learner, the chief was none of these. He was dedicated to his vocation, what he learned became indelible, and was a natural leader who produced loyalty, high morale, and results. He would help make *Calypso* what sailors termed a home, but Starke disliked favorites, so he responded, "You're the executive officer. He's done well before, but speak with him, see what's available, then make your decision accordingly."

Watson nodded unhappily. He took Starke at his word, but the supplicant could be a captain's pet, or asset passed over for no good reason. Starke clearly favored him, but would not trespass on his executive officer's authority. However, several days later, with transfer paperwork complete, the chief and his family were ensconced in a boarding house run by the Newport News rigging loft supervisor's wife.

O'Leary was concerned a boatswain short on diplomatic skills might cause problems because merchant ships were the yard's primary customers and its riggers unfamiliar with Navy ways. He was pleasantly surprised. They informally tested Weaver, concluded his skill equalled or surpassed their own, then accepted him. Osbourne accomplished the same with other shops, and began monitoring tests of *Calypso*'s boilers and engine, although O'Leary remained government lead. Not only did the pair adapt to their present and future relationships, but O'Leary found his future chief engineer an asset familiar with shipyard politics and conversions.

As weeks passed, *Calypso*'s stack was raised, funnel braces rigged, and deckhouse completed. A full day was spent installing ground tackle, with Weaver ensuring each link was struck with a hammer for soundness, properly painted, and accurately marked. One hundred-twenty fathoms of anchor chain was threaded through each hawsehole, then down chain pipes to the locker, where bitter ends were secured by a special staple. When complete, two blackened, stocked anchors were raised from a barge by their davits, secured to port and starboard billboards, then bent to the heavy chain hanging from each hawsehole.

Calypso's full sailing rig was planned but never fitted, and no evidence suggested masts and bowsprit ever existed. However, compatible iron masts and bowsprit were located, barged to the yard, cleaned, inspected, modified, then painted.

To support her masts, six-strand wire rope for standing rigging was unrolled from drums, measured, cut, preserved with boiled linseed oil and red lead, then wormed, parceled, and served to create stays. In dry-dock, the fore, main, and mizzen masts were stepped and bowsprit fitted, including an 1895 silver dollar fastened near the main mast's base. When pine upper masts, yards, and jibboom were barged from the woodworking shop the next day, a tall derrick began their installation. The jibboom came first, then masts, moving foremast to mizzen, allowing each to support the one preceding it. For each iteration, skids were fitted to *Calypso*'s sides to avoid damage, mast sections raised, then rake set using plumb-lines, as stays were fitted and tensioned. With her standing rigging in place, yards were crossed and running rigging started. Once masts were stepped and yards crossed, the sail loft joined in. Panels for a suite of sails had been measured, cut, then sewn together while their running rigging was measured and made up. Throughout, Weaver provided Navy terms and procedures, emerging as the local expert and, O'Leary heard, turning down offers to work at the yard.

While rigging continued above deck, below, and in the deckhouse, yard workers spent equal effort checking boilers, piping, and valves for leaks, insuring ancillary equipment was working, and preparing system tests. Walls and bulkheads were replaced, then varnished or painted; and, pulling electricity from the yard power station, *Calypso*'s searchlights, internal lighting, navigation lights, and other electric equipment were installed and tested.

As completion neared, two work days were set aside for a light displacement inclining experiment that required portable items be removed, bunkers emptied, and fluid systems drained or filled. Delaying until the heavy 4-inch guns were installed was proposed and debated, but cost and schedule prevailed so *Calypso* was positioned where a solid pier blocked river current, three large pendulums mounted main deck centerline, and lead weights staged nearby. On a calm day, steadying lines were removed at slack high water, freeing the ship to float unrestrained as a crane lowered weights to chalked spots on the main deck. The few men allowed on board took pendulum readings, then two tugs standing by returned *Calypso* to her mooring, where the measuring equipment was removed. Using these results and earlier figures, the shipyard drawing department calculated stability. Amongst others, Starke was especially interested in the variance from historical readings, since *Calypso* was never fully rigged, and modern iron masts weighed less than the original design's wood.

Watson was continuing to build the crew and preparing to fit out the ship, when he sparked an imbroglio with the navy yard's equipment office over *Calypso*'s boats. Someone working there circumvented the yard captain and equipment officer to exchange a worn steam pinnace for the new one assigned to *Calypso*. Watson rejected it as deficient since the engine, boiler, and minor components differed from their other pinnace. He refused to acquiesce and reports of his intransigence inexplicably slithered across Admiral Brown's desk. Two captains and a commander immediately summoned him, demanding to know how this reached the admiral. Despite an initially hostile reception, he convinced them no one from *Calypso* was involved and the exchange a backdoor arrangement made inside the yard. Within days, both new steam pinnaces were issued to *Calypso* and the equipment office, albeit less friendly, was more responsive. Starke remained silent as Watson reported this, and might have smiled slightly, although his beard and tightly compressed lips gave nothing away. After letting his future executive officer stew several seconds, he began, "Several people saw fit to bring your sparring to my attention. However, I was confident there were no Watson paw prints on the attempt to involve Admiral Brown. However, when next on *Franklin*'s piers, if you see that particular pinnace, I would avoid inquiring how it got there. Officially, you're not mine until we commission, but in future, keep me informed. I won't necessarily interfere and might offer useful advice, help, or cover."

As *Calypso*'s conversion entered in its final stages, picked coal arrived for boiler tests that took place pier-side. Both were lit off, repairs and adjustments made, then safety valves set and tested. Another day was spent anchored in the James River, operating machinery and equipment, before returning to bend on sails. The final Newport News event was a Navy Board of Inspection and Survey review, required for Admiral Brown to accept the ship and have her towed to the navy shipyard for fitting out, boarding crew, and receiving armament. Starke's eagerness to leave was heightened a short letter from his aunt announcing Captain Albert's invitation to attend the commissioning, which was now added to their summer move to Newport; and Katherine would travel with them.

CHAPTER THIRTEEN
Crewing the Command

Constance Starke watched Washington social activities fade, Congress adjourn, and departure cards accumulate in the silver salver. Meanwhile, family, servants, and guests prepared to summer in Newport, Rhode Island or maintain the mansion until fall. Cynthia would travel by rail to open the cottage, while the family took *Newport News* to Old Point Comfort's Hygeia Hotel. Then, with Constance and Katherine settled in the resort on the bay, Immanuel would visit their West Point shipyard and Jacob's Oxen Grove plantation before *Calypso's* commissioning ceremony.

Immanuel was putting off the distasteful West Point trip when Albert's invitation forced the issue. Still, it was appreciated because Immanuel's nephew avoided ceremonies or social events unless inescapable, required, or orchestrated by others. Even more welcome, Katherine and the entire Albert family would be there, which meant Constance would not demand to accompany him to West Point. Their British guest coming was close run, but initial reticence succumbed to a growing closeness with his wife and prospect of waiting alone until her brother returned from New York City. Even then, she acted unsettled and reticent about the Old Point Comfort hiatus, unlike Abigail who was anything but hesitant. However, the two parties would not travel together since the Starkes were continuing to Newport on a liner steaming north along the coast to New York City, then another through Long Island Sound, while the Alberts went by train.

Katherine and Constance's relationship had strengthened during afternoons in the parlor alcove where they sat upright in loose tea gowns, sharing coffee and cake. During a recent session, conversation paused, allowing the parlor clock's slow, steady rhythm to intensify, while they watched an expensive carriage roll through dancing shade patterns cast from the wind-rustled plumage of young trees lining the street. They already discussed hundreds killed at Czar Nicholas' coronation, Professor Langley's Potomac flight, a supreme court decision allowing separate Colored facilities, Armenian Christians, and Cuba, but not the approaching national elections. Katherine lacked interest, unlike her brother, whose enthusiasm for politics equaled that lavished on business, locomotives, ships, and whatever came his way.

As a carriage passed, Katherine's attention fell on bicycles ghosting down the street, while Constance slowly guided cup and saucer to the polished wood tabletop's white lace doily. Her fondness and respect for the young English widow rose steadily, because, despite a restrained demeanor, she suspected a great deal of the brother lay dormant or suppressed. She also admitted their unexpected relationship substituted for what she once anticipated with a daughter who never came; and now looked forward to Katherine gliding into the parlor, then asking permission to join her by the window.

Constance initially thought Katherine attractive, but austere, rigid, and cold. She now suspected the defensive and disciplined persona shielded an intelligent, articulate woman, formidable hostess, exceptional consort, and restive passion. Smiling, she recalled her probing exchange with the worldly Miss Tarbell, and vigorous dialogue with Miss Evans over women's suffrage. Poised, proper, and refined, Katherine matched most in intellect and force of argument, besides being a voracious reader who shared her nephew's passion for horses; and interest in wheeling. The last raised some concern when the young widow, dressed in the sport's fashionable attire, including bloomers, pedaled surrounding streets. Since this occurred every third morning, Constance considered having one of their men discreetly follow on Jacob's Yellow Fellow, but the idea of any man, especially a Colored one, trailing a fashionably dressed woman riding an expensive bicycle, was quickly discarded. Besides, Katherine claimed a great number of women were about on bicycles without incident, unlike Britain, where female riders anticipated verbal abuse and the occasional stone. Even so, Constance felt more at ease with her equestrian activities. She also thought her a match for Jacob, and surprised to learn they were corresponding. Aware of her nephew's matrimonial misgivings, Katherine's rigid affection for a lost husband, and absence of mutual interest when under the same roof; Constance broached the topic, since correspondence usually preceded or indicated an understanding. The discrete probe began, "May I ask something?"

Katherine lowered her coffee cup, shifted towards her host, smiled, then replied. "Of course, Constance?"

"Does visiting Jacob disturb you?"

Katherine thought her apprehension well-concealed, but already asked herself that question while daydreaming or unable to sleep. She placed cup and saucer on the doily, answering carefully, "I presume it's the correspondence. I write and he responds, mostly about *Calypso*. There's no commitment or understanding."

Constance reached out, gently touched Katherine's wrist, pulled back, then continued, "You and Jacob have Immanuel's blessing, and mine, should one develop."

"I am grateful," Katherine hesitantly responded, similarly touching Constance. But, he's shown no real interest and I've never been beautiful, cannot offer youth, and would not survive long outside England."

As Katherine pulled back, Constance surveyed brown hair pulled to a tight bun, curved eyebrows, firm jawline, unflinching blue eyes, and compressed lips that parted no more than necessary. The tea dress revealed a taut, firm figure easily carrying the heavy, low bust line in vogue with women and, Constance observed, enticing to men. Oddly, she was oblivious to these attributes, and believed male attention the result of an allurement all females offered, her large dowry, and weak resistance anticipated from young widows. Smiling, she responded, "A different country would be a challenge, but the rest's overly harsh, Katherine."

"Constance, I cannot provide the children you, Immanuel, and, someday, Jacob want, so his letters will fade, or end with someone like Cassandra."

Cynthia entered as Katherine finished, refreshed their coffee, contributed an odd look, then closed the double doors to the main hall as she left. Constance did not ask they be closed, but was grateful; Cynthia was invariably well-attuned to atmosphere. Seeing this self-controlled woman's discomfort, Constance suspected Katherine was resisting a growing attraction for her nephew and apprehensive about the Norfolk trip. She could not know if Jacob's feelings were similar, but he never pressed women, if anything, the opposite. Attempting to assuage this, she offered, "You've said nothing that can't be addressed if you grow close. Jacob should marry, but we've never pressured him on choice. You and he must decide."

"And children? I'm barren and can't conceive."

"Children would be a blessing, but that's to the Lord. Besides, what makes you think you're barren?"

"Philip did his part whenever he was home. I felt him often, without result."

Katherine set her jaw as though bracing for a blow after the raw admission. Constance had not anticipated this, but pressed on since a daughter could have led her down the same path. It seemed this attractive, intelligent woman knew little more than basics and saw only failed duty. She and Immanuel began with more knowledge than most, then tried vigorously over the years to conceive, but when it became obvious no children were coming, their enthusiasm continued. Katherine was not unusual, feminine hysterics might be occasionally mentioned between close friends, but beyond that medical complaint, most related topics were seldom brought up and generally downplayed, ignored, or feared. Even her more liberal friends possessed surprisingly little experience or knowledge.

Constance did not know Katherine well enough so, after some tentative exchanges, leaned forward, placed both hands on Katherine's, gently stating, "I'm fond of you and consider Jacob my own. I cannot accept everything you say, and a union would be welcome. Discuss it with Jacob when you're ready, but for now, let's change for dinner; tonight's for packing and selecting what baggage travels with us tomorrow."

Unaware of his aunt's encouragement and assent, Starke sat at his desk on *Calypso* looking over a stores report. They entered Norfolk's navy yard under tow following the successful inspection and survey visit. Captain George Dewey, assigned Lieutenant Commander Seaton Schroeder to review shipyard work, then oversee the inspection and four-hour Chesapeake Bay trial needed before Admiral Brown could accept *Calypso*. The underway portion used the yard's master, deckhands, engineers, and stokers; although Starke and his future officers rode to observe and offer information.

After they returned, yard tugs towed *Calypso* to a navy yard quay on the Elizabeth River's Southern Branch. The large mooring area stretched from the yard's two dry-docks to a timber basin channel cutting deep into the waterfront. Rows of long, red-brick shops lined either side until it ended at a large building. Inshore of the quay where *Calypso* moored was a large open space bounded by dry-docks, the timber basin, and a brick building. Used for staging materials, it had a railroad track along its perimeter and derrick with wooden booms at the timber basin entrance. Across the river was a sawmill that sometimes contributed a whiff of fresh-cut wood, then Berkley; with *Franklin* just downriver. Within days, Admiral Brown accepted the ship.

With their ship shifted to the navy yard, Starke and Osbourne joined Watson at the New Atlantic Hotel. O'Leary joined them after his release from the Newport News government department. Although still short her full complement and quartered on *Franklin*, engineers and sailors began standing watches to deal with flooding, fires, and scavengers. Every day, the entire crew prepared to receive weapons, ammunition, and supplies, so *Franklin*'s steam launches made hourly runs. These commuter launches were fitted with canvas canopies to block the sun. This was especially appreciated on windless days, despite trapping the propulsion plant's steam and lube oil fumes; that were welcome only when passing close aboard the receiving ship's scuppers.

Two letters from Katherine arrived since Starke left Washington; suggesting she posted an immediate response to his. The Old Point Comfort trip was briefly mentioned, but nothing about intentions, which did little to relieve his apprehension and brought Tyson's advice to mind. His friend also wrote, which was unusual, telling Starke the national election postponed any Levant assignment and the Cuban Exposition extended another week. Since Tyson described it as a massive Junta rally, Starke wondered whether his friend's reporting reflected this. If so, it probably fared poorly with Charles Dana, *The Sun*'s publisher, who favored Cuban independence.

Tyson held few people in high regard, but Dana stood out; perhaps because his life's passion was clear, accurate, and true reporting. Tyson also thrived at *The Sun* because he prohibited bylines and never allowed reporters to decline stories on preference, expertise, or reputation. The letter also mentioned a sometimes-reporter and temporary drinking compadre, Frederick Funston, who encouraged him to join the fight in Cuba. The response, no doubt fortified by the silver hip flask, was that an abundance of New York vermin deserved his attention so no reason existed to look for others in Cuba.

Shortly before the crew departed the receiving ship, Starke began meetings on *Calypso*. The wardroom was below her main deck and just above the auxiliary machinery room; which exchanged noise for a smoother underway ride. Watson assigned chairs by rank and position around the long, rectangular table with its polished wood top cloaked in heavy, green cloth. The men reflected Albert's selection and negotiating skills, so no excuse could be made for not fulfilling their promise. Facing Starke around the table was Lieutenant Watson, navigator Walter Dunbar, Gideon Blair with gunnery duties, and Carl Martyn assigned deck. Since there were fewer officers than comparable ships, two naval cadets would fill the ensign gap after Academy graduation: Hamilton Caldwell and Terrence Timme. During their next two years, they would work, learn, study, and prepare for a June examination that separated about a third of the returning graduates receiving commissions from the remainder who would be dismissed with severance pay. Since ship assignment also influenced this, Starke was surprised both asked for *Calypso*. Albert's steam engineer liaison proved equally productive. Osbourne and O'Leary were passed assistant engineers, although Osbourne, with greater seniority, held a relative rank of lieutenant. He would be the ship's chief engineer, but was still too junior to receive the official designation. O'Leary, with the relative rank of lieutenant (junior grade), would be his assistant. In addition, they would have two naval cadets of the engineering division, referred to as engineer cadets; also on a two-year probation, but unlike their naval cadet brethren confident of retention due to demand for steam engineers. Because Navy regulations required cadets be included in the wardroom, rather than a mess, if they stood watch and assumed officer duties, life on *Calypso* would be different from their classmates. Even so, Watson and Osbourne were tasked with instruction, oversight, and morale; knowing Starke would take a personal interest because Philo McGiffin, and others he spent several years studying with were denied commissions.

The ship rated an assistant paymaster, but Albert's quest and contacts returned a passed assistant paymaster with relative rank of lieutenant (junior grade). Matthew Wiggs appeared a dandy at first, even considering a strange flat nose pushed against his face though accident, incident, or whim of nature; but was a procurement virtuoso and exceptionally creative, despite religious and temperance inclinations. Albert also obtained Assistant Surgeon Sidney Conrad, who wore an ensign stripe with maroon band and possessed a University of Michigan medical degree. Soon after reporting he began examining the crew, rejecting three for consumption, then two more for infirmities concealed during their *Franklin* screening.

Albert and Watson did equally well with the enlisted crew, including several holding the new chief petty officer designation. Starke was especially pleased they had a senior gunner; but all would help bridge quarterdeck and forecastle by providing insight on crew morale and concerns. Starke hoped to exploit this, since navy officers remained more distant from their crews to maintain authority than the merchant service.

Captain Albert warned until late May, *Calypso* could receive a corporal's detachment of marines, leaving Starke apprehensive how a marine barracks would fit and, without a marine officer, the additional administration. He planned to assign them a 4-inch mount, until told they were not coming in a telegram from Albert; probably because of Nicaraguan unrest or the requirement to man the battleship *Iowa* that June.

Boy apprentices, of which Starke hoped to steer well clear, caused a brief maelstrom before they were avoided. The program was intended to increase citizens in crews, develop skills, and improve retention. Despite poor results, it had zealous advocates, especially outside the Navy, with several lobbying to add boy training to *Calypso*'s duties. Albert finally subdued them, by suggesting their scheming might end plans for a purpose-built ship.

Enlisted crew quality and numbers improved, not only by Albert's intervention, but Watson's zeal. Because Norfolk was a major commercial port, he approached *Franklin*'s executive officer, requesting permission to recruit in mariners' favorite haunts. Jasper agreed, mostly to avoid not doing so, and the next week saw Watson, flanked by a burly seaman and husky engineer, working the port while weathering cheerful derision on *Franklin*. Soon, the trio known as "Watson's press gang" or "Norfolk's naval crimps" began enlisting seamen, engineers, and landsmen for *Calypso*. Watson gambled this unusual approach might work because merchant berths vanished after the 1893 panic, and an officer possessed greater credibility approaching seamen directly; offering steady pay and better conditions. He also knew, besides fewer berths, American ships had a reputation for parsimony and draconian practices among foreign sailors. A few landsmen also signed on for pay, adventure, travel, or a change; but Watson reported to a perplexed Jasper some enlisted because they had sailed Starke ships, or heard of *Calypso*'s commander.

Calypso's complement ultimately reached 135 enlisted and wardroom of twelve. About seventy percent were citizens, with English, Irish, and Germans predominating; but also Scots, Swedes, British Canadians, a Finn, two Norwegians, several Frenchmen, a Russian, mixed Caribbean races, Japanese mess attendants, several Spaniards, a Sandwich Islander, and one American Indian. Consequently, while his crew might appear European at quarters, closer inspection revealed that continent's northern and southern nations, then Asians, Africans, Hispanics, Negros, Mulattos, Coloreds, and more. This amalgamation had been common for years, and its language cornucopia a constant challenge. Although most quickly acquired basic shipboard English, some ships still assigned officers to teach the language.

Another aspect was their various religious persuasions, as well as none, or finding faith when convenient. With less than two dozen Navy chaplains, *Calypso* was not blessed. This satisfied Starke, who admitted a bias against their single-breasted, dark black or blue coats, and relative ranks. Some were useful instructors, but others constantly inhabited the wardroom; or prowled the ship for converts since most were Methodist or Episcopal, unlike the crews. Religious aspects aside, their presence often brought lodging, custom, and status headaches, which had reached the Secretary of the Navy, especially with a marine officer or excess ensign on board. Their absence, however, meant *Calypso*'s varied pastoral needs fell to Starke. Navy regulations supported Sunday service, but specified no faith and proscribed forced attendance, except for boy apprentices. Some commanders ordered crews to attend for religious reasons or to promote temperance, but most sailors would anyway, for entertainment and singing. Starke wanted a plain service without proselytizing. If he had been a blue-light officer, this could be easily resolved, but, as lapsed Protestant, or Katherine's freethinker, a lay preacher was needed. Paymaster Wiggs brought salvation when Watson learned he was a Baptist deacon who threaded shoal waters between business practices and a wife who strictly adhered to church doctrine. Watson suggested this domestic state might explain his alleged skill avoiding transgression of precise rules, yet achieving a fair amount of creativity within them. Starke designated him after an interview that avoided exploring whether the candidate was a northern or southern Baptist species and convinced Starke he proselytized little, except for a combined mess and temperance.

Watson's last act in the crewing quest required visiting *Maine* before she sailed for Key West. While the primary purpose was to thank her executive officer for Weaver, and take a second run at the trough for a specific seaman, he also wanted to visit the ship, in commission less than a year. Osbourne asked to join him because the Navy's fifth battleship, *Oregon*, was to be commissioned shortly, and he walked that hull after the protected cruiser *Olympia*'s ceremony the previous year, and wanted to compare them.

Unlike the *Indiana* class, *Texas* and *Maine* had similar but obsolete main battery arrangements that sponsoned a large turret from either side. Other than that, their only similarity was a reputation for accidents, incidents, mechanical problems, and design issues. *Maine*'s industrial appearance and peacetime paint scheme of white and straw-yellow, lacked the far smaller *Calypso*'s elegant black hull, yellow masts, and varnished deckhouse, but Watson was impressed when he stepped from the accommodation ladder to the broad main deck, obtaining a clear view of the turrets' twin ten-inch rifles and ship's three superstructure islands.

Her executive officer's quarters was a small steel cell with a riveted overhead segmented by steel girders. Round ventilation ducts crossed the space, then ended with trumpet-shaped diffusers pushing and venting air. Behind green curtains, a porthole was discernible above the varnished wood berth affixed to the hull, with the remaining walls obscured by cabinets, and a desk that swung up to contain contents at sea and lower for work. In the center, was a large high-back cane chair consuming what little floor space remained.

Rising to greet them was Lieutenant Commander Adolph Marix. Watson heard he was a German Jew born in Dresden and appointed to the Academy by President Lincoln; who employed his father as a translator. The balding, round-headed man in undress blues sported a solid but proper mustache and was courteous, but, as every executive officer, overloaded. After a cordial, but brief, exchange, he agreed to Watson's request for the sailor, then offered to provide legal advice, should *Calypso* need it; since he read law and served in the Judge Advocate's office. The interview ended when an ensign arrived to conduct a tour, and Watson obtained assurances the requested sailor would follow shortly.

CHAPTER FOURTEEN
Commissioning and Amour

The Starke party left on *Newport News*, traveled overnight, then disembarked the next morning at Old Point Comfort's large, hexagonal Baltimore Wharf. Passing its central building, they walked the wood pier to the street, where uniformed guards held vendors at bay while porters wrestled steamer trunks and other luggage into carts for the Hygeia Hotel, or slightly closer Chamberlain. Their Hygeia rooms were on the third-floor overlooking Chesapeake Bay and Fort Wool, with a truncated view of the long beach ringing the peninsula. As the sandy ribbon rounded Fort Monroe and the lighthouse, then continued north, the hotel's 700 yards obscured much, while the view west was dominated by the wharf with boats moored to small piers jutting from what seemed a causeway out to it. Almost, directly below the rooms were red and white-striped canvas roofs over the large dining and ballroom pavilions.

Immanuel Starke arranged the next day's baths and other diversions, walked the beach, ate supper, then retired early, leaving the women to themselves. The next morning he was on a Chesapeake & Ohio train for Richmond, then the forty-five minute express to West Point, where he took a Terminal Hotel room overlooking the York River. The three-story edifice with turreted corners was nine years old and served excellent meals, but he took time before eating to study documents sent from the yard. Well prepared, the next morning after breakfast, coffee, and cigar, he met the yard's single-horse carriage, then sat back and watched the open surrey clear an ice delivery van before rolling jauntily along city streets lined with stores, churches, oyster shucking sheds, vacant buildings, and piers with moored schooners and barges. Despite his vehicle's brisk pace, the clean, cool morning promised a warm June day with wharf and river smells portending July.

His West Point and York River relationships began before the war when visiting his brother, Jefferson Starke, at Oxen Grove, downriver from the city. The Oakley plantation produced cotton and tobacco on 3,000 acres with fifty slaves. When Federal cavalry ended that life, most of its people fled to Fort Monroe and the outbuildings were torched. The war, however, was new and awkward, like the cavalry captain who hesitated burning the house, then abandoned his enterprise when confronted by the Negro overseer, Tribbs Jefferson, who stood on the front porch arguing its owners, daughter, and three-year old grandson were in West Point's detention camp as Northern sympathizers; omitting their son by marriage was a Confederate naval officer. Immanuel learned this when sister-in-law and nephew arrived in Washington, after they were freed by a Federal gunboat; then followed McClellan's retreat down the peninsula. His in-laws feared either side might destroy Oxen Grove's remnants without warning, so mother and grandson had been sent to safety with the Starkes.

Until war's end, the Oakley's worked their fields alongside those left, mostly the Jefferson family, growing subsistence crops. Although Oxen Grove was ignored by the Confederates and survived, several tracts were later sold to the Freedmen's Bureau to regain lost capital after Radical Republicans prohibited southern states from paying war debts, and before Northerners known as carpetbaggers could confiscate additional acreage. Starke's mother never returned, having died from typhoid within a year, leaving Jacob to his aunt and uncle, who regularly visited Oxen Grove until the Oakley's joined their daughter.

During one trip, the Oakley's mentioned a local shipyard selling for a fraction of its value, because no capital existed for recovery; and rail lines between Richmond and its port were not yet rebuilt. Immanuel quickly bought it to serve Starke ships and others, since the port saw a brisk trade in manufactured goods, timber, cotton, and tobacco. It remained profitable until the 1893 panic, providing income for twenty-five to fifty people. The small yard broke even after that, then began running at a loss when the railroad shifted freight business to Portsmouth; leaving West Point with fishing, oysters, and some passenger service. Local businesses, including its only bank, began failing, property values collapsed, and the exodus gained momentum.

Beyond West Point, similar shipyards were vanishing for different reasons. Wooden ship building and repair work was drying up as American companies shifted to iron and steel hulls, long after European competitors. Consequently, the yard needed major upgrading to compete for what trade remained, investors would not touch it, and the Starke firm would be put at risk to save it. He hoped to delay its shutdown with *Illusive*'s overhaul, and for that reason, included transfer work in her sale. This plan to close slowly fell apart when insurrectos destroyed the Cuban sugar plantation and mill. With the firm recovering from panic and recession, it could not endure without excising Cuban and West Point operations. In Cuba, buildings, crops and machinery were burned or smashed, oxen confiscated or shot, their local manager killed, and laborers driven off, leaving fallow land and no income. While less dramatic at West Point, the shipyard must permanently disappear. Some working there would find Newport News positions, others might change jobs, and many saw employment as temporary anyway. A handful stood to improve their lot, but incomes would mostly plummet. The yard manager was aware and prepared, but it still made for a tense and depressing day.

The next morning, with a bright sun reflecting off the languid York River, a yard tugboat carried him to Oxen Grove. Standing in the eyes, looking downriver, he watched its blunt bow carve a flat, furrow through the broad waterway lined with trees and fields. This was the best transport to the plantation, even with her justifiably sullen crew. The alternative was a scheduled steamer or pushing down hot, sandy roads flanked by clouds of biting insects endowed with definite speed advantages.

Newman Pearce ran Oxen Grove. Since Jacob's grandparents and Tribbs Jefferson passed, there were several managers, but he alone possessed the knowledge, initiative, and honesty to farm its remaining 1,100 acres without constant oversight. Except for not living in the main house, which his wife maintained, Pearce adopted the property and returned profits, even when those nearby could not. The man's long nose, narrow head, ungainly walk, and slow manner, belied his energy and agricultural skill. Born after the war, then raised along the river, he maintained good relations with sharecroppers and neighboring farmers; White, Colored, or Negro. A deeply religious man, he mostly read the Bible or agricultural periodicals, wrote in a strong hand, and his mathematics exceeded many blessed with greater opportunity. Besides farming, he was an expert trader, never fooled into buying scoured calves, foundered horses, or spoiled seed. After their conference, at the plantation pier extending into the river from a sandy spot below a pine forest, Immanuel wondered if they would meet again. This was probably his last Oxen Grove visit since he was unlikely to return to the shipyard. Besides, he believed Jacob needed to take greater interest or sell; a hard choice with his mother and her family buried there. The diminutive yard tug had him back in West Point by late afternoon, despite plowing upriver.

Across Hampton Roads from Old Point Comfort and the Hygeia, Jacob Starke knew his uncle's party arrived but was unable to greet them since their first days coincided with installation of *Calypso*'s fangs. While the Starke party left *Newport News* for their hotel, a barge burdened with a pair of black, breech-loading, 4-inch rifles lashed down under tarps eased against *Calypso*'s starboard side. Their long barrels, levers, handwheels, worm gears, and breech-blocks bore no resemblance to the black powder, muzzleloading pivot guns originally intended; and only recently withdrawn from Navy service. Those bulky weapons were loaded by ramming a powder bag, wadding, then some projectile down the muzzle; so, despite iron or steel carriages, Decatur or Hull would find them familiar and the very best gun crews still fired three rounds a minute. These successors fired a thirty-pound shell slid into gleaming breeches sealed by hinged breechblocks and, with the gun carriage replaced by a single conical stand, were easily aimed and pointed using polished brass handwheels. Firing eight or nine rounds a minute to 11,500 yards, targets could be hit nearly six miles out with common or armor-piercing rounds. There was no need for canister, grapeshot, and the like, because smaller guns were specifically mounted for close-in work. However, accuracy still depended on gun captains' judgement, timing, and eyesight; which was why Starke spent time unearthing the best gunners.

Mounting consumed a full day and ended main deck activities. Installation began with removing heavy tarps, then rigging to lift and position over six tons of steel. Each gun was hoisted from the barge, transferred above a steel base-ring on the deck, then slowly lowered onto its threaded studs. Once firmly seated, fourteen large nuts were tightened in a prescribed pattern, then a thin second nut, added to lock the first and prevent working it loose when firing or at sea. When the forward rifle completed, the barge was shifted aft and the procedure repeated. Finally, a tampion went into each barrel's mouth and tarps replaced. The next day, *Calypso*'s 3-pounder Hotchkiss guns were installed, Gatling gun mountings added, and final commissioning preparations begun.

These ceremonies normally occurred aft, or on the quarterdeck, but lack of deck space forced Watson to shift to the open area alongside their mooring. He doubted Starke cared where it occurred; and would prefer pausing work to read his orders, then resume. However, a ceremony was required, so Watson arranged it, with a *Franklin* staff officer's assistance. Admiral Brown's barge arrived a half hour before and he quickly vanished into the captain's day cabin with Starke. Ashore, the crew assembled in three groups several ranks deep, in dress white uniforms and flat hats, while being shuffled by officers trying to arrange them by rank, rate, and height. Between this formation and the ship were chairs for Admiral Brown, senior staff, and local notables. To that section's right and left were guest seats for the Starkes, Alberts, and Newport News representatives. Facing this assembly was a podium, with *Calypso*, floating motionless at the quay, proving a backdrop,.

Converted to a small gunboat, and bark-rigged for the first time, two square-rigged masts rose from the black hull, separated by a single large funnel. Aft of the mainmast was a fore-and-aft rigged mizzen. The three masts' lower sections were straw-yellow with the bowsprit, upper masts, and yards blackened. For the ceremony, her yards were squared and sails harbor furled. With full bowsprit and jibboom, clipper bow, and fantail stern, the 245 foot bark's elegance contrasted with two 4-inch rifles peering over her bulwarks. The white canvas used for flying bridge windshields, deck awnings, and wind sails accentuated her varnished oak deckhouse, mahogany pilothouse, and hinged bridge wings. Aft, swinging from round bar davits, or inboard on skids, two whaleboats and a pair of steam pinnaces waited under white canvas covers, while a paint punt floated unseen below the quay wall. Barely visible, an auxiliary boiler's smoke rose lazily from the stack to drift a short distance over the Elizabeth River's Southern Branch before dispersing. An occasional breeze jumbled smells of river, burning coal, shipyard, and lumber mill.

Lieutenant O'Leary was in charge on the ship, where musicians formed on the fantail. Like the rest, they faced heat rising from the deck when each negligible breeze died, but also had to contend with instruments. For this, they wore white gloves to prevent finger sweat causing a wrong note or instrument to slip. Sailors handling flags or manning the rail were well satisfied staying on board and dodging the formation assembling ashore under Lieutenant Osbourne.

The chief engineer, in front of the men standing in ranks on baked-dry grass, dirt, and gravel, shared his commander's views on ceremonies. At parade rest in hot, humid air, with the packed ground reflecting heat, men fidgeted as Watson completed final checks. Periodically, an ensign brought his group to attention, then returned them to parade rest, insuring knees remained unlocked and fainting minimized. Osbourne was going to do it across the entire formation, but welcomed the ensigns' initiative; although self-serving since they stood in the sun, like him, wearing white cotton uniforms with high, tight collars, and swords. The least suffering, mostly Japanese, mess attendants ushered guests from carriages to chairs, then directed drivers to the waiting area near a large stable where horses could water.

With relief, Watson checked his watch, then called everyone to attention as Admiral Brown and Lieutenant Starke left the ship. Once they were seated by the podium, *Franklin*'s Chaplain Morrison opened with an ambitious invocation to the sweating crew and warming guests. Admiral Brown's remarks were brief, then he read his orders to commission *Calypso*, and directed Watson to carry them out. With this, the ensign, jack and Admiral Brown's flag rose simultaneously to hang limp as the band played. When Starke reached the podium, he briefly thanked those present, read his orders taking command, then directed Watson to set the watch. With that, a second deck log entry gave him *Calypso*. Watson attributed Chaplain Morrison's brief closing benediction to his heavy, dark garb, thinking it must feel more hairshirt than uniform in the heat.

Constance Starke, watching from her chair, and sympathizing with those standing, thought the ceremony resembled a church wedding. The Navy Department determined ceremony, Admiral Brown gave the bride away, and her nephew committed his coming years to *Calypso*. Even a somber chaplain was present to add God's blessing to the union. She preferred Katherine over *Calypso*, but unlike a marriage, the ship would have him only a few years.

With ceremony complete, guests were escorted to the wardroom, followed by the crew reembarking. As a merchant ship, *Calypso* was equipped for passengers, so her wardroom was comparatively large. The additional space allowed comfortable leather chairs, secured by short chains to the floor, a buffet along its forward wall and large rosewood table ringed by twelve chairs. Arrayed on it were glassware, wine, cider, and lemonade, replenished by white-jacketed mess attendants, and a small silver service Constance Starke presented to *Calypso* on the firm's behalf. Starke accompanied Admiral Brown until Albert freed him for the customary rounds that insured the new captain spoke briefly with each guest. Although most

Newport News Shipyard participants left when proper, he found his uncle and their conversion manager negotiating under an open porthole. Watson and Osbourne were similarly engaged with Olivia and Isabella Albert, while two ensigns lurked nearby, speculating on whether they were welcome. Wearing travel dresses, Constance, Katherine, and Abigail drifted to a corner where polite laughter elicited a smile from Katherine. As Admiral Brown left, Starke received congratulations from Captains Terry of *Franklin* and McCormick of the navy yard, then, looking up, confirmed Dunbar replaced the admiral's flag with a commissioning pennant, after appropriate honors.

Starke found no opportunity for time alone with Katherine that day, beyond a passing greeting, and within an hour most guests left. While the crew prepared for their promised rope yarn, visitors kept to the wardroom; until Osbourne offered Albert's daughters and Katherine a topside tour, assisted by both ensigns. *Calypso*'s executive officer remained dutifully near, until Starke, mellowed by a glass of cider, sent him to check on the tour. After he returned with them, twenty minutes later Starke escorted his aunt, uncle, and Katherine to their carriage; and invited to the Hygeia before they left for Newport. Meanwhile, Albert coaxed his animated brood into a rented carriage, after telling Starke he would return the next day. Watson and Osbourne stood nearby, obviously desirous of an afternoon away to call on the daughters.

Captain Albert arrived the next morning, then, in the day cabin, asked, "How's your first day in command, captain?"

"Fine, sir. Once our cadets arrive, we'll have a full crew and begin working up."

"Contacted the Academy. If either's unable or unwilling to come off leave, he'll be exchanged for someone who is."

"Yes, sir. We coal tomorrow and load ammunition the following day. With orders, I can be underway for Florida the first full week of July."

"Good. Consider leaving on the fourth."

"*Calypso* can be ready and, with the first quarter started, the paymaster would be in good shape, but what about Independence Day?"

"Why begin a cruise with drunk, hungover, or absent sailors?"

"The usual holiday consequences."

"Precisely, besides your departure early that day would attract less attention."

"Yes, sir."

"Now to the orders."

"Jacksonville, Florida is a likely place to start. Prevailing winds should be off the bow most of the trip south, so you'll steam. If you coal at Port Royal, the Marshals Service might have information on what to expect off the St. Johns River."

"Agree, especially with the new jetties. I understand they completed last year and the channel's dredged to fifteen feet. *Calypso* draws fourteen, making the river passable, although I would prefer high water. Its an improvement over crossing the bar, but the city's a good distance upriver and I've no desire to sit in the St. Johns waiting for high water, or risk being towed off a sand bar."

"What do you intend?"

"Depends on what can be learned about Fernandina and Jacksonville. *Calypso* needs to be seen, but not predictable, so I propose sailing south along the coast, enter the Straits of Florida, cruise the edge of the keys to avoid fighting current, get in a full power run, and look for filibuster expeditions. Afterwards, we might touch at Key West to plant rumors we're headed south and gather information, but instead cruise near the Dry Tortugas to finish working up. Since ships use them for a final landfall before entering the straits or crossing to Cuba, we'll be seen and may get lucky. Then, come back through the Straits of Florida, just north of the Cuban coast, but outside Spain's territory. By then, I'd like to coal."

"How are you handling that?"

"Osbourne and O'Leary will empty bunkers based on source, type, and age, but for now it's all the same."

"Remember, commercial coal's more expensive and the supply uncertain."

"I've considered that. Since shipping lines maintain quality coal stocks at different ports, I spoke with my uncle. He suggested Aron Sharett, a ship chandler both family firms use."

"Can he be trusted?"

"I've done business with him as supercargo, but they've known him for years, and he's expert at quiet arrangements. If we need commercial coal, it can be slipped in with shipments for Starke ships, or my father's. That makes *Calypso* difficult to track using coal orders, or to plant coal torpedos."

"Is Wiggs working out?"

"Yes, I'll put him in touch with Sharett."

"Agreed. When do you plan to contact Sharett?"

"My Uncle sent a telegram requesting assistance, but gave no specifics. With your permission, I'll approach him when I have orders, or just before."

"Agreed, and port arrival reporting?"

"One cable will be sent officially, another as a personal message to you in the Building. Only the coded one to you will contain the next destination. The sender will be *Calypso*, *Cutlass*, *Claymore*, *Rapier*, or *Broadsword*. I've also had those nameboards made up to add ambiguity."

"I've reviewed your written recommendations. The orders will be hand-delivered by the month's end. Did you speak with Admiral Brown as I suggested?"

"Yes, sir."

"Good. Remember, attempts to prosecute Captain Semmes failed because he kept detailed records and stayed scrupulously within the law. We're not in the same situation, but it's a good lesson and the Admiral could better emphasize our risks."

After insuring the cabin window was closed and steward away, Albert added, in a low voice, "An item not in your orders. Should you require, one of *Olivette*'s crew is a confidential courier to Havana, except when his ship goes north for the summer; then it depends whether he's with her or shifts to *Mascotte*, the Plant steamer that stays south. Key West's cable office is also providing information, as is a Havana operator, so I may receive useful information; on the Spanish, anyway."

After covering several minor items, Albert left for the Hygeia, then a train north with his family. That Saturday, with Admiral Brown's permission, Watson took the ship to allow Starke an overnight visit to Old Point Comfort. He took the first Portsmouth ferry, registered at the Hygeia, then joined his uncle's small entourage for a stroll under Fort Monroe, along the beach, then back past Baltimore Wharf and Chamberlain Hotel. After lunch, his aunt and uncle used the hotel baths, leaving Katherine and Jacob reclining in two low, bamboo chairs on a long veranda overlooking Hampton Roads and Fort Wool. Starke chose a lightweight suit, rather than Norfolk jacket, with white cotton shirt, standing collar, and bow tie; the last two a reluctant concession to fashion, as was the light straw hat and new shoes. He found them no improvement over a white cotton uniform in the sun, and preferred shirt, trousers, and boots.

Katherine appeared subdued, so Starke watched men and boys in the shallow water along the beach. They mostly stood or waded, although a few swam short distances. Women along it hovered near exuberant children splashing through the warm water sliding noiselessly back and forth over hot, clinging sand. One or two waded to their waists, but none swam despite it becoming popular exercise. Starke thought more would take it up, except public decency considerations saddled bathing costumes with the attributes of a sea anchor. Katherine reclined beside him in a light, silk-lined tweed waist jacket and skirt that were neither light brown or off-white but straddled both. Beneath, a white cotton blouse closed with a single row of buttons rising to a standing collar held tight against her throat by small hooks. High-topped shoes were mostly concealed by the long skirt, which slipped over her blouse beneath a wide cinch-belt accentuating the waist. Although large hats bursting with replica fruit or flowers were popular, she wore a straw boater tilted slightly forward, shielding her eyes from the reflecting sun, him, or both. A light flowery parasol leaned unused against the railing, should she desire to walk, or sun breach the canvas porch awning.

An awkward silence developed then continued, so his attention wandered to a small pier extending from the Hygeia's dance floor over beach and shore to a canopied platform. Beyond it, assorted schooners, steam tugs, and ship or two moved noiselessly to their next turn or destination. A paddlewheel ferry approached Baltimore Wharf from the west. White steam launches with brass stacks floated along the small piers jutting from the long one out to it; moving hesitantly on light swells until checked by thin mooring lines, or departing with tourists sitting under striped canopies. Katherine ultimately broke the silence, "*Calypso*'s beautiful, a yacht in comparison with Philip's ship."

Looking under the boater's flat brim into her eyes, Starke mused, "She's from another era and outmatched by any modern gunboat."

"It's still elegant. Have you used the sails?"

"Not yet, but I'm looking forward to seeing how she performs under canvas."

"I hope my letters aren't an intrusion? I enjoy yours."

Starke responded, "No, not at all," while groping in a pocket for his pipe, then let it slide back in.

Katherine half-smiled, "Don't deprive yourself. Father prefers a pipe, so I enjoy the scent. Philip favored cigars."

Relieved, he extracted the pipe and tobacco pouch, adding, "Then it's good I recently converted."

She looked directly at him, "Is it?"

The match failed to ignite, leaving him looking directly into her brown eyes without a smokescreen. As they caught the sun, he imagined gold specks mixed with the brown, recovered, readied a new match, and concentrated on lighting his pipe, replying, "I think so."

"You'll continue writing then?"

"Yes."

"Do you swim?"

"Yes."

"Because of the navy?"

"No. They can't decide if teaching sailors is a kindness. Should the ship sink or they fall overboard, some feel it prolongs the inevitable."

With that she turned away. He forgot how she was widowed, "I'm sorry, Katherine."

Still looking toward Baltimore Wharf, she replied, "No, there's always something, and it's an imposition to ask everyone to avoid what reminds me of Philip. He's always there."

"Still ..."

She quickly shifted topics, "I swim. Most women at home can't."

"It's changing here, but those from the country often do. I was told my mother could, and I believe Darius said Cynthia can. I've no idea about my aunt."

"On Brydian Grange there's a large pond where Edward taught me."

"It must be hard to swim in a bathing costume; wool or cotton."

Speaking low and looking away, she answered, "We stopped when I had to wear one."

He changed topics, but they spoke steadily until time to dress for dinner. Both perspired slightly, even in the shade, but there was enough time for one of the Hotel's Russian or Turkish baths. He chose the latter, which was excellent but failed to excise an unsettling urgency about Katherine, whose warm saltwater bath did little to cleanse her of similar sensations.

Jacob waited in the lounge with his uncle until the two women completed dinner preparations. For this evening, he wore the service dress white uniform, which lacked pockets capable of holding a pipe, pouch, and match case. He considered joining his uncle in a cigar, but passed without knowing why. Through rising smoke, Immanuel began, "I'm closing our West Point yard, Jacob. We can't keep it open and there's not enough business potential to sell. Just spent a day with the manager to arrange it."

"And the people?" His uncle detested unions, but was paternal regarding those working for him.

"Severance pay for those with us a long time, and your commissioning ceremony proved useful. Newport News will hire our skilled tradesmen and consider the laborers, since two battleship keels get laid this month. A few may be offered work with our firm, but away from West Point; so I doubt more than one or two will accept."

"I heard the city's bleeding out from the railroad shifting freight business."

"It's bad and won't improve, which leads to Oxen Grove. I reviewed the books and Pearce's plans, but doubt I'll return after the yard closes."

"How does it look?

"Books are good, grounds have changed, but the main house is kept as it was when your grandparents died. When were you last there?"

"Three or four years ago?"

"Then you must decide. Should Pearce leave, it would be hard to recover."

"I can't sell it out from under him, or get more involved without leaving the navy."

At that point, the women entered and Starke's uncle, discarded his cigar, grinning, "Ah, Constance and Katherine. Well then, it would seem you're twice in purgatory."

"Uncle?"

Both men stood before Starke could receive an explanation. As they went to the dining room, he thought his aunt still attractive, how alike the women moved, then realized the two were simpatico. As the aunt's wrist slid through his uncle's crooked arm, Starke felt Katherine do the same, and he enjoyed the sensation. Their table was in front of a large window overlooking the beach, Baltimore Wharf, Hampton Roads, and opposite shore. Its white linen cover was stocked with silverware, flowers, and water glasses stuffed with folded cloth napkins. Extracting Katherine's chair, then easing it forward as she lowered herself, he noticed it was the same style used in the *Newport News* dining and smoking rooms. Several tables away, a massive brick chimney pierced the large room's rustic ceiling. Surrounding it were brass electroliers suspended between beams.

His uncle ordered wine from a white-jacketed waiter, sampled it, then, after glasses were full, sat back as the women ordered off ornate menus with dangling silk ribbons. They selected Consommé Antoinette, then Diamond Back Terrapin a la Maryland, while the men chose prime rib for a main course, with everybody adding baked sweet potatoes and French peas, before finishing with mince pie and fruits.

Table discussion was light and mainly concerned the coming Newport season, with Constance describing the cottage for Katherine. Constructed of wood and nothing like those building along the cliffs, it overlooked harbor, city, and naval station. Starke spent hours there, watching Newport Bay from its expansive yard, or sailing their small, gaff-rigged boat. Across the table, his aunt was apparently gaining headway stirring Katherine's interest, since she turned to Starke asking, "Constance says there's a naval station in Newport. Will *Calypso* visit?"

Caught off guard, Starke pressed a linen napkin against his lips to capture moisture left by the final fork of succulent, rare beef, and gain time, "The North Atlantic Squadron visits most summers, but I doubt *Calypso* will come north of the Chesapeake."

"I see."

When finished, everyone spent a half hour in their rooms before returning to an adjacent dance and concert hall, where the artillery school's band was playing. Resembling the dining room but larger, electroliers suspended on long cables from its beam ceiling lit a waxed parquet dance floor opening to the bay. Outside, dusk turning to night made ships' running and anchor lights visible, while coaxing shore lights from streets, homes, and businesses.

Starke asked Katherine for the second waltz. His aunt and uncle were already gliding over the glistening floor since Immanuel caught Constance's glance when the music first started. After many years, he knew she loved to dance and excelled at it, while he was only a capable partner whose skills were slightly above adequate for business, or pleasing her. Katherine was surprised to discover Jacob Starke danced well, thanks to his aunt, and two military schools where chairs, or other cadets, served as partners. While favoring waltzes, he possessed a respectable repertoire.

Looking across the dance floor at Katherine and his nephew, Immanuel observed both concentrating on their movements, not each other, but without any suggestion this was their first dance. He thought her brother a good man, but Katherine overly reserved, perhaps from losing a husband. She did get on well with Constance, who wanted a daughter as much as he a son. Then, seeing Jacob execute a whisk to avoid another couple, knew if his nephew was what the Lord intended, it was more than satisfactory.

Jacob was everything Immanuel could ask for, but he wished Navy promotions less stagnant and his nephew better able to avoid risky escapades. Some might call them adventures, but he believed that a euphemism for the unworldly having any new experience, surviving what sane people would avoid, or fantasy experienced at a safe distance. Even so, he let Jacob set his own course after the sixteenth birthday when his manipulations nearly cost the nephew's life. Immanuel wanted him to attend university or join their firm, but the cavalry was luring Jacob and he worried a recruiter might enlist him. While the Army avoided educated Southerners as officers since the war, some with Jacob's education, riding, and shooting ability enlisted, along with many recent immigrants. He hoped to discourage this by arranging participation in a relatively safe, but disagreeable, expedition. Aware cavalry duty in the West was especially onerous and his nephew acquainted with the newly commissioned Second Lieutenant Reily, who conveniently transferred from the Tenth to Seventh Cavalry, the Montana campaign seemed perfect. Several thousand troops were gathering to force some Sioux onto reservations, with the greatest dangers being miserable weather, bad food, rattlesnakes, mosquitos, ticks, and fleas. Assisted by Lieutenant Colonel Custer and Reilly, already at Fort Abraham Lincoln in the Dakota Territory, Jacob went along as a civilian packer.

Like the nation, he and Constance were stunned when news of the disaster arrived in the midst of centennial celebrations. They thought Jacob lost for a week, until the wire arrived saying he was safe. They later learned he was with the pack train and several companies dug in on a ridge. It cleansed Jacob of cavalry aspirations and his uncle of manipulation. When Jacob returned home interested in the Naval Academy, Immanuel called in favors for an at-large appointment; thinking the school's academic reputation solid and its naval curriculum might persuade his nephew to join their firm. After receiving a commission, Jacob sailed Starke ships during leaves of absence, but stayed doggedly with the navy. Now, however, Immanuel was becoming anxious about bringing his nephew into the business because he often felt tired, most recently during the easy walk to Oxen Grove plantation from its landing. Watching Jacob and Katherine waltz, he hoped change might be in the air.

Later, when a waltz finished, he felt a tug on his arm then left with Constance who exhibited the impatient affliction she invariably acquired during open air dancing. Jacob watched them enter the hydraulic elevator. It seemed his aunt was tugging his uncle's arm like she did when excited about shopping or sightseeing. Once the door closed, he turned to Katherine and was immediately struck by how the conservative, but fashionably low cut dress, revealed their recent exertions and the warm summer evening. When the electric lights struck just right, he saw a glistening face, shoulders, back, and chest. It also seemed she exuded some strong essence afflicting himself, and several nearby men, although he understood the reserved and cautiously proper Katherine never used more than soap and lemon juice.

Katherine, to her surprise, did not resent his interest, and welcomed a respite from dancing, although Constance's nephew proved an accomplished partner. Given his reserved manner, she anticipated short wooden jerks and, if fortune favored, no more than one or two painful toes. To avoid his gaze, she made a pretense of scanning ballroom, bay, and summer evening stars. Comparing Philip to him, she thought first of her husband's kindness, a less overt quality in the American, although he appeared as much a gentleman. Similarly, Jacob's countenance and spirit seemed more roughhewn and scarred. She also sensed he was far less amenable than Philip, which aroused conflicting feelings of uncertainty, apprehension, attraction, and urgency. When riding in Rock Creek Park, he never abused horses, but was powerful, determined, and kept control. The mouth was often slightly compressed and he seemed guarded, but she admitted they were much the same there. His beard, although not luxuriant, was neatly trimmed and well-formed, which suggested sophistication and reminiscent of her father's as a young man.

Philip, like her brother Edward, preferred a small mustache. Jacob also possessed a lock of rebellious hair and faded blue eyes under dark eyebrows that never flinched when locked on something. She began feeling disgusted with herself because she wanted him to look at her, then grew uneasy from the growing attraction becoming more urgent as she denied it; like a horse she feared mounting but could not forego.

Both were caught off guard when Jacob impetuously invited her to walk the pier, where others were similarly engaged. Without thinking, Katherine responded, "It's warm. I won't need a wrap."

They left for a thin pier spanning a gently sloped shore where small dark waves, laced with minute white crests, constantly caressed beach sand. Replicating the Starkes, Katherine's wrist remained firmly in Jacob's arm as they walked slowly to a small shelter at the pier's head. The night, with its smells and sounds, strangely reminded him of Tyson and another pier, except, as she watched a ferry's running lights enter the Elizabeth River, he unexpectedly wanted this woman heavy with his child. This startled him, while Katherine, unaware, focused on white and green lights moving across the dark bay to control wanton agitation and angst; more virulent than she remembered with Philip, but familiar enough.

Turning to each other, Katherine began, "Are we to continue writing, Jacob?"

Whatever Jacob contemplated, he responded, "It will be difficult when *Calypso*'s at sea."

"Philip and I worked through it. Just know I'm writing, even if they're waiting not at every port."

"I've never been a reliable correspondent, but will do the same."

"We leave for Newport tomorrow."

"Yes."

"Will we meet before?"

"No. I must leave first thing. I've already said good-bye to my aunt and uncle."

"Then, if you'll take me back, I'll do the same."

Fearing a breach in manners, Starke fought an impulse to embrace Katherine as they returned. After an awkward good-bye, she closed the door and he walked past his aunt and uncle's suite. They sounded awake, but he continued on to a bar under one of Hygeia's towers, slowly sipped a brandy, and watched two artillery officers play billiards before returning to his room to pack.

He boarded the first morning ferry after a restless night. Katherine did the same, then, accompanying the Starkes, was soon on an Old Dominion Line steamship for New York City, where they would transfer to a Fall River Line ship for Newport. Standing on the upper deck, she tried looking up the Elizabeth River for *Calypso*, but was unable to see anything. Passing Old Point Comfort, her eyes remained fixed on the Hygeia Hotel and its pier until the steamship heeled slightly starboard. She watched the wake curve until they steadied for the trip south of Thimble Shoal and the Middle Ground, then between Capes Henry and Charles into the Atlantic. As they continued east to the Gulf Stream, the bay's mouth shrank to a small disruption on the light blue horizon, then vanished. Having slept little, she found a vacant deck chair beside Constance, pulled a blanket over lap and chest, then wrestled emotions until the sun's warmth and steamer's throbbing engines caressed her to sleep.

CHAPTER FIFTEEN
Opening Moves

Calypso insured Starke had no time to reflect. During the next three days individual messes were adjusted, berth-deck cooks determined, then coal, ammunition, water, and stores taken aboard. When complete, underway watches were set pier side, boilers lit-off, machinery run, and water rationed. Flooding and fire drills took place, including a coal fire, which entailed breaching a bunker then digging down to a red-painted rock Osbourne planted while coaling. The men simulated cooling with fire hoses, then burrowed down through bunkered coal, extracted the prize, and eased it overboard. Although the black gang proved creative concocting engine, boiler, and machinery room drills, the deck force tackled seamanship with equal enthusiasm. Weaver was everywhere, walking sailors through evolutions, teaching, explaining, encouraging, and, sometimes expressing real or feigned frustration. Both anchors were lowered, raised, cleaned, catted, then secured on billboards. Topmasts and yards were sent up and down; booms shifted; sails bent, reefed, then unbent; and storm sails raised. Even the ungainly tow hawser was snaked out on deck. Quartermasters sorted, updated, and stored charts; then checked publications. Obtaining ranges with stadimeters and angles with sextants was also practiced. Wigwag signals were sent back and forth to people ashore. Gun crews simulated loading and firing every weapon carried, including Gatling guns mounted on carriages. Finally, boats were lowered, the landing party put ashore, then marched to a firing range to check equipment and shoot their unfamiliar clip-fed, bolt action rifles. Although Watson arranged this with Marine First Lieutenant Lejeune, Starke made a point to stop by. While there, the sergeant range master invited him to fire a clip. Despite shooting offhand with an unfamiliar Remington-Lee, Starke grouped five tight rounds, low and right of the black circle, frustrating the man's entertainment, leaving the crew trying to outshoot their captain, and justifying his time spent shooting one in Washington.

Visiting Aron Sharett's Norfolk office, he found the man unchanged. He was short to average in height and balding, with hooked nose and thick accent of a second language, or fluency in several. His light wool suit partially encased a con-stricting satin waistcoat, suggesting earned prosperity. Alt-hough a habitual pacer, he greeted Starke, then settled into a wooden swivel-chair, motioning him to a plain chair nearby, adding it was strange to see him in uniform. His sitting con-cealed short, stout legs supporting a pear-shaped torso with gold chain arcing over a round belly's circumference. Alt-hough bowed slightly, the broad back and shoulders suggest-ed he knew hard, relentless labor, though not recently. Above his substantial neck, constricted by a starched collar, thick lips spewed a vibrant stream of words, thoughts, and ideas over a dancing double chin.

After confirming his uncle's telegram reached the chandler, Starke explained what he could about details and require-ments. When he finished, Sharett lifted himself from the chair, preferring to walk when thinking, speaking, or both, and Starke braced for what would follow. The chandler's cut-and-thrust discourse unbalanced recipients with a flood of state-ments, ideas, concepts, and seemingly unrelated positions. However, each thrust drove home a single point in a coordi-nated campaign, coalescing to the desired objective. Within the hour, Starke had a communication plan, agreement on re-ceiving coal and supplies, and latest information on Caribbean shipping. Like his uncle, Sharett was not supporting filibuster connections, despite disliking Spain for past and present sins, to avoid losing customers or abusing his adopted country.

Calypso spent the next week working up in the lower Chesapeake; anchoring each night in Hampton Roads. They sailed, steamed, adjusted compass compensators, then swung ship to fill a magnetic deviation table. On July's first day they reentered Norfolk to coal, scour the ship, load supplies, then take on fresh water from a lighter brought alongside. When *Calypso* was ready for sea, and word came his orders arrived, Starke took a steam pinnace across the Elizabeth River to *Franklin*. As he boarded, commanding officer honors were rendered before Captain Terry escorted him to Admiral Brown, where he was surprised to find Captain Albert came down by train to hand-deliver them.

Albert was eager to put his plan in operation, and grinned as the large brown envelope passed to Starke, "Your orders, captain. *Calypso* is detached from Admiral Brown and assigned the Special Service Squadron. For operations, you report to me in the Secretary's office; unless I get *Maine* in March."

"Congratulations, sir."

"We'll see," he mused, "but, best of luck. These orders include no surprises, just what we've discussed often enough, so there's no need to review them now. Take your time and let me know if you believe modification necessary," then he chuckled, "I believe Olivia and Isabella are also interested in *Calypso*, if correspondence's any judge."

With less jocularity, Admiral Brown came forward, shook Starke's hand, looked directly into his eyes, "I doubt we'll meet again, captain. This is my last duty station, but when you see your uncle or father, give them my compliments."

Then he paused, without releasing Starke's hand, to add, "I wish you well with your command and, while it's probably inappropriate, good hunting."

Starke left the interview accompanied by Captain Terry. A short man with pronounced paunch, long white sideburns and dark mustache, his appearance better suited a university lectern, especially with glasses. However, he entered the Naval Academy at sixteen, went on the Red River Expedition at twenty, received a small command, then others, and accomplished several impressive actions at sea. He also proved a friend to *Calypso* behind the scenes. As they walked towards the quarterdeck, he smiled, "I hear you're for warmer waters and my XO must find something else to fill time besides Lieutenant Watson's schemes."

At the quarterdeck, Stark paused, grasped his hand, then added "Captain, I appreciate *Franklin*'s help, if I can return the favor, please let me know. With your permission?" Starke then saluted the flag and walked down the brow to the piers where his steam pinnace, doubling as the gig, waited with steam up.

Calypso left Norfolk on Independence Day, normally holiday routine, and a Saturday, usually a half-holiday. Although her sea lawyers had not yet hung shingles, Starke knew they were enlightening individual messes. However, Admiral Brown and Captain Albert emphasized the value of an inconspicuous departure, so she slipped away before the local celebrations. Both main boilers were lit off hours before the pilot arrived with two tugs. Then, under his direction, one breasted *Calypso* from the pier while the other passed a headline to the bow. Once underway, the towing tug belched smoke as her engines demanded increased steam, and the first tug cast off. *Calypso* glided down a glasslike Elizabeth River to Hampton Roads, leaving a long, smooth undulating wake that eventually touched anything moored at piers on either side. As the ferry landing passed, Starke thought briefly of Katherine, then returned to the pilot, river traffic, and wondering how their crew would fare at sea.

Once in Hampton Roads and clear of the channel, the headline was dropped and tug fell off to port; leaving for the yard after several steam whistle toots. Under her own power, *Calypso* gained speed, retracing the course of Katherine's steamer. With Watson having the deck and pilot conning, Starke took time to watch the Hygeia slide astern. Near the bay entrance, *Calypso* slowed, a pilot boat nudged alongside, and Ensign Blair walked their pilot to the bark's waist. With the pilot boat clear, *Calypso* regained speed under a plume of black smoke, and soon thrust into the Atlantic, leaving Capes Henry and Charles merged into the horizon. Watson requested permission to raise staysails despite relatively benign seas, confident the ship would roll less with canvas up, and help the crew adjust.

Starke knew staysails were all they would spread for some time, since *Calypso* must steam against the Gulf Stream, with prevailing winds from southwest or south. Ensign Dunbar prepared a track for Port Royal and was navigating along it, watched closely by Watson and Starke. After steaming far enough east by south into the Atlantic to clear Cape Hatteras, the compass card spun slowly as the helm went over, beginning their turn towards Port Royal. *Calypso* slowly heeled to port, her clipper bow curtseyed into oncoming swells, then she lifted, shook off seawater racing across her forecastle, and steadied on course.

At four the next morning, Starke returned to his day cabin, stripped to undershirt and trousers then wedged himself between commode, washbasin, and water closet. This served to steady small scissors nipping his thin, dark, beard. Assisted by bare toes clawing a foothold on the gyrating, planked deck, he finished trimming, then shaved using a safety razor bought in Norfolk. In the washbasin, a cupful of translucent water slid across white porcelain, failing to gain the rim. Rolling about the bottom, it slipped upward, subsided, then attempted another direction.

Had there been more water, some would have escaped, but this was fresh, rationed to prioritize feedwater and drinking. The minimum allowance of potable water was one gallon each day, since the limited supply was stored in tanks replenished by distilling equipment or, after a medical officer's inspection, lighters. Most *Calypso* sailors owned canteen-like containers to store their ration. However, there was an unlimited seawater supply for washing decks, laundering, flushing heads, and brushing teeth. While it benefited teeth and preserved wood decks, even special soaps refused to lather and residue was left on on clothes and hammocks.

A small hanging mirror slapped and swung against the wall. Staysails helped, but the ship's gyrations were still a steamer's corkscrew motion of pitch, roll, yaw, surge, sway and heave. Driven by a single bronze screw, her clipper bow cut down and forward into each swell, submerged to the bob-stays, then recovered with water spraying up and over the main deck. Intermittently, she would lose rhythm and scoop over a ton of roiling gray-white Atlantic to cascade aft then escape through scuppers and openings under bulwarks. During every cycle, the rising bow rolled to starboard, hesitated, then, while descending, fell off to port as it plunged into an undulating, gray ocean. In this fashion, *Calypso*, met wind and sea nearly bow-on as she steamed south southwest for Port Royal, trailing a light smudge of gray-black smoke. Although their course was possible only under steam, it meant constant pounding, punctuated periodically by her fantail stern slapping the sea with a crash, and triple-expansion engine's constant throbbing that raced to a hammering crescendo each time the four-bladed screw rose from the water, spun free, then took a load as it reentered the sea.

Calypso took a beating throughout the night, but weathered the long gray swells, bald of whitecaps, reasonably well. Despite this, Starke decided slightly altering course and speed might ease the passage and avoid unnecessary strain on ship and crew. Returning his razor to its steel case, he made a note to bring it up with Watson and Dunbar during morning celestial observations. If they acted before hammocks were stowed in steel bins designated nettings by custom, a more sedate ride would make seven-thirty breakfast and ensuing events less challenging. That would be especially welcome today since it was the month's first Sunday, which meant captain's muster and inspection, Articles of War reading, divine service, then afternoon rope-yarn. As the ship lurched unexpectedly, Starke swayed, then caught himself. The motion, and being just out of port, meant a large number would muster in the "or accounted for" column. Most were coming off months on a receiving ship or recovering from their first open ocean night; and gaining sea-legs on steamers took longer than ships steadied under a press of canvas. This included Starke, who kept rock candy in a glass jar on his desk to ward off the first symptoms.

Above him, braced against the pilothouse chart table, Ensign Dunbar entertained similar thoughts as he looked out over the forecastle, felt the ship drop, then rise. He was assigned navigator by the Department and next in line to command after Watson. That meant regulations freed him from deck watches, charged him to relieve watch officers for specific reasons, and placed electrical equipment, including the dynamo room, under his control. While offshore, maintaining

Calypso's position required a navigation regimen with celestial fixes calculated three times each day using stars, sun, planets, and time; with estimated, or dead reckoning, positions plotted between each fix. Nearer shore, they would also pilot, using lights, landmarks, lightships, buoys, and such. His navigator's workday underway, after shooting evening stars, also included drafting night orders for Watson's review and Starke's approval. Both officers usually added a short note before signing, then it went to the pilothouse, and was strictly followed.

Starke preferred his night, and standing, orders, guide rather than direct, but needed to observe the officers first. For that reason, he was often in the pilothouse or, at night, the sea cabin just aft. He also disliked having only two officers assigned deck watches, instead of the three Navy regulations prescribed. On the positive side, it meant both were linked to one of the two enlisted watch sections identified by a shoulder stripe on each sailor's uniform; with Ensign Martyn having the port section and Ensign Blair the starboard.

Engineering was also in two watches, under different officers and orders, with Osbourne taking one and O'Leary the other, since they were an engineer short. Unlike the pilothouse, Starke seldom made nocturnal visits to their spaces, believing it might disturb the subterranean world's rhythm. Days were different, so the previous afternoon, after reviewing the steam log and officers' call, he toured engineering with Osbourne, and planned to make it a habit. That world's denizens were better paid than other sailors, but unable to fully rid themselves of coal dust, and forced to labor in humid temperatures never below ninety, and more often well over a hundred degrees.

Finishing morning ablutions, Starke buttoned the undress blue blouse and rifled through items shuffled inside the slant-top wood desk until Hiroyuki Yamashita, cabin steward, brought a large, white ceramic mug of black coffee. He already knew Starke liked an early morning cup, although captain and crew only breakfasted after morning tasks finished. Like all small ships, *Calypso*'s cabin steward cleaned, cooked, and generally attended his commander. Although pay was lower and work demanding when the captain was present, there was greater freedom and status; along with the temptation to gratify crew curiosity. Previously assigned to *Franklin*, he was aware commanders changing ships could keep their steward, but Starke had none, so requested an interview with Watson and obtained a transfer to the vacant position.

Starke knew very little of Yamashita, besides having a reputation for being discrete, but was comfortable with Watson's selection, since he had been in Far East, and made friends with three Academy classmates from Japan. All were now captains: Serata had *Kongo* after *Katsuragi, Manju, Tenryu,* and *Yamato*; Yenosuke was the naval attaché in China after *Akagi, Tsukushi,* and *Akitsushima*; and Uryu held the same position in Paris after commanding *Akagi*. While his friends' good fortune pleased him, their progress and situations enhanced his uncle's offers. However, playing with a silver napkin ring as the steward left, he admitted most junior lieutenants would give a great deal for *Calypso*, so he stood, adjusted his uniform's white standing collar, checked the blue blouse's buttons, and retrieved a visored cap from the wall rack. Leaving the white mug, with grounds and brown stains patterning its bottom, he climbed to the ship's pilothouse, carefully navigating shifting decks and moving ladders. Before entering, he verified the flying bridge lookout was stationed, his requirement when the officer of the deck was inside the pilot house. Entering the mahogany structure through its starboard side door, he saw the gray and black shapes of the watch, helm, voice tubes, and EOT begin revealing color from morning pre-twilight breaching tall glass windows. It seemed he was just in time for the brief interval stars, planets, and horizon would be visible for shooting their altitudes with sextants.

Watson, Dunbar, and Chief Quartermaster Owen already completed preparations and Martyn was checking the steering compass. Returning salutes, Starke extracted his father's Parkinson & Frodsham sextant from its wooden case, and they climbed to the flying bridge. Dunbar and his chief quartermaster were accomplished, but Watson's surveying experience gave him the edge. The yeoman and quartermaster mates usually participated or assisted, but not today. In future, there would be a naval cadet as well, since they maintained a navigational notebook for the examination board in two years.

While preparing his instrument, Starke concluded he disliked the custom of saluting a captain at each meeting when a hat was worn, although he never considered it before. Saying, "As you were," dispensed with it, but was not always appropriate and equally onerous if repeated constantly. As he finished adjusting his sextant, the ship turned and slowed to ease the ride, then Watson, using a hand chronometer synchronized to the ship's, recorded times for Starke, Dunbar, and Owen as they shot preselected celestial bodies. When *Calypso* resumed course and speed, Starke went to his cabin, leaving the others at the chart table to reduce and compare their sights, obtain a fix, prepare the morning report; then recommend adjusting or maintaining course and speed.

When Starke returned, Dunbar asked to come slightly west. This would place wind and sea further off the port bow and give staysails more bite, which Starke approved since his and Dunbar's positions were close. *Calypso* came several degrees starboard, steadied, and the pounding subsided into a prolonged roll as she shouldered through sea and wind unchanged from the previous day. The turn west also took *Ca-*

lypso toward South Carolina's coastline, rather than paralleling it, so they would now raise it above Port Royal Sound, then turn south, relying on landmarks and buoys until sighting the Martin's Industry lightship, where a harbor pilot would embark. While slightly riskier, especially with a green crew, it did take *Calypso* inshore of the Havana-to-Halifax route sailing ships favored, so fewer head-to-head meetings with them might be expected; and windjammers coming off the Southern Route from the English Channel and Bay of Biscay would likely pass further east.

The change immediately relieved sailors forming to pass hammocks through a one-foot ring, signifying they were rolled tight enough to stow. With an easier motion, they could focus on this and other tasks, without fear of being tossed against their ship or each other. Landsmen were particularly grateful, since poorly wrapped hammocks received no sympathy from petty officers, and could bring punishment. As *Calypso* drove forward, ashes were hoisted, then dumped overboard, and the underway routine continued: colors, watch relief, clothes washing, sweep down, and hosing the decks with seawater. When morning took hold and dark, overcast night passed, *Calypso* cruised easily over Atlantic swells with running lights extinguished and the bright sun sparkling a horizon separating gray-blue sea from a near cloudless blue sky. Rigging creaked and a staysail intermittently flapped, while galley exhaust, sea, and burning coal flavored the day.

Watson held officers call aft of the pilothouse with the Atlantic backing him. His day orders established routine tasks and events, but today's required little originality. Any time available before inspection was taken up preparing full dress uniforms to insure they were clean, correct, and exact. Pride or pressure were common motivators, but any immune to these risked appropriate punishment. Yamashita laid out Starke's uniform in the day cabin, then lightly oiled his blade, honored its care was entrusted to him, because it was an honest weapon, not accoutrement. He knew the captain's uniform must be flawless when inspecting the crew, since they returned the compliment, which reflected on the captain's steward. Starke considered delaying inspection because the crew was adjusting, and roll still pronounced, but ritual was expected, there was no real reason not to, and the crew would be alert for timidity. After this monthly captain's inspection, the Articles of War read, and divine service held, what remained was rope-yarn Sunday for the off-watch.

For breakfast, Yamashita offered fried eggs, ham, rice, and coffee. The rice made sense because it stored better than potatoes, but seemed odd at first. Starke also purchased cabin stores rather than join the wardroom mess. He could do either, but wanted to eat in his cabin and minimize interference with wardroom life, since it served as social club and dining room for officers. Watson appeared relieved and let slip *Winston A. Capps'* commander ate in the wardroom and, with even fewer officers, it was extremely oppressive on the best days. Swirling residual coffee grounds around the base of a white china cup embossed with golden eagle, Starke admitted he also wished to observe Watson's reign. Executive officers were not as fully segregated from their fellows as the captain, so this allowed Starke to see if he curried favor, became a martinet, or achieved balance. Starke was aware the best commands had fair, effective, and efficient executive officers implementing the captain's direction and daily routine. This left their commanders free to monitor execution, act if necessary, and not concentrate on basics. It was common sense, and codified by Navy regulations, but relied on those involved.

While dressing, he decided the inspection would also provide insight into Watson's progress generally. Starke was ready when the master-at-arms knocked at the cabin door; reporting the navigator had the watch, and crew formed by division. Outside, he was greeted by Watson, then guided to deck division, mustered on the forecastle. Chief Weaver stood easily on a swaying deck directly behind Martyn, who clearly saw his immediate future depended on the division and its chief. After snapping a salute, the ensign reported present and/or accounted for, then stated they were standing by for inspection. He was undoubtably coached, or learned, never to say ready for inspection, which could be taken as a challenge.

The formation opened ranks and Starke quickly, but thoroughly, scanned each sailor top-to-bottom, with his yeoman recording discrepancies. Wearing the Medal of Honor, Chief Weaver was instead greeted. The award was especially conspicuous because few sailors, and fewer officers, wore any ribbons or medals. Since the war, these were often awarded for lifesaving, but Weaver's came from a landing in Korea twenty-five years before when sailors and marines took three forts. A landsman then, Weaver was among those assaulting the Hwaseong Fortress on a hill overlooking Asan bay. Inside the fort, his party was surprised by several Koreans and, too scared to run, unintentionally made his stand with pistol and cutlass over a wounded officer; giving observers a different perspective. Starke learned little beyond that, since he preferred talking seamanship, and wore the award only when required.

Each division mustered sailors with minor discrepancies or suffering the inevitable last minute smudge from door or bulkhead as they formed up. Some were landsmen coming off an unsettling night at sea and still perfecting the secrets, shortcuts, and embellishments of neckerchief tying, shoe polishing, and other niceties. Improvement would come, but

Starke was satisfied division officers and chiefs were examining men, uniforms, and equipment at daily inspections.

When that completed, the crew reassembled aft where Starke slowly read the first three Articles of War, which he thought appropriate since the crew was about to be dismissed for divine service. The paymaster read respectfully from Genesis, then finished with the Lord's Prayer. It was a short, forthright observance, since Wiggs held sermons to common moral values, avoided religious harangues, and never evangelized. He was also about right on temperance, although that proclivity merited watching since Watson mentioned he opposed a wardroom wine mess, then joined, despite regulations allowing him to decline.

While Starke shared neither Wigg's abstinence or Tyson's enthusiasm, drink was every command's burden. Distilled liquor was prohibited during the war, except a small medical store, but all ships had wine storerooms built in, and each wardroom allowed a wine mess for meals and social gatherings. Otherwise, beer, ale, and wine were left to individual commanders' discretion. Starke was philosophically inclined to allow rather than deny the crew libations after feeding coal to a hot furnace or spending a day in blistering sun; especially with rationed tank water's distinct, pungent taste. He also suspected prohibition encouraged debauches ashore, but knew many incidents, infractions, altercations, and frictions would be alcohol inspired, with some sailors and officers, lacking restraint. After lengthy consideration, he concluded no halfway measures were possible since asking the master-at-arms to enforce a policy permitting and prohibiting the same drink was perilous at best. Except for a wine mess, *Calypso* would be a dry ship, and, in penance, he would restrict his personal use to special occasions, then drink more tea and coffee to mask tank water's flavor.

Unlike religion, Wiggs proved a persistent evangelist for a general mess to replace the traditional practice of assigning sailors to numerous small ones that elected their own cooks. Under current practice, each sailor's food allowance was split. One part was held for basic food and standard navy utensils, but the rest went directly to them. The second amount was then entrusted to their cook for buying what was needed above the meager basic ration. While allowing choice, quality varied and cooks became a large portion of any crew. There was also no training, and constant temptation to misspend or steal funds. Ensign Niblack, one of Starke's Naval Academy acquaintances, won a Naval Institute prize making the same case as Wiggs. The temptation to free up men by combining messing benefits and problems into one also intrigued Starke, but he was unwilling to experiment with a new crew on a ship not designed for it.

Several hymns were undertaken as *Calypso* cut diagonally, through rolling swells, then rope-yarn Sunday began. Many sailors would spend this time on the main deck, backs against a bulwark or caulking off under a warming sun, free of mosquitoes, gnats, and flies. Yeoman Third Class Matthias Eberhardt would open a midship stall with his portable sewing machine, or hurdy gurdy, to make uniforms for fellow sailors. The ship's library, overseen by the navigator and expanded by Starke's contributions, was also popular. Others smoked in main deck areas set aside for it, and scuttlebutt flourished.

Nothing changed for those standing watch. Steer the ship, navigate, shovel coal, remove ashes, tend feedwater levels, oil bearings, and adjust staysail sheets. Cooks from each mess also worked to prepare the noon meal, stewards the wardroom's, and Yamashita warmed Starke's canned corn beef and cabbage. Just as Starke began eating, a seaman arrived, saluted, waited until his captain's cloth napkin returned to the table, then handed over a small pile of twelve o'clock reports, with the officer of the deck's compliments and request for permission to strike eight bells on time. The cabin's wall clock showed fifteen minutes shy of noon, time enough for the messenger to return to the pilothouse. On the hour, *Calypso*'s bell sounded twice, then this repeated three times to signal the morning watch's end. While eating, Starke resolved to invite officers and cadets to join him in future, one at a time, then left the table for Yamashita to clear. At the slant-top desk, he resumed reviewing and approving various documents.

The morning fix showed eight to nine knots good, which suggested they would raise the Martin's Industry lightship at night, or too late to catch a morning flood, so Dunbar was told to slow the ship after his noon sight. This placed them off the South Carolina coast in early evening. Once there, they would run south along it until early Monday morning, raise the lightship, enter with the flood, go up the river, then moor at Port Royal naval station.

Starke's work was intermittently disrupted by calls to pilothouse or flying bridge for ships passing close aboard. Most were under sail. Some dipped colors, which were promptly acknowledged, but many did not because *Calypso* had a merchant ship's appearance and the States had no mercantile ensign. Those who did, probably spotted 4-inch guns under canvas, or a large, uniformed crew. Coastal traffic increased by late afternoon, but they still raised less than a dozen ships, with few passing close aboard.

Returning to the pilothouse, Starke scanned Dunbar's chart and notes, read the sailing directions, and tried to recall Port Royal. A large river system emptied into Port Royal Sound, with the shipyard on Parris Island, along Harbor River's northern branch just below the city. At the sound's entrance, off a large sand bank fifteen miles northeast of Tybee Light, was the 100 foot schooner-rigged lightship, *Martin's Industry*, with two masts topped by lanterns and reflectors. Moored there since 1892, it would soon leave for refitting and reassignment. Nearby, they would take a pilot, then cross the bar, enter the sound, and head upriver. As they steamed towards the coast, small adjustments were made to arrive at the beginning of a flood tide, since the bar was known for shifting sand, treacherous shallows, and wrecks. With the river little better, entering on a flood would allow the rising tide to lift *Calypso* if she touched.

At the naval station's shipyard, they would coal and water. Wiggs and the cooks would also have an opportunity to go ashore, but Starke decided against liberty since the crew was just settling into sea routine, they would stay only a day or so, and there were few diversions close by. The closest city, Port Royal, survived the war intact because Federals occupied it early to support blockading squadrons, but its neighbor, Beaufort, was burned. That city now had the larger population, mostly Colored or Negro, with its most prominent citizen, the past Collector of Customs and congressman, Robert Smalls. Local plantation families fled the area during occupation, leaving ex-slaves to farm abandoned acreage until reclaimed after their return; and now the population swelled each winter with wealthy Northerners. The more industrialized Port Royal exported phosphate, agricultural products, lumber, and seafood by ship or newly constructed Charleston & Western Carolina Railroad. Between the two cities, Starke guessed a dozen or more local bars were probably in operation, but he had no idea how many allowed sailors.

After supper and eight-o'clock reports, Starke approved the night orders, sent them to the pilothouse, then started a letter to Katherine, but the Hygeia seemed months, not days, past.

Late that evening, *Calypso* turned south and began piloting down a dark coast with shoaling, indistinct coastlines, and local traffic. Despite often being with Dunbar, Starke still slept well, then woke to a clear Monday morning with no weather change and little traffic. Just after sick call and before quarters, he was requested on the flying bridge, where, using binoculars, he could just make out a large dark mound, jerking as if struck from below, with flocks of birds busily walking over it, pecking as they went. Blair, having the deck, approached, "My apologies, captain, it's a dead whale, not a derelict."

Starke looked at the determined face, dark hair, small nose, narrow mouth, and chalky complexion that defied the sun and refused to tan. A derelict was more likely since whaling ships had been forced to the Arctic for smaller right whales, while abandoned wrecks were seen relatively often. Starke let the binoculars hang from their neck strap, "It could easily have been a derelict. Remember, Mister Blair, all captains are at the officer of the deck's service. Think through a decision, then live with it. We'll accomplish some shooting in any case, please clear for action."

Controlling surprise and adrenalin, Blair nonchalantly turned to the boatswain mate of the watch, "Boats. All hands, general quarters."

The boatswain mate acknowledged, lifted the small, curved steel boatswain's pipe dangling from an intricate, black lanyard, piped silence, then the call to action; quickly repeated throughout the ship by word of mouth, other pipes, and voice tubes. Men shot from hatches and doors, then raced forward on the starboard side, aft on the port, to form gun crews, join the repair party, man engine room stations, or fill other watch, quarter and station bill slots. Osbourne relieved Blair to ensure the ship's chief engineer was with the captain, then, as controlled confusion settled to anticipation, Watson reported manned and ready. Starke knew he irrevocably disrupted his executive officer's plans, but that went with the territory, and this would prove worthwhile if some gunnery weakness was exposed confronting a dead whale rather than warship or fleeing filibuster.

Although this mammal's ability to swim was long past and *Calypso*'s hull shape meant seventy-five percent of her speed came with one boiler, general quarters required both. While it would normally take hours adding a second one to the main steam system, it was already lit-off at four o'clock that morning to insure a stable system for entering the sound. After directing Osbourne to slow, Dunbar estimated their position on the chart, and a quartermaster logged it. Turning, Starke smiled easily, "Mr. Watson, let's see how our gun crews shoot. Slow and safe. There's no threat from that gentleman."

Watson replied. He was obviously calculating a shoot's effect on his day orders, since a thorough cleaning always followed, and one that would be especially onerous if black powder Gatlings cut loose. Starke wanted him near the gun crews, since this was not a weekly aiming drill, and felt his gunnery interest might salve this obvious frustration, so he nodded towards the ladder, "Take the guns, Mr. Watson, we'll give you two runs at 500 yards. Mr. Osbourne, I'll remain on the flying bridge."

The executive officer quickly left for the forecastle and its 4-inch mount ringed by a gun crew apprehensively eyeing shells laid out for use. A case might split, one of the guns hang or misfire, and burst ear drums from muzzle blasts, a too common casualty. Below deck, the surgeon and his baymen prepared their wardroom for such casualties, and worse. Once everyone reported ready, Starke called down through the brass voice tube's funnel to Osbourne, "Log the whale carcass off our bow as a navigational hazard."

Osbourne responded, "Yes, sir," while a quartermaster entered the exchange.

Starke followed up with, "Mr. Dunbar, bring up your stadimeter and tables. Let's see how the eye compares with your readings. Mr. Osbourne, please take us upwind 500 yards. That carcass'll be ripe."

Suddenly realizing the noxious implication of freeing gas from more than fifty tons of putrefying flesh, Osbourne, gratefully responded, "Yes, sir," then, "Helmsman, come left to zero-nine-zero, ahead slow."

The ship's wheel spun, then stopped as the sailor caught its thin spokes, then moved it again to steady the swinging bow. The EOT handle rotated until one pointer centered on ahead slow. Someone in the engine room did the same, causing its second pointer to match the first. Reaching little more than bare steerageway, *Calypso* lost way, then began slowly rolling as the helmsman reported, "Steady zero-nine-zero, sir."

Osbourne responded, "Steady, zero-nine-zero, aye," then turned to Starke, "Steady on course, captain."

Starke nodded, checked the horizon, then turned to the messenger, "Tell Mr. Watson, the forward mount has permission to fire two common rounds."

"Permission to fire two common rounds, aye, sir."

Starke and Dunbar were on the flying bridge behind white canvas windscreens laced to lifelines. With a nearly unrestricted view to the horizon, they watched the rolling ship, gun crews, and further out, a swollen whale carcass with water lapping against and sometimes over it. Strong smells of steam mixing with coal smoke and stack heat, enveloped the slowing ship as wind crossing her decks died away. Except for dull engine vibrations, slapping at the hull, lines and blocks striking each other, and the occasional cough, *Calypso* was silent. The carcass passed slowly down the ship's side, perhaps 500 yards off, but Starke thought closer to 400. Several birds on the distorted, leathery mass glanced at the distant ship before resuming their attempt to feed, while others took flight, climbing out and away. A few circled *Calypso* or landed in her wake. Once shed of most surface scavengers, Starke thought the carcass resembled Jules Verne's undersea boat.

From the flying bridge, he watched three sailors in the forward gun crew take station around the blackened weapon, while five supporting them lined up nearby. Already, the protective tarp was off to one side, rolled and secured to cleats along with the muzzle bag that replaced wood tompions at sea. The men were in various states of undress, including bare feet, but designated boarders wore sidearms. Watson stood to one side, letting the crew prepare. He obviously intended to insure safety, but leave the shooting to them. Starke noted that as another point in the man's favor. More than once he watched executive officers gratuitously interfere, and it seldom ended well.

When the gun captain motioned, a 4-inch round, projectile and brass cartridge case, was lifted from a small ready-service magazine, cradled in the loader's arms, then carried to the gun. The breech opened to receive it, was slammed shut, then the breechblock locked with a long lever. Ready to fire, two men moved handwheels that aimed the mount by training it side-to-side, while the gun captain used a smaller one from under the breech to raise and lower, or point, the barrel. Taking aim through iron sights and gauging roll, he suddenly moved clear, said something, then jerked the lanyard as everyone covered their ears.

First came a barely audible click, then an ear-shattering flat crack, brilliant muzzle flash, and gray-black mushroom cloud. Within seconds, smoke settled on the gun crew and spread over the deck. Despite a recoil apparatus, the detonation transmitted through the ship, and Starke felt the muzzle blast against his face. Like a black rock, he just made out the thirty-pound projectile arc towards the whale, pass just above, skip over the water several times, then sink quietly. The second round struck just short of the carcass, skipped over, then struck the sea at a different angle, detonating forty yards beyond in an irregular eruption.

Osbourne ordered, "Starboard your helm, steady two-seven-zero," as Watson left the forward mount and went aft. With the wheel spinning, the helmsman responded, "Starboard your helm, steady two-seven-zero, aye," and Osbourne acknowledged by repeating. When moving this slow, the ship required large amounts of rudder before responding; and holding course more goal than expectation. Starke felt *Calypso* stagger when the rudder finally bit, then heel to port as acrid powder smoke joined an existing coal, steam, and canvas windscreen bouquet. With *Calypso* at bare steerageway, using more rudder initially, then easing it into the turn was best, so Osbourne coaxed the helmsman, "Don't put it in the stops, but use the rudder you need," then acknowledged the response.

With Dunbar calling out ranges, Osbourne swung further out for the next pass; which Starke thought should aid their shooting. As the turn increased, *Calypso* lurched through a broad trough between swells, then settled nearly broadside to the whale. Although both mounts had permission to fire, the aft went first, with the same flash and noise. The projectile struck just above the whale's waterline, penetrated the putre-fying mass, then exploded. Decomposing muscle, blubber, and organs, partly absorbed the blast, but putrid gas already stretched the hide close to bursting, while birds pecking and strikes from below weakened it. The detonation ruptured, burst, and deflated the carcass; launching chunks, pieces, and fragments in all directions. As remnants settled, and water calmed, a second round drove into the sea just beyond to explode in a ragged water burst. *Calypso's* 4-inch guns were firing at short range with relatively flat trajectory, but their shells' detonations still caused Starke to recall a Chinese battleship's twelve-inch rounds creating huge water columns that seemingly hung forever.

Through the voice tube, he told the pilothouse, "Log the whale's destruction, secure from general quarters, and return to base course," then, turning to the navigator, still calling ranges, "Mr. Dunbar, give us a course to regain track."

Starke left the flying bridge for his day cabin; and restoring routine to Watson, Dunbar, and Osbourne. Looking over the expanding wake as *Calypso* gained speed, very little of the creature remained above water, but what did seemed well-marked by eagerly converging birds. The shooting was good, even exceptional, for a first attempt. Green gun crews were unsure what to expect and accuracy still relied on individual gun captain eyesight, timing, and skill with the graduated iron sights. More aiming drills and live firing at longer ranges were needed to improve confidence and hone skills, but the forward gun bracketed their target. If it had been a ship, the rounds would have struck the hull midship, the aft gun's results were roughly the same, but their direct hit earned them bragging rights, and denied the ship's lesser ordnance an opportunity.

Starke returned to the flying bridge when the lightship was sighted off Martins' Industry sand bar, marking the Port Royal Sound entrance. Though binoculars, he studied the forty-year old ship; a short, high-sided schooner with vestigial bowsprit, and two masts bulging at their trucks with lights and day shapes. As *Calypso* closed, its small spencer masts paralleling the main and fore became clear. The mainmast boom swung out over the stern, with the foremast's same appendage angled up to clear a tall, slender stack rising from her deckhouse. Whaleboats hung from rotary davits and the ship's name, same as the station, was painted on her side.

Watson formally requested permission to send the crew to sea and anchor station, then boatswain mates' began piping, although the men were already preparing. Staysails were struck below and a whaleboat swung out on round bar davits, its coxswain and crew standing by to rescue anyone going over. The port anchor, freed from its billboard, was swung out and left hanging from the anchor davit, ready for letting go. Sextant in hand, Chief Quartermaster Owen scanned the coast for usable landmarks while Dunbar called out possibilities and worked the navigation chart. Weaver was on the forecastle, mostly encouraging, but occasionally graphically displaying frustration or feigning disgust.

Starke embraced mornings at sea, especially those like today's, with no real wind, calm surface, warming sun, and the water various shades of light blue and gray. Here and there a bird would descend, fly inches above the ocean, snatch a fish feeding too close to the surface, then soar up and away. Occasionally brown pelicans dove headfirst into the water with such force their necks must break, then surface with a morning meal, or begin their long takeoff to get airborne for another attempt.

Calypso would continue on course just southeast of the lightship, then turn starboard at the channel entrance buoy, to a northwest heading that aligned with the next buoy. The ship swung rapidly since her way was significant, then ahead slow was rung up as they settled on course. *Martin's Industry* passed down her starboard side, close enough to watch the crew work. One or two paused to wave as the tall, black bark ghosted past leaving dark smoke fading to translucent gray before dissipating completely.

As the ship turned, reference points rotated, transforming *Calypso*'s world, and placing the coast off her bow and lightship astern. Distant breakers and swells were intermittently visible to port, and a small schooner, once partly obscured by the lightship, approached, with its booms swung out to catch the light air. It brushed *Calypso*, at the boarding ladder rigged to starboard just long enough for a pilot to grasp it, then half pull, half climb on board. Blair brought him to the flying bridge where Starke, Martyn, and others waited. Except for dry-docks or transiting canals, ship captains determined whether pilot or conning officer controlled, but were held accountable either way, since pilots possessed intimate local area knowledge but not equal familiarity with each ship.

Starke began, "Good morning, captain. Welcome aboard *Calypso*."

"Thank you captain. A fine ship. I watched her round the lightship. Smartly handled. Thought she was a cut-down clipper until seeing your forward gun mount. Nothing large's coming out and not much local traffic yet, so it's an opportunity for one of the youngsters to take her in."

"Appreciate that, captain."

Martyn saw the bearded pilot, a course blend of mariner, fisherman, and farmer, walk towards him; and felt a crushing weight. He anticipated their pilot taking over, but the captain made it clear that was not the case. As the older mariner spoke, he listened closely, with apprehension, to how they would run up a wide channel with shifting sandbars on either side, and several shallow areas in or just off it. When breakers were visible off the starboard bow, *Calypso* would come port thirty degrees, to steer roughly north northwest. More breakers would pass down the starboard side until they entered the sound between two points of land, with Parris Island dead ahead. Coming right, they would travel up the Harbor River's north branch, taking the island to port, follow the river, avoid any shallows, and make small turns to port until reaching the naval station.

As *Calypso* gained speed, a small blue-gray dolphin took station off the starboard side for a few yards, dove under the bow, reappeared, then vanished. Dunbar coordinated the ship's navigation effort, provided information to Starke, and scanned for problems. *Calypso* passed between the points of land, then made her turn, as a strong marsh odor enveloped the ship; mixing with sea, steam, and coal smoke. Starke watched the pilot work calmly with Martyn, offering assurance, confidence, and deliverance. Walking the young officer about, he pointed out landmarks, revealed local currents, and explained what might be expected. Starke fondled an unlit pipe, recalling his introduction to navigating channels. Shores and shallows that appeared distant as an observer, suddenly shrank until it seemed you had marginal control of a huge, unstoppable, awkward object hurtling through a narrow, crooked tube.

The pilot guided *Calypso* upriver of the naval station, where a tug made up to port, then coaxed her around until the bow pointed downriver. She was then eased alongside the coal pier, starboard-side-to, until the hull pressed against two floating camels holding her off the pilings. When the first mooring line dropped over a bollard, the ensign came down from the mainmast at the run, and a second rose from the stern. Starke observed Martyn's tension drain and confidence increase as the last line went over. After mooring at Port Royal's naval station without dramatics, doubling lines began, and their main engine shut down. Observing this, a boat came to take their pilot to an outbound schooner; but before leaving the flying bridge, Starke thanked him and they shook hands.

Once he was away, Starke turned to the ensign, "Well done, Mr. Martyn."

CHAPTER SIXTEEN
Port Royal Hiatus

Calypso lay at a substantial pier, stern upriver, with mooring lines given just enough slack to accommodate the tide's rise and fall. Absent a breeze, she floated in heat and humidity on sedate river currents carrying pungent odors and debris down the port side, past marshland and riverbanks, then into the sound. Beyond the wooden pier, a dirt road paralleled the shore, then passed into the shipyard where two-story industrial buildings partly obscured the commandant's house and dry-dock. Similarly, a large white coaling shed concealed other red-brick, and several white frame, structures. Beyond the dry-dock, a red steam-driven crane with black stack and latticework boom lay idle on rails that wound through the yard and probably linked to a commercial rail line.

Soon after mooring, Osbourne was at his stateroom desk across from two open portholes framed by dark green curtains. Looking up, he thought opening those air ports was more gesture than anything so long as the motionless bark was enveloped by still, hot, and humid air. Wiping a light sweat, he returned to reports and notes spread over a varnished oak surface, then entered coal calculations on requisite forms. One bunker, emptied by the Chesapeake Bay operations and transit, needed cleaning, inspecting, then refilling. Topping off a second would achieve a full load-out, but mixing old and new coal was poor practice. Laying the pencil aside, he recalled newspapers extolling coal as dusky diamonds; clever wording by someone whose experience was small coal stoves or distant observation. Coal grew more dangerous the longer it sat in bunkers, and yet it was tempting to put off opening more troublesome ones. The various coal types and sources also demanded separation, since their handling and properties varied. Some types burned near smokeless, others yielded greater power, several produced mostly clinkers, and a few refused to burn. Ships made do with what was available, or, since many of world's sources were poor, coaled at specific ports and stations where quality coal was stockpiled. His bunkering scheme considered all of this.

Despite choosing steam engineering, Osbourne enjoyed his academy cruise under sail, so long as steam-powered winches, distillers, and dynamos were present and working. *Calypso* especially intrigued him, since her sailing capability reduced coal usage and allowed near unlimited range. Although some hybrids like her were faster under canvas, any ship without steam remained at the mercy of local conditions and confined to global routes set by prevailing winds. Besides, steam was indispensable for short voyages, contrary winds, rhumb line courses, great circle routes, maneuvering, or combat. His black gang gave *Calypso* these advantages to the extent their skill and stamina allowed. Achieving this required experience, practice, and dedication since water tube boilers demanded meticulous care, even when idle.

Osbourne had yet to see *Calypso* under canvas, except briefly in the Chesapeake, but Watson seemed skillful and Starke exceptional. Both were equally comfortable with steam, which was even more reassuring. Starke made it clear officers and naval cadets would sail and steam the ship, which was unusual. Total accountability caused many commanders to limit opportunity and neither train or trust every officer to handle the ship. Even more unusual, Starke included his engineers and engineer cadets; then offered to rotate deck officers and naval cadets through engineering watches. Osbourne expected their commander to follow through, since, despite the brief exposure, he thought Starke enjoyed a unique mix of teaching ability, knowledge, and experience. He never seemed to force officers beyond their capability, but constantly coaxed them past complacency, evolution by evolution. Osbourne felt equally good about Watson, believing him fair, consistent, and interested in the black gang's success.

Besides satisfaction with his fellows, their triple-expansion engine operated flawlessly underway, although the boilers remained questionable. He now understood why he was assigned to work out or document problems and opportunities. Generating high pressure steam for triple-expansion engines, required complex systems intolerant of water level fluctuations and feedwater quality, since their small tubes passing through the firebox not only turned water to steam, but were cooled by it. Because low water or small imperfections could quickly melt piping, feedwater levels required constant attention when steady steaming, then became an art during speed changes or rough weather; and a casualty could destroy or explode the boiler, causing scalding and death. Several of *Calypso*'s tubes already needed replacing, and another was plugged underway, but Osbourne thought it too soon to conclude this was more than teething. The Port Royal stopover was welcome, however, since its navy yard would probably have material and expertise. In any event, a work request through Starke was required to find out, so he signed and forwarded it.

Another report covered a stoker thrown against the port boiler face and burned, along with several coal passers slightly injured excavating coal or moving it to boilers. This was not unusual for a green crew in heavy weather, but none was scalded or more seriously injured, and, excluding the stoker, injuries were mostly severe blisters, cuts, or bruises from holding cart handles carelessly or falling. Even so, they were fortunate in Assistant Surgeon Sidney Conrad, a medical doctor with relative ensign rank who was dedicated to medicine and passionate about cleanliness. Although articulate and intelligent, he appeared inordinately reserved, so it seemed strange Conrad chose a ship for his practice, but Osbourne learned the enticement was travel, since that and medicine were his primary interests, followed by collecting mystery novels, stories, and articles.

The coaling barge would be alongside that afternoon to be readied for the next day. That allowed Wiggs time to complete financial arrangements with Paymaster Ring at the naval station. Like all paymasters, he was busiest in port, replenishing items, obtaining those not available before, and shepherding elected cooks who must bargain with vendors. Wiggs helped anyone who asked, including Yamashita, who ordered quantities of beer, watermelons, and seafood on Starke's account.

The ship's arrival was reported to Albert and the Department in two coded telegrams, then Starke made his formal call on the commandant. Commander Charles Rockwell was a large man with white hair and darker handlebar mustache standing proud above pronounced jowls and distinct chin. The allegedly formfitting uniform draped over his square torso like a tunic, with eyes and eyebrows seemingly dragged back towards the ears. However, his demeanor left no doubt of the nerve that took him to war as a volunteer, saw him commanding a ship by its end, then sustained him during a desperate battle in Florida's swamps near St. Marks; where most of his enlisted sailors received the Medal of Honor. He also fought in the same Korean action as Weaver, and commanded several ships. After exchanging courtesies, Rockwell inquired about Albert, then asked what he needed to know about the captain's scheme. Since Port Royal could prove useful for coaling, Starke outlined his orders and approach while

Rockwell rubbed a button chin before responding slowly; obviously parsing words. Essentially, he saw Port Royal's contribution limited to filling *Calypso*'s requirements, not interfering, then asked if *Calypso*'s commander was related to Jefferson Starke. Nodding when told Jacob Starke was the son, Rockwell smiled and said the father was well known to the Gulf Coast blockading squadron. Before ending the interview, he told Starke the Justice Department's Brian Fields and the revenue cutter *Vanguard*'s First Lieutenant Hunter had come from Jacksonville by train, were staying at a Beaufort hotel, and wanted to talk. Rockwell offered to arrange the meeting, then declined further involvement. Starke was grateful, since others might have inserted themselves as senior naval officer.

It occurred the next morning in a second floor room of the red-brick building nearest the pier. Despite *Calypso* coaling, Starke brought Watson since he might be called upon to assume command. Lieutenant Hunter greeted Starke warmly and with more energy than in Washington. It seemed *Vanguard*'s boiler was under repair, so he joined Field's short excursion. Despite the first Washington meeting's understanding, Fields was chosen to come north because he worked the Southern Florida District, where *Calypso* would mostly operate. Still nondescript and somewhat rotund, his light sack suit replaced the three-piece worn during that meeting with Albert.

When Hunter, Starke, and Watson finished discussing St. Johns River jetty construction, Fields interjected, "I admit expecting little from our March meeting," then turning to Starke and Watson, added, "but a dedicated navy ship might rattle some filibusters."

Hunter smiled, "And, *Vanguard*'s cleared to join *Calypso*. I report to Captain Fischer in Washington rather than a district commander. It's a major concession, but necessary since dealing with filibusters competes with district cutters' regular duties, forces them to ignore other missions, and increases steaming time."

Everyone nodded except Watson, who saw his role as a listener, since captains spoke for their ships. Fields then began, "To ensure we're on the same sheet, please bear with me. Justice collects information from citizens, informants, and, to an extent, Pinkerton detectives. As you know, three Junta-chartered ships were libeled a year ago January in Fernandina. The courts returned them to their owners, and released their cargoes to Nathaniel Borden, owner of N.B. Borden & Company, who swore they were not consigned to insurgents. Untrue, but always impossible to prove until they arrive in Cuba. He was Spanish vice-consul in Fernandina at the time, but now works openly for the Junta's expeditionary section. Our sources are also reporting that office not only ships insurrectionists and military goods to Cuba from American ports, but uses Costa Rica, Dominican Republic, and Jamaica. Already this year, the filibuster, *J.W. Hawkins*, sank off Long Island. *Bermuda* was seized, released, and returned to the trade; where a Spanish gunboat fired on it in April. *Commodore*, *Three Friends*, *Mallory*, and *Laurada* also made runs. The Junta's using false charters, bribes, and has apparently considered seizing transport. These operations are shielded by an excellent legal operation using local attorneys but run by Horatio Rubens, a Jewish New York lawyer. He graduated from Columbia University, same as Gonzalo de Quesada y Aróstegui, a naturalized citizen lobbying for the Junta in Washington. Anyway, filibusters are charged under our Neutrality Act, and his organization's highly skilled at skirting it."

After pausing to daub his face with limp handkerchief, he soldiered on, "We've two items of interest. First, there's rumor a small filibuster expedition is forming along the Florida Keys using an old tug out of Jacksonville or Key West. The Junta prefers tugs because they don't require clearance papers to sail. He'll probably leave port empty, rendezvous with small schooners to load men and military supplies, then make the crossing. Marshals are watching our most likely ports, with *Vanguard* covering the St. Johns River to Jacksonville, and *Maine*'s steam launches enforcing a quarantine and patrolling for filibusters in Key West."

Several questions followed regarding accuracy, timing, and tug description, but it was clear no further information existed. Fields then passed out three envelopes filled with a sheaf of papers fastened by Hotchkiss staples, and looked about for water. He found none, but caught Watson's eye, who rose to open a window, hoping a passing breeze might bless the second floor room; now oppressively hot under a July sun. Fields used the disruption to swallow, wipe face and neck with a stained handkerchief, then resume, "One, maybe two, presidential proclamations on filibustering are expected, which may help; and Governor Lee's appointment as consul-general is welcome, since rumors have Williams nearly worn out."

While Starke recalled Lee's Starke mansion visit, Hunter looked up from the papers, doodled with a pencil on the envelope, then spoke, "Filibusters out of New York, or Charleston, are hard to intercept above Florida without exceptional luck, or a blockade. Besides, unless there's proof cargoes are for the rebels, seizures become shipping delays. Sabers were once claimed to be farm equipment bound for Mexico."

Starke knew it might sound preposterous, and likely a ruse, but swords, cutlasses, and machetes were not always used as intended. Starke recalled a cavalry officer who kept his saber with the pack train for rattlesnakes, and the broad-bladed agricultural tool's Cuban harvest was obvious in Havana's military hospitals.

While considering this, he heard Hunter say, "Lacking reliable information, perhaps we should work from Fernandina through the Straits of Florida. While Tampa and Cedar Key bear watching, it's probably not useful going west of the Dry Tortugas, since any Gulf Coast expedition to Cuba's north shore would pass them for a fix before running in."

Fields leafed through his notes, "True, but *Commodore* left from Charleston this March."

Hunter responded, "Even the area I proposed requires a full squadron, not two ships, so adding the Atlantic coast to New York takes us beyond impossible."

Fields shuffled his papers, "I can't disagree. The areas you suggest are where most crossings occur. *Competitor* left Key West and was caught by a gunboat, Spanish, not one of ours. Some of those on board were shot the next morning, but Consul Williams warned Weyler all American diplomatic contact would end if executions continued, so Madrid blinked. Perhaps that explains why Newcomb claims State's offered to provide whatever assistance we require."

Starke glanced at the closed door, then asked Watson to shut the window, "Sorry, but this can't get out. Captain Hunter's correct. *Calypso* will sweep those areas, plant misinformation, and enter different ports with little or no warning. Captain Albert's working this with State. I've also had false name boards created so the Junta won't be certain how many ships are at sea. *Calypso*'s mission is to disrupt Junta operations, not track down individual filibusters, because we don't have the ships or intelligence."

Fields, attempted to wipe his forehead with the sweat-stained, saturated linen while others searched pockets to follow suite. Starke ignored sweat building on face, wrist, and chest, "I plan to sweep the Straits of Florida's north side, bypass Key West, then enter the Gulf. After working-up off Dry Tortugas, *Calypso* will return along Cuba's north coast, then continue to Jacksonville or Port Royal to coal."

Hunter, thinking aloud, added, "Watch the straits' north side. You can avoid the Florida Current by hugging the coast, but it's easy to go aground." He then scanned Fields' notes again before adding, "Jacksonville's left out, and filibusters find it quite welcoming."

"I'm open to suggestions. Word's out *Calypso* will stop there, but she's fully coaled and provisioned after today, so not going up the river might prove more unsettling. Besides, *Vanguard*'s there, and it's *Boutwell*'s patrol area, so *Calypso* would just be a third ship."

Fields interjected, "Captain, I'd like you in the south, but with the new jetties, shouldn't that city and Fernandina be the focus? Henry Plant supports insurgents and Napoleon Broward, an ex-sheriff and a river pilot, loads his cargos enroute, so we can't apprehend him at the piers."

Starke responded, "Plant ships aren't running weapons and Broward knows the coast too well. *Calypso* would have to remain off the St. Johns, sacrificing her speed and range advantage, to patrol a small area better covered by fast tugs that blend with other traffic and can enter shoal water."

Hunter touched his mustache, "Yes, even *Vanguard* would be more effective."

Fields looked around then lowered his voice, "With that resolved and window closed, my next item's not in your envelopes. Since Cuban insurgents lack gunners and artillery, an expedition may exist to supply them with Hotchkiss field pieces, carriage-mounted machine guns, dynamite cannons, and gunners. The Army claims they need this specific artillery, or their infantry and cavalry will be hobbled by the artillery."

Starke recalled a similar debate in Montana over sending Gatling guns with the cavalry, especially after a scouting party tried. However, taking a fortified town required artillery unless insurgents had incredible luck or accepted heavy casualties; and perhaps they planned to overrun one Weyler declared safe, then slaughter those deemed traitors to weaken Cuban loyalist support. As Starke conjectured, Fields continued, "There's another aspect. This may also be an independent enterprise or major shift in Junta strategy. Filibusters have avoided confrontation by outrunning pursuers, relying on courts, or jettisoning cargoes. It's also rare for one to fire on naval ships, even Spanish patrol boats, for fear they'd be tried as pirates, hung without sympathy, and public support would end."

Looking at the door, then window, he almost whispered, "If this splinter group exists, it believes the Junta too cautious and shipments should be forced through, with anyone interfering attacked. There's little additional information, except rumors the ringleader's a South American or European many Junta leaders dislike or distrust."

Hunter, Starke, and Watson looked at each other, frustrated with Fields, then Hunter responded, "Was Treasury told? Smaller cutters, and even large ones, are at risk."

Starke reached the same conclusion. Was Albert aware or in the dark? Was Fields asking them to act? Looking at Justice's man, he quietly added, "I've similar questions."

Fields leaned forward, "No, you're the first. We want to limit who's approached; and only recently assembled information enough to believe these reports credible."

Starke reclined to a less upright and more comfortable position, carefully stating, "I suggest approaching Captain Albert. He'll take your information to the Secretary."

Hunter followed after his fists unclenched and jaw relaxed, "Captain Fischer's your man. Spencer from your Washington office could approach him and Albert, since they were at the March meeting."

Excluding this brief drama, they finished amicably and agreed meet again, perhaps in Key West. Outside, the Jacksonville contingent's light carriage and cinnamon gelding waited by a small watering trough with the impatient horse swatting flies with its tail, or shuddering to disrupt those feeding and encourage flight. In midmorning heat, he restlessly shifted weight between hooves and occasionally buried soft, dark nostrils into tepid water. With every move, the carriage rocked, suggesting its brake was left off. After untying the reins, Hunter and Fields boarded, waved, then left; leaving small fishtails of nearly white dust and light tracks from delicately spoked wheels. After watching them roll behind a building, *Calypso*'s two officers walked back. There was little work in the yard, so few trades were about and a lethargic, quiet atmosphere permeated its tranquil air. The fitful, half-hearted breeze added little to the shipyard dust and coal smoke ambiance besides brief bursts of river, marsh, or pine fragrance. Partway to their ship, Watson observed, "So much for engine tests and surveying, captain. Looks as though we've more than dead whales on offer."

The boatswain piped Starke on board, followed by Watson, who saluted the limp ensign halfway across, checked the captain's absentee pennant, then walked to the outboard side. A battered two-masted barge, round at either end, was alongside, gently tugging *Calypso* with worn three-strand manila lines angling up through chocks, then figure-eighted on mooring cleats. Compressed between hulls, large rope fenders shifted almost imperceptibly from the lethargic current while sailors above filled line-reinforced canvas sacks using coal forks and scoop shovels. Once full, they were leaned against others until three or four could be lifted together, swung over *Calypso*'s bulwarks, then lowered to her once pristine deck; all directed by boatswain mates using hand signals. Although the ship carried its own spar for this, the barge had two battered booms butted to thick pole-masts and small steam winches. As each lift landed near one of the round deck scuttles for filling and airing coal bunkers, another team sent dusty lumps clattering down its tube.

Then it was up to the entire black gang, working alongside their coal trimmers and passers in the bunker. Waiting between lifts in cramped semi-darkness with nose and mouth wrapped in damp cloth, mouths often stuffed with cotton, and clothing seams tucked, tied, or both; they would see what little outside light filtered through the scuttle blocked, hear coal crash through the pipe, then watch it mound as the space filled with choking dust. When visibility returned, the latest deposit was leveled across the bunker, then the filthy, sweating men attempted a few minutes respite, huddled in a corner, clear of the next injection.

Osbourne and O'Leary saw they were equipped with the best shovel or fork type, whether moving coal or feeding fireboxes, despite Wiggs' perfunctory cost protestations. The crew working the barge, however, found a cornucopia of implements with different pedigrees. Landsman Mallory Hawk cared little about this as he carefully tilted his scoop shovel into a canvas coaling sack held open by another sailor. He disliked the task, but another landsman already complained to Weaver, provoking the homely chief to respond loudly, "In Arab and Japanese ports, women carry coal to ships in baskets, son. When *Calypso* puts in there, they'll handle any work you're not up to." The embarrassed supplicant's interest, participation, and attitude quickly improved, spurred by shipmates' barbs, until he equalled or surpassed their efforts.

Hawk found shoveling coal much like grain, or pitching hay, and disliked all. He did well in school, but was forced to quit in the sixth grade and begin working the Indiana farm full time. His strangled passion for learning became a virulent loathing of farming, unlike three brothers who fell easily into its rhythm of plowing, planting, cultivating, and harvesting. Perhaps his mother once felt the same, but now found solace in Bible study and caring for seven surviving children; while their father did the same in a local tavern. Hawk finally left, worked odd jobs, then drifted to Norfolk, where he fell in with two kindred spirits looking for work at sea. The trio found merchant ship berths, even for those experienced, scarce since the panic, so they finally walked the piers to *Franklin*, where Hawk enlisted as a landsman. The second learned he was consumptive and the third determined unfit for reasons the surgeon refused to reveal. Hawk relished this new life until they entered the Atlantic where he felt weak, drunk, sick, and nauseated in a cramped, unfamiliar and disturbing world that was impossible to navigate.

He recovered as *Calypso* approached Port Royal Sound, and felt ashamed he did not hold up his end at sea; so this miserable work on a hot barge provided an opportunity to make good with deck division shipmates. On the farm he suffered through hours behind threshing machines, with lower back and biceps aching, coated by fine dust, sweat oozing from pores, and head aching. Coaling lacked the onerous need to throw forkfuls high in the air, but there was extra weight, no pebbles to suck, and a cup-like hat with small brim that almost shielded his face from the sun when unfolded. After two hours, he longed for his broad-brimmed threshing hat as rivulets of sweat and dust, from hair, armpits, and crevices, trickled down his clothes until expended or joined with other flows.

During a short pause while four bags went over, he considered some Irish, a pair of Negros and several Germans shoveling. Three appearing Portuguese or Spanish stood apart, sorting and preparing coal sacks. None were from his mess, so he did not know names, but features, mannerisms, and languages gave them away. At the barge's far end, indistinct coal-blackened sailors, wearing uniforms kept for the purpose, were recognizable only by their individual methods of warding off coal dust. Since enlisting, Hawk observed sailors were drawn to those most like them, their messmates, or watch section; although deck seaman and gunners invariably backed each other against the black gang when ashore. Despite this, *Calypso* was home and family, so they stood together for tasks like coaling or facing outsiders, whether locals or another ship. This was strengthened by an executive officer who played no favorites. Today was a good example. Everyone not on the binnacle list was working and those unable to shovel carried water, held bags, or handled lines. Like everything Watson did, it was equitable, so Hawk took a last swipe at his brow with a filthy sleeve, felt grit stick to his forehead, decided all for the ship, then pushed the shovel blade under some coal lumps while giving the handle a quick wiggle as it slid forward with a scraping sound. Feeling the back strain, he lifted, then pointed it towards an open sack held by a man turning his face to avoid the dust.

As coal crashed into the darkness, Dylan Jones, lead stoker, saw new men struggle as he shoveled, watched for slacking, insured none were buried, and kept everyone clear of the overhead chute between black vomits. It was hot, dirty work, but he was not on the barge under the July sun; or down a Pennsylvania coal mine facing bad air, explosions, and flooding after a claustrophobic descent. From a mining family, he accepted it as honest work, until owners cut wages after the panic, then warned they would again. Upset, he studied a Navy recruiting notice for stokers, thought the work similar, but above ground with steady pay, lodging, meals, and travel. After thinking it over, he decided to leave family, friends, and brothers by enlisting. His eldest sibling would have joined him but was married. From his sister-in-law's letters, he learned frustration and desperation deepened until the United Mine Workers struck in the spring. As the panic's effects and strike dragged on, he began sending money home until violence crippled the union, leaving his brother with even less to take home. Meanwhile, Jones advanced from coal trimmer to lead stoker and began studying boilers, especially *Calypso's* water-tube type, hoping to reenlist as a water tender.

The crew paused for a quick lunch on station to keep coal dust above deck, or at least some of it, then finished filling both bunkers. After sailors working the barge stacked shovels and left, they watched a small yard tug make up to it, then use current, rudder, and engine to walk it from bark's side leaving a few minor scrapes for touchup. With the barge away, a sweep down was completed, then fire pumps taking suction from the river sent sparkling water cascading over decks and superstructure until what bled overboard was free of black grit. Even so, dust would still haunt ship, clothes, and bodies for days. This time, however, Osbourne and Conrad wanted potable water tanks drained, inspected, then filled from an inspected water lighter, so freshwater ecstasy took hold on deck, with the crew contriving to get thoroughly soaked until the thin, blackish water pouring from scuppers, waterways, and unblocked deck openings turned gray, then ran clear; and the ship's potable water tanks went dry.

When ship routine was reestablished, Wiggs called the cooks to meet horse-drawn wagons arriving with fish, and river shrimp so plentiful they clogged dry-dock pumps. By evening, *Calypso*'s paymaster, presided over an ersatz general mess and the entire crew ate their fill of seafood, fresh-baked bread, local vegetables, and watermelons. Wiggs was less enthusiastic about arranging for a local brewery to deliver at the pier but accomplished his task; so the master-at-arms issued each sailor a pail of draft beer, smoking was allowed, and a coxswain provided mandolin music.

The crew relaxed ashore, in various states lethargy, with the only mishap, according to Conrad, an Irish seaman's nose, broken against a piling when he tripped. Starke was suspicious and pressed Watson, but everyone, including the master-at-arms and injured party, provided the same account, or saw nothing. Watson did learn rumor had the sailor adding too much morphine to his beer, then confronting a large Negro engineer enjoying a quiet pipe. While subsequent accounts varied between the stoker refusing debate and expressing a contrary opinion; all agreed he was invited to make something of it, just before the seaman fell. Whether broken nose preceded fall, neither Watson or the master-at-arms saw reason to investigate further.

Late that evening, Starke heard the mandolin resume on the main deck aft, broke off drafting a cable to Albert, lit a fresh pipe, and listened. The music's rich tone, tempo, and clear notes suggested the owner's talent matched his instrument. Most crews included one or more amateur musicians, usually playing fiddle, banjo, or penny whistle, but quality varied. These skills were once used to work ships, but sea chanties ended when steam replaced muscle on winches, lines, and capstan. Bugle calls still proved more effective than passing word, but no one on *Calypso* appeared to have that specific skill. He instead settled for enjoying the sweet, soothing notes, then finished his cable and added to a letter for Katherine before sleeping as well and without dreams as though he shoveled with the crew.

Five hundred miles north, Captain Albert was at home, sitting in his row house front room overlooking the street. He was ambivalently satisfied with his new assignment, an extension of the previous one but working for the Secretary. His office also remained the same, although one nearer the Secretary was proposed. That fell through when political types argued placing him closer might be seen as filibuster pursuit receiving more weight, or the administration turning openly against the Junta. While Spain might find either reassuring, they were not voting in the coming election where regaining prosperity and free silver were the accepted campaign issues; and Democrats did not want to oppose Republicans on Cuba since independence was popular with both parties' loyalists. This made little difference to Albert, who found his office comfortable, but worried the assignment might thwart a return to sea, despite assurances *Maine* was waiting when her first commander transferred.

That officer was Captain Arent Crowninshield, from a prominent Boston family with wealth and maritime connections. This possibly helped his promotion somewhat within the seniority system's bounds, but definitely assisted in getting choice assignments, which spoke well for *Maine*, despite her drawbacks, and it was rumored Crowninshield's next billet would include a boost to commodore.

Albert was also aware, despite her efforts to conceal it, Abigail was grateful for additional time with him. She accepted he was a naval officer when they married, but preferred him working blocks away, over a potential three-year absence. Besides, she was from Poughkeepsie, so life in the capital with a husband involved with national leaders, was completely unanticipated. Lately, she also wanted her daughters' father nearby as their interest in men took a more serious turn and recently concentrated on a pair of *Calypso* officers.

Sidney and Abigail ended each day talking in their cluttered front room opposite its small fireplace; so he browsed *The Evening Times* while she was upstairs. It seemed the election was crowding out Cuba and filibuster news, and, sadly, there was another lynching as people nationwide seemed unwilling to trust courts, had enough lawlessness, or settled scores. Today's was in Maryland, where many, including the governor, thought the dead man innocent, or the odds at least even. The Colored community and its lawyers were reportedly upset but calm; while state officials condemned it and blamed outsiders. Southern states were particularly afflicted after occupation, reconstruction, and people flooding south. Besides the opposing camps in these states having little tolerance for each other, northeastern abolitionists were losing favor everywhere after war, occupation, and constitutional amendments; so the nation was leaning towards ending the schism and freeing states to address internal issues. Unlike many, Albert was never forced to choose between state and nation, or viewed the war as a crusade, but was convinced the years since were handled poorly and rising number of lynchings an outgrowth.

Examining another newspaper in his office the next morning, he read a recent filibuster tug's cargo consisted of thirty recruits, a howitzer or dynamite gun with munitions, 1,000 Springfield rifles with a million rounds, quantities of dynamite, and medicine. A more welcome story reported Captain Wiborg, *Horsa*'s ex-master, lost his Supreme Court appeal and would sit in prison for a year. Albert's sources felt this might bolster Presidential proclamations by offering similar accommodations to others flouting the law. There was also a coded message from Port Royal, reporting *Calypso*'s arrival, which meant Starke escaped the shipyard, assembled a crew, and was at sea. It was a start, but more must happen to prove the mission viable. Until then, any Building faction opposing his project, or advocating another, could make a case to end it and assign *Calypso* to them or a squadron commander.

There was also Arliss Spencer's urgent request to meet him and Captain Fischer in a Justice department office. Reading it through twice, he paused, took a pull from his pipe, then recalled Abigail observing on the train from Old Point Comfort that her husband's protege seemed a buccaneer. He thought it whimsy, since she and Constance Starke appeared to have cemented their relationship; but the nephew did oddly effect women; and the English widow, who seemed as enigmatic as Starke, was certainly not immune. However, Albert was relieved Mrs. Ledford was safely ensconced with Constance Starke in Rhode Island, freeing *Calypso*'s commander to focus on mission.

Equally unexpected, Abigail reluctantly declined an invitation to join the Starkes in Newport because her daughters were at home; which resulted in Olivia and Isabella being invited for next year's season. Albert was grateful Abigail would remain with him, but worried she might soon regret it, if heat wave predictions proved accurate, since normal Washington summers were disagreeable enough.

By then, Abigail's new acquaintances had already arrived in Newport, some 350 miles northeast of Albert's office, were settling in, and began mixing with other wealthy New York and Washington families there for the season. Constance's inherited summer home, Thomas Cottage, wood-framed and smaller than Katherine expected, was far less ostentatious than newer ones going up, but nicely fit a shoreline bulge between the harbor and Wellington Avenue. By the time they arrived, Cynthia already opened it for the summer, since Altman stayed in Washington to manage the mansion. She also arranged for a summer cook and locals to augment a couple who maintained the property year round.

From Katherine's bedroom window, Lime Rock Light was immediately to the northwest, with town proper beginning just beyond a small inlet marking the eastern property line. Long Wharf lay directly across the harbor, with City Wharf projecting from it; where their steamer briefly docked on its New York to Providence run. Just offshore, to the west, was Goat Island and Navy Torpedo Station, with launches making regular runs between it and a landing near Long Wharf; or further north at Coasters Island. There, she heard, the Navy War College occupied an old poorhouse, and the permanently moored receiving ship *Constellation* trained boy apprentices.

Katherine was gradually seduced by cool evenings, morning fog on the bay and Lime Rock Light's constant companionship. Newport Harbor also attracted an eclectic gathering of schooners, cutters, and small steam yachts that were moored, anchored, and moving about. They filled the waterfront with energy and activity each day, then, on calm nights, its surface often turned dark and glasslike. When that happened, the near horizon, west and north, flickered with lights from ship and shore reflecting off the water and contrasted with the mostly unlit bay to its east.

The town was inundated by summer visitors with foreign customs, habits, and status, creating a colony separate from locals, who maintained an odd mix of tolerance, association, and separation between the distinct Newport communities. Katherine felt isolated within days because she was a summer person and British. She also found local middle and upper class women aloof and austere, even for her, but Constance assured her it was their way, before adding if you were accepted they became lifelong friends. She also suggested, with an odd smile, their behavior was far different behind closed doors.

Constance promised parties with Fort Adams' officers and local society, but Katherine was comfortable in widowhood and uneasy being out socially. Strangely, Jacob seemed enough, despite their awkward encounters, separation, and reliance on letters. She just finished one recounting her journey north, Edward's New York business, and initial Newport observations. An earlier draft attempted to reveal her feelings on the Hygeia pier, but was torn up, then left in a wicker waste basket. Even so, the replacement letter posted before she received one from him, also seemed too forward.

Women bicycling was less common in Newport than Washington, but there was archery, lawn tennis, boating, and stables. Since Thomas Cottage was on the harbor, each morning she sat on the lawn watching ships and boats; enveloped by smells of bay, harbor, and commerce. It seemed to bring Philip back, along with self-examination and reevaluating their time together. She knew of his profession through talking and letters, but Newport immersed her in the sea and she even began reading accounts by women who went with their men to raise families on board ships.

While Katherine wrestled with Newport social obligations, Starke prepared for a far less palatable Port Royal event. He, and *Calypso*'s wardroom, were invited to midday dinner on the commandant's lawn with naval station officers, local residents, and visitors. Unsuccessfully trying to purge the obligation from his mind, he shaved and shaped his beard while Yamashita placed a mug of coffee on the cabin table then left to prepare eggs, toast, rice, and preserves. Stark thought his steward would have little to do for supper, so at least some-one benefited. While his coffee cooled, reveille sounded at five o'clock then, as he finished, turn-to came at five-thirty, which included dumping ashes. Without being on deck, he could envision clinkers and heavy material dropping to the mud bottom, leaving lighter residue drifting downriver in a gray, scum-like cloud. Breakfast was at seven-thirty, then morning colors at eight; synchronized with the naval station. Quarters was held at nine-thirty, then drills began that were later dis-rupted by tugs bringing a water lighter alongside to fill tanks.

For the afternoon event, Starke drafted Watson, Osbourne, Conrad, Wiggs, Martyn, and all four cadets. After Watson told them the uniform was undress whites, he ensured the host re-ceived their cards then assembled the luncheon detail on the pier just before noon. Once Starke joined them, the group sor-tied; with him in the lead and fully aware those trailing obedi-ently would prefer relaxing on board or working tasks now delayed until evening. These command performances, as the unwilling participants termed them, referred to various func-tions officers were forced to attend, then perform socially once there. Starke almost laughed. He often chafed over these in the past, but was now instigator and, like his captains, unsympa-thetic to wardroom angst. However, three of their number slipped the leash. Ensign Dunbar was left in charge of *Calypso* while he finished underway preparations and assisted by En-sign Blair, who would drive partway downriver. Lieutenant O'Leary plead boiler, not belly, since water tubes were con-veniently being installed and repaired.

Soon after reaching a broad lawn behind the commandant's quarters they were greeted by Paymaster Ring, Passed Assis-tant Surgeon Berryhill, civil engineer MacKay, and Marine First Lieutenant Ingate, all station officers. The industrial area, dry-dock, and *Calypso* were visible to the east from Rockwell's spacious two-story frame house situated on a slight rise west of the shipyard. Its white siding and porches contrasted with red-brick industrial buildings closer to the river, but matched two vacant nearby structures for senior officers and unmarried juniors. Strategically positioned on the carefully clipped lawn were trestle tables ladened with shrimp, fish, vegetables, and fruit. Also included, was a glass punch bowl containing an iced fruit drink, fortified, as Darwin Tyson would say, with spirits of sufficient strength for a pleasing tang that concealed a solid bite. After Starke sipped from his glass, he hoped his officers realized its potency and would avoid refills since the setting, with summer heat pervading lawn and porches, might easily cause the unwary to discover they downed a near lethal dose before its first effects slammed into them. As he considered whether to act, Watson arrived with his sweating glass, smiling, "This concoction's a devilish blend of smooth, sweet, tart, and deadly, captain. Our folks have a two-glass limit, then iced tea or lemonade."

Wiggs soon joined them, as other guests grazed tables with most selecting one or two items after careful consideration, but a few loading plates as though their next feeding was several days off. After surveying the arrangements, Wiggs observed, "This is well done, captain. See the table just off from the seafood and fruit?"

Starke followed Wiggs' nod to a small table where a large beef roast swung from a hook slowly dripping reddish-tinged juice to the flat pan below. Attending it, a steward or drafted sailor, sliced thin pieces on demand, then stretched them across plates as Wiggs grinned, "Never do these without a roast. Sea food, fruits, anything on the buffet table, always disappear. Two or three beef roasts make the difference if a good man's slicing."

Starke sipped the fruit punch, noting Wiggs' experience arranging such affairs, then spied a sturdy woman purposefully towing her reluctant spouse towards them. Closing fast, with Commander Rockwell engaged elsewhere, Starke knew he was prey. Although his uniform blended with the others eating, talking, or sitting on the porch, and nothing he wore indicated position, someone launched her in his direction or she somehow discovered who commanded the ship at the piers below and felt compelled to engage.

"Mrs. Baylee Barrett, Captain Starke, and my husband, Tolbert Barrett."

"Mr. and Mrs. Barrett, may I present *Calypso*'s executive officer, Lieutenant Ben Watson, and paymaster, Lieutenant Matthew Wiggs."

Both officers bowed, shook hands and, Starke suspected, began planning an escape for more favorable ports of call on the lawn or porches. Over her shoulder, he caught a glimpse of Conrad and Osbourne, steering well clear, with Martyn and their cadets staying even further away.

"We're from Philadelphia and Paymaster Ring's guests."

Mr. Barrett was apparently content to leave all to his presumptuous spouse, or allowed no choice. Within several minutes, Watson recalled a critical medical issue requiring an immediate consultation with Assistant Surgeon Conrad, while Paymaster Wiggs, a temperance man, felt the sudden need to refresh his punch. Starke sighed imperceptibly, took a bracing sip of tangy liquid, and prepared to receive. Never a hypocrite, he felt no rancor or disloyalty at his officers' prudent withdrawal; he would have done the same.

Barrett lectured classics at a university and his wife came from a well-off, influential family; which allowed traveling between terms. Indifferent to her surroundings, she declared White Southerners mostly traitors or recalcitrants, and their darker brethren eternally shiftless, with neither worth Pennsylvania's past sacrifices; then enjoined him to explain how *Calypso* would be assisting the Cubans, since Spaniards were worse than Southerners, and Catholic besides. Unable to debate, ignore, or evade, Starke appreciated the punch's deadening effects. Her soliloquy continued, encouraged by his lack of response, which she probably interpreted as acquiescence or agreement; while the professor obviously believed intervention futile or not in his self-interest. Paymaster Ring finally deflected them to a large group surrounding Commander Rockwell, then returned to explain a business associate asked if they could attend since Mr. Barrett wished to tour a naval station. He agreed, thinking it might benefit the Navy, as the wife's family was influential, but had been in purgatory since they arrived and would hear from his commandant the next morning, unless sent to coventry without trial.

Starke did learn the year's first hurricane passed west of Havana, then north through the Gulf before crashing ashore near Pensacola. William Jennings Bryan was favored at the Chicago Democratic Party convention where Tyson was probably cruising; and, unlike Mrs. Barrett, favored Bryan's anti-Social Darwinist position as much as he deplored his prohibitionist stance to the last drop. It also seemed the coming election brought local politics to the boil because Beaufort's Collector of Customs office, a local power center, might revert to Robert Smalls, the previous Republican officeholder whose Democrat antipathy matched his party loyalty.

That evening, relatively unscathed by the day's events, *Calypso*'s officers gathered in the wardroom to review planning for the voyage, since Starke required all officers and cadets to know specifics. *Calypso* would bypass Savannah, Fernandina, and Jacksonville, then enter the Straits of Florida. It was almost certain they would steam most of the trip, but spread canvas in favorable winds, and, once they turned west, complete a full power run along the keys, staying inshore of the powerful current leaving the Gulf.

Later, after Osbourne and Watson reported status on preparations for departure, Starke finished reviewing and signing reports. With that task complete, he finished a letter for Albert, and Lieutenant Commander Wainwright, who relieved Singer as intelligence office head in April. It included information from the Port Royal meeting, excluding the verbal Justice information Albert was alerted to in a coded message sent directly to him. The same cable also advised him *Calypso* would watch for potential filibusters leaving from the keys, although interception was unlikely with the information at hand. Finally, Katherine's letter was brought to a close, sealed, then added to other correspondence for posting before their underway. For some reason, it was longer than those he wrote before their evening at Old Point Comfort.

CHAPTER SEVENTEEN
Against the Stream

The passage downriver to the Atlantic posed a greater challenge than coming upstream to the shipyard. *Calypso*'s speed would be higher, control more difficult, and any anchoring traumatic; since the ship would spin halfway round when the fluke took hold. Starke enjoyed melding man and nature's forces to control the ship, but he was now a commander wanting his officers to learn. Watson would take the ship to Port Royal Sound, then Blair into the Atlantic.

Departure was set to begin as a flood tide swelled the river and slowed downstream current, but it also made grounding worse. Underway preparations began the prior evening, with *Calypso*'s black gang completing sequential tasks or tending their systems. While steaming wore men down, even when boilers were cold or fires banked, valves must be maintained, strainers cleaned, tubes punched, ash-pits emptied overboard, and a thousand smaller tasks addressed. However, by midmorning, boilers were making steam, bearings lubricated, fluid levels checked, valves cycled, and machinery turned over. Topside, Martyn and Weaver pushed their deck force; preparing equipment, sending items adrift to the lucky bag, and readying mooring lines. The starboard anchor was also moved from billboard to cathead; where it hung, ready for dropping. Each time Starke watched their anchor made ready or secured, he regretted stockless anchors were not in the conversion. While less aesthetic, they handled easier and held as well in most bottoms. *Calypso*'s sails would stay harbor furled, but Weaver inspected their lines and halliards, examined stays and shrouds for stretching, then surveyed parceling for damaged or bare wire. He also monitored the ready lifeboat's out-fitting and positioning as it was lifted from chocks and swung outboard between the aft port davits then aligned; before two belly bands were passed around its hull to bring it against the rotary davits and canting slightly outboard.

Naval station line-handlers waited pierside near a small tug with its slow turning engine gently pressing a rope-fendered prow into the battered camel astern of *Calypso*. Except where the tug's screw stirred silt and disturbed a gray-blue surface, the river was flat and glasslike. Now and again a quick gulp or tiny eruption in the pier's shadow marked a water spider or insect struck by small fish. Further off, some gray-white sea gulls and brown-winged ospreys executed long, gliding pass-es just above the river to snatch small, surface-feeding fish, then lift up and away, only slightly marring the flat surface. Along marshland across the river, a wood duck squadron lead by its resplendent drake continued feeding as nature slowed with morning's gentle coolness yielding to a rising sun.

Through his cabin window, *Calypso*'s commander watched a station clerk cross the brow carrying a brown leather postal satchel bulging with correspondence and reports, including Katherine's letter. As he finished a pipe, all hands were called to sea and anchor stations, then, several minutes later, he lift-ed his hat off the hook and left for the pilothouse. After a short climb and half-dozen salutes, he found Watson and Dunbar bent over a chart, studying a mark the chief quartermaster's dividers pointed to. Sailors at the EOT and ship's wheel came to attention, then saluted. Starke returned their salutes, add-ing, "Good morning, men."

Alerted by a lookout, Starke and Watson watched their pilot leave the tug, then amble down the pier to the bulwark gang-way, where Ensign Martyn waited. As the pair left for the pi-lothouse, men on ship and shore eased the station's heavy brow over to the pier. Once it cleared, Watson turned to Starke, "Permission to test engine, captain."

Starke responded, "Very well."

With both pointers resting on ready to answer all bells, the EOT handle swung to slow ahead, and the engine room pointer quickly matched it. It was held just long enough to strain some mooring lines and slack others. After coming to all stop, the process was repeated using slow astern. The steam steering engine was tested next by cycling the rudder right to left, then left to right, easing it gently against the stops. The secondary steering position, primarily used under canvas and manned by two sailors, did the same while the unrigged emergency steering system was being inspected.

When the pilot arrived, Starke recognized him as the one who brought them upriver. It would make the outbound trip easier since he was familiar and already earned their confidence. The pilot surveyed the situation while Starke greeted him and indicated Watson was the first conning officer. Acknowledging this, he grinned confidently, "Mr. Watson, with your permission, I'll make the tug up forward, so we can walk her into the stream."

All pilots were addressed as captain, so Watson responded, "Agree, captain, and the buoy just downriver?"

"Best get well into the channel or the river'll put us on it. Means we can't dawdle bringing lines in." With that, the pilot stepped outside and signaled the tug, which tooted in response, backed into the river, made a Y turn, then came alongside to make up a headline forward of the port anchor. With that complete, Watson ordered mooring lines singled and announced they were getting underway. Starke found a spot to monitor without interfering. Several approaches were possible, but he left that to Watson, who turned solemnly to Starke, "Permission to get underway, captain?"

Starke responded, "Permission granted," and Watson slowly backed until the current was countered then, with wind being of no concern, the rudder was put full starboard and turns increased as all lines were cast off. With prop-wash pushing her stern from the pier and tug pulling her bow out, *Calypso's* steam whistle blasted as she walked into the river with colors lowering at the stern and rising to the mainmast truck.

Aligning a distinctly ragged pier piling with a pilothouse window latch, Watson judged *Calypso* was moving slightly with the current. When they reached mid-channel, and would clear the buoy, he nodded to the pilot, ordered rudder amidships, then rang ahead full for steerageway. The headline released as muddy water billowed from beneath the fantail stern, then, carried by current, *Calypso* accelerated downriver through the marshland.

Ensign Blair was eager to conn through Port Royal Sound, but content to observe his executive officer until then. Watson seemed aware of everything, while carrying on a casual conversation with their pilot. The same held for the captain, who would glance at the chart or nonchalantly observe river traffic. Their final turn on the river came at a single buoy marking shallows to starboard; but nothing similar to port, so the ship's first warning there would be water changing color as bow or screw cleaved mud. *Calypso* turned close enough to avoid swinging wide of the buoy, but with sufficient distance to insure they were not set down on it. During this turn, Blair watched the bow shift rapidly, overshoot slightly, then return to course. He long since decided all buoys were ship magnets, appearing well clear then suddenly crashing alongside, but this one passed without drama. Once steady on the new southern course, Watson explained, he and the pilot used two points of land and an abandoned plantation pier to time their turn; then Blair took over as the ship accelerated down the sound.

Calypso passed two low headlands marking Port Royal Sound's Atlantic entrance, then steamed southeast down a channel with buoys marking its south side, breakers the north, and terminus near the lightship. Halfway through, in a straight, broad section of deep water, they met a small coastal steamer riding high, trailing a black smoke plume, and making for the river *Calypso* just left. Whistle signals were exchanged as they agreed to pass port-to-port, then came crisply starboard, passing close aboard. When abreast, the merchant's ensign dropped, then rose as her colors dipped to the warship. As *Calypso* acknowledged, the pilot slowly waved his cap in an arc above his head, a man on the steamer replicated; then he explained, "That's Smitty, *Claud Jones'* master. Runs between here and Charleston so regular he's his own pilot. A rogue by all accounts. Ran guns during the last Cuban war and met Gómez."

Starke grinned through his beard, "Sounds a character, captain," while observing Blair endeavor to appear impassive despite the discomfort of steering down what he probably felt an impossibly narrow gauntlet.

Trailing a light-gray translucent smoke plume, *Calypso* plowed the expansive, relatively flat, blue-gray surface between buoy sets marking navigable water. Lighter areas or breaking waves warned of sand bars beyond the south buoy line and north boundary. Whatever these buoys' intended color scheme, all were heavily streaked with white bird guano, and larger ones had nests at their peak or wedged in the framing. A loitering schooner finally made to come alongside as Starke walked the pilot aft, thanking him for both trips, since his uncle repeatedly stressed courtesy's value, especially when unexpected or ignored, and his nephew agreed.

Returning to the pilothouse, he saw the elderly, red-hulled Martins' Industry lightship off their port beam. As *Calypso* steered southeast, he used binoculars to scan the stubby, high-sided ship with slender funnel, vestigial bowsprit, and two masts. As she shrank and faded, he lowered them to survey *Calypso*. Using a gun tackle, the anchor was shifted to its billboard and secured for sea as the ship made a brief turn to ease their task and avoid drenching those working forward. With mooring lines stored, Starke left for his day cabin as mess gear was piped. At noon, the crew was called to dinner.

Calypso would track 120 miles southeast, cross the Gulf Stream axis, then turn south, passing west of the Bahama and Bimini Islands. This put stronger currents to the west but avoided hugging Florida's east coast. Starke considered entering the Northwest Providence Channel to Nassau, but judged it a distraction. His father ran the Federal blockade from there, but it was more useful for smuggling into the States and his orders did not allow for boarding European ships. Nassau's bar also required high tide for ships like *Calypso* to cross, anchoring in a deep hole off the town, then running boats. Finally, like other Caribbean ports, the potential for disease was high, while contraband or information less so. However, it could still be used for a run to Cuba, so Starke decided a future visit might prove useful.

Starke slept strong and well in his sea cabin, and with fewer disturbances, as officers of the deck gained confidence, watches coalesced, and his preferences understood. He also had a better feel for the officers. Leading the starboard watch, Ensign Blair's confidence meant he sought help less readily than the port watch's Ensign Martyn, who seemed less sure. Starke suspected Watson would assist easing one towards caution while building the other's self-assurance; and he still wanted to attain Navy regulations' three watch-officer standard, which meant maturing the naval cadets as well.

With obliging weather after they turned due south, and with the ship steady on course, Stark set the jibs and staysails that would not be soiled by smoke or disturb *Calypso*'s slight weather helm. With these drawing well, the bark slowly rose and fell, attended by a gentle, partial roll. Running on one boiler spared stokers, while pilothouse and flying bridge watches marveled at a spectacular night. Windows and doors were opened, the temperature pleasant, and a warm, but not distracting, breeze caressed all it touched. On the horizon, a distinct split between sky and ocean created a circular base for a dome alight with stars; luring engineers on break from the heat and humidity below.

Ship traffic was unusually light. Only one small schooner was sighted, as most deep-water sailing ships turned north-west before the Bahama Islands, placing them further out in the Atlantic or to *Calypso*'s north. Those passing to her west were mostly riding the Gulf Stream from Havana or engaged in coastal trade; placing them beyond visual range, even from a masthead during the day.

Starke remained late on the flying bridge to enjoy it, and avoid retiring. Since 1882, July's eleventh day meant Alexandria's long-dead would return. The Egyptian sojourn began immediately after his commissioning at Annapolis, when Uncle Immanuel handed him the sword from his father. He left immediately by train for Norfolk; and Commander Sydney Albert's steam screw sloop, *Appalachicola*, preparing to join Rear Admiral Nicholson's European Squadron in the Mediterranean. Within days, they rendezvoused with *Nipsic*, *Lancaster*, and *Quinnebaug* off the Egyptian city. Britain's Mediterranean Fleet under Admiral Seymour was already there with the central-battery ironclad HMS *Alexandria*, turret ship HMS *In-*

flexible, seven more battleships, a gunboat flotilla, and torpedo boat. Inevitably, France's Levant Squadron and others arrived, but none matched the British, and even Germany's small squadron of *Zieten*, *Gneisenau*, and *Nymphe* eclipsed the Americans. After scanning the various participants, it was obvious to Starke the European Squadron's flagship, *Lancaster*, although the Navy's most powerful, was incapable of offering the larger warships present more than target practice and could barely stand against most of the gunboats.

After *La Galissonnière*, flying Admiral Conrad's flag, led the French squadron away, Seymour sent an ultimatum ashore and the British were soon bombarding Egyptian forts and striking the city beyond. Americans provided sanctuary from looting and riots, using a liberal interpretation of citizenship, while the redoubtable Charles Chaillé-Long assumed the consular role after its occupant fled. They also sent the first landing party ashore to protect American property and interests. Intending to restore or preserve some order, the fleet landing party was led by *Lancaster*'s executive officer, Lieutenant Commander Casper Goodrich, with Marine Captain Cochrane as executive officer, Lieutenant Waller leading marines, and Lieutenant Denny the sailors.

When Chaillé-Long requested six armed sailors or marines to retrieve an influential family, Starke volunteered. The detail intended only as an escort was forced to fight in and out; so every July, and sporadically during the year, those ghosts visited Starke. On this commission a living one joined *Calypso*. Seaman First Class, Doran Kearney, was one of those with him fourteen years earlier. Watson accepted him from *Franklin* because of his skills and despite a Sisyphean record. The landsman Starke knew at Alexandria should have attained petty officer or chief but instead passed through cycles of advancing, drinking, crashing, then recovery. Watson was unable to put him forward for coxswain or petty officer, despite his value, as another repetition was almost certain.

Starke was awake in his sea cabin before the watch relieved at four, then went to join Watson, Dunbar, and Owen taking morning sights. At sunrise, running lights were extinguished, a forward lookout climbed to the foretop, hammocks were stowed, and the crew prepared to sweep or wash clothes. *Calypso's* berthing surpassed most, with compartments for deck, engineering, and others. Most of the crew rigged their canvas hammocks, or dream sacks, from numbered hooks embedded in the overhead to sleep; then took them down in the morning to roll, tie, and pass them through a sizing ring before stowing in a nettings bin.

The horizon was clear, morning cool, and a pleasant breeze crossed port to starboard as Starke left for his day cabin to change and enjoy the coffee Yamashita would have ready. Sweepers were complete and the crew hosing decks with saltwater, to clean, preserve, and swell wood planking, then lighten it over time. As sea water sluiced across the decks, translucent gray funnel smoke trailed astern, drifted off, dissipated, then settled on a brightening, but still dark-gray sea. Unable to participate physically, but craving exercise, Starke decided to go aloft before an audience gathered. He looked for a convenient place to store his cap, but finally climbed with it since items lying about were declared adrift and turned in. This brought disciplinary action for sailors, who then had to buy back their gear from the lucky bag. He would have done the same to demonstrate no one was exempt, but it was not worth the perceptive risk.

The ship's heel eased his climb to the foretop and using the weather shrouds meant he was blown against them. Equally important, his hands grasped only the parcelled, wire rope shrouds, leaving small, horizontal ratlines for his feet. Only one experience of climbing the lee shrouds using ratlines for handholds was necessary. Novices learned any wind tried to peel them away, and, if a parting ratline did not offer the thrill of nearly falling, the pain of having fingers crushed by another climber's boot was convincing enough. Pausing to look down, Starke's shoes blotted out a large deck section. It always amazed him how the ship and lower mast shrank as you climbed, while shrouds and upper mast grew. Passing though the foretop lubbers hole, since *Calypso* lacked fighting tops with trap doors, he found the barefoot Kearney, who grinned, "Morning captain, sir."

"Good morning, and why's Chief Weaver's leading seaman standing lookout?"

"Well, sir. As it were, the chief sent me up to school lookouts. They'll be arriving after feeding. An agreeable chore on a grand day, sir."

Watson wanted a full stable of skilled lookouts, as did Starke, since they often made the difference. This required instruction as well as experience, and Kearney was the perfect choice to teach. Since Alexandria, he had grown thicker, his short, muscular body toughened, some teeth lost, and a few scars acquired. Starke wondered if his shooting improved. His *Appalachicola* shipmates called Kearney's rifle a shillelagh because targets any distance from its muzzle were quite safe; but he was deadly with butt or bayonet. Surprising Stark, he grinned, "Yes sir, still can't hit a barn much beyond spitting distance, sir."

Kearney scanned the horizon while talking, letting eyes drift, searching for any irregularity warranting scrutiny. Starke also noticed his nose was slightly crooked from being broken long before joining the ship. He was a lapsed Catholic from a family that fled the Irish potato famine for New York, intending to go west and farm; but never left the tenement where Kearney, their youngest, was born and raised. After gaining size and strength, a local tough began taunting him, foolishly braced the young Irishman alone, and paid the price. Since the battered unfortunate enjoyed a gang's backing, Kearney needed to depart rapidly and found a recruiting petty officer willing to oblige by enlisting him as a landsman.

"Settled in, Kearney?"

"Aye, sir. She's the makings of a home, sir."

Starke noticed the rising sun transforming from orange to yellow, then looked down towards the bow where *Calypso's* stem sliced into the swells, then rose with water shouldered to either side, leaving a spray pattern on the ocean to be quickly sucked into the ship's sides. He then glanced aft into the funnel screen. One of the large blackened exhaust pipes from the main boilers was dormant while the second was exuding smoke that quickly drifted to starboard, leaving an acrid scent that was incongruous with sails and lines slapping masts. A staysail collapsed then refilled with a resounding crack as Starke turned back to Kearney, "I believe you're right, she has the makings."

Beyond Kearney's shooting ability, Alexandria held ghosts neither wished to summon, so Starke descended, landed lightly on deck, then went to his cabin; carefully avoiding sailors scrubbing planks under a petty officer's watchful eye. Once inside, he took what his aunt called a whore's bath, then trimmed and shaved as the bark's slow, regular pitching animated the room's movable items. After putting on the fresh blue uniform Yamashita laid out, he found a white mug of coffee waiting. Breakfast arrived soon after; filling a white plate that matched the cup. Fortunately, his steward also rigged the spider, a segmented contraption of wood rails fitting over the tabletop to corral items and prevent their escape to lap or floor. His plate immediately slid against a thin partition, while three animated chairs surrounding the table tugged against lashings, wiggling small ringbolts embedded in the floor.

The wall barometer was steady, but would probably not remain so with the hurricane season opened by that first storm rolling over Cuba into the Gulf a week earlier. He hoped the weather would hold during their two-day run south, but that storm meant more calving across the Caribbean. Watson brought the day orders after breakfast, proposed changes to the week's plan, then, before leaving, asked if anything should be emphasized at the nine-thirty officers' call. Starke suggested the possibility of sighting filibusters along the keys.

When officers' call finished, the ship was cleaned, ashes dumped, crew fed, hammocks stored, and sick call held; all before *Calypso* began the day's work and training. This morning it was singlestick practice. The ship carried a hundred oak singlesticks with leather hilt-guards, along with fifty of the 1860 model cutlasses they stood in for. Starke wanted to join in as it was excellent exercise and could be as strenuous as boxing since no blows slowed the pace, but refrained as the commander. Participants formed a single line for set movements, then paired for practicing attack and defense moves. This usually consumed the allotted hour, but sometimes there were competitions. Starke wanted singlestick practice twice a week, and soon noticed the wardroom was not engaged. After suggesting they do so, it was the surgeon who showed the most interest; although whether from a desire to learn or be close by should the rod-like oak blades strike a head or wrist was left unresolved.

Throughout the afternoon *Calypso* drove south, heeled to starboard with a slow, rocking movement. Starke conducted fewer drills than he wanted, allowing the crew to adjust and discover ship or equipment flaws, but assured Watson that would change, starting with main battery pointing drills that afternoon. Equipment casualties so far were minor, and only the burn and a seasick case remained on Conrad's binnacle list. The surgeon recommended boarding the latter, unless a miracle occurred. The slightest ship movement sent the landsman's stomach in full revolt, then he became disoriented, and, finally, opening unfocused eyes was all that could be expected. Starke disliked discharging him, since Weaver claimed he was intelligent, alert, and willing; but the man only recovered long enough in Port Royal to carry water while they coaled, then crumpled before leaving the sound. Since then, he remained comatose, was racked by dry heaves, and required a bayman trickle water into his mouth. Conrad regretted the approaching departure because his own symptoms had spurred him to research the malady; and losing this patient deprived him of a severe case to study.

Early, on their third morning underway, *Calypso* steamed past Grand Bahama Island, about seventeen miles to port, then into the Caribbean, according to Dunbar's morning sights and dead reckoning. The navigator estimated speed through the water using a simple chip log after *Calypso*'s patent log failed. The modern, fishlike device was towed astern with its propeller sending back electric readings that proved inaccurate at some speeds in calm water, then failed completely on its third use at sea. The traditional method Dunbar resorted to consisted of a triangular plate thrown overboard to hold position while the ship advanced, paying out a knotted line. After knots passing over the taffrail were timed and speed calculated, a solid yank pulled a pin from the plate so it could be retrieved. Meanwhile, engineering offered a second approximation by logging shaft turns and extracting speed from a table developed during trials.

Their estimated position was confirmed that afternoon when *Calypso* passed less than eight miles west of Bimini through a brightening sea becoming less opaque and turning crystal blue. Three hundred miles before entering the Straits of Florida saw the first school of silver-blue flying fish, propelled by tails that launched them up, to glide a yard or more above the surface. At one point, a mammoth hammerhead shark took station alongside with its large brown fin parting the sea like a ship's prow. Then, with Bimini fading off the port quarter, a blue-gray dolphin school closed, paced *Calypso* until bored, then laced back and forth under the bow before streaking off.

Starke had his cabin windows open so the breeze passing through brought smells of ship and salt air, making it almost pleasant to review reports. Passing ships had also been scarce, except near the Northwest Providence Channel's entrance; and Yamashita was trolling from the fantail, so fresh fish might be on the evening menu.

CHAPTER EIGHTEEN
First Blood

Calypso sliced through the afternoon's blue Caribbean waters with her complement sewing, napping, or reading. She had turned slightly southwest Saturday evening, then slowed to raise Alligator Reef lighthouse in daylight. On one boiler, she easily made five or six knots, although the Florida Current, combining with the Gulf Stream held her to four over ground. With speed slow and a languid breeze pressing her sails, there was almost no pitch, but heavy rolls dominated the warm night and life on board; shifting loose items, rattling running gear, and hampering water tenders' efforts to control boiler feedwater. Their track also cut through popular filibuster routes, so watches were given basic information on the description and behavior of *Laurada*, *Dauntless*, *Commodore*, and their fellow travelers; although a sighting was unlikely, and becoming less so, given traffic volume approaching or leaving Havana. This might have created common purpose, but any enthusiasm was damped by the constant rolling, which consumed each watch's attention and stole sleep from the rest.

The *City of Washington*, a New York & Cuba Mail Steamship Company passenger liner, crossed astern about midnight, eliciting little concern in *Calypso*'s pilothouse since her bearing drifted steadily right. On a set schedule, she left New York City's Pier 15, where the Ward Line, as it was commonly known, headquartered. After passing *Calypso*, the liner would race down the coast, raise Cuba, enter Havana, then continue to Mexico and Panama before returning to Pier 15. She was *Calypso*'s vintage, but 300 feet long and 2,600 tons. Designed keel up for merchant service, her compound engine had also been exchanged for a triple-expansion type to increase speed and reduce costs. Despite a reputation for reliability, the owners retained her hermaphrodite brig sailing rig, mostly to comfort passengers. For those on *Calypso* watching with naked eyes, she was a dark, amorphous shape with two white masthead lights, green running light, and several lighted cabin windows. Those with telescopes or binoculars could make out a black-hulled silhouette with straight stem, extended counter, conspicuous rudder, and single amidship stack supported by funnel stays and ringed by ventilators. At night, her long, white deck cabin appeared gray and a line of rectangular ports forming a promenade bulwark for staterooms under the main deck could just be seen. While the Ward Line's two thin, white stack bands were invisible, the liner's white-hulled boats hanging from davits above the deckhouse stood out, as did a canvas awning rigged aft.

Under that awning, a solitary third class passenger, Manuel Valencia y Gomis, who just escaped his confining third class bunk, was finishing a cigarette when *Calypso* slipped past. Using false identification for passage to the Mexican port of Veracruz, he wanted time above deck before Havana, where he must remain below. Valencia was an anarchist, and Spain was purging the movement's violent adherents, along with its advocates, philosophers, publishers, and sympathizers. Martial law had been invoked after Santiago Salvador tossed explosives into a theater of wealthy Barcelona opera patrons. That was reprisal for executing Paulino Pallas, who attempted to blow up General Martínez-Campos y Antón during a parade. Valencia assumed his friends taken by Spanish police were denouncing others to save themselves, knew he was safe in New York embracing international anarchism, and probably gave up his name. Being hunted also convinced him class oppression and anarchist suppression must suffer direct, violent action; and Cuba was promising since the Junta included a small anarchist faction. They persuaded him the island quagmire that drove the government to bleed Spain's treasury and conscript thousands unable to avoid the draft could bring down the monarchy and inaugurate the class war needed to bring oppressors to book. To achieve this, he organized a filibuster expedition, obtained support, and chartered *Rafael Riego*, an old, but fast, tug also on its way to Veracruz.

Unknown to Valencia, between him and Veracruz another filibuster tug, *John Gwinn Williams*, lay anchored off Bahia Honda in the Florida Keys; where a less utopian Fachtna Harler concentrated on his expedition, which was not going well. After slipping past Navy launches enforcing Key West's quarantine, he languished two days at anchor near a deep channel with treacherous currents coursing between keys. Each night, red warning flashes from the Sombrero Key and American Shoals lighthouses reminded him the exposed anchorage was precarious during hurricane season. Most of his time was consumed watching the brilliant sun illuminate a small green island's narrow sand beaches. Like most keys, where it lacked a beach lapped by minute wave crests, mangroves held back the sea. Further out came shoals under multiple shades of green seawater that grew darker, then turned blue in the distance, where a deep current rushed into the Straits of Florida.

Along Florida's keys and west coast, Fachtna Harler was known as Captain Buff, short for Captain Buffalo, despite never setting eyes on the beast. The complete sobriquet came after his first passage as master, before then it was just Buffalo. Like the namesake, he carried a thick matting of black hair, that once thickly coated his entire body, and exposed skin tanned light brown. Since then, the beard was gone, the head mostly bald, and hide damaged, burned, or tanned from a life at sea. Both powerful hands were scarred from hard fishing, fighting, and the work that fashioned a burly physique, with protruding lozenge-shaped belly. While his demeanor could resemble his namesake, in many ways it did not. He was intelligent, cunning, and no herd animal, but tolerated few barriers, was unstoppable in a brawl, and shook off tremendous punishment.

Over both days *John Gwinn Williams* sat anchored, Captain Buff's traits and skills were essential for starting Sunday's run, since anything not on board Saturday night must be abandoned, or the start delayed to Monday. The Junta employed small sponging schooners to ferry machetes, pistols, and rifles to mother ships because the masters knew these keys; but there was a drawback. This close, insular sponging fraternity might dress shabbily and split evenly between races, but was extraordinarily devout, so absolutely no Sunday work was possible. Unlike the cargo, his passengers came off a large schooner traveling between Jacksonville and Key West that hove to off St. Augustine for boarding insurgents; mostly young men from Florida cigar factories. Unlike them, Captain Buff was neither adventurer or idealist, and held no grievance with Spain; although he saw no reason Cubans should not throw out the Dons. Having watched his own South crushed trying to exit a union voluntarily entered, it did not surprise him they must fight their way out. Besides his lacking moral reservations, the Junta paid exceptionally well for each trip, while Spanish shipments offered only the customary fare. This was a significant motivator as he approached his mid-fifties and wished to build funds for later years; perhaps a small Key West bar. Unlike other smugglers, the well-organized Junta minimized risk by arranging for ships making runs to receive cargo and passengers from separate sources at sea or relatively safe locations along the coast. To further insure security in a voluble culture, only the master and Cuban leader knew precise destinations; and nondescript tugs like *John Gwinn Williams* were preferred because they could leave port without clearance papers, further complicating prosecution.

While Captain Buff and his engineer clashed over the state of the tug's worn boilers, *Calypso*'s crew resigned themselves to a full power run disrupting their Sunday rope-yarn. Following quarters, and Wiggs' sermon, which Starke thought perilously near a temperance speech, Alligator Reef's framework light house broke the bright horizon, signaling the course change required before their full power run. Once settled on a heading that set a straight course five to eight miles off the reefs, but inside the Florida Current, *Calypso* would steam full out on both boilers from Alligator Reef to Key West. If fourteen or fifteen knots were achieved, the Key West lighthouse would pass down their starboard side around three-thirty that afternoon.

To accomplish this, *Calypso* would take in all sails, set her EOT to four bells, or ahead fast, then hold it using their best helmsmen to steer the straightest course using least rudder. Speed through the water would be measured by engine turns, the chipboard, and taking positions on lighthouses or distinct land features. All main steam would go to the engine, with donkey boilers used for winches, distillers, and other equipment. Every black ganger would participate, and anyone not directly involved must stand by or avoid interfering. Since steam plant limits would be stressed, Watson orchestrated all pilothouse activity, mustered a fire party on the fantail, then rigged steam and manual fire pumps.

Osbourne, O'Leary, the engineer cadets, and engineering watch section had lit-off the starboard boiler some hours before. For this, a small amount of kindling wood and coal were carefully piled in the firebox, then set alight by glowing coals taken from the port boiler. It warmed, grew hot, then began generating steam as more fuel was added over several hours. When its pressure matched the port boiler, a second stop valve to the main steam system was opened, allowing both long, white and dull-silver boilers to feed it. To fire them, trimmers and passers staged West Virginia Pocahontas coal in precise piles on the steel deck between them. Sweating stokers with streaked faces then worked shovels under these black mounds, before lifting the exact amount required to spread evenly across the firebox through six stokeholes. For builder's trials, where partial knots over contract speed reaped huge bonuses, yards would lighten ships then use hand-picked men and coal lumps. Osbourne could do neither, but merged watches to obtain the best water tenders, stokers, passers, and trimmers available; leaving the rest to assist. Knowing black gang excitement ran so high most would work to exhaustion, or collapse in damp heat exceeding 120 degrees, before reporting to sick bay, Assistant Surgeon Conrad set up a main deck relief station near the boiler room access to treat those seeking a brief respite topside.

The funneled brass voice tube between pilothouse and engine room remained busy until, steady on course, with Alligator Reef lighthouse dropping astern, the EOT swung to ahead fast and engineering walked up the ship's speed, balancing heat, steam pressure, and water levels. While the helmsman held his compass card at the lubber's line, Starke climbed to *Calypso*'s flying bridge. Standing near clustered brass voice tubes surrounding the binnacle with its gimbaled magnetic compass, he steadied himself on railings made uneven by lashings constraining white canvas windscreen panels bulging inward from the air's press. To starboard, low-lying keys surrounded by sandy beaches or mangrove roots rose slightly above a blue-green translucent sea with several fishing schooners ghosting along, seeking a day's catch. There was no visible traffic to port, where the straits grew dark blue near the horizon. Under squawking sea gulls, a dolphin streaked along one side, plunged under the bow, then disappeared. While Watson's fire party stood by on the fantail, sailors worked running rigging or wove boat fenders along the main deck, because Watson forbid anyone but lookouts going aloft; to prevent an overboard ending the run.

Every role and movement in the boiler and engine rooms was choreographed with trimmers digging out coal, often by hand, then coal passers moving ungainly loads that regularly topped 140 pounds to the boiler flat, where stokers served a blistering fire box by smoothly feeding the exact amount of coal needed. The water tenders standing nearby were intent on sight glass and gages as valves were slowly turned in one direction or the other. The feedwater these valves controlled would enter the firebox, turn to steam for the three-cylinder engine, then pass through a condenser to become water again.

Besides hellish heat, bilge gas, a cacophony of scraping shovels, roaring fires, black lumps being cracked, coal passers' dumps, slamming doors, and steam's piercing hiss; coal dust permeated the atmosphere despite continuous sweeping. To survive, men wore what clothes suited, and most added a bandanna across their face to filter dust, or one encircling the forehead to prevent sweat rivulets from burning eyes. However, one tribulation *Calypso*'s black gang did avoid was forced draft steaming, since she was not fitted with tall stacks or steam-driven blowers. Pressurizing boiler rooms sometimes added a knot or two, but wear on equipment and men, was substantial. For all this, the black gang was paid more, but only those who never entered their spaces at sea begrudged them.

Lead stoker Jones worked with water tenders to balance fire, water, and steam as boilers smoothly rose to maximum pressure, then held. With *Calypso* running all out, he judged when to open a furnace door, releasing a short burst of flame into the space, while ensuring each shovelful went evenly across the firebox and the middle stokehole was not overfed; being lower than the other two. As temperature climbed to 140 degrees, sweating stokers levered shovels on knees and limited movement to that absolutely necessary for thrusting coal into the firebox during the brief interval a door was open. This was never long, to minimize escaping heat and prevent water tube ends from weakening. Even with perfect firing and the best coal, clinkers developed and required extraction. For this, and precisely arranging dark lumps interspersed by devouring red, yellow, and white flames, each boiler's fire irons included a long rod with one end curved to a circle.

Osbourne changed teams every two hours during full power runs, so Jones was soon relieved by Delmar Kemp, the imposing, amiable Negro; a man who was respected and not one to confront with fists, as a deck seaman's broken nose attested. Although neither Jones or Kemp were designated petty officers, those holding these positions were weak, so the pair emerged as unofficial leaders. O'Leary watched them help shape the department by molding his trimmers, coal passers, and stokers. With some misgiving, he turned a blind eye to his chief machinist mate surreptitiously supporting their efforts, frustrated he could not bypass petty officers and preserve discipline.

Once relieved by Kemp's group, Jones and his men climbed to the main deck where a July sun provoked the aquamarine ocean to shimmer and sparkle. While a warm, caressing breeze passed down the ship's length, slipping around deckhouse and masts, *Calypso*'s bow wave climbed the forward sheer, creating a frothy mound alongside, which spread into an expanding V astern, past the whitewater tail extending out from her counter, then settling into a straight wake. Even so, Jones heard Ensign Blair admonish the helmsman to steer small, supporting his opinion Osbourne and O'Leary were better officers. Near the forecastle, Chief Weaver spotted his group and nodded. The chief took exception to faint black footprints despoiling his deck, but made allowances today, and Jones repaid him by keeping his men from grasping paint or canvas. Engineers emerging from below staggered or collapsed, then began gulping lukewarm water that cut meandering paths where it dribbled or spilled on skin thick with coal dust; then left dark blotches on clothes. As Jones raised a pail to drink, he saw Starke on the flying bridge, while below him, on the collapsible bridge wing off the pilothouse, a small group watched the Florida Keys pass.

Calypso's commander looked out over the main deck at men from assorted faiths, cultures, and countries coalescing into a crew. While more modern ships were less diverse, long-serving Navy officers often dealt with disparate crews; and it was the rule on most merchant ships. However, once a crew came together, comrade and ship easily trumped speeches, jingoes, race, nationality, and more. To achieve this, *Calypso* enjoyed the advantage of more continuous-service men than most. Experienced sailors usually left after serving three years, disliking the service or realizing no pension waited at career's end; but many deserted, accepting they would never obtain naturalization papers, or lose their right to vote if already a citizen.

Starke returned to his day cabin at noon, looking forward to Yamashita's steamed dolphin. He met Osbourne on the way. The chief engineer's grimy uniform showed he was not sitting in the wardroom receiving status reports. Starke also noticed a petty officer directing two landsmen hosing down deck space near the canvas awning rigged for stokers. While they carefully directed the stream to miss the surgeon and his operation, a dark figure stood nearby, barely controlling his movements, while two more squatted with heads between their knees.

In his cabin, Starke saw Yamashita's dolphin, caught on a hand-line before the ship picked up speed, was extremely small. As the steward cleared the table, he asked, "Did you get any, Yamashita?"

In rapidly improving English, the small, lithe steward smiled, "Not today, captain, but fishing will get better. Maybe a turtle."

Starke went from table to desk, where he worked until Surgeon Conrad interrupted to report eight engineers treated for heat exhaustion, with seven returned to duty, and the burn patient showing no sign of infection. Their seasick case was still dehydrated, so there was no chance of keeping him.

As *Calypso*'s stem knifed through blue water, thrust forward by three progressively larger pistons spinning a single shaft, Starke finished an inventory report, then opened his personal log. Just after one o'clock, Watson requested he come to the pilothouse. Stepping outside, he saw Sombrero Key nearly abeam in the distance and *Calypso*'s large bow wave rolling water over a nearly flat turquoise sea, merging with the midship wake, then melting away astern. Coming through the door, he heard, "Captain's in the pilothouse," which lifted Watson, Dunbar, and Martyn's heads from a chart.

Watson gestured through open windows past foremast and bowsprit, "Captain, that red tug off the bow was leaving Bahia Honda or Big Pine Key, reversed course to starboard, then headed north. Smoke's increased, she's pushing hard, and sits low in the water. No sign of fire, so it could be flooding or shifting cargo, but she seemed startled and eager to reach shoal water."

Deciding it was past time to end Watson's informal probation, Starke used the more casual term for executive officers, "Filibuster, XO?"

"Her movements are strange, sir. Ensign Martyn reported the turn, and we've observed her master watching us, but held to the full power run. Dunbar and Owen say we could close the keys somewhat, but must feel our way in. It shallows quickly with reefs and coral heads that fellow's probably familiar with."

Starke studied the chart. The engineers completed over two hours under full power, so useful information was obtained using excellent fixes from the Alligator and Sombrero Key lighthouses. The tug behaved strangely, but would *Calypso* be chasing or aiding, if she followed? Either way, it meant closing treacherous shoal water surrounding the reefs and small islands strung west from mainland Florida to Dry Tortugas. Lighthouses were constructed along these keys, which reduced the wrecking trade, but ships still went aground. Alligator Reef was named for a Navy schooner that struck it, was then burned to deny pirates the carcass, and still lay off the lighthouse. Risking the deep draft *Calypso* was unpalatable, but the tug's maneuvering smacked of distress or nefarious activity. Making the call, Starke faced Watson, "XO, tell Osbourne we'll take what we have on the full power run, be prepared to answer all bells, and standby to turn. Also, alert Mr. Conrad, then send word to man a forward Gatling gun on either side and ready the lifeboat."

"Aye, aye, sir. General quarters?"

"Not yet, XO. Let's see what our friend does."

Easing into a smart starboard turn at speed, *Calypso* heeled well to port, uprighted, then steadied on course to intercept the tug. That tug would see the pronounced heel as tall masts converged, then, with binoculars or telescopes, a white mustache form under the bowsprit; telling the master help was coming, or he was *Calypso*'s prey. More black smoke poured from the smaller ship's single funnel, hung briefly above the sea, then settled on sparkling blue-green water. Watson turned to Starke, "Make a signal, captain?"

"I believe we have, XO; besides there's no war and we're obviously not a pirate. He may be a filibuster, but odds still favor him making for shoal water to put out a fire or go aground before flooding. Either way, he's no interest in trading flag signals."

Watson replied, "Aye, sir," then returned his attention to the tug.

As *Calypso* gained, the chase drew idlers and the off-watch forward. Below deck, word must have reached the engineers, since speed actually increased slightly. A dolphin school also joined in with glistening blue-gray backs effortlessly slipping through the water. Starke was confident maneuvering room remained, although vanishing rapidly as tug, ship, and dolphins raced towards shoal waters sown with coral reefs. Chief Owen's normally buoyant face looked strained as he turned to Dunbar, who was struggling how to best approach his captain, or attract Watson's attention. Starke was aware a fine line existed between discipline and alienation, so he asked, "Thoughts, XO?"

"Another half-mile, mile at most, then we must slow or turn. I doubt we'll overtake him before he enters the shallows between Big Pine Key and Bahia Honda, sir."

Starke turned to the navigator, "Mr. Dunbar. Check the channels between Big Pine Key and Bahia Honda, then have Chief Weaver prepare the hand lead. We may need water depth and bottom."

Through binoculars, it appeared the tug's last years had been hard, and she was not making much over ten knots, despite black smoke billowing astern. There was a cluster of animated men on the fantail, near crates stacked against the deckhouse, and two more arguing on the upper deck, aft of the pilothouse. Far too many people were topside without purpose for a normal crew, so Starke suspected they had stumbled on a filibuster, but shoal water was closing rapidly. Lowering binoculars, Starke scanned the horizon, but found only three small fishing schooners, anchored off a channel between the keys. However, he could tell the bark was about to cross the danger line between Loo and Sombrero Key, so *Calypso* must turn and slow, or run aground. Starke wanted to overtake their quarry, but the chance meeting already thwarted a Junta expedition. He could use the 4-inch rifles to halt the tug, then board with a steam pinnace, and *Calypso*'s appetite for the hunt seemed whetted, but it was still possible she was in distress. Raising binoculars, Starke looked for a name on her stern, but saw only an indecipherable smudge; so it was faded or covered. To risk driving aground for a better look was beyond rash, since *Calypso*'s hull would rip open at this speed then be torn apart when her iron masts went overboard; broken or bent. Starke reached for his unlit pipe, then turned to Watson, "Ahead slow, XO."

As *Calypso*'s engineers acknowledged, a large puff of white steam burst through black smoke billowing from the tug's stack, followed seconds later by a dull report. Raising his binoculars, Starke saw men milling in confusion on the tug's main deck while others struggled with two dirty gray boats. As *Calypso* coasted to bare steerageway, he told Martyn, "Steer towards her, but don't cross the line between Loo and Sombrero Keys," then to Watson, "lower the ready lifeboat and put the second whaleboat to the rail, XO."

Just before reaching the line, *Calypso*'s rudder was put hard to port and engine stopped. At bare steerageway and nearly broadside to the tug, the first whaleboat entered the water and towed obediently alongside to port by a sea painter made up to a small inboard cleat just aft of its bow. Starke lowered his glasses, "Send the first boat, XO; then lower the second. Tell our crews they're racing sharks, but use caution."

Starke considered using their steam pinnaces, but knew the stricken ship's end would come before they reached operating pressure. He also regretted his boat crews were less than fully seasoned, but despite that, the first whaleboat closed quickly with steady, confident stokes. Through binoculars, Starke confirmed their progress, then shifted back to the tug. The distance might entice neophytes to think there was little damage, since no flames were visible and the tug's stack smoke rose lazily up before drifting slowly away, but the pregnant waddle signaled flooding in an old tug that lacked watertight compartments. There was probably a rudimentary crash bulkhead and, perhaps, something fore and aft of her engineering spaces, but nothing more. Her end would come quickly, so he hoped the coxswains also realized this, would stand off, and not risk boat crews.

As the tug's fantail settled and bow rose, her efforts to launch boats ended and the stern crowded with people waiting for *Calypso*'s whaleboats. The first coxswain evaluated the risk, took his boat within forty feet, then stood in the stern sheets urging them to swim, or go over with anything that floated. A number did and soon clung to its gunnels as more arrived than his whaleboat could carry, so he backed carefully away as men remaining on the tug urged the boats to come alongside. The second coxswain succumbed and his whaleboat shot forward until its bow touched the tug's quarter, nearly capsizing as men rushed to climb aboard or, failing that, grab hold of its gunnels. He quickly backed away to follow the first coxswain's example.

The boats were just clear and command to hold oars given when blue-green water poured over the foundering tug's aft bulwarks forcing her stern down rapidly as she rolled to port, away from *Calypso*, almost to her beam-ends. Although pilothouse, main deck, and some red hull were masked; black planks below her waterline, streaked with marine growth and marred by bare areas were clearly visible. As the fantail submerged, she fought to upright herself and stay afloat. Half under and settling deeper, the dying tug righted, with its bow pointing skyward, fantail under water, and venting compressed air that roiled water above any opening. Soon, only the tug's thick oak stem, foremast, and stack top remained above the surface, supported by compressed air pockets and buoyant wood. Seconds later a boiler ruptured, planking separated, and inrushing water pressurized the remaining air, causing windows, portholes, decks, and bulkheads to rupture. She slipped quickly below, encircled by white water erupting in small geysers, leaving a boil quickly filling with sea water and surrounded by expanding surface rings. Within minutes, only discolored water, floating debris, struggling or floating forms, and whaleboats recovering from her dying convulsions' rough handling remained.

As rescue boats came alongside *Calypso*, Surgeon Conrad, his apothecary, and baymen waited while sailors lined the side throwing out lines and helping survivors. Chief Weaver directed the first whaleboat under its davits, then, after those clinging to its gunnels were taken aboard and falls attached, everyone available took hold of the manila boat falls to raise it fully loaded to the rail, dripping water from the keel. The second enjoyed the same reception. Most men arriving from the tug swallowed saltwater and, although some required no assistance, others were in acute pain and a few were laid out unmoving. As the boats lowered for a second trip, sailors who rigged the heat exhaustion area now turned it into a dressing station while Conrad passed from one man to the next, not tending wounded as they arrived, but selecting some while leaving others to his apothecary and baymen.

The unloaded whaleboats returned to the floating debris where they began retrieving weak and lifeless forms by standing off, then racing in to snatch a prize. This needed steady nerves since buoyant items, including one of the wreck's boats, intermittently shot to the surface and occasionally into the air. After several minutes without either boat moving in, Starke obtained Watson's attention, then said, "Recall our boats, XO, but don't bring them on board. Log the position and pass a well-done to the crew."

Starke experienced similar scenes, unlike many of his crew, and knew medical people would earn this day's pay. Leaving a sinking ship exacted a toll. Almost everyone would be sick from swallowing seawater, with other injuries ranging from abrasions to compound fractures; and scalding if a steam ship. For some, little attention was necessary beyond ensuring they were not left too long in the sun.

After waiting thirty minutes, a single whaleboat was dispatched to what little debris still floated, intermixed with sea gulls bobbing amid the flotsam or circling above. After smashing holes in the tug's overturned dinghy, *Calypso*'s boat held position as it slowly rose and fell on a slight swell. After several minutes, it was once more disturbing gulls by pulling in one direction, stopping, moving off in another, then coasting to a halt. In ten minutes, a body was retrieved, after another twenty the boat was recalled and brought on board. With both whaleboats in chocks under their davits and secured, Starke scanned what debris remained with binoculars, then said, "XO, make for Key West at best speed."

Watson turned to Dunbar, who quickly responded, "Recommend west southwest, XO. That clears shoal water and sets us up to enter Key West through their Southeast Channel. Estimate a bit over thirty miles to turn."

Watson ordered ahead two-thirds, until reaching steerageway, then had his helmsman put the rudder full over and gave him the new heading. *Calypso*'s bowsprit slowly slid across the keys until it paralleled, then began opening them. Considering Dunbar's latest calculations, Starke added, "When on course, XO, bring us to full speed. With luck, we'll turn about six and be through the channel before dark. If the tug's master is able, please request he visit my cabin." With that, Starke left to record the afternoon's events in his personal log. Watching him, a quartermaster turned to his shipmate whispering, "God, that tug sank and the captain seemed about as excited as leaving Port Royal."

His friend, late of the British navy, smiled, "A queer fish that one, but he'll do us, I'm thinking."

Starke was writing when Watson entered, "Captain, this is Fachtna Harler, *John Gwinn Williams*' master, but goes by Captain Buff. Ensign Blair has the bridge and starboard watch."

"Very well, XO. Please pass the word for Yeoman Pond."

The man malevolently eyeing Starke seemed a clean-shaven, hard-case, nearly bald, with whatever black or gray hair left cut short. As he thrust past Watson, Starke saw the sunburned neck was little more than compressed rolls, bearing close resemblance to a snapping turtle, as weathered paws clenched then unclenched. Watson moved to intervene, since their guest appeared willing to strangle his captain, who rose ominously from the chair without extending a hand. Captain Buff's small, nearly black, eyes blazed with barely controlled rage, and Starke thought him an arrogant tartan, made worse by the tug's loss. While waiting for Yamashita to return with Yeoman Pond, the two eyed each other without speaking, as if each willed their adversary to break eye contact first. When the yeoman arrived, Starke surrendered his seat, saying, "Use my desk, Pond, we'll take the chairs."

Returning to his irascible guest, Starke added, "Please have a seat, captain," motioning Captain Buff to a chair. The master dropped heavily into the nearest.

"For our log, captain, I would appreciate an initial statement, then Lieutenant Watson, my executive officer, will stand witness."

"I'm damned if I'll have dealings with the bastard that sank my ship."

"You'd best explain. *John Gwinn Williams* was not fired on or molested."

"You chased her 'til the boiler exploded."

"So you had no emergency when you came about and ran for shoal water?"

Captain Buff saw the trap too late. Losing ship and cargo in this manner left three distasteful paths: say nothing until a Junta lawyer was present; claim a fatal equipment casualty and thank the lieutenant; or admit filibustering. His quick temper just closed any opportunity to claim a casualty, although it was not his nature to lie, and the third option meant arrest at the next port. That left the first, since *John Gwinn Williams* signed a six-man crew, but carried twenty-odd more, along with a hold and deck load of military goods; which might still be salvaged by the Junta, or authorities, if she settled inshore of the shelf.

Starke saw this as well, so he ended the interview, stating, "Yeoman Pond will log *Calypso* observed *John Gwinn Williams* trying to reach the shallows at speed. This command, unwilling to ignore what appeared a ship in extremis, went to assist, but was only able to recover survivors. Their number and condition will be added when I've heard from our surgeon. That should serve our purposes for the moment, captain."

Captain Buff had a question he longed to put to the lieutenant, but knew there was no chance of an answer unless the man was a complete fool; and asking condemned him outright. Recalling *Calypso*'s sudden arrival running full out, he was convinced the bastard knew *John Gwinn Williams* was a filibuster, while he mistook *Calypso* for a merchantman that would pass astern. Once the bark maneuvered, he was forced to let them board or run inshore and hopefully gain time to jettison the cargo in shallow water. He could have made shoal water using bacon slabs like blockade runners did oiled cotton, but a boiler blew when, despite the engineer's resistance, he ordered safety valves locked down, dismissing all protestations. Since his friend was still inside the wreck, he also believed it possible someone sabotaged the tug while others orchestrated the events delaying *John Gwinn Williams'* departure until the warship's arrival.

"One other thing, captain."

Through gritted teeth, Captain Buff growled, "Yes."

"Your homeport and registry?"

"Key West."

"Thank you. Yeoman Pond will escort you aft to your crew, or you may rest in my at-sea cabin."

"I stay with my crew."

"Very well. We should make Key West by evening."

After Pond and the sullen master left, Starke turned to Watson, "Insure our guests are disarmed, knives included. Post guards until they're with the U.S. Marshal, or Key West customs collector. We'll report the facts and leave it to the courts to unravel. Captain Buff's in the bag, the Junta's out *John*

Gwinn Williams, and we're better employed elsewhere. Also, please ask the surgeon to stop by when convenient."

"Yes, sir."

After Watson left, Starke selected, then lit a browning meerschaum pipe to calm himself. Thinking it fair to assume it was the Junta that lost *John Gwinn Williams* and a weapons cargo, he was confident Captain Buff would not offer gratuitous information. Consequently, he reordered his notes between soothing draws, completed a statement, then started a coded message for Albert. It would accompany the standard arrival telegram to the Department; followed by a full report that would include his suspicion the livid master might erroneously suspect betrayal, which could unsettle the New York Junta.

Surgeon Conrad knocked on Starke's door just before afternoon officer's call, looking all the more haggard because of a clean uniform. *Calypso*'s young surgeon was heavy without fat, had large eyes, and robust cheeks, with demeanor and countenance that promised a dominating effect when he fully matured. Summoning a tired smile, Conrad began, "Good afternoon, captain. I've prepared a casualty list."

With that, he handed over a sheet of paper Starke placed unread on the desk before saying, "In your own words, Mr. Conrad."

"A Spanish, or possibly Cuban, gentleman from Key West confirmed twenty-three passengers and crew of six. I prepared a short medical note on each, excluding any missing and the master. He was not examined and said I could go straight to hell."

As Starke looked, Conrad straightened, then added, "I told him better men were being treated and preferred spending time on them anyway."

While he expected some rebuke or warning, Starke smiled so slightly his thin beard barely moved, then said, "I considered something similar myself."

"Yes, sir."

"Please continue."

"Yes, sir. It seems they left Key West with twenty-nine, although the XO suspects we'll find six reported. Two remain missing, including their engineer, and four came aboard deceased. Their stoker was badly scalded and won't survive if his burns infect. Two have broken arms. One's a clean break that's been reset and bound, but the other's a compound fracture requiring amputation. The XO says Key West has a Marine Hospital, so it's best done there to mitigate shock, but the wound's been cleaned and dressed. Two have broken ribs from being crushed by heavy crates sliding aft. They're in tight bandages, so time will tell. The serious cases have been given laudanum. Almost all ingested saltwater and may be sick for a day or two. We're treating cuts and abrasions now, and they should all should be ready for transfer by Key West."

"Tough day?"

"No, not really, sir. It's medicine. I would amputate the arm now, except we're near a hospital. My father regularly removed limbs at the railroad yard. I sometimes assisted and have done several since. Scalding's more distressing since everything beyond cleaning and laudanum falls to God."

"Well, Mister Conrad, if it's any solace, Captain Buff's a filibuster and the gentlemen a Cuban army officer, Junta leader or insurrectionist official. While some are dead, or may die, these men hoped to inflict similar suffering on others and knew the risk, or should have. Unfortunately, most were probably comfortably rolling cigars until a few weeks ago. They may see things differently now, but that's to them. I did the same myself, years ago."

"Yes, sir."

"Mr. Watson is correct, the Marine Hospital's just up from Fort Taylor and has its own pier. The dead and those you judge fit will be turned over to the authorities when we arrive; and the remainder transferred to hospital in the morning."

Starke thought Conrad was doing well for his first cruise, but he was a medical school graduate who might easily succumb to a more comfortable and profitable shore practice. Raising the pipe to relight it after the surgeon left, he concluded the doctor's dilemma was much like his own, and yet he remained in the service.

CHAPTER NINETEEN
Key West

Osbourne entered Starke's cabin before the Key West sea and anchor detail to report with a grin, "Captain, she made over fifteen knots most of the run, and nearly sixteen chasing the tug. I can't yet speak to reliability or maintenance, but based on existing records, our triple-expansion engine, with the replacement screw, squeezes out a little more speed from the hull. Between that and new boilers, coal consumption's also lower."

"Well, done. Send your report from Key West, and I'll add a note."

With Osbourne off, Starke began changing. He directed *Calypso's* crew be in whites for entering Key West, although blue uniforms were preferred, even in the tropics. Arriving in the pilothouse, he compared the entrance chart to visible landmarks. The Southeast Channel and shelf's edge were marked by four irregular keys barely above water and partly flooded. The first was Speculator Shoal followed by the three Sambos, Eastern, Middle, and Western. Beginning just beyond Western Sambo was the narrow channel lining up on Key West Lighthouse and marked by two red buoys that would pass to starboard at roughly a hundred yards if steering northwest by a quarter north.

Starke entered the port several times, but still consulted the *United States Coast Pilot* with Dunbar, Watson, and Osbourne; then, though open pilothouse windows, observed the deep blue water fade to light green as it shoaled and grew less distinct with evening approaching. Although the island's two Martello towers and barrier key were just visible, Blair struggled to locate the first red buoy. Starke glimpsed an indistinct shape low on the water just off the starboard bow, almost certainly the buoy, but said nothing. There was time, and Blair's temporary discomfort did him no harm. Besides, the Sand Key and Key West lighthouses were visible, as was Fort Taylor's imposing bulk.

Being late Sunday, pilot boats were not off the port entrances, where they usually drifted or circled just outside shoal water. When this occurred, the custom was to signal for them to come out, but Navy ships did not require pilots and Starke wanted to pass through the tight channel between shoals and coral heads before dark. He might have considered waiting for one, or remain offshore until morning, if they had arrived later or were not carrying dead and wounded.

When Blair finally reported he could just make out a numeral two on the red nun buoy, Starke turned to Osbourne, "Feel comfortable taking her in Mr. Osbourne?"

"Yes, sir."

"Then Mr. Watson may take the deck and Mr. Osbourne the conn. Mr. Blair, you'll bring her out. In the meantime, back up the navigator. Mr. Dunbar, we'll anchor below the yellow buoy, just above Fort Taylor, and wait to be boarded; which I doubt will take long."

Starke knew Blair was disappointed, but the Key West approaches were known for sharp turns in narrow channels, and they could not see what waited after clearing Whitehead Spit. While *Calypso* slowed, Dunbar called out estimated times to turn as the small nun buoy drew closer; guano-stained and riding the slight swells.

Calypso steamed nearly parallel, but seaward, of the miniature keys while Osbourne timed his turn. Too soon and they would strike rocks or clip the buoy, but hesitation could take them into shoal water on the channel's far side; and anywhere between usually called for corrections to gain the channel axis. When the bow was nearly abreast the buoy, Osbourne ordered a solid starboard turn to northwest by a quarter north. The serious-looking helmsman spun the wheel, then, once the bow began swinging faster, countered to reduce momentum before stopping the turn. Once steady on course, he called it out. Several in the pilothouse and forecastle waited to judge if the turn was early or late, but *Calypso*'s bowsprit lined perfectly up the South East Channel as the red buoy flew down their starboard side. Soon after, halfway up the first leg, a second red nun, carrying more guano than the first, passed close aboard to starboard, offering a barely readable numeral four.

Weaver watched the port anchor, catted and ready for dropping, shift slightly as *Calypso*'s keel glided just feet above the sandy bottom. Several coral heads and reefs lay just outside the channel, barely above or just under the water. Those submerged or awash were becoming visible only when the fading light struck right, or, if near the surface, hosted a mix of sea gulls, terns, and brown pelicans. Looking at the clustered birds, and others floating between them in a clear, calm evening flavored by coastal smells combining with the sea, Chief Weaver breathed deeply, chastised a landsman who just stepped in a line's bight, then grinned at Mr. Martyn.

For the next leg, they lined up on the Hawk Channel Turn Buoy, a black and white, vertically striped can. Its condition mirrored the others, clearly showing local birds had no prejudice or favoritism regarding shape or color. While it could be left to either side, Stark, being more familiar, said, "Take it to starboard. Either side's safe water, but the current makes it better to turn south. Pass close aboard, and you'll gain a touch more room."

Osbourne again precisely executed the turn, leaving the buoy twenty-five yards to starboard. On the new west by north course, *Calypso* moved along the island, passing White-head Point with sailors above deck enjoying a close look at Fort Taylor, Key West Lighthouse, and the western Martello Tower. City proper, wharfs, and naval station were further north, but much closer sat a massive white-hulled ship with stacks and upper superstructure painted straw-yellow. She was anchored south of the naval station, west of the ship channel, and north of *Calypso*'s planned anchorage. Her accommodation ladders and boat booms were rigged, with several white-hulled pinnaces and a large barge tied to her port boom. Further north, a steam launch was making for the starboard accommodation ladder's lower platform.

The battleship *Maine* was unmistakable. Only she and *Texas* carried en echelon main batteries in turrets, and hers were more widely spaced, with two blackened barrels. Only Brazil, in the Americas, had similar battleships, and their hulls were black. *Maine* was the first battleship designed by the Navy and attempted to leverage thirty years of overseas experiments. The design proved unsatisfactory, partly because she became obsolete during the years spent in construction, which was often true in Europe. Consequently, the Navy's second battleship to commission was too slow for use as an armored cruiser but insufficiently armed and armored for a first class battleship; especially with three *Indiana* class ships joining the fleet. The solution was to designate *Maine*, and somewhat swifter *Texas*, second class battleships.

After clearing the next buoy, showing a barely readable numeral six, *Calypso* turned north, passed Fort Taylor, continued between two more buoys before anchoring northwest of the Marine Hospital's pier. As the anchor struck bottom, *Calypso*'s ensign shifted from main truck to stern, Osbourne backed, and Weaver veered anchor chain until sufficient rode lay across the bottom to bury the fluke and hold *Calypso*, without entering *Maine*'s stern circle.

Starke waited to ensure the anchor was holding and bearings taken to check for dragging. Finally, he nodded to Watson, who requested to secure, then signaled the engine room to shut down. Signing the rough log, Osbourne left to change, then join his black gang, Conrad prepared patients for transfer, and Starke remained with Watson waiting for *Maine* to reply to their flag signal reporting *Calypso*'s arrival. Soon, colored flags and pennants breaking from *Maine*'s foremast requested he report on board immediately. Looking north to the battleship, then west to an orange sun sinking into a distant horizon beyond some small keys, he turned to Watson, "Very well, acknowledge. Since the whaleboat's at the rail, she'll do for a gig this evening."

Despite their unplanned arrival, Starke had been reasonably confident of departing for the Dry Tortugas after making courtesy calls, turning over survivors, and sending the dead ashore. However, his intent to leave the following day, vanished during the interview on *Maine*; leaving *Calypso* indefinitely at anchor northwest of Fort Taylor, west of the ship channel, and slightly southeast of the battleship.

Maine's Captain Crowninshield had been senior navy officer present in Key West since early June and therefore exercised temporary control over *Calypso*. This authority usually entailed coordinating local ships' exterior routine and relations, so Starke was not surprised *Maine*'s first flag-hoist requested him to visit, but its urgency did. The wording suggested something important afoot or petty subterfuge to put a junior officer through his paces. Whatever reason, it did not matter. The whaleboat gig was lowered and Starke rowed to *Maine* where her executive officer, Lieutenant Commander

Marix, met Starke at the accommodation ladder then led him to the captain's cabin.

Located on the main deck aft, above the wardroom and beside a vacant twin intended for a flag officer, the large cabin's steel walls were painted white and trimmed with dark varnished wood. On the outboard side was a line of rectangular windows; each equipped with a steel shutter that swung up and out to shield their thick glass and provide shade from the sun. The living area included a substantial desk, circular pedestal table of dark wood, and matching buffet. The four corners of a square tablecloth, similar to Persian-style rugs on the floor, nearly reached the deck. Crowninshield obviously preferred the table for work and had gathered papers spread across it into a single pile while Marix was meeting Starke. He rose as the two men entered, shook Starke's hand, then offered him a leather-backed chair at the table. Marix took another, as Crowninshield resumed his seat.

Maine's commanding officer considered his junior over the table and disrupted paperwork, then, with probing eyes accentuated by bushy eyebrows, spoke through a prominent walrus mustache at odds with the thinning, center-parted hair, "Saw *Calypso* anchor. Nicely done," then quickly added, "Mister Marix says your XO poached two good men from us in Norfolk."

"I believe so, sir. Lieutenant Watson harvested an excellent crop from several sources."

Nodding to Marix, who listened attentively, but was obviously weighing this discussion against competing demands, he added, "Then we're both fortunate in that respect."

"Yes, sir."

"We've several cables for *Calypso*, but I assume your unannounced entry here means plans have changed?"

Starke realized *Calypso*'s cruise was truncated as Crowninshield continued, "One's in a code we don't have, but others direct you to remain at whatever port entered to await further instructions. There's a third to your XO requiring a statement for Captain Albert. Although circumspect, I suspect it concerns the *Winston A. Capps* grounding on Cay Sal Bank. You passed too far north to see the wreck, but a merchant saw her go aground and rescued the crew. Ship's a loss, but injuries minor. However, there're rumors her commander's wired a lengthy diatribe charging her officers and many of the crew."

"I'll inform Mr. Watson, and hopefully a statement's all that's required."

Commander Marix added, "Tell Ben I'm available should he want a legal review before submitting. This doesn't sound like a routine inquiry."

Starke thanked him, then added, "Captain, I must report while doing a full power run along the keys we observed a red tug in distress, or fleeing, and altered course to intercept. Her boiler exploded when we were closing and she was lost. I've survivors and bodies on *Calypso*. By tomorrow, I'll submit a written report and cable for your review, but some of her survivors require immediate medical attention."

"*John Gwinn Williams* and Captain Buff?"

"Yes sir, how did you guess?"

"Slipped through our picket boats enforcing quarantine. There's smallpox in the city and a detention camp constructed. About twenty-eight cases. No ships can leave without certifying the crew's vaccinated. Since many locals refuse, and city police force small, the Army and Navy are assisting. We've small boats patrolling with orders to stop anyone leaving without vaccinations, or engaged in filibustering. Which reminds, the quarantine officer should board *Calypso* directly.

Incoming ships must declare they've not entered a tropical port, no yellow fever's on board, then pay a fee that goes in local coffers, so they're quite diligent. A Spanish cruiser planning a port visit left after learning their stay would consist of watching the city from its quarantine anchorage. Decided to forego Key West and spend their quarantine in Port Tampa."

"We've come direct from Port Royal so quarantine's no issue, but Captain Buff, his crew, and, what are probably insurrecto recruits, should be put ashore and casualties sent to the Marine Hospital."

"Yes, the incorrigible Captain Buff. One of our less popular filibusters, I understand."

With that, Marix looked slightly, but respectfully, askance, caveating, "Suspected, captain, we've no solid proof."

"Suspected it is then, XO,"

Crowninshield then returned to Starke, "Which reminds me, you've probably not launched your steam pinnace. XO, let's make ours available to run the wounded to hospital this evening; and you should probably take the captain, or his XO, to the customs house for instruction regarding their other guests."

Marix accepted this unanticipated task with a nod as Crowninshield continued, "The XO's excellent relations with them. The Collector of Customs is Jefferson Browne, and Judge Ramon Alvarez is special deputy. They'll probably wish Captain Buff went under with his ship and became a local martyr. Don't expect much. Building any filibuster case is difficult, but a trial here would be exceptionally unpopular since locals support the insurrection and resent outside interference. Key West politicians know better than to argue against an independent Cuba. I understand Republicans roughly equal Democrats, with most elections seeing Southern sympathizers balancing Union men, Coloreds, and Negroes. That means most island elections hinge on the Cuban vote. The Junta may operate from New York, but its roots here are deep, and customs house positions go to the party controlling Washington."

After further small talk, mostly about Port Royal, Starke returned to *Calypso*, where Watson was conferring with a quarantine officer. Twenty minutes later, *Maine*'s steam launch was alongside and their injured en route to the Marine Hospital; a white building not quite due east of *Calypso* and behind a masonry seawall with protruding dock. Surgeon Conrad accompanied his patients, to confer with the hospital surgeon, Dr. White. Later that evening, a large steam launch brought the customs officer to identify and gather healthy survivors for release; lifting that responsibility from *Calypso* much sooner than Starke anticipated.

During the first week in port, Starke was often at the customs house, a large building with a distinctive red-brick exterior trimmed in stone and terra cotta. Sited next to the naval station, it fronted a small triangular park, with its rear grounds sloping to the customs piers and ship channel. Several times Starke climbed stairs from the first floor's Customs and Postal Service offices to a third floor room above the Federal courthouse where a consensus matured. Captain Buff had taken *John Gwinn Williams* out of Key West with a small crew and no cargo, completed loading, met *Calypso* off Bahai Honda, then ran for shoal water. The evasion failed when a boiler burst from unknown causes. No one doubted he was filibustering, but successful prosecution was thought unlikely without tug, passengers, and cargo; which was precisely why expeditions received insurrectionists and arms separately after departing port. The survivors were not speaking and relatively safe from arrest unless the un-manifested cargo was salvaged. It was also accepted that should this be accomplished, no proof existed Cuba was the military goods' destination;

and local Junta lawyers would have no difficulty concocting a story any Key West jury would accept.

The United States Marshal and others took the position it was best to let *John Gwinn Williams* rest undisturbed off Bahai Honda. Except for her dead, insurers, and the Junta; most participants benefitted by avoiding an investigation. A speculative court case might delay or risk her owners receiving an insurance payout that would help replace a tug whose useful life was nearing its end anyway. Local officials would not risk an unpopular trial just before elections. Spain's local consul, Manuel Garcia y Ruiz, would not complain, since this arsenal was rusting in warm saltwater and never see Cuba, the expedition had been derailed, and a ship lost to the Junta. Even Captain Albert would be satisfied since neither *Calypso* or her wardroom would be ensnared with an extended court case.

Starke also viewed it as convenient, since, with this decided, *Calypso* would be released to continue Caribbean operations against filibusters. Believing time was short, he finished a letter to Darwin Tyson, began a more awkward one to Katherine, now well into Newport's summer season, then paused to stand at a cabin window watching the Caribbean sun slide quietly below the horizon between Key West and Veracruz, Mexico.

AUTHOR'S BIOGRAPHY

Born in Lapeer, Michigan and raised on two farms near Davison, Michael Ribble received his bachelor's degree after attending Central Michigan University and University of Colorado, Boulder. His first work experiences included road construction, farming, helping construct a feedlot, working cattle and riding fence in the Rocky Mountains, harvesting sugar beets, teaching marksmanship as a camp counselor, and working in a combination gas station and sporting goods store. Enlisting as a seaman recruit, he attended basic training in San Diego, served on two minesweepers, a cruiser, destroyer, and frigate before retiring from active and reserve duty as a captain. After receiving a Master of Business Administration degree from Florida State University, he held various integrated logistics, program analyst, and cost estimating positions in the nation's capital; at Naval Sea Systems Command then Department of Homeland Security. Besides a Guantanamo Bay tour, he was involved with towing de-fueled nuclear submarines, taught naval science at Northwestern University, facilitated a statutory Naval Reserve policy board at the national level, and completed the United States Naval War College's continuing education program. Qualified as a Surface Warfare Officer, he served on steam and diesel ships, and crewed in several annual sail races down Chesapeake Bay. His material has been published in university publications, newspapers, and the United States Naval Institute *Proceedings*.